In a post pandemic world where women are bought and sold, Harper Crain has come of age.

Sold to a stranger with the highest bid, Harper seeks to change her own fate. With help from her brother and a handsome outsider with secrets that could destroy them all, they run.

But Harper's rich and powerful fiancé isn't willing to let her go easily and is prepared to hunt his prize to the ends of the earth.

Pursued by forces that would enslave her, can she be freed by love?

Unholy
Copyright © 2021 Rowena Wren
ISBN: 978-1-4874-3045-0
Cover art by Martine Jardin

Published by eXtasy Books Inc or
Devine Destinies, an imprint of eXtasy Books Inc

Look for us online at:
www.eXtasybooks.com or www.devinedestinies.com

Unholy

By

Rowena Wren

CHAPTER ONE

I sat with my head hanging between my knees and took in long slow breaths.

"I don't think I can do it," I moaned as my stomach lurched.

"Don't be ridiculous, Harper. You have an obligation to your country." Mother jerked my head up and twisted my long brown hair into a bun.

I had never been vain, but I knew I wasn't ugly. In fact, I had been told I was actually kind of pretty, with my emerald-green eyes, shapely figure, and straight nose. However, being put on show was something I hated, and this was going to be the biggest show of my life.

I tugged at the skin-tight white jumpsuit I was being forced to wear. The outfit left nothing to the imagination, as it clung to every curve and bump on my five-foot seven-inch frame. "I just want it to go on record that I think I might throw up."

My mother tugged my hair a little tighter, putting more force into the movement than was necessary. "It's natural to be nervous. I was nervous when I was tested, but since the Pandemic it's our responsibility as women."

The Pandemic she was talking about had claimed two thirds of our nation's population over a century ago and mutated another quarter of the surviving humans into what had become known as the *Unholy*, which the government then went to great lengths to eradicate. The Pandemic hit hardest among the female population of the time. Its effects had something to do with the reproductive system. For every one man

1

who died, three women did, leaving much of the human population in ruin. When the dust settled and the scientists finally found a vaccine, they realised there were barely any women left.

By all reports from those early days, the men turned savage, women were kidnapped and brutalised, and many reports of incest began flooding in. That was until Praeses, the leader of our great country, the *Nation*, sent the army in to round up every female, young and old, and made mandatory DNA sequencing compulsory for every female on their eighteenth birthday. They tell us it is so we can be paired with the best genetic match, but none of the men who can afford the DNA sequencing for a potential bride are under thirty.

My mother says that if they can afford the DNA testing and have the other financial qualifications, such as a house and savings as well as the government taxes, then they can afford a wife. But, of course, the prettier girls were usually selected by the wealthier men. And no Unholy would ever qualify to take a wife.

My mother took a step back and looked me over with a critical gaze. "I expect you will be matched with a very handsome and wealthy man."

"I'd feel better if I got to choose my own husband," I grumbled, tugging on the high neck.

My mother shook her head and mumbled something about *silly girls* as she ushered me out to the waiting car, where my father sat. He glanced over at me, giving me a smile and a wink as I slid into the passenger seat.

"Now make sure you behave yourself. Don't open your mouth unless spoken to, and for goodness sake, don't fidget," my mother scolded before closing the door harder than necessary.

If she were permitted at the DNA facility, she would have jumped in the car with us so she could chastise me about my manners or lack of, but only the females who were to be tested were allowed to be present. My father waved at her while pulling the car away and guiding it down the long driveway to the main road.

Our local DNA sequencing centre was only two hours away in the city, which wasn't too far to go, considering other families in our region had to travel more than eight hours to get there.

"You nervous?" my father asked.

I nodded as I glanced over at him. "What if they find something in my DNA that makes me unworthy to be married?"

"Then you become a *Bride of the state*." He shrugged.

A Bride of the state was a woman whose DNA was unsuitable for marriage. Those women were turned into government servants such as cleaners, secretaries and women who service the unmarried men, or as I had once heard them called, prostitutes. I didn't envy those poor girls. They would never have a home or family of their own and by all reports were forced to have a surgery that left them barren.

"Don't worry, I'm sure you'll be matched," my father said in his calm voice.

My kind-hearted father always spoke calmly and had an aristocratic bearing. If it were up to him, I would be allowed to stay unwed and live at home for all my years, but the law was the law and my father never broke it.

I sat in silence and watched the world slip by. In all my eighteen years, I'd rarely left the farm. It was too dangerous for a woman to venture out alone and rare for one to go into town, even in the company of a man.

My father hired young men as farmhands, but etiquette decreed I wasn't to speak to them nor they to me, so the only males I ever spoke to were my father, my older brother, Bernard, who everyone called Birdy, and Mr Winter, the foreman on my father's farm.

Birdy and I had a love-hate relationship, especially when it came to cake. I *hated* the fact that because he was a boy, he always got the last piece and he *loved* to rub that in. But apart from that, we got along great.

Small houses occupied the outskirts of the city and grew larger and more compact as we neared the centre, until eventually the buildings towered over us in gigantic columns of steel, glass, and grey concrete.

"The building we're looking for is on the next block," my father said as he turned a corner and pulled into an underground carpark which was so big I couldn't see the other end.

My father found a parking space near a bank of elevators and ushered me out.

"Just remember what your mother said, behave yourself. We don't want you to become a Bride of the state," my father said quietly as we crossed the carpark to the steel doored elevators.

I nodded. There was no way I wanted to service men for the rest of my life. It sounded icky and revolting.

The elevator pinged as the doors open and we stepped inside. The doors had just begun to close when a hand jutted through the gap and forced the doors open before a tall broad-shouldered man stepped in. He had dark hair and eyes so dark blue they almost looked black. He was handsome.

The man looked me up and down. His gaze made me feel naked in my skin-tight bodysuit as his perfect lips stretched into a grin.

I dropped my gaze to the ground. Why the hell was I looking at his lips?

"Are you here for the DNA sequencing?" the man asked in his cultured voice.

I glanced up, but he wasn't talking to me, he was talking to my father.

"Yes sir, my daughter will be turning eighteen in a few

weeks," Father replied with a smile.

Then the man looked at me again. "She has good child-bearing hips, decent mammary glands and a pretty face." He sounded as if he were judging a prized cow and not a woman.

I wanted to snap his thick neck.

"She should fetch a decent amount of interest, if her sequencing isn't flawed," the man continued.

That was it. "I'm not a cow at the sale yards!" I snapped.

The corner of the man's lips curved slightly more. "Indeed," he said mockingly.

"Harper!" my father barked angrily.

It was the first time since I was a child that he had spoken to me in such a sharp tone.

My father turned to the man "I apologise for my daughter's behaviour. I believe her nerves have gotten the better of her."

The man nodded at my father "Quite," he said as he glanced back at me. His eyes showed an assessing and almost amused expression.

I dropped my glance back to the ground. I knew I had misspoken — it wasn't a woman's place to object to a man, and in reality, he had given me a compliment by saying I had good hips and breasts.

"I apologise, sir," I said. The heat of embarrassment burning my cheeks.

He didn't say anything, but I could feel him watching me.

The elevator doors opened, and the man stepped out before my father snatched my arm and followed him.

Father gave my name to a man at a desk as I was ushered away, which left my father to sit with the rest of the waiting chaperones.

"Name?" a man asked as I was pushed through a door.

He was short, balding, and had wire-rimmed glasses balanced on his beak-like nose.

"Harper Crain," I told him while he punched the keys on

his computer.

"Are you eighteen?"

"I am in two weeks."

More typing.

"Stand against the wall," he barked as he stabbed a hairy knuckled finger toward a white wall with numbers painted down the sides.

I stepped to the wall and turned back to the man, but before I had time to register what was happening a bright flash startled me, forcing me to blink back stars.

"Turn left," he barked.

I turned.

Flash!

"Now to your right."

I turned.

Flash!

"Now face the wall."

I felt like a criminal.

Flash!

"Go through to the next room," he dismissed me.

In the next room, a skinny man with a slicked-back hairdo and oily skin ran a tape measure over every part of my body while he called out numbers to an equally greasy looking man who was sitting behind a desk.

"Lift your arms to the side," he ordered before running the tape across my breasts, which he seemed to take more time doing than he did with my arms and waist. It was the same when he measured the inside of my thighs.

I felt violated by his slimy touch and glad when it was over.

"Move to the next room," the man said finally.

The next room had eight white padded chairs, four against one wall and four opposite, all facing toward the centre of the stark white room.

Two of the chairs were already occupied, one by a bronze skinned girl with an atrocious overbite which made her jaw look as if it had receded into her neck. In the second chair was a girl with short red hair, big brown eyes, and a sprinkling of freckles across her nose.

I took a seat opposite them while a man who looked to be a hundred years old tottered over pushing a stainless-steel trolley with needles and glass vials on it.

"Name?" he asked.

"Harper Crain."

He wrote something on a clipboard before he turned back to me. "I'll be taking blood and saliva. He slipped an elastic band around my arm and pulled it tight.

My arm began to feel strange as he wiped the inside of my elbow with a small wet square of gauze before he lined a needle up with my raised vein. His hand shook slightly, which made me wince.

"Don't move, or I could do you damage," he told me.

I clenched my teeth and looked away as a sharp sting bit my arm, but I didn't flinch. He changed the receptacle vial three times, each time leaving the spike of the needle in my arm while he unscrewed one and added another. He finally withdrew the spike and stuck a small round patch over the puncture mark. Next he held out a long stick, which looked like an oversized ear cleaning bud.

"Open your mouth," he told me.

I did.

"You have good teeth," the old man said while he scrubbed the inside of my cheeks with the swab, then popped it into a long thin vial.

Now I really did feel like livestock.

My father could tell the age of a horse by looking in its mouth. The further the teeth sat forward, the older the horse was.

"Wait here until you're called," the old man said as he pushed the trolley with my blood and spit through a side door.

The two girls across from me sat demurely, their hands folded neatly in their laps and their eyes downcast. *They* had obviously been well trained, because *I* had to fight the urge to squirm or tap my fingers.

Another girl entered the room and took a seat beside me. The old man returned and went through the same routine, except the girl yelped when the old man put the needle in her vein, and he didn't tell her she had good teeth.

Time seemed to crawl by, making me anxious, and I had to keep reminding myself not to shift around in my seat too much. The other three girls didn't seem to be half as restless as me. They sat perfectly still like statues while my mind wandered.

The door from which the old pathologist came and went opened, and he stepped out followed by two men in white coats and rubber gloves. The old man pointed to the pretty red-haired girl who was seated across from me.

"That one," the old man said with disgust in his voice.

The girl went stiff as the two men in white approached.

"Come with us," one of the men ordered.

The girl glanced around, her big brown eyes confused. "Is there something wrong?" her voice quivered.

"You Unholy think you can get away with trying to marry good, hardworking, normal folk so you can spit out your spawn of hell," the old man sneered with disgust.

Oh, my goodness, I was sitting across from an Unholy and I didn't even know it. She looked so normal.

The girl beside her shifted away, as if scared she might catch something while the men in coats escorted the redhead away.

The redhead sobbed and protested that she was normal and they must have made a mistake.

The room felt icy. I wondered what they were going to do

to the redhead. I had plenty of time to wonder, because we sat there for another half an hour at least, while three more girls filed in and the old man went through the routine again. All three girls yelped at the needle.

Was I the only one who hadn't yelped? It stung, but I'd had worse from a bee.

The door at the end of the room opened and a man in a neat plain black suit stepped into view. He was maybe forty with silver starting to touch his dark hair.

"Ladies, please follow me," he said in a calm, authoritative voice.

We all stood and followed the man into a long wide hallway with floor-to-ceiling mirrors on either side. Some of the girls primped themselves in the mirrors as we walked, but I barely glanced at them. I know it might sound strange, but it felt like we were being watched by many eyes hidden behind those very mirrors.

"Ladies, please form a line behind this one," the man leading us said as he tapped me on the head.

The other five girls scrambled into a line behind me.

"Now, everyone, turn to your left," he said as he motioned his hand to the large mirrored wall to the left.

We all turned to face the mirror.

"Now lift your heads, and please look at your own face in the reflection," he ordered.

I did and the feeling of someone watching us grew stronger, like if that mirror weren't there, I would have been looking directly into someone's eyes.

"Now ladies, please turn around and do the same in the opposite mirror."

We all turned and stood for a minute, my back ramrod straight with my chin up while I tried not to shift my weight from foot to foot. This made me uncomfortable, because I then knew for certain we were being watched, I just didn't know how.

"Please follow me," the man finally said. We all turned in unison and followed him to the end of the hall and out to where our male chaperones waited for us.

Chapter Two

I sat on the old tree swing under the shade of the Mulberry tree. The dry summer heat was oppressive as I watched my father and Mr Winter discuss farm business while my brother Birdy approached with a handsome young man who I knew was a farmhand.

Birdy looked a lot like our father, with his dark hair, dark eyes and broad stocky build, but the young man who was standing beside him was taller, with a trim fit body, not skinny but not bulky. His honey blond hair looked messy, which contrasted with his bronzed skin and dark brown eyes. He had been working around the farm for the past six months, but I'd never spoken to him. I hadn't spoken to any of the farmhands, but I did remember my brother calling him North.

Birdy looked over and smiled. "Shouldn't you be learning how to bake a cake?" he called out.

"If I could bake cakes, you'd be fat," I called back.

North looked over at me, and I dropped my head.

Mr Winter and my father were used to Birdy and me having digs at each other. Mr Winter was pretty much part of the family, but I had spoken in front of the young man whom I didn't know and in an unladylike manner.

North looked at me, amused, while I pursed my lips together.

Birdy laughed as I quickly stood.

"Harper, did you forget your manners?" my father asked.

I kept my head down, my gaze fixed on my shoes. My father wasn't an unkind man, but he understood that not every house or every man was like him. Most husbands expected complete obedience and submission, and I always had trouble with both.

"You may wish to sweep and mop the entire house for speaking out of turn," my father told me.

I nodded, keeping my eyes firmly downcast before I turned and walked inside.

A trickle of sweat rolled down my back as I tipped the mop bucket out over my mother's rose bushes. I would probably get into trouble for it if she caught me, but she and father were in the office at present, and I doubted anyone else would snitch on the boss's daughter. Besides, it was still only mid-afternoon, and most of the farmhands wouldn't be in until dark.

I looked up in time to see North striding across the lawn. He looked like a blond Adonis from mythology. He was one good-looking young man.

"Harper?"

The sound of Birdy's voice startled me. North looked over and caught me watching him. I turned away and pretended to take in the roses instead.

"Father wants to see you in his office," Birdy called.

I nodded and went inside as I held back the desire to steal one last glimpse of North.

Father was seated behind his large desk while my mother hovered by his side.

"I finished the mopping," I told him wearily.

"Good, good," he said with a wave of his hand to indicate I should take a seat.

I did. I felt so tired.

"I have good news—your DNA test came back and there have been seven matches." He smiled.

"Seven? I was hoping for two or three, but seven!" I

exclaimed as all the fatigue left my body in a rush of shock and excitement.

It was an honour to get any matches, but seven was almost unheard of.

My mother beamed. "We are very proud of you."

"All seven men have expressed interest in meeting you, but only one is financially stable enough to honour the current bidding amount," my father told me.

The bidding amount was the amount the man was willing to pay for the honour of the woman's hand in marriage.

"And how much is that?" I questioned, unsure whether I wanted to hear it.

My mother's smile widened further. "Because you had so many matches your bidding price has gone up to two hundred thousand."

My mouth dropped open. The most any girl's family had ever been offered was four hundred thousand, and despite mine only being half that, it was a far cry from the usual twenty to thirty thousand.

I was glad I was sitting down, or I probably would have fainted.

"I know. We can't believe it either." My mother beamed. She looked as if she was about to jump out of her skin with excitement.

"I can believe it," my father said calmly. "I think she is worth more."

He didn't mean financially—my father wasn't a stupid man who frittered away money, but he loved me, and I knew he meant that I was priceless to him, in a heartfelt way.

My mother disregarded my father's comment. "Father has arranged for the gentleman to join us for dinner tomorrow night. We'll have to get you a new dress and do your hair— oh, and we must arrange a couple of servers, maybe a couple of the farmhands could do that," she rattled off while she hurried out of the office to start making arrangements.

My father waited for my mother to be out of earshot before he leaned forward over his desk and spoke in a hushed tone, "Mr James is younger than the rest of the candidates by at least twenty years and is exceedingly wealthy. He would easily be able to support you in a lavish lifestyle. He outbid the other candidates by seventy-five thousand."

And the one-hundred-and-twenty thousand my parents would receive after taxes would go a long way on the farm was what he didn't say.

I knew it wasn't about money, but knowing I was being bought and paid for still disturbed me. I nodded at my father. I knew as long as this man, Mr James, had all his fingers and toes, my father would accept his offer.

The day went by slowly despite the dress fitting, hair styling, makeup torture and the incessant chattering of my mother about lady's etiquette.

At quarter to five I was sitting on my bed wearing a black evening gown which fit so snuggly that eating anything was out of the question. My long brown hair had been pulled up into a fancy bun and my makeup was done to perfection. I felt like a child's doll being dressed up, but my mother insisted I looked wonderful.

There was a knock at my door, and Birdy stepped in. He assessed me for a moment before he smiled. "Wow, you don't scrub up half bad."

I sighed. "Yeah, but I can hardly breathe in this thing."

Birdy's expression turned more serious. "You know you can tell father you don't want to marry this guy if you don't like him."

I looked at my hands folded in my lap. "No, I can't. The farm needs a new tractor, and he is the youngest candidate, the rest are old men."

"You could run away," Birdy told me.

I laughed until I realised Birdy wasn't laughing with me.

"You can't be serious?"

"I know the government makes it sound like the entire world works like us, but it doesn't. In other places women choose their husbands because they love them, not because they are a genetic match or the men have money," Birdy explained in a low voice.

It was the first time I had ever heard him speak like this.

"I want my wife to love me, not be obligated by a computer program," he continued. "If you choose to marry this man, I will respect your choice. But just know I will leave in a heartbeat if you want to, Harper."

Breath caught in my throat. What Birdy was saying was paramount to treason, but it made me feel better to know my big brother was on my side.

"Thank you," I told him, and I meant it.

Birdy walked me down the steps at precisely five o'clock. I had to blink when we were greeted by the tall dark-haired man with the dark-blue eyes I'd seen in the elevator at the DNA centre a few days earlier.

He smiled as he gave a shallow bow of his head.

The man was devastatingly handsome in his perfectly tailored black suit, black shirt, and red tie, but there was something about his eyes that made me want to turn tail and run.

It's just nerves, most girls would think him a dream husband. So why was I thinking I should dash back up the stairs? I had been waiting and preparing for this day my entire life. I had been told over and over that the day I met my husband would be the happiest day of my life, but I just wanted to vomit.

"Mr James, please let me formally introduce you to my daughter, Harper," my father said.

"Please, call me Sabastian. After all we are almost family." The tall dark haired man smiled.

Mr James sat to my left, his back straight while he engaged

my father in small talk about the farm. He was cordial, refined and elegant throughout the entire dinner, despite the feeling I got that my father's home was a large step down from his usual surroundings.

"Harper." My father smiled after dessert. "I think you and Mr James should take a stroll around the garden and better acquaint yourselves."

This was his way of saying he liked Mr James and would most likely sign the marriage documents as soon as possible. A man who wasn't family didn't take strolls with a young lady without her father's blessing.

I stood, giving my father a small nod before I turned to Mr James. "Sir, if you would please follow me."

Sabastian James stood and gave a small nod to Harper's father before he followed her outside.

He'd thought her pretty when he'd seen her in the elevator, but now in the tight dress with her hair and makeup done, she was perfection, just like her DNA results.

He had chosen Harper Crain to be his wife partly because she was beautiful, but mostly because of her unusual results, which he recognised immediately as special.

Sabastian stayed a few feet behind her as they strolled through the rose garden. He wasn't admiring the rows of flowers, but the way her ass looked in that tight black dress.

In a few days you will be mine to do with as I want.

"Are you the gardener, Miss Crain?" Sabastian asked in his smooth rich voice.

She stopped walking and shook her head. His gaze fixed on the nape of her long slender neck.

"I'm afraid not, sir, that honour goes to my mother." Harper half-turned to face him, her gaze cast down.

"Do you think me handsome?" he asked in a mocking tone. He knew he was handsome, but he wanted her to say it.

16

Harper took a moment. "Very," she said softly as her cheeks blushed pink.

That was what he wanted to see, that slight discomfort in her face. But even if she didn't think him handsome, it was the correct answer. Any woman would have been a fool to tell a candidate he was unattractive, especially one as rich and powerful as Sabastian James.

Sabastian smirked with contentment.

"Please may I ask a question?" Harper asked.

It wasn't a young woman's place to question a man, and Sabastian thought it imprudent of her. He would have to teach her some manners, but for now he would be the gentleman. There would be plenty of time once they were married and away from this dump to instruct her on a woman's place.

"Of course," he said with a smile.

Harper lifted her head and looked him in the eyes. "Why me? I mean, I'm not as well versed in society as you would be accustomed to."

Sabastian fought every cell in his body not to snap at her as she looked at him as though she was his equal and she had the audacity to question a man's choice—his choice. Oh, he would have fun breaking her into the wife he surely deserved, and she would bear him beautiful children.

The thought of having her in his bed on their wedding night made him smile.

"You are what I've been waiting for," was all he told her, and he meant it. He didn't want a lapdog, he wanted a challenge, but most of all he wanted her DNA in his children.

Harper looked at him as if she expected more of an answer. "That doesn't tell me much," she said dryly.

Again, she'd spoken out of turn, and he wanted to slap her. His hand itched for it. She was insolent. Oh, how he was going to enjoy every inch of her.

"A man's reasons are his own," Sabastian said, letting his

mouth stretch into a tight smile.

I saw a look in Mr James's dark eyes which told me he had a cruel streak, but father liked him, and I could do worse for a husband.

"I'm sorry I spoke," I apologised, even though I didn't feel at all sorry.

Mr James offered me his elbow. I hesitated for a moment, then linked my arm with his.

"Your manners are a little unorthodox, and I may need to send you for elocution lessons, but you are very pretty, and we did have the highest DNA match out of everyone, so I'm confident you will produce attractive children and bear me a son to take on my family name," he said.

I fought a shiver. Sabastian James made me feel uncomfortable, and the thought of lying naked with him had me wanting to run away. I reminded myself he was a great catch for all intents and purposes. I could have easily been paired with a man older than my father.

We rounded the house in a slow walk while I thought about my wedding night. I had little idea what to expect. It wasn't something polite society talked about, and there was no way I was going to ask my mother about it.

North strode across the yard in front of us. His jeans fitted tightly around his ass and accentuated his long muscular legs. I watched him as he glanced over at us. The corners of his mouth turned up into a small smile. I smiled back before I dropped my head.

Mr James's grip on my arm suddenly tightened until it hurt.

"You're hurting me," I yelped as I tried to pull my arm away.

"You are never to look another man in the face again," he

said, the words cold.

I tugged my arm, but he tightened his grip even further.

"Do you understand?" he snarled through clenched teeth at me as he pulled me in close to his face.

"Yes," I said meekly.

He released me.

My arm hurt as I lowered my head to look at the ground.

I knew that North would have seen what Mr James had done. He'd been only meters away. I felt embarrassed and scared. This was the man I was going to marry — if he was this cruel now, how bad would he be once I was under lock and key?

Mr James gripped the top of my arm again in a firm hold and walked me on through the garden while I kept my head down.

"Good evening, farm boy," Mr James said, and without looking I knew he had been speaking to North.

North admired Harper as she strolled through the garden with a tall dark-haired man who looked to be in his mid-to-late twenties. He thought she looked beautiful, but he thought her prettier without all the makeup and fancy hair, although the dress was definitely something he liked. It was so tight he could almost imagine her naked, something he had thought about many times before when in the privacy of his own room.

He strode across the yard a little quicker than usual so as not to interrupt the couple. He was jealous that it wasn't him walking with Harper. He couldn't help but take one last glance at her, and to his surprise his eyes met with her beautiful emerald ones, and he smiled at how enchanting she looked. She smiled back and they both quickly looked down. Then he heard Harper's voice.

"You're hurting me."

North looked over at them. The dark-haired man was gripping her so tightly that he was sure he was going to snap her fragile arms.

"You are never to look another man in the face again," the dark-haired man told her as he pulled her in close to his face.

North had to anchor himself to the ground to stop himself from knocking the man out. No man should ever treat a woman like that.

"Do you understand?" the dark-haired man snarled as North watched Harper cower.

"Yes," Harper said, her voice tiny and meek.

North's jaw was set so tight he could have bitten through steel. He wanted to beat the shit out of the man, his hands itched for it, but he knew he was a farmhand, and it wasn't his place to interfere with the boss's daughter's business. Hell, he had no right looking at her in the first place. But no man should ever touch a woman like that.

The dark-haired man gripped Harper's arm, making her flinch while she stared at the ground, her face twisted with fear as the dark-haired man strolled past North and gave him a cruel, twisted smile. "Good-evening farm boy."

North didn't reply. He was too angry that someone who knew they were bigger and stronger could hurt someone as beautiful as Harper Crain.

CHAPTER THREE

I sat on my bed and looked at the bruises on my arm which showed the precise spots where Sabastian James's fingers had dug in. It hurt, but it didn't seem real. Girls were always told that their husbands would be perfect gentlemen, feed, shelter and father their children. In return the wives were expected to be obedient, subservient and compliant to her husbands every whim.

My father had taken Mr James into his office when we returned from our walk and had given his blessing to him, which was as good as a done deal for me to marry him. If my father backed out of the arrangement now, he would likely have to pay Mr James a substantial amount of compensation.

My father had money in the bank, but not Sabastian James's kind of money and I was betting Mr James wasn't the kind of man that would take kindly to being denied.

Mr James had left looking pleased with himself, while I wanted to throw myself out the second storey window, although I thought probably the worst injury I would do myself would be a broken limb and that certainly wouldn't stop me being forced to marry him.

I had changed out of the form-fitting dress, choosing instead to wear my black leggings and a black, fitted short-sleeved top. I figured a girl in mourning for her own life should wear black. It was a self-pitying gesture which I wasn't accustomed to, but it seemed appropriate under the circumstances. My father had informed me I was to become Mrs Harper James in two days. I was so stunned I could have spat acid. In shock, I questioned the haste. He told me he had made up his mind and I would do what he wanted because I was a girl and I had to learn my place. I had never heard him speak so harshly to me or so coldly.

My mother proceeded to lecture me on a woman's place and how I didn't deserve a husband as fine and aristocratic as Mr James. Then I was punished by having to scrub the kitchen from ceiling to floor and everything in between.

It was one in the morning. My arm hurt. I had washed and scrubbed with the ferocity of a demon scorned, grateful the walls of the house were solid enough to withstand it or I would probably have destroyed the kitchen. I thought about Birdy's offer to run away with me, but surely he was jesting, as he had a good life here. He was the boss's son, who would one day inherit the entire estate and have enough money to buy a wife.

Buy a wife. The words rattled around my head. Birdy had said that outside our country, women could choose a man because they loved him. Birdy didn't want a woman to be his slave. He wanted to be in love with the woman he chose to be with.

A smile crossed my lips. *My big brother is a romantic.* That thought suddenly grew painful. If I went with Sabastian James, Birdy would stay here, and the only way to gain a wife here was to buy one.

My heart sank a little. He would lose his romantic heart if he stayed, and it would be my fault. I couldn't do that to him or myself.

I slipped off my bed and down the hall to Birdy's bedroom door, the faint sound of his snoring breaking the house's deathly silence as I pushed his door open and slipped inside.

"Birdy, Birdy," I whispered as I gave him a small shake.

He made a snorting noise, rolled onto his side and resumed

snoring.

"Birdy." I shook him a little harder. "Wake up."

"What?" he groaned, a little too loudly.

"Shh," I hushed as he rolled to face me.

"What's going on?" he grumbled.

"Were you serious about running away?"

"Yeah." Birdy's sleepiness suddenly dissolved as he sat up. "Do you want to?" he asked while he flicked on the bedside lamp to look at me.

"I can't marry Sabastian James and I can't ask father to call it off — he doesn't have the money to compensate him," I said in all seriousness.

Birdy raised an eyebrow. "He's rich, good-looking and has impeccable dress sense, I thought he'd be a girl's ideal husband?"

"He's also a brute." I held up my arm to show him the bruises.

"He did that to you?"

I nodded.

"That sonofabitch," Birdy bit out, "I'm going to rip his head off and shove it up his ass."

"No, you're not. You're going to get us both out of here so we can live the lives we want with the people we want."

Birdy looked at me, and I could see the cogs ticking in his head — he was thinking about it. "We can't leave tonight, because I have to make some arrangements and get some money together."

"I am to marry Sabastian James the day after tomorrow."

"Then we'll leave tomorrow night. Don't mention a thing to anyone, do whatever you usually do and be ready to leave after dinner."

I nodded at Birdy, "Where are we going?"

Birdy shrugged, "Away from here."

That was good enough for me.

Sabastian sat in his luxury sports car enjoying the smooth ride. He had called in a favour to expedite the funds transfer to Mr Crain's bank account. Once that was done, Harper was all his, but for the small matter of her father's signature on the government wedding licence.

In less than twenty-four hours he would be married, and then he would have her. He smiled just thinking about planting his seed in her, but first she had to learn to be obedient. That would be a fun lesson to teach her. Maybe he could do both at the same time, plant his seed and discipline her. His smile widened at the thought. After all, she was going to be his wife, and she would be expected to fulfil his every whim.

He pulled his phone out and dialled Mr Crain's number.

"Hello," Mr Crain answered tiredly.

"Hello, Mr Crain, this is Sabastian James," he said delightedly. "Our agreed price has been deposited in your bank account, and the relevant taxes and paperwork have been filed with the government department."

"So soon?" Mr Crain sounded shocked, and Sabastian couldn't help smiling to himself. He wasn't a run of the mill businessman. His company developed the computer systems and weaponry for every government department in the Nation, including the DNA research facilities, the armed forces, and national security departments. He had access to more private information than any other man on earth, and he relished it.

"I was hoping to visit with my bride to be," Sabastian said.

"Of course."

He could hear Mr Crain almost falling over himself to oblige.

"Thank you, you're most kind. Expect me in an hour," he told the blithering old man.

Once he and Harper were married, he would leave this wretched corner of the Nation and head back to his house near the Capital, never to return. It had been sheer luck that he'd been called to the DNA facility to oversee one of the new computer systems when he ran into Mr Crain and his daughter in the elevator. He had watched her, along with the rest of the potential bidders, through the showroom's one-way mirrors. She stood ramrod straight, looking defiant, and Sabastian suspected that Harper somehow knew she was on show. Whereas the other girls in her group had primped and preened, she hadn't. Instead, she'd looked determined and strong. A challenge.

"Would you join us for lunch?" Mr Crain asked.

"I'd be delighted," Sabastian said, although he could barely stand the thought of eating such rustic food. He was accustomed to the best, and these country bumpkins seemed to think roasted lamb and potatoes was fine dining. Oh, how he couldn't wait to take his bride home and have his chef cook him something edible.

I wanted to protest when father informed me that Sabastian James would be joining us for lunch. My mother, the sensible woman she was, started to flap her arms about while she ran in circles. "Oh, what will we serve him? We can't give him leftovers," she babbled before she turned to me. Her glance caught on my pink shorts and blue top with a mark down the front from where I'd spilled bleach earlier, "Go get changed, girl, that top is a disgrace, and do something with your hair!"

"But I haven't finished the bathroom," I told her, half hoping she'd lock me in there until I was finished.

"I don't care about the bathroom. Go clean yourself up!" she snapped as she finally decided on a direction to take and headed for the kitchen.

I looked to my father with pleading eyes.

"Do as you are told," he said sternly.

I let out a sigh of surrender as I trudged up the stairs. Maybe if I showed Mr James how unladylike I was, he'd withdraw his offer and Birdy and I wouldn't have to run away. No. If Mr James withdrew his offer, then the next man in line would be here trying to court me, and even if I managed to dissuade all of them, I would then become a Bride of the state, and there was no way I wanted that.

I jumped in the shower and washed the smell of bleach from my skin. I could play this game for one more afternoon, then tonight Birdy and I would slip away, and they could all go jump off a bridge.

I dressed in my pretty creamy-white dress with the lace trim and tied my hair into a ponytail before I brushed on some mascara and peach lip gloss. I didn't look as fancy as I had last night, but I was sure even Mr James wouldn't expect me to look like I was going to a formal dinner all day every day, and I didn't care if he did — I liked this dress.

When I went downstairs, my mother was rushing around barking orders at several of the farmhands who were doing their best to help.

"Go help in the kitchen," my mother ordered as soon as she saw me come down the stairs, "And for heaven's sake, why didn't you put some makeup on? And why are you wearing that old dress?"

I thought about telling her I did put makeup on, but she wouldn't be happy unless I was done up to the hilt.

The kitchen wasn't busy, only North stood stirring a pot of something which smelled amazing. He glanced up and saw me, a faint flicker twitching his lips before he turned back to the pot on the stove. I dropped my gaze, took a fresh loaf of bread out and began to slice it as I tried not to glance over at him, which was almost impossible.

North tried to ignore Harper and the way she looked almost ethereal in her lacy white dress, but the scent of her perfume had him mesmerised — soft, sweet and completely feminine, just like her. He had never in his life seen anyone as perfect as Harper Crain, and he couldn't help secretly stealing glimpses of her slicing the crusty bread. He reflected that if he were a rich man, he would give every cent he had just to spend an hour gazing into those beautiful green eyes.

North mentally slapped himself for what he was thinking. he could never be DNA tested or have anyone as beautiful as her. She was perfection, and his secret would disgust her.

Harper stopped slicing, put down the knife and swept past him. She brushed against him ever so lightly on her way to retrieve a large ornate plate for the bread.

That single faint touch sent an electric buzz through every cell in North's body. Holy cow, she was way out of his league and due to marry that dark haired man tomorrow. He couldn't be thinking about her. But still, he stole another glance and wished with every cell in his body that he could take her away from here and make her his.

I could feel every time North glanced over at me, which made me wonder if I had something stuck to my face or maybe there was a mark on my dress I hadn't noticed. Still, I had inadvertently brushed against him when I went to fetch the plate, and it felt kind of funny, like an electric shock, but in a pleasant way.

I glanced over at him again. He was handsome and strong with a well-defined square jaw and honey blond hair. He turned his gaze on me, and for a moment his deep brown eyes looked straight into mine. I felt like a deer in the headlights. I was transfixed. I was held by his gaze and time seemed irrelevant.

"So, what are we eating for lunch?" Birdy's voice snapped me back to the present.

We broke eye contact and I glanced over at the door just in time to see Birdy walk in before turning my eyes back to the bread. I was sure my cheeks must have been beet-red from embarrassment. My dear brother would see it in a heartbeat and probably guess what I was thinking.

"Lamb stew," North said.

I had never heard him speak, and his voice surprised me. It was masculine, with a slight hint of a northern accent. I hadn't heard many accents except when the farmhands were talking, and they only spoke when they didn't know I was around, so I couldn't tell where his accent was from exactly.

"It smells great," Birdy said cheerfully.

I picked up the plate of bread and the butter and carried it out to the dining room.

Through the large windows that faced the driveway, I saw an expensive black sports car pull up. My heart sank in my chest as the handsome Mr James slid out and was warmly greeted by my father and mother.

The way my parents fawned over the man, you'd think they were stray dogs and he had a bag of bones just for them. The sight angered me. I was being sold to the devil, and they were licking his boots.

If Birdy couldn't get us out of here, then I would be married to Mr James by lunchtime tomorrow.

Chapter Four

Sabastian shook the eager Mr Crain's hand. The older man had obviously checked his bank balance today and had probably started spending it in his head. Maybe if Sabastian could get the old man to sign the paperwork this afternoon, he could take his new bride today and be done with this place. *No.* As tempting as that sounded, he still had business at the DNA facility tonight, and he didn't want to have to deal with worrying about keeping his investment secure while he worked.

"Welcome." Mr Crain grinned, while his wife vibrated on the spot like a nervous lapdog.

"It is most kind of you both to grant me a visit at such short notice," Sabastian said.. "I hope it isn't an inconvenience?"

Sabastian didn't actually care if it was—he had paid a lot of money, and these people would be stupid to refuse him anything. Not that he thought they would. In fact, if he told Mr and Mrs Crain to lick his boots, he was sure they'd crouch down and do it in a heartbeat.

"Please come inside," Mr Crain said as he ushered him up the front steps into the house.

Sabastian smiled when he saw Harper Crain standing by the window looking out at the garden in a simple white dress, her silhouette perfectly framed. By tomorrow evening they would be in his luxurious home near the Capital, and he was going to enjoy her, all of her.

"We will give you a minute with your bride-to-be," Mr Crain said in a low tone as he left them alone.

Sabastian watched her for a moment longer, simply enjoying her perfection. "Miss Crain."

She turned, and Sabastian marvelled at how pretty a wife he had chosen. Even with very little makeup, she was exquisite. His business associates would be green with envy when they saw her. They had all chosen well, but Harper was exceptional. The best thing about her was that she didn't know just how exceptional she was, and he planned to keep it that way.

I could feel Sabastian James watching me while I stared out the window at North striding back to the farmhands' quarters on the far side of the expansive lawn. I waited until he was out of sight before I turned to face my betrothed. Mr James was wearing a perfectly tailored pair of charcoal dress pants and a cream three-button shirt. His clothes said casual, but I was sure that this one ensemble probably cost more than every stitch of clothing in my wardrobe.

"Mr James." I diverted my gaze to the ground.

"Please, call me Sabastian. After all, we will be officially man and wife tomorrow."

The thought of being this man's wife chilled me, but I couldn't run away yet. I had to play nice, for now.

"Sabastian," I said softly while I tried not to gag on his name.

"Now, isn't that better?" he cooed as he walked over to stand next to me by the window seat. "Shall we sit?" His tone was still aristocratic, but lighter and filled with amusement.

I took a seat as I flicked a glance out the window, but thank goodness North was nowhere to be seen. I didn't want a repeat of last evening's tirade.

"My dear Harper, I must apologise for my behaviour in the garden," Sabastian began while he took my hand in his.

I fought the urge to pull away.

"I behaved like a barbarian," he said. "It is just that you are so beautiful. I know that how things are done in the country may not be the same as in the city, so I have arranged for an etiquette teacher to work with you when we return to my house near the Capital."

My head sprang up, and my eyes met his dark-blue ones. "The Capital? I thought you lived near here."

Sabastian grinned, but not a pleasant grin. It was full of something that made me want to curl into a ball and cringe. I dropped my gaze to my lap.

He chuckled softly. "I am going to enjoy training you."

"Maybe you need a dog, not a wife," I mumbled, trying to pull my hand away, but he gripped it tighter, while his other hand grabbed my ponytail and yanked me close to his face.

I wanted to fight and scratch and scream abuse, but I bit it all down. I had to just get through this lunch, and tonight I would be gone.

"You will learn to hold your tongue," Sabastian whispered, his breath hot against my cheek before he suddenly licked the side of my face.

I squirmed in disgust and fear as I tried to free myself.

"Mmm, you taste delicious. I can't wait to taste the rest of you."

The thought of him touching me again sent acid burning the back of my throat. For such an attractive man, he was completely revolting.

Footsteps echoed outside the open door. Sabastian suddenly released his grip on my hair.

"Mr James," Birdy greeted him as he entered the dining room, "How nice to see you again."

Sabastian released my hand and stood. "Master Crain, a pleasure to see you again."

Birdy was smiling, but I knew he was watching me

intently. I could tell he knew something was wrong. I wiped the slobber from the side of my face and tried to fix my hair. Now all I had to do was get through lunch, have a shower, and remind myself that I would be gone after dinner and this bastard would have to find another girl to torture. That thought stopped me cold. How many men were out there like Sabastian James? Men who would control a woman with brutality. And worse still, how many women were forced to live with it?

I was grateful when lunch was finally over and Sabastian had to return to the city on business. I took myself up to my room to enjoy alone time. It was after supper time, and my stomach growled ferociously, but I couldn't eat, despite the amazing smell of the lamb stew and the high praise everyone gave it.

Sabastian had even looked shocked to find something so delicious on the table. But I couldn't eat a bite all day. My stomach had twisted itself into a tight ball of nerves, especially with Sabastian sitting so close and giving me grins that would flash freeze the Nile in summer.

"Harper," my father said from the doorway, "are you all right, my girl?"

I gave him a small smile, "Of course, I'm sure it's just nerves."

"Well, it's to be expected—you are about to marry one of the richest, most eligible men in the entire Nation. I'm sure you will be attending balls and dinners every week." Father sat himself down on the bed beside me. "I always knew you were destined for greatness."

"Thank you," I said automatically.

I wanted to tell him how nasty Sabastian had been.

"Isn't Sabastian a wonderful man? And to think he chose you, my beautiful daughter. He has even transferred the money into my bank already."

That was it, it was a done deal. I had been bought and paid for. If Birdy didn't come through this evening, I would steal one of the cars and run away by myself.

"Thank you, Daddy," I said as I leaned forward and hugged him. If all went well — or even if it didn't — I would never see him or this farm again.

"I will miss you, my darling girl." His stoic voice trembled slightly while he patted my shoulder before he stood, wished me goodnight and left me alone with my dread and fears.

I was leaving one way or another, and I would miss my parents.

North sat on the ground with his back against the garage door while he looked up at the light still burning in the room he knew belonged to Harper. The rest of the house had been dark for at least an hour, which wasn't unusual, but it wasn't common, either. He was guessing she was either nervous or excited about marrying that rich idiot he'd seen hurting her in the garden. Staring absently at the light, North sighed — he wished he was the one who was marrying her. He often watched her window late at night, imagining her reading a book or brushing her beautiful long silky brown hair, until the light would go out and he would return to his bed to dream of her. He lamented that this would be the last night he'd do this.

Her light blinked out, and North sat for a moment longer, something akin to heartache burning in his chest. He was usually so sensible. He'd had to be, and he hardly knew Harper. How could he be so stupid as to pine for her?

He exhaled and pushed himself up off the cold ground. He had barely taken a step when he heard the faint sound of the house door opening and two sets of feet tiptoeing down the steps. To anyone else they scarcely made a sound, but North wasn't normal. He had heightened senses thanks to his genetic faults.

North froze against the building and waited to see who was sneaking out of the house so late at night. He caught her scent first—he would know it anywhere—and then he smelled Birdy's. In the low light he could see Birdy gripping his sister's hand as he pulled her across the yard.

"What the—?"

I gripped tightly to Birdy's hand as he pulled me across the yard toward the garage. It was so dark that I was scared I was going to run into mother's rose bushes and shred myself to bits before we had even left the farm.

Birdy had left his SUV down the driveway a bit so the noise wouldn't wake anyone and alert them to our escape.

My heart pounded, and I wasn't sure I could do this, but the thought of Sabastian James touching me, or more to the point brutalising me again, spurred me on.

We were passing the garage when I felt someone watching us. I turned and let out a gasp at the huge shadowy figure standing against the wall mere meters away. Birdy spun and put himself between me and the figure. For a moment I wasn't sure if I should run, scream or vomit. I knew if I screamed, I would wake the house. I gripped Birdy's shirt tightly, but it took me only a moment to realise the figure was familiar.

"North?" I whispered, my beating heart so loud in my ears I wasn't sure if my voice was audible.

"What are you doing out here?" Birdy asked as he pulled out the handgun he'd slipped into his hip pocket on the way out the door and pointed it at the tall blond man.

North raised his hands without a word. There was a long moment of silence as the tension grew so thick I could taste it.

"Shit," Birdy finally protested. "We have to take him with

us."

"What? Why?" I asked.

"He saw us, and if we leave him, he'll be obligated to tell Father."

North's face was in shadow, but I could feel his gaze so heavily that it was an anvil on my shoulders.

"Birdy, we can't take him. He'll be accused of kidnapping me," I protested.

If the authorities thought we had run away that was one thing, but if they thought North had kidnapped me, then they would hunt him down like a rabid dog and execute him.

"I'm sorry North, we'll drop you a few towns over. By the time you walk home, it'll be morning, and you can tell my father and the authorities whatever you want," Birdy apologised.

North pondered the brother and sister. Harper looked so fragile and frightened. He would do anything not to see that look on her face, but the fact remained that this brother and sister were out here in the middle of the night, obviously running away. He had heard tales of incest on his travels, but he would never have picked Birdy and Harper as being so revolting.

"Are you two," North began, trying to choose the right words, "involved?"

It took a moment, and then Harper gasped. "Oh yuck, don't be so disgusting, he's my brother."

Harper's honest reaction gave North some relief.

"Look, we need to get as far away from here as possible before morning. That's all you need to know," Birdy told him flatly.

North knew Birdy meant as far away from Mr James as possible. He couldn't blame them. He had disliked the pompous brute the moment he saw him hurt Harper in the garden.

Without a word, North started down the driveway. He'd seen Birdy's SUV parked away down and thought it odd at the time, but now he understood.

I let out a sigh as we followed North down the long driveway. I felt bad that we had to involve him in our escape, but Birdy was right, if we didn't take him with us, then his obligation was to immediately notify our father of our absence, and then our father would have to contact the authorities. Missing girls were a high priority for the authorities, and I would be top of the list, considering the amount Sabastian James had just paid for me.

"Can you drive?" Birdy asked North as we reached the car.

"Yes," he answered, while Birdy ushered me into the back seat.

"Good, then you can get us out of here," Birdy said, holding the gun on North.

North slid into the driver's seat while Birdy ran around the car and got into the passenger seat beside him, gun in hand. North turned the key, and the car sprang to life. I had never driven a car. It wasn't a skill most females had. Women couldn't go anywhere without a male escort anyway.

North drove to the end of the long driveway and stopped when he came to the main road. "Which way?" he asked.

Birdy looked in both directions. He probably hadn't thought too much about it, and it was obvious to me the decision was hard.

North quietly cleared his throat, "If I was trying to get my sister somewhere safe, I'd head north toward the border. The country to the south has an extradition agreement with ours, while up north barely has a government, and they hate the laws of the Nation."

Birdy looked over his shoulder at me, as if questioning me

on my thoughts—head south where we could get extradited, or north where there were barely any laws?

"I trust him." The words sounded foreign as they left my mouth. "We go north."

CHAPTER FIVE

Sabastian admired himself in a full-length mirror and thought how lucky Harper Crain was to be marrying him and how he would be enjoying her perfect body very soon. He might even bring her back to his apartment in the city to enjoy her before they flew back to the Capital. A grin stretched across his face. Harper was so perfect that Sabastian was sure several of his business associates would offer to pay him for her time, which wasn't uncommon amongst his wealthy colleagues. He himself had been given several of his business associates' wives while they were begging for various contracts. All the women he'd been offered were certainly beautiful, but Harper left even the prettiest ones in the doghouse. He would never share his gorgeous trophy wife with anyone. He would be the only man who would ever enjoy her. Sabastian adjusted his tie as he marvelled at his own perfection.

His phone rang displaying a number he didn't know.

"Mr James?" a deep male voice asked.

"Speaking," Sabastian answered, irritated that his morning had been interrupted.

"This is Agent Fairchild from the Missing Girls Department."

Sabastian felt his blood pressure rise. There was only one reason for MGD to be calling him.

She wouldn't dare!

"We've been called out to the Crain property. It appears that Miss Crain is missing," Agent Fairchild said.

"Was she kidnapped?" Sabastian asked, but he had the feeling she had run.

"We're not sure. Her brother Bernard and one of the farm-hands are also missing."

Sabastian instantly thought of the tall blond man he'd seen in the garden, but he would never have suspected Bernard Crain. He had thought the boy had no backbone. He smiled. He always enjoyed a chase, and it would be all the more fun when he caught her, and then he would teach her never to betray him again.

"Mr James, how would you like us to proceed?" Fairchild's voice penetrated Sabastian's thoughts.

"I'll be there shortly," Sabastian said. "I'll be arriving by copter."

My limbs felt stiff as I opened my eyes. I was lying across the back seat of Birdy's SUV, and the sun was already high in the sky.

North was still at the wheel driving us through the lush green countryside while Birdy slept in the passenger seat, the gun resting loosely on his lap.

I sat up and stretched.

The sound of a man's dreary voice played through the radio while he read the news in a slow methodical voice.

'Praeses, our Nation's great leader, has announced the building of a new DNA research facility to develop a vaccine against the Unholy. If successful, he plans to inoculate every man, woman and child in our great Nation.'

North's fingers tightened visibly on the steering wheel.

'In further news, the MGD has reports of a missing girl. She is believed to be in the company of two men. Authorities have grave fears for her wellbeing. MGD spokesman Agent Fairchild asks the public to be on the lookout for a black SUV, number plate Z . . .'

North reached over and turned off the radio. "Shit, I

thought we'd be further away than this before they put out the broadcast."

"I'm sorry, we should have left you at the farm," I apologised. "They're going to think you're involved."

North had been driving for five hours straight and it was still at least another five hours before they would be out of the state.

He glanced over his shoulder at Harper, and her emerald-green eyes looked mournful.

"I could have pulled over four hours ago when Birdy fell asleep and just walked away," North told Harper.

"So why didn't you?"

North shrugged. He had his own reasons, but the one that would sound least stalkerish was probably the best one. "I don't agree that DNA sequencing is the best way to determine someone's happiness, and I don't think that women should be treated like commodities to be bought, swapped and sold to the highest bidder."

He glanced in the rear-view mirror and saw Harper slump back in her seat, cover her eyes and silently sob.

North's heart felt tight. Had he said something to upset her?

He turned the SUV off the main highway and down a narrow country road bordered by thick trees on either side. He swung the car off the road and pulled as far as he could into a dense thicket of trees until the forest hid the SUV from the outside world.

Birdy stirred in the passenger seat and blinked groggily. "What's going on?"

"The MGD just put out a bulletin on us and the SUV," North told him.

Birdy swore.

Sabastian's pilot and right-hand man Mr Kleve landed the copter on the lawn behind the Crain house.

When he'd woken up that morning, Sabastian had expected Mr Crain would officially hand over the marriage certificate and daughter after breakfast, but the plans had changed.

Mr Kleve slipped out of the copter while several men in black fatigues waited by the house. Sabastian smiled to himself, aware that all gazes fell on Mr Kleve as he rounded the copter to open his door. He thought about how often people misjudged Mr Kleve due to his height or lack thereof.

Mr Kleve was only four feet tall with a lot of muscle, but Sabastian hadn't hired him because people misjudged him. He had hired him because he was the best sniper in the business and was as placid as a cut snake.

If god had made a human Pitbull, Mr Kleve would be it.

An older man in black fatigues made his way over with Mr Crain by his side.

"Mr James, it's an honour to meet you, sir, I'm Agent Fairchild. And I'd just like to say, thank you, sir, your surveillance equipment has made our job easier over the years."

Great, a sycophant. He detested brown-nosers, but he would endure it as long as he needed the man's resources.

"Thank you, Agent Fairchild," Sabastian said before he turned to Mr Crain. "But let us get straight to business. When did you discover she was missing?"

"Around six this morning," Mr Crain answered as he fidgeted nervously.

"Did you call the MGD immediately?" Sabastian asked, although he doubted he would have—he would have waited until he'd searched the property. Mr Crain wouldn't have wanted his daughter's disappearance on her wedding day to become public knowledge.

Mr Crain looked sheepishly at a piece of paper in his hand. "No, I called them around seven. I thought she might have been taking some private time before your wedding today."

Sabastian glanced at his expensive watch — it was now nine-forty. Agent Fairchild had called him only half an hour ago.

"Why wasn't I called when the MGD was called?" Sabastian seethed.

Mr Crain took a step back. "I was hoping that we would find this was all a misunderstanding." He held a piece of paper out to Sabastian. "I am aware that my daughter's infraction would be marked as a breach of our contract. Although I signed the wedding certificate not long after you left yesterday, I completely understand you're not going through with it and I suggest you shred it. I will transfer the money back into your account by the days end."

Sabastian stared at the signature on the piece of paper, the corners of his lips curved as he thought about it. With her father's signature, she was legally his.

"Mr Crain," Sabastian said while he rolled the paper into a tube in his hands. "Let us not be hasty." He turned to Agent Fairchild, "Has the broadcast been released?"

"Yes, sir, about twenty minutes ago, and we have set up roadblocks on all the major roads."

"How far out are the roadblocks?" Sabastian asked in his smooth tone.

"A hundred kilometres."

Sabastian tried not to sound too disgusted. "I don't mean to sound critical, but one hundred kilometres? Even if they were moving slowly, they would have covered that in a few hours. And since it is safe to assume they departed before six this morning and it is almost ten now, I would say they are far beyond that range. They're probably also listening to the in-car radio, which means they will likely be aware that the MGD is looking for them, so it's unlikely they'd be keeping to the main roads."

Agent Fairchild shifted uncomfortably, which made Sabastian pleased. He loved nothing more than to make others uneasy.

"Perhaps I should suggest road-blocks on the state borders," Sabastian said calmly before turning to Mr Crain. "Does your son have a mobile phone, or does his car have a GPS locator?"

"He doesn't have a phone, but he does have one of those GPS units on his dashboard," Mr Crain said helpfully.

Sabastian grinned. This was going to be too easy.

"What the hell did you do to my car?" Birdy yelled as he paced back and forth. "We could have used that GPS to find the back roads out of here!"

"I told you, if you can locate a position on the screen, then someone can locate you," North said without raising his voice.

"So, what did you do with it?" I asked.

North glanced over at me as a hot blush heated my cheeks. "I threw it out the window about three hours after we left the farm."

"You threw it out the window." Birdy rubbed his face, grumbling something about North being the male offspring of a female dog.

I went to the back of the SUV and opened the boot. Birdy had loaded it with food, water, blankets and our own personal belongings. I felt bad. North had nothing. We had taken him without a single scrap of his own personal belongings.

"I'm going for a walk," Birdy grumbled as he stomped off into the trees.

"Sorry about Birdy, he gets a bit . . ." I started to say, my gaze fixed to the ground.

"You don't have to apologise for someone else's behaviour," North said quietly.

I chanced a glance up, and our gazes met for a moment before I quickly diverted them to the boxes of food in the back of the car. I felt suddenly shaky inside, not scared, but nervous—as if North could see right through me. It both thrilled and frightened me.

North leaned against the car watching Harper. She was too fragile. Maybe he should have turned them in when he had the chance. *No.* That dark-haired man she was expected to marry would have made her life a living hell. He knew where he was going to take them once they crossed out of the country—he had grown up there. The only thing was, would Birdy and Harper despise him if they found out what he was?

"Are you hungry?" Harper asked him while she pulled out a loaf of bread from one of the boxes.

"Starved," North replied.

He watched her butter the bread and smear peanut butter across it before she handed him one of the sandwiches. Their hands brushed lightly, and that same electric jolt nipped his skin.

My fingers buzzed where they'd inadvertently brushed North's hand when I handed him the sandwich. It was an odd sensation, almost pleasant, yet foreign at the same time.

I took a bite of my peanut butter sandwich, remembering how I couldn't stand the taste of peanut butter or the way it stuck to the roof of my mouth.

I chuckled to myself thinking of how spoilt I must seem.

Food was food, and I couldn't complain when I had some in my hand.

I glanced up to see North looking at me, his eyebrow raised in question. He must have heard my chuckle.

I lowered my head. "Sorry, I'm not very fond of peanut butter, and I was just thinking you would probably think I was spoilt."

I heard North laugh. I had never heard his laugh before, and I found it pleasant and warm. I lowered my head again, feeling embarrassed that I had spoken so frankly to a man I wasn't related to. His laugh stopped, and silence claimed the trees around us.

"Harper," North said softly.

The way he said my name sounded almost musical.

"Please look at me," he urged quietly. "You are a free woman now. You don't have to look down for anyone, especially me."

I lifted my head slowly and looked into his deep brown eyes. He smiled. North was handsome on a good day, but seeing his smile sent him into devastatingly gorgeous territory.

"I should probably confess I'm not a fan of peanut butter either," he told me earnestly. "I just didn't want to hurt your feelings."

I laughed. "I'll remember that for next time."

CHAPTER SIX

Sabastian snarled as he looked down at the black device, no bigger than a deck of playing cards, lying by the side of the highway.

"Guess we can't track them that way?" Agent Fairchild shook his head. "And they could be anywhere by now."

Sabastian thought Agent Fairchild and his team incompetent fools, but he could still use them to find her.

"On the contrary." Sabastian smiled coldly. "We know they are heading north, so you should reassign all available men to the northern border."

Agent Fairchild looked dumbstruck. Sabastian fought the urge to slap the older man up the side of his head to see if he had any brains in there.

"The Crain farm is to the south. This particular highway leads to the north," Sabastian explained slowly as though speaking to a child. "So, we can assume they are heading for the border."

"But if they cross into the northern country, we haven't got any extradition agreements," Agent Fairchild said worriedly.

Oh, how Sabastian wanted to pull out his gun and lodge a bullet in the man's head.

"That is why you are going to close the border," Sabastian told him through gritted teeth.

He wasn't used to having to play nice. He was used to issuing an order and everyone jumping as if their asses were on fire.

Agent Fairchild reluctantly pulled his phone out. "We need

to close the northern border. It is possible that two men are trying to smuggle a girl out of the country."

Sabastian shook his head and wondered if all of MGD were as incompetent as Fairchild and his subordinates.

The first thing he was going to do when he had Harper back in his possession was develop an injectable GPS tracker so he could keep close tabs on her. Maybe he could introduce it to all women who passed through the DNA facilities, or have the devices injected into newborn girls so that none could slip through the cracks and disappear before their eighteenth birthdays. He'd have to develop a nationwide computer tracking system to go along with the injectable GPS, but that shouldn't be too hard for a man of his talents and then the inept MGD agents might actually be able to find a missing girl.

I lay in the reclined passenger seat trying to nap while North slept soundly in the reclined driver's seat. He had driven all night and was exhausted. But still it felt weird lying next to a man, even with Birdy sitting just outside with his back against the tyre. I tossed and turned as I tried to get comfortable, and finally settled on my side so I could watch North sleep. There was something captivating about him, and I found myself studying every curve of his face as though it held some secret.

He shifted slightly, and I closed my eyes, pretending to be asleep as I lay still for a moment before slowly reopening my eyes. He was still asleep, but his soft honey-blond hair had fallen across his forehead. My hand reached out, my fingers gently brushing his soft hair from his face before I could stop myself.

North opened his eyes and smiled.

Heat burned my cheeks as I quickly withdrew and rolled over.

What must he think of me touching him? A woman never touches a man who isn't her family or husband.

"Are you all right?" Birdy pushed himself off the ground.

I looked over at him and nodded. "When are we leaving?"

"We can't move until its dark, and even then we're going to have to try to find some new plates or another car," Birdy said, as though it were obvious.

"There is also the issue of fuel," North said as I heard the driver's door open. "We're getting pretty low, and I'm not sure how much further we can go on what's left in the tank."

"Great, we'll have to find a fuel station and hope no one listens to the radio," Birdy said sarcastically.

I thought about it for a moment. Everyone would be looking for two men and a woman with long brown hair. I walked to the back of the SUV and rummaged through the bags before I pulled out a pair of scissors. I took a deep breath and began chopping my hair off in chunks.

"What are you doing?" Birdy screeched as he tried to snatch the scissors from my hand.

"They are looking for two men and a woman," I snapped while I yanked the scissors out of his reach. "If I cut my hair and wear some of your clothes, I'll look like a boy."

Birdy swore.

"It's just hair," I told him as North rounded the car and looked at me before holding his hand out for me to give him the scissors. I hesitated only for the briefest moment before handing them over. He stepped behind me, lifted a section of hair and cut.

North thought Harper would be beautiful with her head shaved bald and wearing a brown hessian sack, but he hadn't expected her to just cut it off. Maybe she wasn't as fragile as he thought she was. He lifted a section of her soft hair, which smelled sensual and feminine like her, then without hesitation he cut it off before moving to the next bit.

"What are you doing?" Birdy growled.

"Either I cut it, or your sister does. And I'm fairly sure I'd do a better job," North told him.

Birdy began to pace back and forth. "She still has . . ." He moved his hands to indicate Harper's breasts which, although weren't massive, were still generous.

North bent over Harper's shoulder looking down at her and did his best not to smile.

"I could strap myself," Harper offered while she squished her breasts flat with her hands. "There are some bandages in the back."

North was impressed by her willingness to do whatever she could to conceal herself while he lifted another piece of hair and cut it. He had long imagined himself running his fingers through her hair, but this wasn't what he had in mind.

Birdy sighed and went to grab the bandages out of the car. "I guess it might work," he finally conceded.

North trimmed the last of her hair. It was on the longer side for a male, but short for a female, and he doubted it would fool anyone. Harper was way too feminine to look like a boy. She was simply beautiful.

I stood in a puddle of my own hair wishing that I had a mirror to see the end result, but not entirely sure I wanted to. I wasn't vain, but I'd had long hair as long as I could remember, and the shortness now felt odd.

Birdy gave me a once over, sighed and handed me the bandages.

I thought about trying to be modest by slipping behind a tree to bind my chest, but I knew from experience I would need help.

My mother had strapped my chest when I'd first started developing breasts so my father and the farmhands wouldn't know. I was never sure exactly why she did it, and she never explained it, but I always thought it was probably because she didn't want the unattached male farmhands to notice I was growing up and had breasts. After all, we lived a long way from town, and many of the men were chauvinistic pigs that seemed resentful that they would never have the chance to marry. They treated all women, not just the Brides of the state, as chattel.

I reached for the hem of my top and pulled it off. Birdy and North both instantly turned their backs.

I rolled my eyes. "I'm going to need help."

"She's your sister," North said to Birdy.

"That's right, she's my sister, and I'm not touching her. That's just wrong!" Birdy spat in disgust, jammed the rolls of bandages into North's hands and walked away.

I wrapped my arms around myself as I tried to cover as much as possible, but I knew my navy-blue bra was exposed for the world to see. I bit my bottom lip and looked at North's broad back.

"Do you have a problem touching me?" I asked, instantly regretting how it must have sounded.

North shifted uncomfortably. "Umm, can't you do it yourself?"

"I can do the front, but I need help passing it across my back."

North turned slowly, but he didn't look at me. Maybe my body disgusted him.

I turned my back to him. For a moment I wasn't sure if he was even still behind me, but then I felt a tingling sensation buzz through me as his warm fingers touched my skin just above my bra strap.

"Lift your arm," he said softly. The remnants of his breath brushed across my shoulder. He was so close, and some silly notion in my head wanted him closer.

North's fingers fumbled clumsily with the bandage, his gaze caught on Harper's soft skin and long delicate neck as he touched the gauzy bandage to her bare back. She was so silky soft under his fingertips. His work-worn hands were such a contrast that she almost didn't seem real beneath his touch, but the warm buzzing sensation said she was. Something about her made his entire body hum.

"Lift your arm," he managed to say as he passed the gauze into her hand before she passed it over her chest, then back to him.

"It needs to be tight," Harper told him as she pulled the gauze until it was taut.

"You won't be able to breathe if we do it much tighter," North told her. He didn't want her to suffocate.

"If we don't do it tighter, than it won't flatten me out."

North sighed. The only way they were going to get it tight enough was if he wrapped her himself. "Lift your arms, I'll have to wrap you."

She hesitated for a moment then lifted both arms, exposing her bra.

North pulled the gauze tight and began circling her, trying not to look at the curve of her breasts or almost bare torso.

I slipped an oversized baggy shirt on and a pair of jeans which were way too big. They had to be secured with a belt that Birdy punched extra holes in to make it fit me.

"What do you think?" I asked when I was ready.

Both men looked at me and shook their heads before Birdy grabbed his favourite old hat out of his bag and slapped it on my head.

"I swear if you grew a moustache and a beard you'd still

look like a girl," Birdy said with a shake of his head.

I turned to North. "What do you think?"

North glanced over at Birdy before answering. "I think you could be wearing a bag of garbage and smell like a skunk and you would still look like a woman to me."

My cheeks instantly blushed and I looked to the ground.

"And men don't blush or stare at the ground. Gee, Harper, if you're going to pretend you're a man, you have to act like a man," Birdy told me with a sigh. "This is never going to work, you're too girly."

I lifted my head and looked at the reflection of myself in the car window. I thought I looked boyish, maybe more teenager than man, but still male.

"Just keep your mouth shut and your head down," Birdy told me. "At least then people may have half a chance of mistaking you for a boy."

Chapter Seven

Sabastian sat in the copter with Mr Kleve ready to take off. He had wasted time with the incompetent MGD agents and was losing patience fast.

The blades began to whirl as the engine primed. The newer copters were quieter, stealthier, but they still made a low humming noise.

Sabastian watched Agent Fairchild answer his phone while he stuck his other hand over his ear to hear the caller. The older man's glance darted to Sabastian, and he knew there was some news on his missing bride.

"Wait" Sabastian barked before Kleve could lift off.

Agent Fairchild hung up and jogged over. "A car fitting the description was seen turning off the main road about six hours ago. The gentleman said he was sure there was a woman in the back seat. He thought it odd to see a woman but didn't give it much thought at the time."

Sabastian's heart sped up. "And we're only just getting the report?"

"The gentleman said he didn't realise it was significant until he got home and saw the bulletin on television," Agent Fairchild said as one of his young counterparts handed him a GPS unit. "By this time, they're about two or three hours ahead of us."

Sabastian swore under his breath.

"We have men en route to the location. It's a dead-end road — if they're there, we'll find them," Agent Fairchild continued.

"Get in," Sabastian ordered, thumbing his finger at the copter.

I sat silently in the back seat while Birdy pulled back onto the highway with North in the front passenger seat. Birdy had wanted to dump North on the side of the road, but I had convinced him we would need him once we crossed the border. But honestly, I just wanted him close because he made me feel safe for some reason. I knew it was probably mad, considering I didn't know him, but there was something about him, something I couldn't explain which seemed to draw me in.

Birdy drove along the highway, which was almost deserted at night. People tended to only travel during the day. My father had told me that in some parts of the Nation, groups of men would lay barricades across the roads to stop travellers so they could rob them, steal their cars and sometimes murder them. The thought made my stomach clench with fear.

The faint silhouette of distant hills faded slowly with the falling dark until only the light of the headlights separated us from the blackness outside. It felt lonely and frightening to be on the road.

A sign flashed by advertising a fuel station a few kilometres ahead.

"Pull over," North said. "If we drive in there someone is likely to see the plates. I'll run up to the fuel station and see if I can get us some plates off another car."

Birdy pulled to the side of the road, down a small culvert and turned off the headlights. The glow of the fuel station shone just beyond the next rise. North and Birdy slid out and unscrewed the plates. North took them and jogged away up the road while Birdy and I watched his silhouette fade into the darkness.

Birdy turned to me. "When we go in there, I need you to lie on the floor, and I'll cover you with a blanket."

I didn't protest. To say I was scared would have been an understatement of epic proportion. If even one man saw me and recognised me or the car, the jig would be up. I didn't want to think about what would happen to Birdy and North, and come to think of it I wasn't sure what happened to girls who ran away of their own free will either. It wasn't something anyone talked about. In fact, it was something that was never mentioned. Women didn't run away, they were always kidnapped. I thought about that for a moment. I couldn't be the only woman to have ever run away — there had to have been others.

We sat and silently waited for North to return. Waiting made me nervous, but we couldn't move until he returned.

A lone figure appeared, jogging toward the car. I held my breath as I sank down in my seat. In the dark the person wouldn't be able to see me, but if it wasn't North then we would likely be in trouble. The figure drew closer, the tall muscular figure was outlined by the dim glow of the fuel station beyond the crest of the hill. *North*.

Birdy slipped from the SUV.

"Got them," I heard North say as he slowed to a walk. "I swapped our plates for a truck's."

The two of them attached the plates before Birdy opened the back door, reached into the back and pulled two blankets out, while I curled myself on the floor behind North's seat, making myself as small as possible.

"Whatever happens, stay out of sight," Birdy ordered while he tossed the blankets over me.

My beating heart felt too heavy and confined by the tight binding around my chest, making each breath shallow.

We were entering the lion's den.

North had run several scenarios through his head on his jog to and from the fuel station packed with long haul trucks. If he took the SUV in alone, it'd look suspicious. Even men didn't travel alone at night in this part of the country, and leaving Harper on the side of the road while he and Birdy made the short trip wasn't an option either. She might have cut her hair, wrapped her chest and donned boy's clothes, but her features were too delicate to be that of a boy. If some creep saw her, he'd snatch her in an instant. No. She had to stay with them at all costs.

Birdy drove into the fuel station, pulled cash from his pocket, and handed it to North.

"I'll pump the fuel, you go pay for it when I'm done," Birdy told him as both men slipped from the SUV.

North agreed it was a good idea to get them in and out as quickly as possible.

Birdy began pumping the fuel while North wandered inside, trying to look casual. Birdy finished pumping and North went to the cashier to pay.

The cashier gave North a speculative look. "Don't I know you from somewhere?"

North shook his head. "I don't think so," he said softly. He doubted that the authorities had a photo of him. In fact, he didn't think a photo of him existed.

"Aren't you the boy who works out on the Birch farm?" the cashier asked as North saw his glance momentarily flick to the waiting SUV then back to him. "Yeah, you work . . ."

North turned and saw two men holding guns at Birdy. One of them slipped into the passenger seat and the other into the seat behind him. North ran for the SUV, but before he could get there the engine caught, and Birdy drove away.

"Sonofabitch," North growled.

That bastard cashier had distracted him while his mates

hijacked the car. North stormed back into the store, grabbed the scrawny, weasel faced man through the gap in the partition and dragged him out.

"Where are they taking him?" North growled between gritted teeth. He was furious, his skin prickled and he knew he was barely in control.

The weasel shook with fear.

"Tell me, or I'll rip your head off your shoulders," North snarled, knowing it wasn't an empty threat—he had the strength and his secret to back him up.

"M-M-Marble house," the weasel stuttered, his arm flinging out to point the direction. "Three kilometres north, take Kemp Road, it's at the end."

North slammed the weasel's head into the wall, knocking him out so he couldn't call his buddies then dumped him on the ground. He just prayed he would get there in time.

My mind executed a full stop. The man's voice I was hearing wasn't North's, and he didn't sound friendly.

"I think you're sitting in our car," the man said. His voice was gravelly and had a twang.

I lay perfectly still, my breath caught in my throat.

"Get out!" the gravelly voiced man ordered.

"NO! Get your own fucking car," I heard Birdy snap.

"Just shoot him," a second man's voice said impatiently.

"We can't shoot him here, someone will see," the gravelly man said as the sound of the front passenger door opening and closing filled my ears.

"Get the fuck out of my . . ." Birdy began.

The sound of something metal clicked, and I was sure it was a gun. Another door opened and the smell of a filthy, unwashed man filled my nostrils, which made me want to gag as someone slid into the back seat by my feet.

"Now drive or I'll shoot you right here," the gravelly man ordered.

The engine caught and the car began to move.

My mind raced at a million miles an hour, but the only thought that terrified me more than knowing two strangers were in the car was where was North? And had they done something to him?

Sabastian noted that the local MGD was slightly less inept than Agent Fairchild. They had found a track that led from the narrow road into the wooded area and set up lights to better see a pile of long brown hair which was lying discarded on the ground and two half-eaten peanut butter sandwiches that were now mostly covered in ants.

Sabastian picked a clump of the hair up and sniffed it. It had the soft, perfumed scent of her on it. He smiled. She had cut her hair, most likely to try to look more masculine, but Sabastian doubted she would. Harper was far too pretty to ever be mistaken for a man, but he was interested to see how she looked with shorter hair. Perhaps he'd like it and make her keep it short for a while.

Sabastian pulled out his phone and dialled his office. "I need you to take that photo of Harper Crain I sent you and doctor it to give her shorter hair, something a boy would wear," he told the person on the other end before disconnecting.

"Her kidnappers must know we're onto them and are trying to cover their tracks," Agent Fairchild said.

Sabastian had no doubt that they knew they were being hunted, but he doubted Harper had been kidnapped. In fact, he was almost sure that Harper and her brother had taken the blond farmhand on the spur of the moment. All of his clothes and a few thousand dollars were still in his room back at the

Crain farm. But in no way did he think the young farmhand innocent. No. Sabastian had seen the way the boy looked at Harper—he would have gone willingly enough. But why did Bernard Crain decide to slip away in the middle of the night with his sister? Was their relationship that of incest?

Sabastian almost smiled at that thought. No. Harper was a virgin. He could tell by the way she held herself and the way her skin prickled under his fingers, unused to a man's touch. No man had plucked that sweet flower, yet.

Sabastian kicked one of the discarded sandwiches and sent the ants scattering before he leaned down to feel the bread for freshness. It felt slightly stale. He noted the larger bite marks before moving to the second sandwich, where the bite marks were smaller. His and her sandwiches.

He wondered if the farm boy was still with them or if he had been abandoned somewhere along the road.

"I figured they're going to need fuel at some point," Agent Fairchild interrupted Sabastian's thoughts. "So I had my men canvas every fuel station from here to the Crain's farm. No one fitting their description or the car was reported. The local agents said the next station is about an hour and a half north of here. I'm betting they'd have to stop there."

"Unless they brought fuel with them," Sabastian interjected, but there was no harm in investigating—they were heading that way anyway.

Mr Kleve had taken the copter to refuel, which left Sabastian the choice of waiting for Kleve to return in a few hours or riding in one of the MGD cars with Agent Fairchild and several of the local MGD agents.

Sabastian buckled himself into the front seat.

CHAPTER EIGHT

My head hit the door as the SUV turned sharply, forcing a gasp from me.

"What was that?" the gravelly man's voice asked as the blanket was lifted and an ogrish, round face looked down at me.

"We have a stowaway," the ogrish man said as he grabbed my arm and yanked me up with a painful jolt to sit on the seat beside him.

A grizzled, wiry haired old man, who was sitting in the front seat, swivelled to look at me. His coarse features were mostly lost in shadow, but the darkness in his eyes was clear as day.

"Leave my brother alone," Birdy said from the driver's seat as the car bumped along the gravelled road.

"He's a young one. He don't even have any face hair yet," the ogrish one said as he grabbed my chin and yanked my face to his.

I flinched away and kicked out at him. My foot sank into his flabby stomach and he let out a whoosh of air with a grunt. His massive hand came down across my face, releasing an explosion of pain through my cheek that jerked my head back into the door with a solid thud.

"You little . . ." the ogre started, reaching for me.

"Now, now," the gravelly man said while I held my face and tried not to cry like a girl. "You don't want to damage him. If he's too beaten up, Clement might not want him as a toy. And you know how much Clement likes the young boys."

"But he kicked me," the ogre protested.

"Like you don't have enough padding there to take a kick from a kid." The gravelly man laughed at his own joke.

"If he tries anything again, I'll beat his skull in," the ogre growled, unhappy with the gravelly man's response. "And what about him?" He indicated Birdy.

"We'll see," the gravelly man said, a glint in his black, beady eyes.

The headlights caught an old, rundown house. Its roof sagged as if the weight of the world rested on its rafters.

"Stop here," the gravelly man ordered.

The ogre snatched my arm. His fingers dug in painfully as the car came to a stop in front of the house.

"Take that one in to Clement, and I'll take this one over to the barn," the gravelly man ordered while the ogre pulled me from the car.

"No!" Birdy protested, but the gravelly man smashed him in the face with the butt of his gun. Something crunched as blood spirted from his nose, and Birdy grunted in pain.

I struggled against the ogre, but he was too strong. He yanked me out of the car and tossed me across the driveway toward the house as if I weighed nothing.

"Behave yourself," the ogre ordered.

I lay on the ground, stunned. I felt like every ounce of breath had left my body. The ogre stalked over, clamped my shoulder with one huge hand and hoisted me to my feet before dragging me into the rundown house.

In the dim light cast by an old lamp, the ogre looked bigger and more grotesque. Thinning sandy-blond hair sat on top of his pear-shaped head. His defined brow protruded over narrow close-set eyes, a wide flat nose spread across his bulging cheeks and beneath that, large fleshy lips scowled at me.

I'd thought him younger in the car but in the light, he

looked to be in his forties at least.

"Clement," the ogre bellowed through the house.

A door opened, and a man as thin as a rake with the same sandy-blond hair and beady eyes stepped out of a room. His skin was sallow, his face gaunt and he looked deathly sick.

"We got you a present." The ogre sounded happy with himself. "This one don't even have face hair yet."

The pasty Clement smiled, showing me three rotten grey teeth and a lot of gum. "Put him in my room and make sure you put the chain on properly. We don't want him to be thinking he can try and make a run for it like the last one," he said in an oddly feminine voice.

The ogre dragged me through a door into a filthy rubbish-littered bedroom. Dirty, mottled brown sheets lay crumpled on the bed.

The ogre tossed me on the bed and fastened a chain around my leg. The sallow man stood in the doorway watching with a gleeful smile on his hideous face. He licked his lips.

"You know, this one's almost too pretty for me," Clement said as he squinted at me. "But I'm sure I'll enjoy him anyway."

I felt sick to the stomach. This man liked to have relations with young boys, and he thought I was a young boy. Oh, what a shock he was going to get.

North ran, tearing off his clothes, as his body shifted into his *Unholy* animal form of a giant black furred wolf. He could run fastest in his full animal shape as rage and terror gripped him. He had to get there in time. He couldn't face the consequences if he didn't.

Ahead, the dim lights of a farmhouse came into view while his claws gripped the ground, pushing him forward. He could see a large figure moving across the yard toward a barn close to the house just as a screech of pain shattered the silence of the night.

Birdy.

They must have them in the barn. North accelerated forward on silent paws.

The large figure slipped inside the barn. North's body warped in mid stride, turning from full animal to his half-wolf, half-human form without missing a step. North tore the barn door off its hinges, tossed it across the yard and dove inside.

Birdy was strapped to a pole with a long gash across his left bicep. Two men stood, mouths agape, staring at North with horror in their eyes.

North didn't hesitate. His massive clawed fingers ripped the throat of the larger man. The smaller man lifted a gun, the sound of a shot rang out, and North's claws raked his stomach. Blood and guts poured out. The man screamed in agony as he gripped his stomach and tried to hold everything in as he collapsed to the ground.

"Where's Harper?" North snapped at Birdy.

Birdy looked at him with terrified eyes before he finally stammered, "House."

North raised his clawed hand and swiped at Birdy's restraints. Birdy dropped to the ground before North turned and ran toward the house, praying nothing had happened to her.

My stomach lurched into my throat as the disgusting Clement pulled a small knife from a sheath on his belt and moved toward me while he licked his crusty old lips. The short chain didn't even allow me enough length to put my foot on the floor.

"Aww, so young and fresh." The old man grinned while I

tugged at the chain trying to free myself. "If you struggle, you'll just hurt yourself, and you won't enjoy it as much."

"Stay away from me," I growled through clenched teeth as I tried to kick out at him with my free leg.

Clement smiled wider and with preternatural speed lunged at me, grabbed my leg, flipped me onto my stomach and sat on my back. He wasn't very big, but he was bigger than me, and his weight and strength pinned me. I bucked and railed under him as I tried to throw him off, but he just laughed.

"Oh, I do like it when they fight me," he cooed in my ear, his fetid breath filling my nose, making me want to vomit. "Now hold still, boy, I want to enjoy this."

There was a sharp prick against my shoulder and the sound of ripping fabric. He suddenly stopped as cold air washed over my back.

"What's this?" he said as I felt him tug at the bandage binding me and then my bra strap.

Something loud crashed outside, distracting him. I rolled and threw him off balance so that he flopped onto the bed beside me. His knife dropped over the edge. I dove for it, but the chain yanked me back.

It was just there. I stretched. My fingers had just grazed the knife when I felt hands tighten around my throat, choking me.

I couldn't breathe. I clawed frantically at the fingers around my neck trying to inhale, but they gripped tighter.

"You're no boy!" he screeched in my ear.

In a last-ditch effort, I flung my head back. I connected with something solid and it crunched. The hands around my throat instantly let go.

I rolled onto my back and gasped for air while Clement gripped his face, blood pouring from his nose. I kicked out as hard as I could and sent him tumbling back off the bed. There was a hollow sound as the back of his head hit the hardwood floor.

I turned back to the knife. I strained as my fingers just skimmed it and I teased it a little closer, then a little more before I could finally grab it.

A scream echoed from somewhere outside. Those bastards must be torturing Birdy. I had to get to him. I had to save my brother. I yanked at the chain, my ankle raw and bloody from my effort to free myself.

Clement began to stir on the floor.

I grit my teeth and pulled at the chain again. It felt like something was tearing as pain gripped my ankle, but I pulled harder, fighting the tears before suddenly my foot came free in a burst of torturous agony.

I wanted to scream and cry, but I buried the desire to curl into a ball and sob—I had to help Birdy.

I leapt to my feet, the pain in my ankle almost unbearable.

Clement sat up, his focus unsteady. I hobbled past him to the bedroom door, the knife in my hand. I didn't want to fight him. I just wanted to get Birdy and get out of here. I swung the door open. Something made me look back just as Clement surged up and tackled me onto my back in the hallway. It knocked the breath out of me.

"You fucking little whore," he snarled as he ripped at my clothes and bandages.

I pushed him away and scrambled back, but he grabbed my shredded ankle and pulled me back. I screamed in pain and instinctively swung the knife as it drove into the side of his neck with all the force of my fear and horror.

Clement's eyes went wide with shock. He sat back as he gurgled and gripped his throat, a look of panic on his gaunt face.

I scrambled back on my ass. My tattered shirt and sagging bandages hung from me. I watched what little colour he had leech from his sallow face before he toppled forward.

My back brushed something furry. I darted a look over my shoulder. Huge muscled legs covered in fur greeted me. My gaze followed them up until I saw the unmistakable half-human, half-wolf face of an Unholy.

It moved to crouch beside me.

I opened my mouth to scream, but in the blink of an eye North's naked form enfolded me. He picked me up and held me against his strong, bare muscular chest.

"Is she all right?" I heard Birdy's voice call as North swung me around and passed me to my brother.

The edges of my vision wavered and grew darker.

"We have to get out of here," North's voice said before everything went black.

Sabastian crouched by the fuel station attendant, who was holding an icepack to a lump on his head.

"So, did you see the men or didn't you?" Sabastian questioned.

He was losing patience with the uncooperative cashier.

"Like I told the other guy, an SUV came in here with some out of state plates. There were only two guys in it. Then the big blond guy came in to pay, and he attacked me. I didn't see no third guy or girl," the cashier said.

Sabastian looked at the man's hand resting on the ground and stood, "Did you see where they went?" he asked in a calm, casual tone.

"No, I told you, I was knocked out."

Sabastian brought his foot down on the man's extended hand. Bones crunched under his foot and the cashier dropped the bag of ice with a scream.

"Mr James!" Agent Fairchild barked.

But Sabastian didn't lift his foot. Instead, he pulled his

phone out and punched in a number.

"Frederick, I am sorry to disturb you at this late hour, but would you have a word to Agent Fairchild about my involvement in this MGD case," Sabastian said smoothly as the cashier thrashed about under his foot. He calmly handed the phone to Agent Fairchild.

"Hello?" Fairchild said into the phone and what he heard made his back visibly straighten.

Sabastian smiled to himself. It was often handy to be on first name basis with the heads of every department in the government. Even the exulted Praeses, leader of the Nation, expected his calls occasionally.

"Yes, sir, of course, sir. I will, sir," Fairchild blathered, almost falling over himself, before he hung up the phone and handed it back to Sabastian.

"Agent Fairchild, please find the video surveillance disk, I want a copy," he ordered as he nodded at a camera mounted in the corner of the room before he turned back to the cashier, his smile wide with satanic delight at the prospect of further coercion. "Now, are you going to tell me where they went?"

CHAPTER NINE

North pulled on a pair of Birdy's sweatpants and a shirt while Birdy drove like a bat out of hell, trying to get them as far away from the farm as possible. The deserted highway stretched off out of the headlights' view while Harper lay on the back seat, her ankle swollen and her clothes torn, but otherwise unharmed. She'd fainted, and for a moment after she passed out, Birdy had started freaking out, sure she was dead.

"You're an Unholy," Birdy said. It was a statement, not a question.

North had hidden it so well until now. He had always been so careful and conscious not to let anything slip, but the thought of Harper in danger had flipped a switch in his brain, and he couldn't help it—his animal form took over, and so did the savagery. He had gutted one man and ripped the throat from another.

The old books had called them Shapeshifters or Were-wolves. Until tonight, he had thought himself only human, but when Harper had looked up at him in sheer terror he'd felt like a monster.

"So how does it work? Can you change at will?" Birdy asked, sounding almost excited.

"Aren't you scared of me?" North questioned.

Birdy glanced over at him, "You worked on my father's farm for months, and if you'd wanted to kill us you could have done it last night when Harper and I were sleeping, or today in the forest, or pretty much anytime you wanted."

North thought about it for a moment. Maybe if Birdy was

taking it so well, Harper would too.

"So, can you change at will?" Birdy repeated.

"Ahh, yeah." North felt a trickle of blood down his arm. The bullet the man in the barn had fired had grazed his arm. It stung, but not enough to make Birdy pull over. They had to get as far away from this place as possible.

"So, do you just change into that big human dog thing or can you change into other things?" Birdy asked.

"We call the *human dog* a half-form. I also have the full animal form," North told him.

"Animal?"

"I can turn into a wolf," North explained. He had never had an open conversation about what he was with anyone that wasn't an Unholy, and it felt weird.

"Are you contagious?" Harper's voice said from the back seat.

North turned to see her pushed against the far door, her injured leg tightly tucked up while her slender arms covered her exposed bra.

She looked so afraid that it hurt his chest.

"No. It's a genetic mutation, not a viral disease," North explained as he slipped his shirt off and offered it to her.

Pain lanced his arm, and he winced as Harper's emerald-green-eyed gaze went to the blood on his arm, then back to his eyes, but she didn't move.

"So, do you get fleas?" Birdy asked.

My mind ran at a million miles an hour. I had always been told that the Unholy were inhuman feral creatures without a soul, but North was human, and he'd been kind.

Is what I've been told my entire life a lie?

North had been injured, probably trying to save Birdy and me from those horrible men.

My mind executed a full stop again.

"I killed someone." The words sounded foreign coming out of my mouth. "Oh geez, I killed a man."

"Shit, Harper," Birdy swore, "that man was trying to kill you."

My entire body shook, tears blurred my vision, and nausea gripped my stomach.

"Pull over, I think I'm going to be sick," I told Birdy.

"Keep driving," North told him as he climbed into the back seat with me. "You're having an adrenaline let down," he said calmly. "Put your feet on the floor and put your head between your knees."

I did as he said, unsure if I could trust him, but scared if I didn't do what he said, he might turn into that creature again.

North's warm hand rested on the back of my neck, which sent weird tingling sensations down my spine.

"Push against my hand and breathe," he said softly.

I did as I was told. The nausea eased, and a rush of fatigue washed over me.

"I'm all right," I told him after a few moments. "Now I just feel tired."

"Good," North told me as he took my face in his hands to examine the spot where the big ogre had hit me. He gently touched it.

"Ouch, that hurts," I snapped while I tried to cover my exposed bra.

"I don't think your cheek bone is broken," he said as he moved his gaze to the gravel rash on my arms which were covering my chest. "We should clean those wounds when we get a chance," he added.

I slipped the shirt on and instantly felt less exposed.

"Can I have a look at your ankle?" he asked, his voice calm and soft.

I hesitated for a moment, then leaned back and lifted my leg onto his lap.

His fingers moved toward it

"Don't touch it," I said, scared of the pain it might release.

North withdrew his fingers and examined my ankle visually. "Is there any disinfectant?"

"There's a medical kit in the boot, but Harper used the bandages on her chest," Birdy said while he drove as fast as he could safely manage along the abandoned highway.

"It's all right, we still have the bandages." North said. He gently lowered my foot to the floor to give himself room, then turned around in his seat to search for the medical kit in the back.

Sabastian looked at the knife buried in the throat of the old man lying dead in the house's filthy hallway. He had seen the bloody chain attached to the bed, the shredded fabric that littered the hall, and the small, bloody handprint that marked the floorboards.

"My darling Harper, you killed a man. I'm impressed," Sabastian said to himself with a smile of satisfaction.

He had hoped she would be a surprise package, but killing a man was ruthless, and he felt himself aroused as his pants began to feel too tight.

"Mr James," Agent Fairchild called from the front door. "You might want to come have a look at this."

Sabastian groaned and stood. That blithering idiot couldn't even let him enjoy his hard-on over the thought of Harper Crain killing a man. Sabastian strode across the yard toward the barn as the dawn light brightened the sky.

Inside the barn lay two mutilated bodies, one with his guts sprawling out, the other without a throat.

One of the young MGD agents dashed past Sabastian before the sound of vomiting erupted just beyond the shattered doorway.

Sabastian rolled his eyes in disgust. These men were supposed to be trained to deal with any circumstance, not go running at the sight of some guts and the inside of a trachea.

He glanced around the room and noted the shredded ropes that dangled loosely from a pole and the deep claw like gouges in the wood before he walked over to the big man without a throat. Sabastian glanced around the putrid barn until he saw the rest of the man's throat lying in a bloody clump on the other side of the room.

"It was an Unholy, wasn't it?" a young agent with red hair asked while he stood at parade rest in his black tactical pants and fitted shirt.

"Yes," Agent Fairchild said. "That thing took out a decent hard-working family."

Sabastian had seen the video footage from the fuel station which identified the two dead men in front of him as the carjackers, as well as the blond farmhand dragging the cashier through the serving window in a rage. These men weren't decent—in fact, Sabastian hated them. They had obviously injured his bride to be, but he thought himself lucky he'd picked a girl as resilient as she was, or she would have been violated by this repulsive family.

"Don't feel sorry for these men," Sabastian said coldly. "These repugnant creatures would have murdered the Crains if they themselves hadn't been killed."

Agent Fairchild shifted uncomfortably. Sabastian grew tired of the man's ineptness and presumed his move up the ranks had been due to luck or the favour of a friend, not competence.

"How far is the state border from here?" Sabastian asked.

Agent Fairchild looked to the younger red-haired agent.

"Less than fifty kilometres." He shrugged.

"Are the road-blocks in place?" Sabastian questioned.

Agent Fairchild looked again to the younger agent.

"No," the redhead said. "The order was to close the northern border to the country, not the state."

Sabastian swore, pulled out his gun and shot Agent Fairchild right between the eyes.

The redhead and two other agents pulled their guns and pointed them at Sabastian. Sabastian didn't flinch, instead he slowly pulled the phone from his pocket and dialled, "Frederick, I am sorry for the earliness of this call, but I should inform you I just shot Agent Fairchild in the head. His complete incompetence was beyond manageable."

"Put on the next in charge," the low heavy voice of Frederick Mills said with a sigh.

Sabastian handed the phone to the redhead.

The redhead cautiously took the phone and placed it to his ear, "Hello?"

Again, Sabastian admired how a man thousands of kilometres away could make an underling like the redhead in front of him straighten his spine with just a few short words.

The redhead barked, "Yes, sir," and disconnected. He handed the phone back, holstered his gun and ordered the other agents to lower their weapons before he informed them that from now on Sabastian James was in charge of the investigation.

Sabastian smiled.

Chapter Ten

I sat with my foot propped up on the dashboard. My ankle ached and the car smelled like disinfectant. North had cleaned me up and wrapped my injury. I swapped Birdy for the front passenger seat so he could sleep in the back while North took a turn at driving. Poor Birdy was so exhausted after the manic night and the adrenaline come-down, he could barely keep his eyes open.

I stared out at the rolling green fields and distant mountains. The sun had risen hours ago, but barely a car had passed us along this open stretch of road. Despite the calm beauty of this place, my thoughts were scattered and scary, I had left everyone and everything I knew for the unknown. Scariest of all was that I didn't have the faintest idea of what was out here waiting for me.

"Do you know where we are going?" I asked North, breaking the long silence.

"There's a settlement a few hundred kilometres north of the border."

"Have you been there before?"

"I grew up there," he smiled.

"Oh," I said unsure how to word my next question without sounding naive or insulting. "So, is there . . . umm?"

"If you're asking if the entire town is made up of Unholy, then no, but there were a few who escaped the Nation and settled there with their families," North told me. "People are more accepting over the border. They don't see the Unholy as anything different."

"So why did you leave?"

"Some things are the same everywhere," he said wryly. "My parents wanted me to work on the family farm, marry one of the girls in town and produce babies to carry on the legacy."

"Instead, you moved to the Nation and worked on someone else's farm where you were forced to help a spoilt girl runaway. If we count Birdy as the baby, then I guess that would be your trifecta," I joked.

North glanced over at me and smiled. "I'm not changing his nappy."

I laughed before I remembered my face hurt. "Ouch," I winced as I gingerly touched my fingers to my cheek.

"Are you all right?" North asked as he reached over and touched my hand. His fingers ignited that pleasant buzz I had come to expect whenever he touched me, no matter how brief or light.

"How do you do that?" I questioned.

"What?"

"That buzzing thing you do whenever you touch me," I told him before quickly adding, "Don't get me wrong, I don't mind, it actually feels kind of nice."

North glanced over at me. "I'm not doing anything. You're the one who keeps zapping me."

I shook my head. "If you don't want to tell me, then you don't have to—I was just curious."

North looked over at me. "I get the same buzzing sensation when you touch me, but I'm not causing it. I thought you were."

I thought about it for a moment, but there was no logical reason for it. It wasn't like a sharp, painful static-electricity shock. No, it was a weird buzz which felt nice, pleasant even, and I looked forward to it happening.

I reached over and touched North's leg. The instant my

fingers made contact, the pleasant buzzing started.

"Are you sure you aren't doing that?" I asked as he lifted my hand into his and heat began pouring up my arm.

"It isn't me, but I like it," he smiled.

I liked it too, but I wasn't sure if I should let go of his hand or if he'd mind me holding it a little longer. North didn't let go, so neither did I. We drove in silence, the weird buzzing warmth flowing through me.

Was this what it was like to touch a man? I wondered. Then I thought back to Sabastian James. No. When he had touched me, even before he showed his cruelty, there was indifference and perhaps dubiousness, but no warmth. North made me feel the strange desire to curl up on his lap like a cat.

North had been looking out for the correct turn for the past forty kilometres, but when he felt the buzzing heat flowing from Harper's hand, he almost forgot why he'd come this way in the first place. Damn. He could barely concentrate on driving with her holding his hand, but he sure as hell didn't want to let go of it.

"I told you it was you." Harper smiled and gave his hand a light squeeze.

North glanced over. He returned her smile, but just looking at her made him feel he'd failed her. Harper's beautiful face was bruised, her long hair cut short, grazes adorned her arms, and her ankle was in a bandage resting on the dashboard, but worst of all, she had been forced to kill a man, and that kind of thing scarred not only the mind but the soul. North should have been there to protect her from that.

He slowed the car, released Harper's hand and turned down a long driveway. The warm buzzing instantly disappeared, which left North feeling almost empty without her touch. He glanced over and thought about taking her hand again, but it rested comfortably in her lap, and grabbing it would be inappropriate.

North followed the long driveway over several hills.

"Where are we going?" Harper asked, sounding anxious.

"A friend's," North told her as he wound the SUV down into a wide-open valley and up to a homestead which overlooked a tranquil lake.

North hadn't been here in a few years, but nothing had changed. He didn't bother wasting time parking the car and going to the door to see if anyone was home. Instead, he pulled the SUV in through the open garage doors and slipped out. He tapped on the window above Birdy's head to wake him, then rounded the car to help Harper out. North opened Harper's door and was about to pick her up when he felt the cold steel of a gun barrel against the nape of his neck.

Harper's face paled.

I saw the barrel pointed at the back of North's head and felt the blood drain from me.

"God damn it, you're freaking her out!" North snapped as he spun with preternatural speed.

I barely saw him move.

One moment there was a gun pointed at the back of his head, and the next he had it in his hand and was emptying the bullets out onto the ground.

"I see you haven't lost it," the young woman said. She had long blonde hair tied back into a ponytail, olive-brown skin and a perfect hourglass figure. She wrapped her arms around North's neck in a hug. He squeezed her, lifted her off the ground and spun her around.

I know he had said his parents wanted him to marry a girl from their town, but being stupid and naïve, I didn't ask him if he had. I had also neglected to ask if he had a girlfriend.

After all, he wasn't from the Nation, and he himself did say that things were different over the border. Hell, I had no idea if we had already crossed it or not.

North planted the blonde's feet back on the ground and kissed her forehead. "Geez, I've missed you."

"So you show it by bringing me an injured kid," the woman said while she looked over at me, then peered in the back window at Birdy. "And sleeping beauty."

"I am generous," North joked.

I had never really heard him joke, but then up until a couple of days ago I hadn't heard him speak.

"So how have you been?" North asked.

"Well, I haven't needed my husband." She winked at him. "Although now that he's back I could use a hand with a couple of things, starting with one in my bedroom."

My heart sank. Did she just say he was her husband and she wanted him in her bedroom?

I wanted to kick myself. I had been eyeing and pining over a married man. Of course he'd be married. He worked hard and probably saved every dollar he made, and he was unbelievably good-looking.

I took a deep breath and carefully pulled myself out of the car. I felt like the ugly stepsister to the gorgeous blonde as I hobbled over to where they were both talking.

The blonde was beautiful. Her body looked perfect in well-fitted jeans and a stretchy girly top that curved around her generous breasts. I still wore Birdy's jeans that sagged off me and North's shirt with the bloodstain which he'd given me to wear last night. Not to mention the attractive swollen and bruised cheek, grazed arms and bandaged ankle, topped off with the sweat and grime of not showering for three days and a boy's haircut.

Yep, I was never going to win a beauty contest, especially if this woman was my competition.

North's back was to me, but the blonde smiled when I approached. I leaned my hand against the car to take the weight off my ankle and smiled back.

"Well." The blonde grinned, looking me over before looking at North. "What have you brought me? She's definitely not a kid — or a boy."

North gave me one of his smiles, which catapulted him into unbearably handsome. "Charli, this is Harper, Harper, this is Charli."

"It's very nice to meet you," I said, remembering my manners.

The back car door opened, and Birdy stepped out and stretched. He stopped when he saw the pretty blonde.

Charli looked Birdy over, then looked to North, then me.

"Charli, may I introduce my brother Birdy," I said. "Birdy, this is Charli."

"My lady," Birdy said as he gave a short bow.

"Pleased to meet you." She smiled. "Now you all look like you need a bath and some warm food." Charli turned to go back to the house, while Birdy followed like a pup following its new master.

I took a few tentative steps, but the pain burned my ankle.

"Do you want a hand?" North asked.

"No, I should be fine," I told him while I forced a smile and tried not to wince with every step.

Without warning he bent and scooped me up. My arms instinctively wrapped around his neck, and that warm buzzing sensation washed over me. I had to tell myself that he was a married man.

Sabastian waited on the lawn outside of the dilapidated house, thinking that only an incendiary device would make this place bearable. He couldn't wait to be gone, and once Mr

Kleve had retrieved the knife from the dead man in the house, they would be. He had wanted it to DNA match, just to make sure it had been his Harper who had killed the man. He surely hoped it was.

Sabastian's pants tightened at the thought of his betrothed actually fighting back.

There had been no reports of any sightings of her for over eighteen hours, but that didn't surprise him. The areas in the north of the Nation were less densely populated following the Pandemic over a century before, but still, they should be getting close to the border by now. That thought pained Sabastian. Once they were caught, the hunt would be over, and he had enjoyed hunting her. Still, once she was caught, she would be his.

A smile festered on Sabastian's cruel lips. He would have her. He remembered the marriage certificate Mr Crain had given him, already signed and ready to go. All Sabastian had to do was sign it, hand it over to the government, and she was legally his. His, to do with as he pleased. Once he caught her, she became his problem, and he had the right to punish her. With his connections, he could kill her if he wanted to, and no one would think twice about it. Sabastian let out a contented sigh, his pants now so tight it almost hurt. The thought of strangling her made him as hard as a rock.

"As requested," Mr Kleve interrupted Sabastian's thoughts. He held up a clear plastic bag with the short-bladed knife in it.

"Excellent, Mr Kleve," Sabastian said. "Now, let us leave this putrescent hovel."

"Yes, sir," Kleve said, walking over and opening the door of the copter for Sabastian. "Where are we going?"

Sabastian thought about it. He had a feeling Harper wasn't going to raise her head for a few days, and he'd neglected his work. He wanted to get started on the injectable GPS unit he had envisaged while hunting her. "Home, for now."

North stood in the middle of Charli's bedroom looking at an old set of drawers.

"I left the window open, and the rain came in, which made the wood swell with the wet, and now I can't open them," Charli explained as she closed the bedroom door behind them.

North rattled the top drawer. Then he tried banging it with his fist to dislodge it.

"So, are you going to tell me what's going on with the girl and her brother?" Charli asked as she crossed her arms.

North banged the drawer again with more force. "Harper was meant to marry a guy, but he's a sadistic asshole, so Birdy helped her run away," he grunted. He focussed on what he was doing, so not to give away any emotions, like the fact he was happy she had.

North heaved the top drawer with a grunt and it popped open. He slid it in and out a few times, then started banging on the next drawer down.

Charli raised an eyebrow as a smile played across her face. "You like her."

North felt himself blush. He never blushed. *You like her* didn't begin to describe how he felt about Harper Crain. From the moment he first saw her, he had been captivated, and the more he learned about her and watched her, the more he wanted her.

"Is it that obvious?" North asked as he paused his assault on the drawers for a moment.

"Yes." Charli's grin widened. "You're a good man, North. You deserve to be happy. For goodness' sake, when my husband died, you risked yourself by pretending to be him so I wouldn't get turned into a Bride of the state or sold off."

North tugged at the drawer and huffed. He remembered back to that time. He'd come to the farm to find work when he first crossed the border. Finn, Charli's husband, had been an old alcoholic with a heavy hand on his young wife. One night after Finn had drowned himself in a bottle of his own homemade whisky, he'd fallen down the back steps and cracked his head open.

North had helped Charli dig the grave in the back paddock. When two farmhands had called on the house three days later, looking for work, North had pretended to be Charli's husband. As it turned out, the two men were actually lovers and were trying to go north over the border to escape persecution in the Nation.

"Are Lloyd and Blane still here?" North asked, before giving an audible *grrrrr* when the second drawer loosened and flew open.

"They're over the other side of the lake mustering the cattle," Charli said. "I don't know what I would have done when you left if they hadn't been here. Lloyd's pretended to be my husband a few times now."

North smiled. "He is a better choice than Blane."

They both grinned at that.

Blane was in his early thirties, with a mass of curly blond hair that made him look like a cherub and mannerisms that would put even the most elegant woman to shame. Lloyd was older, closer to fifty, with salt and pepper hair, a deeper, more masculine voice and a square jaw.

North kicked the bottom drawer a few times before kneeling down and tugging at the handles. The set of drawers rocked, and a hairbrush and a few trinkets hit the ground. "I'm almost there," North grunted as the set rocked.

Charli braced the top and the drawer suddenly gave way, jerking open.

"Oh wow, you're fantastic. I can't believe you did that!"

Charli squealed in delight. She went over to her closet to retrieve some of Finn's old clothes for North to change into.

"So, are you going to tell Harper how you feel?" Charli asked, as North reached for the door.

"She is way out of my league," he told her. "She's the most beautiful woman I have ever seen, and I'm an Unholy."

"Does she know?" Charli asked.

North nodded. "Yeah, I lost it when she was taken last night. I couldn't control myself."

"You might be surprised," Charli offered. "I don't think she's as shallow or fragile as you might think."

I sat at the kitchen table sipping a cup of tea while I inadvertently listened to the banging and grunting coming from behind the closed bedroom door. I had been so stupid to think he may have been interested in me, or maybe it was my growing infatuation with him that had blinded me.

Something crashed behind the closed door, followed by more banging and Charli's excited voice. "Oh wow, you're fantastic. I can't believe you did that!"

I felt like a pervert sitting there listening to a married couple making love in the next room. If Birdy wasn't in the shower, I would have been in there washing my heartache away.

The bedroom door opened and for a moment, North's gaze caught mine before I cast my gaze down into the milky tea in front of me. He had just made love to his wife, and I was scolding myself for wanting it to have been me.

The bathroom door opened, and Birdy stepped out in a flourish of steam, a wide smile across his face.

"Wow, I feel like a new man." He beamed while he strolled over to the table where I sat.

"Harper?" North asked. "Would you like the next

shower?"

I shook my head. I kept my head down so he wouldn't see my embarrassment at my own foolish thoughts written on my face. "I'll have the one after," I told him, happy my voice didn't break.

If I could have walked more than a few steps without my ankle feeling as if it were on fire, I would have run away.

North crossed the kitchen to the bathroom and closed the door behind him.

Charli appeared in the kitchen with her blonde hair looking perfect. She gave me a wide, toothy smile. It was easy to see why North had taken his wife straight to the bedroom. She was gorgeous, busty and obviously knew her own mind.

"Are either of you hungry?" Charli asked as she moved around the kitchen.

"I'm starved," Birdy said as the water started in the bathroom.

I watched Birdy almost falling over himself while he followed Charli around the kitchen like a lovestruck teenager. Later I would have to tell him that North and Charli were married, so he wouldn't make a complete fool of himself or destroy his and North's friendship.

Chapter Eleven

North paced outside the bathroom door while he waited for Harper to finish in the shower. He wanted to be in there holding her up so she wouldn't hurt herself, but he couldn't.

Charli and Birdy had taken plates of food out onto the veranda a few minutes before, and he could hear them talking, but North was worried Harper might slip in the shower. He turned and did another lap past the closed door.

Harper suddenly yelped, and there was a thud. Before North could stop himself, he had opened the door, "Are you all right?" he asked as his gaze landed on her huddled naked form in the bottom of the shower.

Harper's face blushed bright crimson. Suddenly, he realised his misconduct and turned his back.

"I slipped," she said shakily.

North wanted to wrap her in cotton wool and hold her so that nothing could ever hurt her again.

"Are you all right now?" he asked without turning.

Another thump.

"Umm," she said, her voice low and soft. "I . . ."

North had to fight himself not to turn around.

"I'm a little embarrassed, but I can't get up. The shower is too slippery," she said in a small voice.

North glanced back at her, stealing a look at her bare silky skin, and thought himself an asshole for admiring her while she was so vulnerable, but he couldn't leave her sitting there getting cold either. North averted his eyes while he reached over Harper to turn off the water, then wrapped a towel over her hunched shoulders.

"I'm so embarrassed." Harper's voice sounded mournful and weak.

"Don't be embarrassed," North told her softly while he slipped his hands under her bare legs to scoop her up. "I'm the one who should be embarrassed. I barged in here without your permission."

North carried her out of the bathroom and down the hall to her room, the buzzing he felt coming from her almost too much to bear.

He lowered her gently onto the bed, careful not to let the towel slip so as not to embarrass her further. His glance flicked to her ankle. It looked a little better now it had been properly cleaned, but the raw deep wounds around the front of her ankle and down her heel looked painful and swollen. The bruise on her cheek was turning a mottled purple-blue, and he could now make out light yellow-brown finger marks around her long delicate neck where that asshole had tried to strangle her.

He'd kill him a hundred times for touching her, but she had beaten him to it.

"I'll get the bandages to wrap your ankle," North said as he suddenly realised he'd been standing there staring at her.

I pulled the towel tighter around myself, unsure of my own will power.

He was looking at me, probably pitying me in my current state. The debutant bride all battered and bruised and pathetically unable to get myself up out of a shower of all things.

"I'll get the bandages to wrap your ankle," North said before he turned and walked from the room, leaving the door open.

I was all but naked, sitting on the bed with only the towel to cover me. A tall older man with salt and pepper hair walked past the door and stopped as he looked in at me.

I pulled the towel tighter, adjusting it to cover as much of me as possible.

"Well, hello there." He smiled. "You must be Harper."

I must have looked like a deer in the headlights, while he looked casual as he leaned against the door frame.

"I'm Lloyd, Charli's husband." He smiled.

Confusion struck me. "Wait, what?" I managed. "I thought North was her husband."

The older man chuckled. "Sometimes he is, sometimes I am and once even Blane was. But Blane, as much as I love him, isn't exactly husband material. Doting housewife yes, manly husband, no."

"Lloyd," I heard North say in the hallway.

"North, it's good to see you, it's been too long." Lloyd smiled as I watched them hug briefly.

"Charli said you were over the other side of the lake."

"We were, but you know what Blane's like, he wanted to get back so he could put the roast on. Then we found out you were here with company and Blane has started preparing a banquet." Lloyd grinned. "Charli said you managed to wrangle those darn drawers open in her room. She told me you bashed it and grunted at it for twenty minutes."

I felt my cheeks flush. He'd been wrestling with a set of drawers, not having sex, and what exactly did Lloyd mean when he said that they were all her husbands? Was this a bigamist thing?

Lloyd glanced over at me still sitting on the bed, his glance flicking from my face to my ankle. "You sure look like you must be a fighter," he said to me. "Your brother said you were one of the bravest women he knows."

"She is," North smiled.

I dropped my head.

I hated when he looked at me like that. It made my stomach twist and I still wasn't sure who was married to whom, or if he even liked me. Geez, I felt stupid. A man was nice to me, so I thought I was in love with him. *Wait, what? Did I just think I was in love with North? Shit, I did.*

"I'll let you two be, just wanted to get changed out of these clothes," Lloyd said. "Nice to meet you, Miss Harper." And he was gone.

North stepped into the room and closed the door behind him. "Charli said to put this on to stop an infection," he said as he held up a jar of dark brown ointment.

North sat on the end of the bed while Harper extended her injured leg and rested it on his lap. The familiar warm buzz flowed through him wherever they made contact.

North opened the jar and took in the smell. It smelled like tar and looked as thick.

Harper wrinkled her cute nose and smiled. "It doesn't smell great."

North's sense of smell was heightened by the Unholy gene in his body, and the ointment was almost overpowering, but he could still smell Harper's clean scent over all of it.

Harper winced while his finger gently smoothed the ointment over her tortured heel.

"Sorry," North apologised, withdrawing his hand.

"It isn't your fault, it's just tender." Harper said without an ounce of malice in her voice. "Do you think it will be better in a few days?"

North shrugged, "I hope so."

He finished applying the ointment and began wrapping the clean bandage around it.

I almost sighed with each brush of his fingertips. Tingling heat rushed up my leg in tantalising waves, each one feeling stronger and more pleasurable than the last.

North's fingers stopped when he secured the bandage and I felt like screaming. Something overtook me then, and I had to kiss him.

Without thinking I grabbed his hand, pulled him toward me and dropped my towel. His eyes widened, and for a moment I was afraid he'd pull away, but he came willingly as I wrapped my arms around his neck. His lips brushed mine as a ball of heat curled in my stomach, then moved down between my thighs. He kissed me harder, his tongue licking my lips as I opened to him, his taste setting every nerve on fire while he laid me back against the soft pillows, our lips locked in need-filled desire.

I tugged at his shirt. "I need to feel your skin against mine," I told him, my breath catching in my throat. He sat back just long enough to tear his shirt away before leaning back down to press his bare flesh against mine. My body hummed against his.

He moved as he kissed a line down my neck, which sent shivers through me.

My fingers clumsily fumbled to undo his pants. I needed him naked, and there was too much material between us. The belt came undone in my hand and I flicked his pants button open.

North's tongue licked my bare nipple as a jolt of electricity shot through me.

I moaned.

He lifted his head, his dark eyes looking into mine. "Did I hurt you?"

I didn't answer as I slid my hand inside his pants to feel his hard length. It felt like steel sheathed in soft velvety skin.

North gasped, his eyes almost rolling back in his head as I

ran my hand along him, stroking him.

I had nothing to compare it to, but he felt big in my hand.

"If you keep doing that, I won't be able to stop," he moaned.

I leaned up to kiss his shoulder. "I never said I wanted you to stop," I whispered.

The words sounded like they were coming from someone else. When had I become so brazen?

North looked down at me. "Are you sure this is what you want?"

"Aren't you?"

Sabastian studied the tiny device through the microscope. It was no bigger than a single grain of rice and was powered by the body's own electromagnetic charge, but this tiny GPS could track the recipient's exact location within a metre. Now all he would have to do is inject it under Harper's skin. Then she could never run away from him again—or maybe he'd let her try. It might be fun.

Sabastian looked at the official marriage certificate lying on his desk. He was considering signing it. It would make the hunt more legal if any judicial law agent should ever question his authority or motivation on the case.

He picked up the pen with a flourish and signed it.

Harper Crain was now his legally wedded wife.

"Kleve," Sabastian called to his henchman, who abruptly appeared. "I need this notarised and presented to the government office." He handed Kleve the piece of paper.

Kleve took it and headed for the door.

"Oh, and Kleve, can you go to the gentlemen's service centre and find me some entertainment?" Sabastian continued as he crossed his luxurious office to pour himself a glass of whisky.

"Do you want a blonde, brunette or redhead?" Kleve asked.

Sabastian smiled, "Get me a brunette, and if possible, I want one that looks like my wife."

I pulled the towel around me, to cover my bare skin.

"I don't mean I don't want you, every cell in my body wants you," North said while he paced back and forth. "I just mean I don't want you to regret being with me."

I looked at my lap, not wanting to see the rejection or disgust in his eyes. I had just thrown myself at him and acted like a harlot let loose in a brothel, how on earth did he think I didn't want him?

North paced some more. "I'm an Unholy, and you're so perfect."

"You could have just said you weren't interested," I said. My voice was quaking with embarrassment as I carefully shifted off the bed and hobbled over to my clothes, then grabbed a shirt and a pair of sweatpants from my bag.

I wanted to tell him that if I thought for a moment his genetics were a problem, I wouldn't have made a fool of myself by hurling myself at him, but I couldn't even look at him.

"Is it Charli?" I asked while I pulled the towel a little tighter around myself.

"What? No. I just don't think you've thought this through."

"I know I haven't known you long," I said, my voice low and shaky. "And you'll probably think me silly, but I'm pretty sure I'm in love with you."

North went quiet and his pacing stopped.

I wasn't game to look at him in case he was about to laugh in my face.

The air in the small room felt thick and heavy while I waited for him to say something, anything.

His feet moved into view and my breath caught in my throat.

"Harper, I—" he started, then there was a knock on the door.

"North?" Charli's voice called.

North's feet moved out of view as I heard him cross the room and open the door. "Yeah?"

"Lloyd asked if you could give him a hand feeding the cattle, Blane is too busy in the kitchen and I've got to put the chickens away," Charli said. "We've had some problems with foxes lately, guess they're trying to fatten up for winter,"

"When?" North asked as I stole a brief glance at him.

The door was open, but the bulk of it shielded me from Charli's view.

"Now. He's already loading the truck."

I looked back at the floor.

"Yeah, sure," North agreed, and he was gone.

CHAPTER TWELVE

North sat across the table from Harper, who was sitting between Lloyd and Birdy. He had been remembering the feel of her soft skin and the way her lips tasted, playing every moment over and over in his mind since he left her earlier. He had wanted so desperately to make love to her but had stopped himself. She was perfection, and he was an Unholy. That fact should have disgusted her, but it didn't seem to. Then out of nowhere she'd told him she was in love with him. His mind seemed to do a full stop at that point, unable to comprehend that the woman he had watched, fantasised over and dreamed about since his first day on the Crain farm was in love with him. North wanted to kick himself for not telling her that he was in love with her too.

Harper was looking silently at her lap, as if unable to look at the people around the table for fear she might be scolded for making eye contact with any of them, like North had seen Sabastian James do to her.

North's blood burned remembering the odious man who had hurt Harper in the garden, and the only thing he hated more than remembering the pain on Harper's face that day was the fact he had stood by and done nothing to stop it.

Birdy leaned over to his sister, and North heard him whisper, "We aren't at home, you are allowed to speak at the table if you want."

Harper flicked her eyes up to glance at North for a millisecond before leaning to Birdy. "I've already acted inappropriately enough, and I'm sure you and North have heard my voice enough in the last few days to last a lifetime," she whispered, so low that even North found it hard to hear.

He hated himself, sure she had withdrawn back into her shell because of him.

"So, Harper. Birdy said you grew up on a farm, can you ride motorbikes?" Lloyd asked.

Harper didn't look up as she silently shook her head.

"We didn't have them on our parents' farm," Birdy answered for her.

"Did you have horses?" Charli asked.

"Yeah, a couple," Birdy answered again.

"Did you ride, Harper?" Charli asked, obviously trying to engage her in conversation.

North saw her sink her head a little lower as she shook it. "No."

"Our parents didn't allow her to ride. They thought it unladylike to straddle a horse, and we didn't have a side saddle," Birdy explained.

The conversation around the table broke into talk about which saddles were best for what jobs and how everyone thought a side saddle was ridiculous.

North stood and moved around to Harper so he could lean in close to her ear. "Would you like some fresh air?"

Harper shook her head and remained seated beside Birdy. "No."

"Would you like to retire for the evening?" Birdy asked in a low tone.

Harper nodded her head. "Yes."

North stepped back while Birdy stood and addressed the table. "Pardon us, Harper is feeling a little overwhelmed. I'll help her to her room."

North watched as Birdy helped his sister from her seat and down the hall to her room. He felt like a complete asshole.

"So, North," Charli began. "Will you be fox hunting tonight?"

Sabastian grabbed the brunette's long hair, wrapped it around his hand and pulled her back against him, driving his hard length into her from behind while she leaned her hands against the edge of the bed. She was no Harper, her body wasn't as smooth or perfectly curved, and her face, despite being pretty enough, looked plain compared to his new bride's.

Sabastian drove himself into her again and she let out a small whimper.

"Come, my dear, I haven't even built up a rhythm yet." He smiled as he pulled her hair back and pushed deeper into her soft core.

Sabastian knew he was well endowed. He prided himself on it, but listening to the brunette's pained moan at his length made him excited. He withdrew and effortlessly flipped the woman onto her back on the bed before delving into her again. He wanted to see her face when he buried himself in her.

Sabastian closed his fingers around the woman's neck as he imagined Harper in her place and his excitement grew, his thrust harder as her face began to turn red, then purple, while he squeezed her throat. She clawed at his hands as she struggled under him. He liked when they fought. He thrust deeper and his body clenched with excitement as he emptied himself inside her before releasing her throat.

The woman choked for air, coughing under him.

Sabastian withdrew, stood, and wrapped his robe around himself before walking to the bedroom door.

"Kleve!" he called.

Kleve appeared. "Sir?"

"I'm finished with her for now. Make sure she is thoroughly washed and ready for me when I want to use her again."

"Yes, sir, may I . . ." Kleve almost smiled.

Sabastian rolled his eyes. "Fine. Consider it your Christmas bonus. But make sure she's thoroughly cleaned after you're finished."

The short man grinned widely and rubbed his hands.

Sabastian wouldn't ever share his wife, but the whore lying in one of his spare rooms wasn't his wife, and Kleve was a loyal servant. Besides, he was sure she'd be dead by morning, in fact he was looking forward to doing it. The thought aroused him as he headed up the marble staircase of his luxurious mansion to wash the stench of the cheap woman from his skin.

I sat on my bed in the dark and looked out at the way the moonlight rested on the placid lake. The sounds of the dinner conversation floated through the still night air. I couldn't make out what they were saying, but the bellowing laugh of Lloyd would occasionally echo out. The sounds of the voices eventually died down as people retired for the night. I didn't feel tired, I felt sad and forlorn. I had run away to find a better life and be free, but now I felt more trapped than ever. I couldn't go back. I would be a disgrace to my parents, and I had no idea how to move forward. And worse still, I felt dirty. I had acted in such an unladylike manner that I was sure it had disgusted North.

A sudden thought occurred to me — what if he told everyone what I had done?

I grabbed my pillow and stuffed it over my face to stop myself from screaming out in humiliation. No wonder North didn't want me. I was an unclean woman. He must have thought me revolting.

I needed air.

I slipped off the bed. My ankle protested my weight as I slowly made my way out the bedroom door and down the dark, empty hallway. Everyone had gone to bed leaving me alone with my thoughts.

Outside, the darkness was thick and heavy with only a quarter moon and the billions of tiny stars to light the inky-black sky.

I made my way down the steps, across the dew-covered lawn and out along the small jetty that jutted out into the flat, glassy, black lake. The water was so still that it appeared that the heavens had sprouted within the depths of the earth forming two universes, one above and one below. In all my years I had never seen anything as enchanting or wondrous.

I suddenly felt a prickle at the back of my neck, the weight of someone's gaze weighing on me. I turned to look back at the lawn, sure that was where the gaze was coming from, but all I could see was darkness. Something in the back of my mind told me it was North.

North lay on the grass in his animal form silently watching the chicken coop while he waited for the fox to show its head. His heightened senses gave him an advantage. His sense of smell was the best, his vision sharper than a human's, and his coordination more honed. He had long ago recognised he was a predator, thanks to his Unholy blood.

The faint sound of the veranda door opening, then closing to his left caught his attention, and he glanced over.

Harper made her way down the steps, gripping the old handrail for support before crossing the lawn to the jetty that stretched out into the lake.

Her ethereal beauty reminded North of a dream while he simultaneously scolded himself as an idiot for not making love to her when she had asked him to. He wanted to go to her, but if she saw him in his giant black wolf form, he was sure she'd scream.

Harper stopped at the end of the jetty, then turned to look right at him. He knew she couldn't see him from where she stood, but he froze, feeling as if he were a deer in the headlights, her dark silhouette framed by starlight.

"North, I know you're there," Harper said, her voice calm.

North remained still, convinced she hadn't seen him.

Harper waited with her slender arms wrapped around herself. After a long silence, she slowly turned back to the lake and looked up at the stars. Then with a long slow breath she stripped off her top and sweatpants.

North's heart faltered in his chest as her smooth skin almost glowed in the pale moonlight. Then without warning, Harper stepped to the edge of the jetty and dove into the black water.

North sprang to his paws and sprinted to the jetty as his body twisted furiously to transform back into his human form while he scanned the black water for her.

"Harper!" he called, unsure if she could even swim.

About ten meters away, something broke the surface.

Harper.

"What are you doing? It's the middle of the night!" North barked as adrenaline pumped through his veins.

Harper smiled, "I'm being a free woman."

I stripped off my clothes as the reality set in, I was free. I didn't have to bow my head or hold my tongue with anyone anymore. I could do what I wanted, when I wanted.

I dove into black, cool water, letting it slide over my naked body like cold silk. It felt exhilarating.

I heard my name being called as I broke the surface.

I looked back at the jetty where a figure stood in the

darkness.

"What are you doing? It's the middle of the night!" It was North.

I smiled, taking in a breath of cool, clean air. "I'm being a free woman," I told him as I floated on my back and looked up at the stars. I felt the weight of the world drift from my shoulders and even the pain in my ankle felt less intense.

"You are naked, swimming in a lake in the middle of the night," North called.

I didn't expect him to understand how I felt, and it didn't matter. I was free.

"Yes," I told him, "and the stars are that much brighter for it."

"You are going to catch a cold."

I laughed. "If you're so worried about it, come and drag me out."

There was a splash and I looked up to see North was swimming towards me. He stopped a few feet away. We looked across the water at each other.

"So, do I have to drag you back to shore or will you swim by yourself?" he asked.

"Drag me," I dared him.

North moved closer and slipped a hand around my bare waist, setting an electric charge off through my entire body before he quickly released me.

"You're naked," he said with a half-smile.

I reached out and touched his hard, muscular body and felt the ridges of his stomach beneath my fingertips. "So are you," I told him before I languidly rolled away and began to swim back to the jetty.

Harper climbed from the water while the pale moonlight played over her wet, naked body before she picked her clothes up off the jetty and glanced back at him.

"Are you coming?" she asked.

In that moment North knew he didn't have a chance against her.

He left the water almost hypnotised by her perfect form, but he could see Harper's foot was still hurting her.

North stepped forward, scooped her up in his arms with a strong, fluid motion, and started toward the house. Harper let out a faint sigh and wrapped an arm around his neck. Despite the chill of the water and the cool night air, her skin felt warm against his.

North tiptoed lightly through the house and into her bedroom. He quietly closed the door, laid her on the bed and leaned over to look into her mesmerising emerald-green eyes.

He knew he was hanging onto his control by a thread, and Harper was the knife that could cut it.

North moved to leave, but Harper jumped to her knees, grabbed his arm and pulled him back onto the smooth sheets before hurriedly straddling him.

Harper smiled and lowered herself against him as he moaned at her touch, the electric buzz of their bodies amplifying between them.

"You're not going anywhere," she whispered.

I had no idea what I was doing but I knew I didn't want him to leave. I was a free woman who made my own decisions, and my decision was, I wanted him. I grabbed his arm, pulled him back onto the bed and quickly straddled him so he couldn't leave.

"You're not going anywhere," I told him.

I leaned forward as my bare nipples brushed against his firm chest and kissed him. The taste of him ignited every cell in my body while his arms closed around me to grip me tighter.

He wanted me as much as I wanted him.

North rolled me onto my back and kissed a line down my neck to my nipples. His tongue swirled around them, tantalising them while his warm hand moved lower, sending electrifying currents through me. His mouth followed the line of his hand, kissing and nipping his way down over my stomach. His fingers found the sensitive spot between my thighs, followed by his tongue.

I gasped and gripped his wet blond hair. My back arched as he took a long slow lick before he dipped his finger inside me. The sensation was so foreign and arousing as waves of buzzing heat rushed through me.

"Make love to me," I gasped.

North lifted his head as his fingers continued to tantalise me. "Are you sure?"

I gripped his hair and pulled him up my body. "Yes."

He positioned himself as his hard length rested against my core. If he didn't make love to me right now, I was sure I'd explode.

"It might hurt," he whispered. "If you want me to stop, tell me."

He was taking too long.

I lifted myself up and felt him slide inside me a little.

I gasped.

"Are you all right?" he asked.

"Yes."

North slid a little deeper, his hard length slowly filling me as he kissed my neck, then my jaw and on to my mouth.

He was moving too slow. I lifted myself and forced him deeper. Stifling a yelp, I felt a short, sharp pain.

We both froze.

North lifted his head as his eyes asked the question.

I leaned up and kissed his hot, tender lips as I shifted

against him, taking him even deeper before I felt his hips against mine. It was his turn to gasp.

I felt so full.

"Make love to me," I whispered against his mouth.

North rocked inside me, slowly at first before he built to a smooth steady rhythm. The hot buzzing sensation was building. The feeling was so consuming it could become addictive as I moaned against his mouth.

"Am I hurting you?" he whispered.

"No," I gasped as I kissed his neck. "But can we move a little faster and harder?"

He smiled down at me but did as I asked. His beautiful body pumped harder into my eager core as a hot pressure rose, each intoxicating thrust building on the last until my body felt sure to explode.

I panted as my body tightened around him, sending pulses of electrifying heat buzzing through me in a rush of pure pleasure.

North groaned and thrust deep inside me as his body shook above me and I knew he was feeling that same electrifying buzz I was.

North gripped me and rolled as he pulled me on top of him, our bodies still connected.

I rested my head on his chest and listened to his heartbeat as he pulled the blanket up over us and wrapped his arms around me.

For the first time in my life, I was completely happy.

Sabastian looked down at the dead woman lying naked on his guest bed with her head drooping to one side. He would have to send one of his servants out to buy a new mattress when the shops opened.

He remembered the look of terror in the woman's eyes

when he had entered the room for the second time. She had told him she would do anything to please him, and she had.

He smiled.

He had enjoyed it, but the dead woman wasn't his wife. Not that he wanted to kill Harper — no, but he did want her to want to please him, giving herself over to him in every way he desired her.

Sabastian pulled up his pants and buckled them at the waist while he looked out the window at the dawn light, before making his way back upstairs to his bedroom to wash the smell of the dead whore from his skin. He had a meeting to attend in the Capital in a few hours, and he still hadn't perfected the GPS tracker, although that wasn't entirely his fault. Many of the outdated satellites that orbited the earth were ill equipped for his modern technology, leaving large patches of unmonitored areas, especially to the north where many of the escapees tried to flee. Sabastian thought he would have to address this issue with Mark Lucas, Head of the Nation's Defence Network.

He thought Mark Lucas an obsolete old fool. He hadn't updated the Nation's Defence Network in the forty years since he had taken the position. Much of the old monitoring equipment could be easily hacked by the outside world and was on a regular basis. But still he had the ear of Praeses Connelly, the Nation's leader.

Sabastian smiled at the thought of the two old men talking about their inflated prostates and their inability to satisfy their rumoured harems of young wives.

That thought tantalised Sabastian. Bigamy was illegal among the general population, but if he were Head of the Defence Department, he would have a harem of young, beautiful wives to satisfy himself. Then if he killed a few, there would be plenty more where they came from. But all he really wanted was one girl, Harper. Beautiful, perfect Harper.

Chapter Thirteen

North lay with Harper next to him, his arm wrapped protectively around her waist while the early morning light crept into the room.

He had fallen asleep in her bed, but the sound of footsteps in the hallway woke him with a start.

Shit. He didn't even have any clothes in her room.

"Harper," North whispered. Sleepily her body rolled over to face him, her emerald-green eyes unfocused, but she was smiling.

North thought that no other woman on earth could look so beautiful, even with her mussed hair and sleepy eyes.

Harper reached over, cupped his cheek and kissed him softly on the lips.

"I have to go," North whispered.

Her brow furrowed. "No, stay."

"I can't, everyone will be getting up soon and I think Blane is already in the kitchen."

He kissed her forehead, rolled out of bed and snagged a towel that was hanging over the back of the dressing table chair. North took one last look at Harper lying in the bed. He wished he could have climbed back in there with her, but he knew he couldn't. He silently pulled open the bedroom door and slipped out.

North tiptoed down the hall to his door and had one hand on the handle when Lloyd stepped from his room, taking in the towel wrapped around North's bare hips and smiled.

"I'm guessing it's been a good morning?" Lloyd chuckled.

North gave him a flat stare. He thought about telling the older man not to mention anything to anyone, but that would be insulting. He knew Lloyd wouldn't say anything. He was more discreet than that, but it didn't mean he wouldn't give North shit in private.

"I guess this means I can count on you helping out with the fencing this morning, considering you're already up." Lloyd's smile widened. "We'll be heading out after breakfast."

North nodded. He knew Lloyd meant his mouth was shut, but that didn't mean he wouldn't take advantage of the extra help he could derive from this awkward encounter.

North watched Lloyd walk off down the hallway before slipping into his room. When he was dressed in an old pair of jeans and a faded shirt, he made his way to the kitchen. There he found Harper sitting at the table talking with Blane, while Lloyd leaned against the sink with his coffee in hand.

"So, you and Lloyd are husband and husband?" she asked, looking a little confused.

Blane nodded at her while North poured himself a cup of coffee.

"So, figuratively speaking you both wear the pants in the relationship?"

"Oh no, sweetie," Blane said in his gentle voice. "Lloyd definitely wears the pants, I just tell him which ones to wear."

Lloyd burst out laughing, slopping coffee on the floor. "That sounds about right."

Sabastian smiled and shook hands with General Mark Lucas, Head of the Nation's Defence Department.

It had taken longer than he had anticipated getting the GPS tracking unit to a state he felt comfortable presenting. All the while he had been thinking about his wayward wife.

The older man gestured to one of the chairs in front of his

broad oak desk.

"Please, have a seat Mr James," the old man said, as he moved to the high-backed chair behind the desk and eased himself down. "I have to admit, I was a little surprised to get a personal call from you this morning. We are both busy men."

Sabastian gave the blithering old fool a cordial grin.

"Yes, quite, that's why I'm going to get straight to the point. I am developing an injectable GPS tracking unit."

"How do you see it being used?" General Lucas asked, leaning back in his chair.

Sabastian leaned forward a little. He had anticipated this question and knew that the general wouldn't be interested in treasonous females. That was the MGD's problem.

"It could be injected into troops, security personnel and field operatives. Each unit would be able to track its host to within a meter of their location, and the information would then be able to be called up by a central computer within seconds," Sabastian explained.

The general thought about it for a moment. "How do you see it benefitting our great and powerful Nation?"

Sabastian leaned back. "You could track soldiers in undesirable locations, locate field operatives, and if you suspect that one of your spies is actually a double agent, then you could monitor his movements."

"Sounds like you've thought this through. What do you need from the government?"

He had the general on the hook. There had been several breeches of national security, the weight of which had landed squarely on the general's shoulders.

"I have identified two key satellite black-spots within our borders. The most significant one is to the north near the border, where I fear treasonous runners might attempt to flee, and the other is to the south-east. I would need those black-spots eliminated if we were to track our villainous country-men efficiently," Sabastian said, sounding as patriotic as he could.

The general leaned an arm on the desk, tapping his fingers. "How long would it take to develop this technology?"

"I already have a prototype, and my factories are mostly automated, so it would only require me to input the blue-prints."

The general nodded his balding head. "Let me see if we can move a couple of the satellites around, and I'll get back to you."

Sabastian kept a cool expression on his face. "Thank you, I'll look forward to hearing from you," he said as he moved toward the door.

"Just one last thing," the general said as Sabastian turned to him. "Would it be possible to incorporate a remotely acti-vated poison into the device? Just in case we do find a traitor in the ranks."

Sabastian wanted to kick himself. Why hadn't he thought of that? "I'll get to work on it immediately."

I sat on the veranda with my foot propped up on a pillow. North, Birdy and Lloyd had headed out in the old rusty farm truck to fix a break in one of the fences. It had been weeks since we had arrived here, and at first, I was anxious to get over the border, but now I couldn't imagine leaving. I spent every night with North, making love and sleeping wrapped in his arms, and every minute of every waking moment think-ing about him.

"I can't believe how hot it is," Blane sighed, leaning against the rail, his blond curly hair glowing like a halo in the sun-light.

Charli walked up the back steps holding a gun and

stopped. "Have you ever shot a gun?"

I shook my head.

My father hadn't allowed me to shoot guns. He thought it unladylike, but I was an excellent archer. He thought archery more feminine and he said it promoted good posture. He had been right. I had practised for hours, shooting at targets, and my posture had improved because of it.

"Come on, I'll show you how," Charli encouraged.

She led me across the yard to where she had pinned a piece of paper to a tree and drawn a smiley face.

Charli raised the gun, took aim and fired. A quiet *POP* announced the shot as she put a hole through the smiley face's cheek, then handed the gun to me.

"Okay, this rifle is a newer defence model. It can hold twelve shots, has an inbuilt sound dampener, and doesn't have the usual kick back," she told me proudly. "So all you have to do is press it to your shoulder, look down the barrel and gently squeeze the trigger."

I did as she said. I lifted it to my shoulder, taking aim along its length at the space between the smiley face's eyes and pulled the trigger.

The bullet punctured where the smiley face's left ear would have been.

"Wow, that was good for your first attempt." Charli smiled. "Try again. There are ten more bullets in there. I'll be back in a minute, I'm just going to get a drink."

I readjusted my aim, lifting it slightly and aiming a little further to the right. I had arrows at home which were slightly bowed and didn't fire straight. I presumed guns would be the same.

I squeezed the trigger. The bullet left a small hole between the eyes just a little lower than I wanted. I readjusted my aim and shot again, hitting it dead centre. I took two more shots, widening the hole in its forehead a little before deciding to make a line down the centre of its face. A couple of the shots were a few millimetres off, but for my first time I was pretty happy.

The gun finally clicked empty, I lowered it, pointing the barrel at the ground. I turned to see Charli and Blane standing a few feet behind me with their mouths open.

"Did I do something wrong? I'm sorry if I did," I said, looking back at the piece of paper.

Blane slowly closed his mouth. "I thought you said you hadn't fired a gun before."

"I haven't," I told him before turning to Charli and handing her the gun. "Thank you for teaching me. I'm sorry I used up all your bullets."

Charli looked at me, then the smiley face with a look of what I would describe as shock. I hadn't thought that making a line down a piece of paper would produce such a reaction, or maybe my inaccuracy with the bullet holes in the line was the problem, they were a little off.

"I'm sure I'd get better with practise, and I can draw another smiley face if you want, just show me where the paper is," I offered, unsure of what else to say or do.

Charli slowly shook her head as I lowered mine and slowly hobbled back to the veranda.

"Harper," Charli called as I reached the bottom step.

I turned to look at her.

"Where did you learn to shoot that good?" Charli asked, something akin to awe in her voice.

North wiped the grimy sweat from his brow while Birdy threw the last bundle of old wire in the back of the truck.

"So, what's the story with Charli?" Birdy asked, trying to sound casual while he and North slipped onto the seat beside Lloyd.

"That was as subtle as cracking an egg with a sledgehammer." Lloyd smiled, starting back to the house.

North chuckled.

"Charli's a tough, hard working woman who isn't into all that girly stuff," Lloyd said. "And if you're interested in her, you have to be prepared to work as hard as she does and not expect her to dress up in frilly frocks and act demurely. It's just not her."

The house came into view, and North felt his heart speed up a little at the thought of seeing Harper. He had thought about her almost every second since he'd left that morning, hoping to be back by lunchtime, but the job had been bigger than expected, and it was now almost dinnertime.

Lloyd parked the car in the garage, and all three men slid out and went inside.

"Where is everyone?" Birdy asked

The house was quiet and empty except for distant giggling. "I can hear them out by the lake," North said, heading for the back door with Lloyd and Birdy in tow.

North was anxious to see Harper again. It had only been about ten hours since he saw her that morning, but it felt like decades had passed. North pushed open the back door and stopped so abruptly that Lloyd and Birdy bumped into him.

Tiny fairy lights hung from the big tree and a table was set out like a dinner party sat beneath it. But it was Harper sitting at the table in the same creamy-white lace trimmed dress she'd worn when she sliced bread in her parent's kitchen that caught his gaze.

"Wow, this looks amazing," Lloyd said, pushing North forward so he and Birdy could slip past.

North wanted to stride across the grass, pick Harper up and kiss her. He looked down at his filthy hands and clothes — if he so much as brushed against her, he'd ruin that angelic dress.

He quickly turned and headed for the shower. He desperately wanted to be clean so he could touch her.

I had once heard about a rich couple hosting a dinner party under the stars, and when I had suggested it to Blane and Charli, they both jumped on the idea. I was sure Blane just wanted to cook a feast, and Charli liked the idea of wearing a dress. She said that it had been years since she had an excuse to do it and she missed *girlying* up.

Blane and Charli had set to work hanging lights in the tree almost immediately before they dragged the dining table downstairs to set up under it.

I felt redundant as I struggled to carry one chair down the steps while they carried the rest. However, after Blane had carried out everything that I'd told him I needed to set the table, I was finally of some use, and then Charli had asked me to do her hair and makeup. I was in the middle of pinning her soft blonde hair into a French roll and discussing which dress she was going to wear when she tried to casually ask me if I thought Birdy preferred pink or blue.

I smiled. "I don't think he would mind either," I told her, "but the pink one makes your boobs look great."

Charli chose the pink one.

Blane had also decided on a pink shirt with black dress pants and had asked me to style his unruly hair into a quiff at the front — it had taken a lot of hair gel and spray, but we managed to tame the curls.

Now we were sitting by the lake, my sore ankle propped on a stool with the rifle by my side. Charli had left the rifle with me because she wanted the fox dead and told me I was a better shot than she was.

Blane poured us each a glass of his homemade schnapps while we sat back and enjoyed the sunset over the lake.

"So, my dear Harper, what exactly is going on between you and North? Because I've seen the way you look at each other," Blane asked, sounding tipsy.

"What kind of man asks a woman that?" Charli interjected. "Besides, that was my next question, now what am I going to ask her?"

We all burst out laughing as I heard the back door open and looked up to see North standing there gazing at me. He was so ruggedly handsome in his work clothes.

I smiled at him.

North suddenly turned and almost ran back into the house.

Had I done something wrong?

"This looks amazing." Birdy grinned, but he wasn't looking at the lights, the table or the food, he was looking at Charli and the pink dress which did credit to her already ample breasts.

I sat staring at my glass of schnapps while Blane took Lloyd inside to show him the cake he had made, and Birdy talked to Charli about the fencing. I was sure Birdy would get around to talking about other things, but my brother wasn't a smooth talker.

I turned the glass in my hand, watching the way the light played through the liquid, but my thoughts were interrupted when a shadow fell over me.

I looked up to see North in a white button-through shirt and black pants. His hair was ruffled, and he smelled of soap. He smiled at me.

"Now you smile at me?" I asked.

"I was filthy, and I didn't want to get that dress dirty," North said, sitting down beside me, taking my hand.

"It's just a dress."

North shook his head at me and smiled. "No, that was the dress you wore when we were both in your parent's kitchen and you were slicing bread."

I smiled, surprised he remembered.

North leaned a little closer, his hand slipping up under my skirt. "I *really* like this dress."

"Seriously," Birdy said, holding up the piece of paper with the smiley face I had shot. "My sister did this? Like as in Harper?"

I dropped my head.

"What is it?" North asked, sitting back, his hand resting high on my thigh.

Birdy handed him the piece of paper.

North looked at it, then at me and smiled widely. "You never cease to amaze me," he told me before he forgot all proprieties and kissed me.

"What the hell?" Birdy suddenly shouted, snatching my shoulder, jerking me away from North.

Birdy's fingers dug into my arm. "Birdy, you're hurting me," I told him, but he wasn't listening, he was looking at North.

"You sonofabitch, keep your hands off my sister!"

North rose from his chair beside Harper, unsure what he should do next. He knew if he and Birdy got into a fight he would win. Birdy might have had the bulkier muscles, but North had preternatural speed and he had been forced to fight for his life more than once. The downside was that Harper would be likely to hate him for hurting her brother.

"Birdy!" Harper snapped, trying to pry his fingers from her arm. "Let me go. I'm a free woman now."

"It doesn't mean you have to throw yourself at the first man that comes along," Birdy shouted, yanking Harper to her feet.

Harper yelped in pain and North had to use every ounce of will power not to knock Birdy out.

"You talked about finding a wife you could love and would love you, well guess what, I love North, and I'm fairly sure he loves me too!" Harper yelled back.

North felt a swell in his heart, she loved him and had told everyone here that she did.

Birdy looked to North. "You can't be serious, he's an Unholy."

Harper finally managed to pull free of Birdy's tight grip. "I know, and it doesn't make any difference to me." Her voice dropped as she glanced back and smiled at North.

North almost grabbed her and kissed her again. The woman he had been in love with, who he'd thought would be running for the hills when she found out what he was, was standing just a few feet away telling the world she loved him and didn't care what he was.

"But—" Birdy started as Charli gently stepped in close and took his arm. Birdy turned and looked at her.

"I think you are missing the point here. Your sister is happy," Charli said gently, tugging at his arm. "Come take a walk with me, and if you feel like arguing later, then I'm sure you can."

Birdy snarled at North. "Keep your hands off my sister," he ordered before he turned and walked away.

Charli looked to Harper and North. "You two make a cute couple, and I bet your babies will be gorgeous." She turned and followed Birdy off into the darkness along the lake's edge.

North suddenly had a sense of dread—if he got Harper pregnant, their child could be an Unholy like him.

Harper turned and looked at him. "I'm sorry about Birdy," she said, lifting her hand to brush North's shaggy hair from his face.

"I shouldn't have kissed you in front of him," North said.

Harper just smiled at him. "I'm glad you did. Now it's all

out in the open. Birdy will be all right when he calms down, he's just never been good with surprises." She stepped forward, wrapped her arms around North's body, and rested her head against his collar bone.

North held her to him. He'd never let her go — she was *his*.

CHAPTER FOURTEEN

Harper

I had eaten more food than my body could possibly handle, and still Blane piled more onto my plate.

"Really, I can't eat any more," I told him.

"But you didn't try the chicken yet," Blane complained.

I had tried the chicken three servings ago, and now the sight of it made me feel sick. North reached over and stabbed the chicken off my plate, giving me a quick smile. I laughed. He was like an eating machine, and it saved me from listening to Blane complain that there was food going to waste.

Charli and Birdy hadn't come back from their walk yet, and I was kind of hoping they wouldn't for a while longer. I didn't want to argue with my brother. I was certain I was in love with North, or at least a good way there, and that was that.

With dinner finished, Blane, Lloyd and North cleared the leftover food from the table, insisting I not help so I could keep my foot up. Lloyd thought I might have torn a ligament or dislocated the bones, given how painful it was. I tended to agree. If I had just scraped it up, it wouldn't have hurt as much, and it had been nearly a month since we'd arrived here, time enough for the scrapes to heal.

I sat staring out over the glassy black water just thinking. I had a suspicion, or maybe just a hope, I was carrying North's baby, and the thought made me smile. I imagined a little boy the spitting image of his father, or a girl with his beautiful blond hair.

A small tug on my senses pulled me from my thoughts. I could feel something was creeping around in the dark just beyond the lights of the house. Two shiny eyes looked at me, glowing red in the low light. The fox.

I slowly lifted the gun and took aim between the red eyes. *POP.*

A single shot, and the eyes jerked back.

I heard footsteps running through the house before North burst onto the veranda.

"I heard the gun," he said, looking at me as I lowered it.

How the hell had he heard that all the way inside? It was so quiet.

"Fox," I told him pointing in the general direction. "Charli said she wanted it dead."

North looked at me before jogging over to the shadows. He bent to pick something up off the ground as Lloyd and Blane emerged from the house. North carried the reddish-brown creature into the light, examining it, then looked to me with a smile.

Lloyd and Blane went to have a look at the fox before their eyes also turned to me.

"I told you I wasn't exaggerating," Blane said with pride, before coming over to sit next to me.

"You shot it dead centre between the eyes," Lloyd said, a shocked expression on his face. "That must be at least a forty-metre shot."

North's gaze didn't leave mine. "You are full of surprises, Miss Crain."

Sabastian sat back in his office chair wondering why the red-headed MGD agent hadn't called him in weeks with an update on Harper. He presumed she hadn't tried to cross the border yet and was still hiding out somewhere to the north. She would likely try to cross at night, because that was what he would do, but the question remained—would she still have her brother and the farm boy with her? Or had she done away with them? The thought of her killing her own brother twisted his lips into a smile. He himself had killed his older brother when he was seventeen so he could take control of his father's fortune. He then handed his widowed mother over to the government like a good citizen should.

Sabastian's phone rang.

"Mr James," General Lucas said in his rough voice. "I have been informed we have one satellite that isn't currently being used for defence purposes and can be shifted. But it won't cover the entire northern region, and it still leaves the area you pointed out to the south-east in a black-spot."

Sabastian sighed. It would have to do until he could convince the government to launch another satellite.

"As a military man, I'm sure you're aware that the northern area is a greater threat than the south, where our neighbours shield us from a lot of the rogue elements," Sabastian conceded, although secretly happy.

"Of course. We can't have renegades jumping back and forth across the border," the general said. "Now I need you to come in so you can show a few members of the government your prototype, perhaps even demonstrate it so we can see how it works."

"When would you like me there?" Sabastian asked, glancing at the tiny rice-sized prototype sitting in a glass tube on his desk.

"In the morning, around nine."

"I'll be there." Sabastian grinned before disconnecting.

He had done exactly what the general had ordered—he had added the remotely activated poison and already had his factory manufacturing thousands of the tiny devices. The poison he had chosen to use only needed a tiny drop to be lethal and was almost undetectable. Once he located Harper, she would never get away from him alive again.

North studied the line of Harper's nose and the way her lips curled into a perpetual smile even when she slept. North felt as if he must have died, because to him this was heaven.

Harper moved, nestling herself against him, her silky-soft skin warm and electric against his. He loved her. He would die for her, but he didn't think it right to stay with her, because eventually Harper would want children, and that was something he couldn't give her. The Unholy gene had all but died out over the years since the Pandemic, occasionally casting a throwback from two normal parents four or five generations down the line, but the children of an Unholy had a fifty/fifty chance of being born with it. He and one of his brothers had been born with it.

North had decided long ago, when he began to understand what he was, that he would never have any children because he didn't want his children to be ostracized as he had been.

He decided he would get Harper and Birdy across the border and take them to his parents' house so they would be safe, and then he'd have to leave. The thought made him sick to the stomach. But the longer he stayed with her, the harder it would be to leave her.

He loved her and knew Harper loved him, but he just couldn't do it to her.

North started planning out the route they'd take in his head. Lloyd had told him that all the roads over the border had been closed, but they weren't far from the border, and North knew another way to cross. He just hoped Harper's ankle would be healed enough to make the trip within another month.

Once they were over the border, North would call one of his brothers to come collect them, but he couldn't do it from here. The Nation's phone lines were notoriously tapped.

North gently brushed the hair from Harper's face and kissed her forehead. He had only just found her, and in a month, he would have to let her go. He decided that while he had her, he would make every moment count.

CHAPTER FIFTEEN

Sabastian sat easily in the government boardroom. He had become accustomed to talking to the bureaucrats and paper-shufflers that ran the Nation's government. They were the men who signed the cheques and ticked the boxes.

The overhead lights reflected brightly off the general's balding patch while he waffled on about national security and treasonous traitors. It was the usual stuff heads of departments spouted when they wanted the devoted approval of their underlings, but Sabastian knew the final word would be the general's. He had the power of *yes* or *no*, but he was sure the general would agree after the demonstration he had planned.

"Mr James, if you would," the general finally said, taking his seat at the head of the long conference table.

"With pleasure, sir." Sabastian nodded. He commenced his speech about tracking lost soldiers in hostile territories and how it could be used to better guide agents to their targets before he moved onto double agents and spies. "We can only assume that our enemies have spies everywhere. They are cunning and devious villains," Sabastian said, moving to the closed conference room door to open it.

Mr Kleve pushed a skinny emaciated man through the door with an electrified cattle prod.

"This is Mr Hull, otherwise known as Mr Fledge. He is one of those spies we were just talking about, and he has been working in the government's information processing office. He was discovered by my company about three months ago sending out classified documents to the north," Sabastian said calmly while he picked a syringe up off the table.

"I didn't do anything. You have the wrong man," Mr Hull begged.

"Of course we do, and I wanted to bring you in here to apologise for such an abominable mistake and give you an injection that will help with your recovery," Sabastian said, snatching the man's withered arm and injecting the GPS device just below the surface.

Sabastian released the man's arm while Kleve handed him a disinfectant wipe, which Sabastian used to wipe his own hands.

The man stood rooted to the floor for a moment. "So, I can go?"

"Certainly, you may. And the best to you and yours," Sabastian told him, motioning to the door.

Sabastian had to stop himself from laughing when the idiotic fool practically ran from the room.

"Do you want to explain the meaning of this?" A stocky man with wiry white hair barked.

"I merely gave us a target to track," Sabastian said casually, picking up his glass tablet and tapping in the code for the GPS he'd just injected.

He'd already tested the device on several of his servants and knew it worked perfectly. He had even tracked one of his servants while he went to a bargain store to buy yet another replacement mattress for the downstairs room. The servant obviously thought his employer wouldn't notice, so no doubt he pocketed the difference on the deal. Sabastian watched the little red dot on his screen and waited like a cat for the ping of his servant's tracker to approach the store's counter to pay. He pressed the *Execute* command. After twenty seconds, the little red dot blinked out, the man's own electric charge gone.

Sabastian knew he really had to stop killing whores on his

expensive mattresses.

The general looked at Sabastian while he tapped a button on the tablet, then the large screen at the end of the conference room lit up, displaying an overhead view of the building's transparent blueprint. A red dot blinked its way down one of the hallways.

"As you can see, we have eyes on Mr Hull, and he appears a little frantic." Sabastian tapped a button revealing a heart rate monitor. He had added it as a last-minute detail just before sending the final specs off to his factory. He thought it would be handy to see the agitation levels in someone he was tracking if need be. Though for himself, he wanted the pleasure of seeing their final heartbeat. The idea had come from watching the red light of the servant he had disposed of simply blink out on the screen. No. Sabastian wanted to see the panic they felt as the poison entered their blood stream.

"So, are you just going to let the traitorous spy go?" The man with the wiry, white hair complained irritably.

Sabastian smiled. "Not at all, but I should let General Lucas have his moment in the sun. After all, it was he who suggested the most auspicious addition."

Sabastian hated sharing the limelight for his invention, but he had to keep the general happy, and it didn't hurt his end goal to do so.

"Sir," Sabastian said, handing him the control panel. "Just tap on the red dot."

The general pressed it. The image on the large screen zoomed in, a list of commands overlaying it.

"Now all you have to do is press the button with the skull and cross bones and confirm *yes*," Sabastian instructed.

The general pressed the skull and crossbones button. A box blinked onto the screen with two buttons, *yes* and *no*, above which *confirm?* was written in bold lettering. The general pressed *yes*, and Sabastian leaned over the general's shoulder, pressing the heartbeat monitor so all could see. For a moment nothing happened, then there was suddenly a spike of the heartbeat. The blinking red dot zigzagged down the hall then went still, the heartbeat racing before it slowed and blinked out.

"What happened?" the white-haired man demanded.

"The general saw it as fortuitous to add a kill switch," Sabastian said, taking the control panel back. "I think it was a marvellous addition and would be handy if one of our agents was captured or tortured for information. We could simply eliminate him before he could divulge any secrets."

"Quite right," the general agreed. "I think this should be rolled out as soon as possible."

Sabastian nodded. "Of course, sir, I will have the first batch available in a few days."

"Very good, now this meeting is over," the general ordered, and as one, his underlings stood and filed out of the room.

Sabastian waited a moment before speaking. "Sir, I know it isn't your department, but a thought just crossed my mind, what if we use the device to track girls? I mean they do sometimes get kidnapped, and it is our civic duty to return them when possible."

The general thought about it for a moment. "I guess we wouldn't have to activate the device unless one goes missing, and it would give many of our wealthier husbands peace of mind. They could even keep an eye on them and make sure their wives are where they are meant to be." The General rubbed his chin. "Of course, I wouldn't want poison in the ladies' trackers."

"Of course, and eventually if we inject the device into baby girls, they would all grow up safer," Sabastian said casually.

"Quite. You'd better schedule a meeting with Frederick Mills, he's head of that department," the general said, nodding his bulbous bald head.

Oh, how Sabastian hated having to play nice with the blithering old fool, but at least he was easy to manipulate.

North had been preparing for their trip over the border for nearly a month now. Harper's ankle was getting better, but it still pained her to walk too far. He knew they'd have to leave soon before it got too cold, but once they left the farm it was only a matter of time until he would have to leave her. He didn't feel he had a choice.

North watched Harper sitting on the veranda talking with Blane. Her short brown hair was held back with a pale-blue ribbon while her nimble fingers shelled a mountain of peas.

Harper looked over and smiled at him. North didn't know how she did it, but she always seemed to know when he was looking at her. It seemed to be her own special talent. He'd miss that.

North went back to stacking the load of firewood he and Lloyd had collected.

"Are you going to tell her, at least?" Lloyd asked quietly.

North looked at him. "Tell her what?"

"Don't play the fool with me, North, I've known you too long, and I've seen the way you look at her, it's like you're already out the door," Lloyd said. "That girl doesn't want anything from you except your love, and she accepts you fur and all, without question."

North glanced back up at Harper. "She deserves better than me."

"That's bullshit," Lloyd barked. "If I thought she was just a girl you were using to get your dick wet, then I would have told you from the start she was too nice to play Casanova with, but you love her, and I know she loves you."

North looked at the old man. "You don't know shit."

"Then explain it to me."

North ran his hand through his hair. "What if I get her pregnant? It would be a mutant like me."

Lloyd shook his head. "You're the only one who sees you as a mutant."

"I don't expect you to understand — you've never been different."

"No, I've never been different," Lloyd said sarcastically. "It's not like I grew up fancying boys in a society that would have lobotomised me or put a bullet in my head if they knew."

"That's not the same. I'm talking about her having my babies. She would hate me and them," North said, the ache in his heart so strong it felt like it was tearing him in half.

"Shouldn't that be her choice to make?"

North shook his head. "She shouldn't have to make a choice," he said, before he turned and walked away.

I watched North and Lloyd from my seat on the veranda. It looked as if they were arguing, but their voices didn't carry.

"Do you think I should go and see what the problem is?" I asked Blane.

Blane shook his mop of curly blond hair. "Those two have a strange relationship — they're more like father and son than friends."

North glanced over at me, a pained look on his face, then looked back at Lloyd and continued the argument. Something told me the argument was about me, and a heavy feeling settled in my stomach. North had been different these last few weeks, distant. My mind had blocked out the feeling of impending doom. Instead I had been concentrating on how to tell him we were expecting, imagining his excitement at the news, but not now. Now something else threatened to take me over. It felt like sorrow.

North suddenly walked away from the argument.

I pushed the thoughts away. It was probably just hormones, after all.

After dinner North and I sat out under the stars, my head leaning against his shoulder while he wrapped his arm around me. I thought about telling North about the baby, but something made me wait.

"I saw you and Lloyd arguing," I told him. "Do you want to talk about it?"

"No," North told me softly, squeezing me to him. "I just want to sit here with you."

He felt warm. The electric buzz he sent through me felt so natural now when I was with him, but the emptiness it left when he was gone was almost unbearable.

"Are we still planning to cross the border?" I asked.

North took a breath, exhaling softly. "Yeah, as soon as we can."

Something in the way he said it made me pause.

"We could stay here until spring, I'm sure my ankle should be better by then," I suggested, not mentioning that being pregnant might slow me up.

North kissed the top of my head. I heard him take in my scent as he had done a thousand times before, like he was memorising me, but with that one simple gesture something clicked in my head and I knew he was leaving me. It suddenly became abundantly clear that was what the argument was about and why he had been acting so distant.

Something inside me shattered, and tears slid silently from my eyes, the heat burning my skin, but I didn't dare move in case he saw me like this. I just wanted whatever time I had left with him. I wouldn't tell him about the baby — that might make him stay out of obligation, and I didn't want that to be the only reason he'd stay.

"Are you ready to go in yet?" he asked softly, lifting his head off mine.

I couldn't speak. My world was crumbling, and I couldn't make a sound. I stood and walked back inside, wiping the tears with the back of my sleeve so he wouldn't see.

We made love, and it was the most passionate we had ever been, as if we were each saying goodbye to the other's body.

North fell asleep holding me in his warm arms.

In the darkness I watched him sleep. He was everything I had ever wanted, but I mustn't have been what he wanted. I was a lovestruck fool, but he was the most beautiful man I had ever seen and the only man I would ever love.

I had to leave.

I pressed his sleeping hand to my stomach. "We love you," I whispered before I slid out of bed, dressed and took a few clothes from the cupboard. I picked up my shoes and slipped out into the hallway.

I thought about waking Birdy, but I didn't dare. He would likely cause an argument and wake the house, and besides, I thought he and Charli were good for each other.

I tiptoed out to the kitchen and found a note pad.

I scrawled a few words on a page, folded it, wrote *North* on the front and left it lying, lonely on the table. I grabbed a loaf of bread and a few apples before heading out to the garage. Charli had been teaching me to drive the old farm truck, but I was still learning.

I heaved four of the large fuel cans into the back of Birdy's SUV, slipped into the driver's seat and started the engine. The SUV roared to life and I was sure I'd wake the entire house. I quickly reversed out of the garage, jerkily jammed the brakes on, put the car into drive and accelerated up the driveway before flicking on the headlights.

Tears streamed down my face and I had no idea where I

was going.

I couldn't head toward the border—it was closed and a woman travelling alone would be too obvious.

The driveway ended and the black ribbon of the road stretched off in both directions.

I turned south and prayed I would find somewhere I could hide for the rest of my life, for the rest of my baby's life.

North woke suddenly with a jolt of pain through his chest like his very life essence had been ripped from his soul.

He heard the sound of a car driving away up the driveway. He turned and felt the bed beside him. It was empty—she was gone.

North vaulted out of bed and ran through the house, bursting out the front door, his body warping into his animal form as he dashed after her.

Harper couldn't leave him, he loved her.

His pawed feet pounded up the hill. he could see the headlights ahead in the darkness. He prayed she wouldn't turn toward the border.

North pushed his legs as hard as he could. He needed to stop her.

The car pulled out of the driveway, turned south, and accelerated.

He chased after the car, but the lights grew further and further away until he lost sight of them.

North stood in the middle of the road in his giant black wolf form staring down the dark road. Harper was gone. The woman he loved more than life was gone. North collapsed on the ground, his body twisting back into his naked human form, and he screamed as tears rolled down his cheeks.

CHAPTER SIXTEEN

North kicked open the door. "You fucking sonofabitch, you had no right to tell her!"

"What's going on?" Blane asked, turning on a side lamp.

"I didn't tell her anything," Lloyd yelled back. "But she isn't stupid, she saw you moping around and knew something was wrong. Maybe she can read you like a book, like I can!"

"What's going on?" Charli asked, running into the room. She quickly glanced at North and turned away. "You're naked."

North looked down at himself. He had shifted back to his human form but hadn't dressed.

"Where is Harper now?" Lloyd asked as Birdy walked into the bedroom.

"She's gone," North cried, clenching his fists. He was so close to losing control that his skin prickled, ready to sprout hair.

"What the fuck do you mean, Harper's gone?" Birdy shouted.

"She took your SUV," North said, his legs suddenly too weak, and he sat down heavily on the end of Lloyd and Blane's bed and put his head in his palms.

"What the fuck did you do to her to make her run away in the middle of the night?" Birdy exploded.

Charli put herself between Birdy and North.

"I think we all need a cup of tea," Blane offered, slipping out of bed, grabbing his robe and gently wrapping it over

North's shoulders.

Lloyd was the first person to see the folded note sitting on the table. He picked it up and handed it straight to North without reading it.

North looked at his name written in Harper's perfectly curved handwriting before opening it.

North,
I'm sorry and please forgive me, but I love you too much to watch you walk away, so, I'm leaving first.
    Yours eternally
    Harper

North felt the air leave his lungs. The sensation of suffocating was nothing compared to the ache he felt inside.

Harper had known what he was thinking and had walked away to spare herself the pain, but North now realised he would never have been able to leave her. He loved her.

Harper was the stronger of the two of them, and he knew it. He had to find her. He had to get her back.

My tears had all but dried up, leaving me with a headache and a load of regret.

What if he wasn't planning on leaving me? No. I knew he was. I just obviously loved him more than he loved me, or maybe he didn't love me at all. Maybe he didn't feel that amazing electric buzz whenever our bodies touched, and it was all in my head.

I turned the car west away from the rising sun. I had no idea where I was going. I just knew I couldn't stay.

I drove and drove on autopilot. When the car ran out of fuel, I pulled one of the cans out, filled the tank up, climbed behind the wheel and drove again.

Day turned to night, but I only stopped to refuel. The

landscape had turned from flat and open to snow-capped mountains before night had fallen. The SUV strained up the dark winding road. Fatigue began to set in.

I felt so tired and alone.

I turned a tight corner to find a huge boulder in the middle of the road. I swerved, hitting the rail. I jerked the car back, the rear tires whipping out as I frantically tried to pull the SUV under control. I saw the wide trunk of a tree and slammed my foot on the brakes, but it was too late.

Sabastian stood sipping his morning coffee while he watched thousands of little red dots blinking on his monitor. The GPS injection program was going along better than planned. However, not a single female had been injected. General Lucas had insisted that his soldiers and agents be implanted first as a matter of national security before the MGD could start the female injections and monitoring program.

Sabastian smiled while he prepared for yet another meeting with the tedious General Lucas. Today was the day the general got his GPS tracker. At first, he had objected to the idea, saying he was above reproach and shouldn't be monitored like a common criminal. Sabastian had coerced him by making the injection to sound more like a safeguard in case some heathen radical group somehow managed to kidnap him. The army would need to find their leader to rescue him. The general eventually agreed, adding that he only expected to be monitored by the control room if such an event happened and that he didn't want *that* remote-controlled poison. Sabastian agreed to the general's terms. He had a closed-circuit monitoring device installed so only he could watch the general's movements, added an audio transmission upgrade, and instead of using *that* poison he had replaced it with an enzyme which was completely undetectable and would cause a massive coronary.

Sabastian would have the inside run on every defence department contract. And if he got sick of the old man, he'd simply eliminate him. He smiled at the thought.

He looked at the manila folder on his desk with the MGD profile photograph of Harper pinned to the front cover. It had been almost two and a half months since his dear wife had vanished off the face of the earth, but he knew she was still out there. He could feel her.

Sabastian's phone rang.

"Mr James, sir, this is Agent Twain from the north-east branch of the MGD," the voice said.

Sabastian remembered the redheaded agent, as he'd been expecting a call for months.

"We had a report come across our desk. A truck driver reported seeing what he thought was a young woman with short brown hair pulled over on the side of the road, refuelling a black SUV with out of state number-plates," the young Agent said. "It could be nothing but . . ."

"It's her." Sabastian smiled. He knew she couldn't stay hidden for ever, and now the hunt began again. "Send me the coordinates."

He wanted to fly out immediately, but he had the appointment with the general and he couldn't miss it — if he did, the blithering old fool might change his mind. "I'll leave as soon as my meetings here are done for the day."

"Yes, sir," the eager young Agent barked down the phone before disconnecting.

Sabastian took the glass tube with the GPS device in it and headed for General Lucas's office. He wanted to get this over and done with quickly so he could leave.

A pack of reporters were loitering outside the defence department's building when Sabastian arrived in his sleek sports car.

"Ahh, Sabastian." The general smiled.

He had taken to calling him by his first name which Sabastian detested. He only expected someone to use his first name if he had invited them to do so and he certainly hadn't invited the general. But there was an upside to such familiarities, and that was that the general thought him a friend and confidant, something Sabastian could use against him.

"General," Sabastian said in a happy, friendly voice, grinning widely at the old man. "You're looking well."

"I look the same as always, and I've told you, call me Mark." The old man chuckled, slapping Sabastian's back.

Sabastian wanted to wrench the old man's arm out of its socket, a feat he was more than capable of doing. He had been trained by his father, who'd been a Black Ops specialist. His father was convinced that the radical factions of the world would one day destroy the Nation. Sabastian had also served the Nation as a specialist covert agent in line with his father's wishes.

"I noticed some reporters outside," Sabastian said casually.

"I invited them so they could see you inject my GPS transmitter. I thought it would help dissuade the Insurgents and give the general public peace of mind about the devices," General Lucas said proudly.

It was obviously meant to be the general's brainchild, but Sabastian thought he could use it to his advantage. If the general public were convinced it was good enough for the soldiers, then they might be convinced it would be a good way to keep track of their wives and daughters. The men would drive their females into the DNA research facilities just to have them tagged. The MGD wouldn't even have to set foot outside to have every female in the Nation monitored.

"That is a fantastic idea, Mark." Sabastian smiled. "Every father that sends his son off to the Army will have peace of mind."

"Quite right." The old man lifted his chest to match his inflated ego.

Oh, how Sabastian yearned to burst that bubble.

"Now if you would stand beside me while I speak to the press, and then you can inject the device," the general said, motioning to the door.

Sabastian felt almost giddy. This was working out better than he'd planned. "It would be my pleasure."

North paced back and forth across the kitchen. It had been almost twenty-four hours since he'd chased Harper up the road. They had searched for her and the car all day, but there was nothing, not even a hint of her scent. "We have to find her."

Birdy scoffed at him. "You were going to run off on her after ruining her virtue, and now you want to chase her down." He snorted with disgust. "You're just pissed Harper left you before you had a chance to leave her."

North had given them a brief rundown of his previous plan before Birdy lunged across the table at him and had to be restrained by Lloyd. Now Birdy was sitting on the far side of the kitchen, arms folded, obviously simmering with rage at his once friend.

"I realise now I could never have left Harper," North protested.

Blane stood from his chair, brushing back his floppy blond curls. "Let me make some phone calls."

"Who does he expect to ring? The Praeses?" Birdy asked mockingly as Blane left the kitchen.

Lloyd smiled. "Blane is a man of many talents and he has connections that most folk don't even know exist. He was helping men and women disappear when I met him."

North paced. He doubted Blane's connections would know

anything unless Harper had been picked up by the MGD. He stopped pacing, his blood suddenly icy in his veins. She had to be all right—he couldn't live with himself if she wasn't.

"I put the word out with Harper's description. They said they'll send out an alert to all the groups, but they haven't heard anything yet, and some of the groups are pretty isolated, so they might not even get the message for months," Blane said from the doorway.

North wanted to punch something—he felt utterly helpless. He had done this. He had pushed away the most perfect woman in the world because he was scared, and now Harper was out there somewhere alone.

"North," Charli said quietly. "Walk with me."

North didn't want to walk with her, he wanted to find Harper, but despite himself he turned and followed her outside.

"When I first met you, I thought you the hardest man I had ever seen," Charli said softly.

"I'm not hard," North objected.

"You were. You carried the weight of the world on your shoulders and you thought yourself a monster."

"I am a monster. An Unholy fucking monster," North snapped.

Charli stopped and shook her head. "I never saw you as a monster, and no one here does."

"Except for Birdy."

"No, he sees you as an asshole that used his sister," Charli corrected.

"I'm definitely one of those."

"I know you love her, and for a time, I admit, I wished you would have looked at me that way."

North looked at her, shocked. He had only ever thought of Charli as a kind of sister.

Charli raised her hand in a stopping gesture. "But I know that what you and Harper have is more. The energy you two produce when you're close is . . ."

"Electric," North finished.

Charli nodded. "I have never felt that from any other couple. You're meant to be together, and you will find her."

"How?" North's voice cracked, tears blurring his sight.

Charli wrapped her arms around him. "I don't know, but where there's a will, there's a way."

Sabastian was seated across the table from General Lucas, Frederick Mills and several underlings while they discussed the MGD's nationwide roll out of the GPS trackers. Neither of the older men seemed to be in a hurry to end the meeting, and it was now approaching midnight.

Sabastian had been caught up in media interviews with the general. Mark had wanted him by his side, presenting him like a first-born child, despite not actually requiring Sabastian to speak, just to be there on show.

"Gentleman," Sabastian said finally. "I must apologise, but if I don't retire for the evening, I am afraid I will fall asleep at the table"

General Lucas chuckled. "Well, we can't have our *Star* sleeping on the floor like a common street person."

Sabastian said his goodnights. It was too late to fly halfway around the country now. His trip to meet Agent Twain would have to wait until morning.

He pulled his phone out and dialled Kleve.

"Get me a virgin. With brown hair and green eyes," he ordered, sliding into his car. If he couldn't have his wife, he'd have a substitute, for now.

Chapter Seventeen

Harper

My head felt groggy. I lifted my hand to a spot on my fore-head. Rough material stopped me from touching the skin, but I could still feel the lump underneath it.

"Hey, I think she's coming around," a young voice shouted as I opened my eyes and tried to focus on the blurry face hovering over me.

It was a boy, maybe fifteen with black hair, who I didn't recognise. Panic suddenly gripped me. I looked around frantically. Two more people, men, stood close by.

"Calm down, we're not going to hurt you," a big man with russet hair said, pressing my shoulders back as I realised I was on a bed, in a bedroom.

Are they going to rape me?

I lifted my legs and kicked him as hard as I could, sending him stumbling back. I scurried off the bed, my legs unsteady as the second man came at me. I swung, punching him as hard as I could, his nose crunched under my fist. Blood spurted.

"Fuck!" he screamed, gripping his face.

Two broad arms wrapped around me, pinning my arms to my sides. I pushed off the ground, throwing my head back, the back of my head connecting with something hard. The arms instantly released me, dropping me to the ground.

I looked around. Both men were holding their faces and swearing as blood poured out between their fingers. Only the fifteen-year-old boy remained standing, a wide, goofy smile playing across his lips.

"That was awesome," the boy said, as my legs wobbled under me and the world tilted.

I grabbed the wall, trying to stay upright as two more figures appeared in the doorway. Another russet-haired man, older, and a woman my mother's age with a round face.

"What the hell happened in here?" the man said disapprovingly while I tried to scan the room for a weapon, but my focus wavered.

"She beat up Travis and Todd," the young boy said cheerfully. "It was awesome."

"For goodness' sake," the woman huffed. "You boys better get out of here and leave the poor girl alone before I give you more than a broken nose."

The two men with the broken noses shuffled past me. I pressed myself to the wall, terrified of the retaliation I would receive once the tears and blood had been wiped away.

"You too, Billy," the woman told the boy.

"But . . ."

"Go," the woman ordered, pointing a stiff arm out the open door.

The woman waited for the older russet-haired man to leave as well.

"First off, no one here is going to hurt you," the woman said calmly. "This place is a sanctuary of sorts, and my name is Elisabeth Hall, but most folks call me Beth."

I looked around the room, unsure whether I should try and make a break for the door. The only problem was I wasn't sure my legs would hold me.

"So, what's your name?" the woman asked gently.

I didn't want to tell her my name. If I did, she could ring the MGD and tell them she had Sabastian James's fiancée.

Shit, I had barely thought of Sabastian since I ran away. Now he could be waiting right outside that door, and I wouldn't be able to do a thing about it.

I kept my mouth closed.

"You don't have to tell me if you don't want to. Many folk here choose to leave their old lives behind." The woman smiled.

It was a disarming smile.

"Now you're probably wondering how you got here," Beth said, sitting down in a chair beside the bed. "You were in a car accident, Travis found you unconscious a few hours ago and brought you home. You've got a nasty bump on your head, but that seems to be the worst of it."

A knock came from the door, and the older russet-haired man entered carrying a bowl of soup, the smell instantly made my mouth water. I hadn't eaten before I left the farm a few days earlier and I hadn't wanted to.

The big man set the bowl on the bedside table and nodded at me.

"This is my husband, Joe. He doesn't say much, but he's a darn fine cook." Beth smiled, rose from her seat, took a step toward the bowl and spooned a mouthful in. "Mmm, you have certainly outdone yourself this time."

The big man smiled at her before turning to leave the room, Beth followed, stopping momentarily at the door.

"You are free to leave anytime, but you are also free to stay as long as you like," she said before she walked out, leaving the door wide open.

My legs gave way under me and I sat down hard on the floor, my back against the wall. I buried my face in my knees, exhausted and afraid.

"You should eat," a voice said, as I jerked my head up to see the boy Beth had called Billy squatting in front of me with the bowl of soup. "I know Beth told you Joe's cooking is the best, but really it's pretty average. I think she just says that so she doesn't have to cook."

Billy slid the bowl across the floor toward me. I thought he might be scared he'd be the third person to receive a bloody nose.

I was so hungry. I took the bowl and spooned some into my mouth, it was delicious. Forgetting all proprieties, I ditched the spoon and drank straight from the bowl.

Billy laughed. "Slow down, you'll end up wearing it."

I paused, remembering my manners, and picked up the spoon, wiping it on my pants before I resumed eating at a normal pace.

Sabastian stood on the side of the road looking at the long expanse of empty black bitumen with distant farmhouses dotting the horizon.

"We started a sweep of the area," Agent Twain said, leaning against his car.

Sabastian doubted they'd find her out here, but it was as good a place as any to look. Harper was like a ghost — she appeared, then disappeared, but Sabastian was patient. He would wait, gather intelligence and find her.

"You said the truck driver saw a woman alone?" Sabastian asked, curious if Harper had killed her brother or merely left him behind.

He was hoping Bernard Crain was lying dead in a shallow grave somewhere. The thought twisted his lips into a sadistic grin.

"The driver said from a distance he thought it was a boy, but when he got closer he noticed she had breasts and a very female face." Agent Twain held out his hands indicating large boobs before pulling a photo out and handing it to Sabastian. "This is a still image we pulled from the truck's dash-cam."

Sabastian took the photo. It was grainy, and the woman's hair was shorter, but it was unmistakably Harper.

Sabastian's phone rang. He glanced at the number then back to the photograph before pressing connect. "General Lucas."

The young agent stiffened, pushing himself from his car.

"Sabastian, I know I've told you a million times to call me Mark."

"Mark," Sabastian said. "What can I do for you?"

"I was hoping I could impose on you to join me for dinner at my house."

Sabastian looked at his watch. It would take four hours to fly back to the Capital, another hour to shower and change and it was already one o'clock in the afternoon.

"I'm not in the Capital at the moment, but if you can hold dinner until six or seven, I should be able to make it," Sabastian said in his carefully cultured voice as he slid the photograph into his pants' pocket.

"Seven it is, then," the general said, sounding pleased.

Sabastian disconnected and shook his head as he turned to Kleve. "Fly me back to the Capital. I'm dining at Mark Lucas's house tonight."

"Like *the* General Lucas?" Agent Twain asked, his eyes wide.

Kleve stepped forward, forcing Agent Twain to look down at him. "General Lucas and Frederick Mills are close personal friends of Mr James, so you might want to be discreet and find his wife before you find yourself on the wrong end of a judicial enquiry into your MGD unit's dealings with this matter."

Agent Twain's face whitened. "We'll commence a thorough search of every property within fifty kilometres."

"Make it one hundred kilometres," Kleve told him.

Sabastian liked having Kleve as his right-hand man. It was like having a Pitbull with a voice and a sniper scope for a pet. Although he was certain Harper wasn't out here — no, she was only passing through, perhaps heading for the coast, maybe to find ship passage north because of the closed border. Or was he giving her too much credit? After all, she was only a woman and women were only good for two things in his eyes. And neither of them involved thinking.

"If my wife was heading west, she might be trying to find an alternate route over the border, maybe by sea," Sabastian suggested.

"I'll let the port authorities know to be on the lookout for stowaway girls," the young agent said helpfully while Kleve and Sabastian walked back to the copter in the paddock.

Sabastian had a dinner to attend and possibly a heart attack to inflict if the general's dinner turned out to be as tasteless as the general.

I woke curled up on the hard, wooden floor with a pillow under my head and a blanket over me. Daylight flooded into the small room through a large window, and outside I could see trees. I sat up and looked around the room. The bed had been made and the blood from the men's broken noses had been cleaned away.

I looked at the door. It had been closed all but an inch.

I pushed myself off the floor. My head felt sore, but the wobbliness in my legs had subsided, leaving me only a little shaky.

A note had been left on the bed.

Kitchen is to the left,
Bathroom is to the right

I tiptoed to the door and peeked out, expecting to see one of the big men standing guard, but there was only an empty hallway. I needed to use the bathroom desperately, but I wasn't sure if it was a good idea.

Oh, stuff it, I need to pee.

I carefully pulled the door open and crept down the hallway to the right. I passed two bedrooms. One looked as neat as a pin, while the other looked like a bomb had exploded in the laundry basket, sending clothes scattering in every direction.

I kept going and found the bathroom behind the third door.

Aww, sweet relief.

When I was done, I walked as silently as I could back down the hallway past the bedrooms and out into a large open-plan living area with a kitchen off to one side.

"Glad you're awake," a voice said. I spun to see the younger russet-haired man sitting at a desk in the corner. His nose was swollen and both his eyes looked black.

I backed away, bumping into the kitchen counter.

"I know he's ugly, but don't freak out," Billy said, walking through the door carrying two skinned rabbits and a rifle.

I thought about tackling the boy for the rifle, I was an excellent shot, but the way I was feeling, an ant could beat me up and steal my lunch money.

Billy set the two rabbits on the counter, laying the gun down beside them. He didn't seem worried that I'd try to take it. Maybe he assumed because I was a girl I couldn't shoot, or maybe he trusted I wouldn't.

I looked at the two dead rabbits, neither of them a clean kill. One looked like it had been shot through the side, while the other had a bullet hole through its flank.

"I can see you're impressed with my hunting skills." Billy beamed, holding the rabbits up for me to see. "If you want, I can teach you to shoot."

"Billy. Would you mind if I had a word to our guest alone?" the young russet-haired man asked as he stood.

I took a step back, my hands protectively covering my stomach.

Billy smiled at the russet-haired guy. "See, I told you, you were ugly, Travis. She's less scared of me with a gun than she is of you with that face," he said, picking up the rabbits and the gun before disappearing through a doorway.

The russet-haired man took another step forward and I stepped back, glancing across the counter tops for a weapon. A knife block sat on the far bench. If I was quick enough, I could grab a knife before he could get to me.

"The knife at the back of the block is a cleaver," the russet-haired man said, standing still and folding his arms across his broad chest. "If it makes you feel better you can grab it, but I will tell you you're perfectly safe here."

I moved another step back, then another, my eyes watching him, but he didn't move.

My hand reached over, pulling the handle of the meat cleaver, which slid easily from the block.

"You feel better now?" he asked, then casually turned and walked over to a dining table sitting next to a large window. He took a seat at the far end and waved his hand indicating a seat at the other end.

I hesitated.

"You have a knife, I'm unarmed," he said, patting down his shirt to prove it. "Please take a seat."

I moved slowly, finding my way around the kitchen counter to the table and stood behind the seat he had offered, my white knuckles gripping the handle of the meat cleaver.

"Fine, don't sit." He sighed. "Let's start with introductions, I'm Travis Hall and you are?"

I didn't answer.

"You have a name, don't you?" he asked.

I stared at him defiantly. I wasn't giving my name up.

"Fine, if you don't want to give me a name. I'll just call you *Car Crash*, seeing as that's where I found you."

He could call me anything he liked. I wasn't speaking to

him or anyone else.

He sighed again. "Fine then, Crash, this place you've landed yourself in is called Haven. It is a community of outcasts and runaways. We have little communication with the outside world, and we don't judge a book by its cover." Travis nodded at the window.

I glanced out. The house was set on the side of a hill, below other houses sat amongst the trees. Beyond, rocky peaks jutted above the tall trees.

"You are obviously running from something or someone, but I promise you're safe here. We don't judge and we don't ask questions about your past. That is up to you to talk about. If you choose to stay then you will be expected to work," Travis said in a very matter of fact way. "I understand you're scared, and I don't hold it against you, but violence isn't permitted here. However, you are required to learn self-defence and to shoot a gun as a precaution in case we are ever raided by the MGD or the military. Not that we ever have been or that I think you need it." He touched a finger to his nose and winced.

Had I died in the car crash? This place sounded too good to be true. Maybe it was a ploy to get me to talk or give myself away.

"Have you got any questions?" Travis asked.

I stood silently. I had a million questions, but I kept my mouth tightly shut.

"Very well, I'm going to stand up and walk to the kitchen to make you a sandwich. Don't stab me, and we'll get along fine," Travis said, slowly rising from his seat and walking past without a sideways glance.

Travis made me a peanut butter sandwich. I thought about telling him I didn't like peanut butter, but I'd eat it if it meant I didn't have to talk.

Chapter Eighteen

Harper, six months later.

My breath made foggy clouds in the early spring air. Winter was over on the calendar, but someone had forgotten to tell Mother Nature to turn up the thermostat.

I restacked the firewood and thought about North. It seemed like every waking moment and most of my dreams held thoughts of him. My growing belly was a constant reminder of the time we'd spent together, and it was getting harder to hide it. Thank goodness the winter coat Beth had given me was bulky and five sizes too big, or it would be obvious, even to a layman.

"I know I said I like Gail, but I think I changed my mind, because Felicity was looking at me yesterday, and I like her red hair," Billy said.

I had started off not talking so I wouldn't give myself away, but now it had just become a habit. The only time I spoke was when I was alone in my room. I'd tell my baby what his daddy was like and how much I loved and missed him. My silence didn't seem to bother anyone—they talked to me regardless. Occasionally I felt like the confessional at a church, listening to people's confessions and sins, their problems and solutions.

"Yeah, I think I definitely like Felicity now," Billy told me, resting against the stack of wood, the rifle propped next to him.

The gun looked to be identical to the ex-military one Charli had back on the farm. The government had probably sold off thousands of them when they released the newer models. I hadn't yet been allowed onto Haven's firing range, but I didn't mind. I wouldn't give a mute stranger a gun either.

"You want to shoot it? I can teach you," Billy said, noticing me looking at the gun.

He picked it up and handed it to me.

"Okay, first thing is tuck it into your shoulder," he told me as I lifted it up, pushing it against my shoulder. "Now just look along the length of it and see that pinecone hanging from the tree, try to shoot it."

I sighted the pinecone and squeezed the trigger. The familiar quiet *POP* filled my ears and I smiled, remembering how proud North looked when I had shot the fox. The bullet nipped the bottom edge of the cone, sending it swinging slightly. The sight was pretty straight, if not a little low.

"That was great, do you want another go?" Billy asked excitedly.

I took aim adjusting the height and *POP*, the bullet hit dead centre.

Billy's usual chatty persona vanished. I turned to see him standing, mouth gaping open.

I smiled, lined up another shot, and *POP*, I hit it in the exact same spot.

I turned, handed Billy back the gun and resumed stacking wood.

It took Billy a full five minutes to regain his voice, a new record for him.

"How'd you do that?" he asked.

I looked at him and smiled while I picked up a bundle of logs and carried them up to the house with Billy running ahead of me.

"Travis, I think you just got out-done as Haven's sharpshooter," Billy said, bursting through the door.

I followed him in, kicking the door closed behind me.

Travis looked over at him. "I know you're getting good, but you still have a way to go," he said patiently while he and Beth set the table for dinner.

I sat the wood down and warmed myself by the fire.

"Not me—Crash. She's awesome. She hit a pinecone from like a hundred metres away," Billy said.

I looked over at him and raised an eyebrow. The pinecone had only been about fifteen metres away.

"Fine, it was like twenty metres, but the point is she's good and she could go hunting with me," Billy said excitedly while Beth, Travis and Joe all looked over at me.

"Can you shoot?" Travis asked.

I shrugged and nodded.

Travis walked around the counter and took the rifle from Billy, nodding for me to follow him outside.

My shoulders dropped and I sighed. I didn't want to go back outside—it was cold, but I followed anyway.

Travis stood on the veranda waiting for me while Joe, Beth and Billy followed us out.

I felt like a peacock on display.

Travis handed me the gun before he walked down the steps, picked up a fist sized rock and walked it down to where a clump of pine trees stood about twenty or thirty metres away. He sat the rock at the base of one of the trees.

Something moved in the bushes behind Travis. Suddenly a massive brown creature crashed through the bushes. Travis turned stumbling back, but he tripped and fell on his ass. Beth screamed as Joe bolted down the stairs toward Travis. I jerked the gun up just as the beast reared on its back legs, towering over Travis.

POP. POP. POP.

I fired three bullets, aiming for its heart.

The creature roared and stumbled back. Travis jumped to

his feet and ran toward the house.

I kept the gun fixed on the creature as it collapsed to the ground. I was almost certain it wasn't getting back up, but I was ready if it did.

Travis and Joe both stopped running and looked over at the brown creature lying unmoving on the ground. I lowered the gun muzzle to the ground. The two men edged over to the beast and looked down at it, then up at me.

North would have been proud of me, and he would have smiled, but both Travis and Joe stood open mouthed.

Several people came running from a nearby house. They had probably heard Beth's scream.

The way Joe was toeing the creature with his boot made me presume it was dead, so I handed the gun back to Billy, wrapped my arm around Beth, who had turned deathly white, and walked her inside to make her a cup of tea.

Sabastian watched a petite young girl receiving the GPS implant through a two-way mirror. He had presumed that more fathers and husbands would bring their females in, but in the last five months since they had started injecting the females, less than thirty percent of the Nation's females had been injected.

"So, what do you think?" Frederick Mills, Head of the Missing Girls Department asked.

Sabastian leaned against the wall and crossed his arms. "I think we should make it mandatory and every female from adult to infant should be tagged. I also think your field agents should be doing a door-to-door search, especially in the northern region along the border, to locate my wife."

Sabastian was a patient person, and he didn't think Harper was in the northern region anymore. The last time she had been seen she was heading west, but if he could find where she had been hiding, then perhaps he could find where she was going.

Frederick looked as though he was thinking about it. "We could offer a reward for information. Maybe whoever is helping her might be motivated by money?"

"What about the door-to-door search?"

"As a favour to you for all the work you've done getting this GPS tracking system up and running, I'll fast-track the mandatory implanting of all females and send out several teams of agents to the northern area, past that farm where the mutilated bodies were found, to start implementing the new laws. They will have the authority to tag any females they find and do searches of the properties," Frederick told him. "It will be a two-for-one deal."

Sabastian smiled. Manipulating Frederick Mills was so easy.

"I'll get my agents to take photographs of every female they think is aged between sixteen and twenty-five so you can go through them and see if any are your wife," Frederick said. "But I should warn you, it is unlikely the poor girl is alive, and if she is, it's unlikely she has been spared her virtue."

Sabastian had thought about that, but the truth was he didn't care. He knew something about Harper's DNA sequencing that even Frederick didn't know and *that* made her even more special. He had found himself the perfect, most beautiful wife, and he intended to find her and keep her all to himself.

North stood on the end of the jetty looking out over the thawing lake. He had chased every lead, every whisper Blane's friends had reported, but none of them were Harper.

He needed her so desperately it hurt.

"Staring at the ice won't make it melt any faster," Lloyd

said, wandering up to stand beside him.

"It won't melt slower either," North replied.

"I know you're missing her, and if she's out there, you'll find her."

"She isn't dead," North snapped.

Lloyd sighed. "You know that's not what I meant."

"I know, I'm sorry. I just . . ." North sighed. "What do I do if I can't find her? Or worse, if she's found someone else?"

"Are you insane? That girl would never move on from you, she loves you."

"She left me."

"Only to save herself the heartache of you leaving her," Lloyd told him — he had read the note Harper had left and he understood why she did it.

"You want to hear something crazy?" North said, shaking his head. "Sometimes I dream that Harper is lying next to me and she takes my hand and places it on her pregnant stomach. Sometimes I could swear I feel the baby kicking, and for a moment I'm happy, and then I wake up and remember that's the reason why I was going to leave, because I didn't want to do that to her. I didn't want to give Harper a baby that wasn't as perfect as she is."

"Did you ever stop to consider that Harper might have thought you were perfect?" Lloyd asked, slapping him on the back.

"Perfectly stupid." North shook his head.

Lloyd wrapped an arm around North's shoulders. "Come on up to the house. Blane's making pumpkin soup and he's baking a fresh loaf of bread."

"I'll be up in a few minutes," North said, turning back to the lake.

"Don't be long. I don't want to have to chip icicles off you," Lloyd said as he headed to the house.

North stared at the slushy ice sitting on top of the water, it was hard to think that only eight and a half months ago he had dived into that water because Harper was swimming naked in the middle of the night, and that night was the first time they'd made love.

He closed his eyes, recalling the smell of her skin, the way it felt under his fingertips, the curve of her lips when she smiled and the colour of her eyes, those beautiful emerald-green eyes.

North turned and walked back up to the house.

"Really, how long until the roads open again?" Blane asked, scribbling something down on a piece of paper. "Hello? Hello?" he said, taking the phone away from his ear and looking at it before pressing it back to his ear again. "Hello?" He waited a moment and hung up. "Darn reception."

"What was that about?" North asked.

"One of the guys I know had to deliver some supplies up to an off-the-grid community in the mountains southwest of here. I couldn't catch everything he was saying because the phone had horrible static and the line kept dropping in and out, but what I did catch was there is a girl at this place with brown hair and bright green eyes."

North's heart pounded in his chest. "When can we leave?"

Blane looked to Lloyd and Birdy before looking back at North. "There have been several landslides and the road is closed, but he said they are going to start working on it and it should be reopened in a month or two."

"I can't wait that long," North said, beginning to pace.

Blane looked out the window, his handsome jaw set tight.

North stopped pacing. "There's something else, isn't there?"

Blane didn't look at him. "I didn't get all the details, but what I could pick up was that the young woman had been found unconscious in a car crash. She woke up, but she hasn't

153

spoken since she got there," he said softly.

North's heart faltered in his chest as the air was sucked from the room.

"Did your friend say if she has a brain injury?" Charli questioned, asking what everyone else was thinking.

"He didn't say, but he said she shot a bear dead with three clean shots to the heart," Blane told her.

"That has to be her. I don't know anyone else that could do that," Birdy said. "I need to go get my sister. Where is this place?"

"I told you, the road is closed," Blane said.

"Then we'll drive as far as we can and walk the rest of the way," North told him as Birdy nodded in agreement.

"The place is called Haven," Blane said, knowing there was no point arguing.

I woke with tears rolling down my cheeks as a sharp pain tightened my stomach. I had the dream again. The one where I took North's hand and placed it on my stomach so he could feel our baby growing inside me.

It was still dark outside when I slipped out of bed and waddled down to the bathroom for the millionth time before returning to my room.

Another pain tightened my stomach, and I gripped the mattress.

I had heard several of the women around the community talking about Braxton Hicks, and from what I could gather, it made the stomach tighten and was like a false labour.

The pain eased.

I knew I wasn't going to get any more sleep, so I grabbed my dressing gown and headed out to the kitchen to make myself a hot chocolate before I took it out onto the dark veranda to look up at the stars.

Another pain came, more intense than the last. I gritted my teeth until it began to ease off and I could breathe again.

I had only been sitting for a few minutes when the door opened and Travis stepped out. He wrapped a blanket around my shoulders and sat down next to me.

"I have no idea why you come out here to look at the stars when it is so cold," he half-whispered.

It was still an hour until dawn, and we were likely the only ones awake in all of Haven. I liked it like that. I liked the people here and looking at the stars while the world slept was magical. Even if I chose to speak, I wouldn't tell him how North and I swam in a lake that looked like its own universe or how I used to lie in North's arms for hours and watch the stars.

I glanced over at Travis, his russet hair messy from sleep.

"I wish you'd talk to me. I know you can, I've heard you whispering when I've walked past your bedroom late at night," Travis said.

He had heard me. I put my head down.

"Don't worry, I couldn't hear what you were saying, it was too soft," Travis added quickly. "But will you at least tell me when you go into labour?"

I looked at him. I thought I'd hidden my swollen stomach well.

"I know I said that we don't ask questions here, but I need to know, did you love the guy who fathered your baby?"

I smiled at him and nodded.

"Crash," Travis said softly. "Would you marry me if I asked you and let me help raise the baby?"

I reached over and gently touched his cheek before slowly shaking my head with tears welling in my eyes. It was the kindest offer, but I didn't love him like that, like he wanted me to.

"I didn't think so," Travis said softly, taking my hand and

kissing my palm. "If you change your mind, just speak up."

I gave him a weak smile as another pain gripped my stomach and I tried not to show it on my face.

North woke with a tear rolling down his cheek and a tightening pain in is lower stomach. He had experienced the same dream he'd been having since Harper left, the one where she took his hand and placed it on her pregnant stomach. At first in his dream her stomach had been flat, but over the months since she left it had slowly grown, making her even more beautiful to him with the thought of her carrying his child inside her.

Usually Harper was smiling at him in his dreams, but this time she was crying. She looked so sad that he wanted to cry with her, and then there was the pain he felt in his stomach. He hoped he hadn't eaten something off.

North sat up in the passenger seat of Lloyd's truck with Birdy behind the wheel and looked out at the darkness.

"How long have I been asleep?" North asked.

"A few hours. I stopped about twenty minutes ago to re-fuel, so we should be all right for a while," Birdy told him. "And at this time of the morning, without a single car around I can pretty much do whatever speed I want. I'm guessing if I keep this up, we might even get there by lunchtime."

North stared out the window at the stars while he remembered Harper floating naked in the lake, looking so enchanting with the stars reflecting off the glassy black water around her.

Another pain grabbed him as he gritted his teeth. He couldn't let Birdy see he was sick—he would probably turn the car around and take him back to the farm. They had already had to convince the others not to come, using the argument that Birdy and he would be quicker without them. If

North had to crawl over broken glass and not make a sound doing it to get to Harper, he would do it in a heartbeat.

The dark sky grew lighter as the long straight road along the plains gave way to twisting foothills. North's pain got worse, coming in more and more frequent waves. He could feel the sweat dripping from his forehead, but he gritted his teeth while Birdy concentrated on the winding road, driving them deeper into the mountains. Eventually they turned off the main road onto the unassuming dirt trail that was on Blane's map.

Then suddenly without warning the pain stopped, and for a moment he could have sworn he heard Harper call out his name. He slumped in the chair, his stomach muscles tender from tensing them. By lunch time they had reached the sight of the avalanche and parked the car. North had recovered from his pain as if it had never happened.

"How far is it from here?" Birdy asked, slipping from the driver's seat.

"I don't know. By the map I'm guessing a couple of days walk," North told him, grabbing his backpack and the extra water bottles.

Climbing across the landslide took longer than they thought, but once on the road on the other side it was easier. Then it was just a matter of getting to Haven, to Harper.

CHAPTER NINETEEN

I could barely stand the pain as it came in stronger and stronger waves with less time between. I was so worried that there was something wrong with my baby.

Dawn had broken, and the sun was peeking over the tops of the trees. Travis had gone back to his bedroom, but I was still sitting on the veranda as another wave came and tears rolled down my face. Gritting my teeth, I waited for it to pass and pushed myself up and waddled inside to find Travis. I knew he wouldn't be asleep yet.

I knocked on his door. Just as he opened it, another pain gripped me, and hot fluid gushed down my leg and puddled around my bare feet.

I groaned, half-buckling over to grab my stomach.

Travis caught me and lifted me up.

"I guess this is your way of telling me you're in labour," he said, stepping over the puddle as he carried me down the hallway to Beth and Joe's room.

Was I in labour? It was too early. I was sure the baby wasn't due for another two weeks.

Travis kicked the bedroom door a few times with his foot in way of knocking.

Another pain bit into me and I sobbed, cradling my stomach.

"Wake up!" Travis called through the closed door. "Crash is in labour!"

The door opened and Beth looked out at me, a wide smile on her face. "Well, I knew it had to be coming soon, you've looked like you were going to pop for the last two weeks."

Did everyone know I was pregnant? Well, that was a shot to my ego. I thought I was being discrete about my baby bump.

"You can take her into her room while I go and get the rubber-backed sheets from the linen cupboard," Beth said, hurrying past.

"Watch out you don't slip over, Crash's water broke in the hallway," Travis called after his mother.

Beth stepped over the puddle. "Joe, can you clean that up?"

Another more intense pain gripped me, and a whimpering growl escaped me.

"I think that's the most noise I've ever heard you make," Travis said, carrying me back down the hallway.

Billy's door opened and he looked out, sleep still clinging to his eyes. "What's going on?"

"Crash is having the baby," Travis told him as we passed by.

Another pain enveloped me as I curled into a ball in Travis's arms.

"It's about time," Billy said.

Wow, they must all have known, and not one of them had said a word to me.

Travis carried me into my room, where Beth was stretching a white rubber-backed sheet over the bed. He gently moved to lay me down, and another pain filled me.

I gripped his arm and gritted my teeth.

There was barely a break between each pain now. The pain subsided, and I released Travis's arm so he could lower me onto the bed.

"You'll be all right Crash," Travis said softly. "Mum's delivered half the kids in Haven."

I nodded at him, but I was so scared, and it didn't feel like it was going to be all right. I wanted North here. I needed him with me.

Another sharper pain engulfed me as sweat poured from me and I gripped the sheet, unable to breathe.

"Get me a bowl of water and a face washer," Beth told Travis before turning back to me. "There is no need to be stoic now. You can scream all you want, and no one will think less of you."

Another pain.

Travis came in carrying a glass bowl full of water and a cloth. He dipped the cloth into the water and squeezed the excess from it before dabbing it across my forehead.

Another pain.

"That baby is sure in a hurry to come out," Beth said, draping a sheet over my stomach and legs before lifting my night dress. "I'm going to take your panties off now."

I looked at her, then Travis. North was the only man that had seen me.

"Don't worry about Travis, he's up that end and he can't see anything," Beth told me as I felt her tug my panties down.

Another pain, and suddenly I didn't care if the entire world saw me naked.

I groaned, gripping Travis's hand while I prayed for the pain to stop, but it didn't, it just kept getting stronger and stronger before an overwhelming sensation came to push.

"You're doing well, Crash, I can see the top of the head," Beth said from between my legs. "Okay, breathe."

I panted rapidly until another need to push came. It hurt and burned, and I was sure that this wasn't right.

I felt something give.

"Okay the head's out," Beth said. "Now you just have to get the rest out.'

I wanted North here, I needed him.

As I pushed, his name slipped from my lips in a pain filled cry. "North!"

A tiny cry echoed through the room as Beth held up a tiny baby from between my legs, covered in blood and white gunky stuff.

My body felt utterly spent. I lay loose-limbed on the bed.

"You did well," Travis said softly, then he bent and kissed my forehead.

Beth tied the cord and wrapped the baby in a towel while Travis gently lifted my back and propped pillows under me to sit me up.

"You have a son," Beth smiled, handing me the tiny bundle.

Tears rolled down my face as I looked down at the tiny wisps of blond hair and a set of dark eyes. He was so beautiful, so perfect, just like his daddy.

I kissed the top of his tiny head as I cradled him in my arms.

"What are you going to name him?" Travis asked.

I didn't look at him—my gaze was on my perfect baby. "Wolf," I told them and kissed my baby again.

North wished he could shift into animal form and run the entire way, but he'd leave Birdy behind in two strides. No. North had to walk like a human, but that didn't mean he had to walk slowly. They had already walked through the night, not willing to stop, and he knew he could go for days without rest or sleep if he had to. It was one of the only upsides of being an Unholy. The closer they got to Haven, the more strongly he felt that Harper was there.

He and Birdy had driven halfway around the Nation in the last six months, chasing down every whisper of a brown-haired woman, but North would do a million more trips like that if it meant he'd find Harper.

North took a gulp of his water bottle.

"You know how Blane said the girl had a car accident and wasn't talking?" Birdy asked, half-jogging to keep up. "What if it is Harper and something is wrong with her brain?"

North felt himself stiffen slightly. "Then we'll take her back to the farm and look after her."

The thought had run through North's mind too, but even if he had to feed and wash her for the rest of his life, he would do it gladly. He loved her, heart, body and soul.

"Just checking," Birdy said.

Birdy had despised North when Harper first left. He'd thought North was a heartless asshole who didn't deserve his sister, but as the months rolled by and Birdy saw North's unwavering devotion to find her, he gained respect for him. It didn't take a genius to see North loved Harper with every fibre of his being.

The road stretched off in front of them, twisting its way along the side of the steep mountains.

The hairs on the back of North's neck prickled. He could smell several men up ahead.

"We are being watched," North said softly as they continued to walk.

Up ahead two men stepped from behind a tree, levelling guns at them.

"This is private property," a man in his twenties with russet hair called out.

"We're looking for a place called Haven," Birdy called back.

"Why?" the russet man asked.

"We are looking for my sister. We were told she might be there."

"What's her name?" the second young man called out, but he was more of a teenager than a man, with black hair and a mischievous face.

"Harper," North said.

"There's no one in Haven by that name," the russet haired man called out. "Describe her."

"Short brown hair, emerald-green eyes, very beautiful," North said.

"That sounds like Crash," the teenager said, lowering his gun.

"Crash?" North asked.

"Yeah, Travis here found her after she crashed her car into a tree. And she never talks, so we don't know her real name, so we just call her Crash," the teenager said.

Breath caught in North's throat.

"Was it a black SUV with out of state plates?" Birdy asked.

"Yeah, how did you know?" the teenager asked.

"That was my car," Birdy said, his voice suddenly shaky.

"Can we see her?" North asked, feeling anxious.

"How do we know you aren't government agents?" the russet-haired Travis said, still aiming his gun at them.

"You don't, but you have our word we aren't," Birdy replied.

"We don't take the word of strangers here, you could be trying to set us up," Travis called.

"Yeah, we need proof," the kid said, as if punctuating Travis's words.

North lifted his hand, concentrating on it as fur and claws sprouted. "Is that proof enough?" As far as he knew, he was the only Unholy that could change just one part of himself while the rest of him stayed human. Everyone else he knew could only turn into their half or animal forms completely. Some even had trouble forming the half-form, turning straight to animal.

"Holy cow, how'd you do that?" the younger boy asked.

"He's an Unholy," Travis said lowering his gun slightly. "It still doesn't mean I trust them. It just means they aren't government agents."

"So, can you take us to her?" Birdy asked while North returned his hand back to normal.

Travis nodded. "We're having a new life celebration, so she should be at the clearing."

"Yeah, every time a baby is born here, we have a bonfire," the teenager said excitedly. "And now I'm an uncle, I might even get a glass of the home-brewed alcohol."

"Billy!" Travis snapped.

The boy looked at him, registering he had probably said too much in front of the strangers.

"Billy, you can lead the way," Travis told the boy.

North didn't care about their celebrations or the fact Travis had put himself behind them with the gun, he just wanted to get to Haven and find Harper.

They walked for about twenty minutes through the forest, the sounds of many voices growing louder until they stepped out into a wide clearing with a bonfire mound waiting to be lit in the centre.

People stood around in groups talking and laughing while children ran around them.

"Where is she?" Birdy asked as the men scanned the clearing.

North smelled her soft delicate scent before he saw her. She was sitting with her back to him by the unlit bonfire. Her short brown hair was longer, almost to her shoulders, but he would know his love anywhere.

Harper suddenly stiffened in her seat and slowly turned her beautiful face, looking over her shoulder at him, her emerald-green eyes meeting his.

North sprinted toward her as she stood and turned. In her arms there was a bundle of cloth with a tiny sleeping face sticking out.

North stopped, hesitating for a moment as his brain registered the sleeping baby. He had dreamed of this so many times and he wasn't sure he wasn't dreaming now.

He stepped forward, taking Harper in his arms and kissed her.

The charge of electricity that ran between them was almost overwhelming. North felt like he had just come home out of a dark night into the light. Harper reached up, wrapping one arm around his neck as they broke from the kiss.

"I love you, please never leave me again," North told her as he rested his forehead against hers.

Harper smiled, tears filling both their eyes. "I love you too," she half-whispered while North looked down at the bundle in her arms.

I was quietly sitting, thinking about how I could sneak back to the house so I didn't have to be here, but this bonfire and the celebration was for Wolf and me.

I liked the people of Haven, and I was sure my child and I would be safe here, but I knew the only place I would be truly happy in was with North. The only problem was I had no idea how to find him or Charli's farm. I had been in such a daze when I left, and then I had driven on autopilot for most of the way before crashing Birdy's car into a tree.

"Crash, would you like a hot chocolate?" Beth asked, pulling a thermos from a basket she had brought down from the house.

She had been mothering me and helping me with Wolf since I gave birth yesterday morning and probably would have organised the bonfire for last night so she could show off the newest addition to her household, but Travis and Joe insisted I needed to rest.

Travis pretty much jumped to attention every time Wolf made even the slightest of noises. He paced outside the bathroom door while Beth showed me how to bathe him, then brought me cups of tea while I nursed. If my heart wasn't devoted entirely to North, I would have considered Travis's offer to marry him. He would make a doting husband and father, but I couldn't do that to him. I would never love him like I did North, and that would be unfair to both of us.

I was kind of glad when Joe had got an alarm call telling him there were two people approaching Haven on foot because I knew it was Travis and Billy's turn on guard duty, meaning his doting would have to be put on hold.

I smiled and nodded at Beth while she pulled two cups out. I guess retreating to my bedroom to adore my baby and dream about North could wait until after the hot chocolate.

Suddenly I felt a shock of electricity run up my spine.

My back stiffened.

I must be hallucinating—it couldn't be him. How would he ever find me here? I didn't even know where *here* was.

I slowly turned and looked back over my shoulder. Like a dream, he was standing there, across the other side of the clearing, looking at me with those beautiful hypnotic brown eyes.

North suddenly sprinted toward me, and as if in a trance I stood and turned toward him.

He stopped just short of me, his eyes wide as he looked down at Wolf, bundled in my arms. I had almost forgotten about him for a moment when I saw North.

I had been cruel and hadn't told him I was pregnant before I left, and now I stood in front of him holding his newborn son.

North stepped forward, wrapped his arms around me and kissed me. That electric buzz that seemed to touch my soul pulsed between us as if the universe had been broken in two but had now been made whole again.

I reached up, wrapping one arm around his neck as we broke from the kiss and he leaned his forehead against mine, tears flooding both our eyes.

"I love you, please never leave me again," North said, the words crackling with sorrow and happiness.

I couldn't help but smile as tears of happiness ran down my face. "I love you, too."

North looked down at Wolf sleeping in my arms between us and smiled. Tears streaked down his face.

"This is Wolf," I told him quietly. "Your son."

North carefully took him from my arms. His hands looked so big and strong against Wolf's tiny body.

"I dreamed about you," North whispered quietly to Wolf before turning to me and kissing me again. "And I dreamed about you every night."

"Harper," I heard my name called.

I looked around North's broad shoulders to see Birdy jogging toward me, with Billy and Travis following him. Travis looked like he was ready to murder someone, and I suddenly realised Birdy and North must have been the intruders that set off the alarm.

I smiled at Birdy as North turned to him with Wolf in his arms.

Both Birdy and Travis stopped.

North smiled at Birdy. "You're an uncle," he said with such pride I thought he might burst. Then he leaned over and kissed me on top of my head.

"You had a baby?" Birdy looked shocked as his gaze moved to North. "Did you know Harper was pregnant?"

"No, but I used to dream she'd put my hand on her pregnant stomach," North said.

I looked up at him and he smiled down at me. "I had the same dream."

Beth stepped up beside me, handing me a cup of hot chocolate. "So you're North. Up until a moment ago your name and Wolf's were the only two words I heard pass Crash's lips in the last six months. It is nice to put a face to the name," Beth said. "I'm presuming you're the father of this beautiful little boy?"

Travis looked like he'd just chewed on gravel and was ready to spit it out. "I thought you said you were her brothers," he snarled.

"I'm her brother, that's her lover," Birdy corrected.

The comment didn't make Travis look any less pissed. He turned and stalked away.

"Hey Crash, did you know your baby's daddy is an Unholy?" Billy asked.

I nodded at him.

Billy looked as if he was considering something for a moment. "Are you an Unholy too?"

I smiled and shook my head.

"Awe darn, that would be cool if you could sprout fur and fangs and stuff like your boyfriend," Billy said, sounding disappointed.

North adjusted Wolf in his arms, then wrapped an arm around me. "Is he serious?" he asked.

"Yes, and he'll probably ask you to turn into your animal form next." Beth smiled.

"Can you do that? Can you show me?" Billy bounced excitedly.

"Billy, leave our new guests alone," Beth said, shaking her head before turning to North then Birdy. "I'm so sorry about Billy. We don't have any Unholys living here at the moment. Would either of you like a cup of hot chocolate?"

CHAPTER TWENTY

Sabastian straightened his tie and adjusted his suit while he slid from his expensive sports car. He had been invited to attend a dinner with Praeses Connelly, the Nation's leader.

Since he had manipulated Frederick Mills to make the GPS implant mandatary and made sure that the hefty fine and possible prison time for noncompliance was advertised, men had flocked to the DNA sequencing facilities with their wives and daughters to get them implanted. His manufacturing plant was working around the clock to fill the demand, but it was worth it now that almost ninety percent of the known females in the Nation had been tagged. Even General Lucas's three wives had been fitted with the implant.

General Lucas admitted that he often sat at his desk and spied on them, although they never actually did anything. They were too well trained.

Sabastian thought it juvenile to waste so much time watching women just sitting dormant, but then again if he had Harper tagged, he would probably do the same thing. In any case, the general's current wives weren't as pretty as Harper and didn't have her genetics.

Sabastian thought about Harper's DNA profiling — she was literally perfect, as if her DNA was Angelic in itself. In all the years he had been programming the DNA facility's mainframes, he had never seen that before. Most women had a break here or a miss there, but he had only ever heard about perfect sequencing once by an old lab tech.

He had said, "Since the Pandemic, there are normal

humans and of course the Unholys, who have mutated genes that turn them into monsters. Then there is the rarest gene group, the Angelics. They have the perfect genes. No one knows if they have any special biological advantages, except they never catch a cold and they have an advanced degree of adaptability. They are like the modern proverbial needle in a haystack."

Even though the other men at the DNA sequencing facility had looked at Harper's results with vested interests and lustful groins, it was only Sabastian who had seen her DNA results for what they were. He had known he'd found his shining needle in the haystack, and she was beautiful.

Sabastian entered the Praeses's grand mansion, following a servant to the dining room. He noted that the house was richly furnished, but his house was much more refined and spacious.

"Mr James," the aging Praeses greeted him, holding his hand out for Sabastian to take.

"Praeses Connelly," Sabastian greeted with a smile. "Please call me Sabastian."

"And you may call me Irving," the old man said in a distinguished voice similar to Sabastian's own. "Please have a seat."

Sabastian took the seat on the Praeses's right. He had expected at least a few people to be joining them, but the long table had only been set for two.

The old man flicked his napkin and laid it on his lap.

Sabastian noted that the old man's body still looked fit, even though his dark grey hair gave away his age.

"I hope you don't mind that it's just you and I for dinner. I can't stand half those jackass heads of departments. They are mindless puppets that can be manipulated with mere suggestions," Irving said in disgust before looking Sabastian over. "You, on the other hand, Sabastian James, are a puppet master."

Sabastian wasn't sure if he should act offended or proud that the Praeses had said such a thing. He thought he'd go with modest.

"I think you give me too much credit," Sabastian said casually.

"No, I've been watching you. You wanted the general to use your GPS tracking units, so you played on his fears of traitors and spies. Then you wanted Mills to implant all of the women in our Nation, so you played on his insecurities about a man being able to track his wife's movements. Now you have Mills bending over backward, eternally grateful that he did the job he was appointed to do in the first place, and as a reward for his inept handling of your wife's disappearance, Mills has finally sent a small army of agents up north to track down your wife. Which he should have done in the first place." Irving paused. "Did I leave anything out?"

"I don't think so," Sabastian said calmly.

"I think you are ruthless, cunning and clever. That's why I would never trust you to implant one of your devices in me." Irving shrugged, leaning back in his chair.

Sabastian recognised it wasn't an insult. It was a compliment. "Thank you, sir."

"General Lucas told me he got you to make him his own special implant that didn't have the poison in it, is that true?" Irving asked, while two servers came out and placed a plate of Beef Wellington in front of each of them.

"Yes, he did ask me to leave out the poison and yes, I did comply," Sabastian answered honestly. "I used an untraceable enzyme instead."

Praeses Irving Connelly burst out laughing and instantly Sabastian knew he was a man after his own heart.

When Irving's laughter died down, he looked at Sabastian. "I would have been tempted to use it by now. That man is insufferably dull and has a tendency to listen to himself talk far too often."

Sabastian smiled. He had the same opinion of General Lucas.

"I have to ask," Irving started. "If you were General of our Nation's Defence Network, what would be the first things you would change?"

Sabastian had many things he would do differently, but there were a few that stood out more than others. "First I would upgrade the antiquated computer networking system and link all the departments to it so I could monitor what the other departments were doing and build my defences around that. Next, I would do full psychological screening and testing on all highly classified military personnel to make sure they are both stable and incorruptible. The current vetting program is inadequate for determining such decisions. Then I would introduce a two-year minimum compulsory service for all men aged eighteen years to twenty-five, so we can boost our defences and build our dwindling army."

Praeses Connelly nodded. "Do you think the masses would accept compulsory service?"

"They will if they can't even look at marrying until they have served their time. Most men in our Nation work their entire lives to buy themselves a wife, while rich men's sons stroll out the front door and purchase the prettiest ones. If the general public sees the rich men as having to do the same as them and earn their wives, then we may have more control and be able to shape how our young men think," Sabastian said, slicing through his Beef Wellington with surgical precision.

Irving studied Sabastian with interest. "It sounds like you've given this some thought, but tell me, how do we pay for all these mandatory soldiers?"

"We train them and send them out on deployments around

the world. At any one time there are at least a half dozen conflicts happening overseas. I'm sure countries would pay handsomely to have these disputes resolved."

"An army to hire, and once they return, they can marry and produce more soldiers and wives, while we gain a trained military man in every house for our own defences," Irving summarised. "What about the Unholy?"

"I have seen them fight. They are vicious, cunning and fast. I think instead of euthanizing them, we should train them as specialty weapons."

"So, you want those disgusting creatures to be able to marry when they return home from service?" Irving frowned, looking revolted.

"Goodness no, they would be the ones we send into impossible situations and if somehow they do survive their service, then we kill them ourselves. Of course, we don't inform them of that," Sabastian told the old man.

Irving rolled his wine glass around in his hands. "I'm retiring General Lucas in two months. He doesn't know it yet, and I was going to make it a permanent retirement. To be honest, I've wanted to kill that man for the last twenty years." Irving chuckled. "How would you like the job?"

Sabastian placed his knife and fork on his plate and leaned back casually. "Why me? I'm sure you have commanders and generals who would happily be your lapdog."

"I don't need lapdogs, I need men who can run a country, not sit on their hands talking about the good old days and be so blindly inept they can't even see when a young upstart is manipulating them."

Sabastian was sure that Praeses Connelly had been cut from the same cloth as him. He didn't tolerate fools and was far from stupid, which in Sabastian's eyes made him both an enemy and an ally. He would have to watch his back with Praeses Irving Connelly.

Sabastian smiled. "I guess I start in two months, then."

"Oh, and find that darn wife, use whatever resources you need. You can't have that kind of loose end floating around."

"I will, sir." Sabastian's smile widened—he had just got permission to use the Nation's army to hunt down Harper.

I leaned against North, unable to separate myself from him for more than a few moments, and I was sure he felt the same way. He alternated between looking at me and looking at Wolf while we sat by the bonfire.

"I can't believe we made something so beautiful." North smiled as he stared into Wolf's dark eyes while the baby looked up at him, firelight dancing across their faces and reflecting in their eyes.

"I can. He was made of love," I told him softly. "And he looks like his gorgeous father." I added as I leaned over and kissed him.

North looked at me, his eyebrows furrowed. "Why did you call him Wolf?"

"Because a wolf is a strong noble creature, they are loyal to their pack and would fight to the death to save the ones they love, they also mate for life"—I reached over and gently brushed his cheek—"and I love both of my wolves."

North looked down at Wolf. "Is he a . . ." The words sounded shaky.

"I think so."

"How do you know? My Unholy traits didn't come out until I was five, and most other Unholys said theirs didn't show up until puberty."

I know he hated being different, but to me he was perfect, I just wished he could see what I saw in him.

"It's hard to describe, but I can feel people's energy, and I'm fairly certain Wolf has your wolf energy," I said. "But if it's all right, I'm going to call him a Werewolf because I don't think anything as beautiful as him or you can possibly be Unholy."

Tears flooded North's eyes. "Can you forgive me for giving you a son that isn't normal?"

I wrapped my arms around him. I wanted to take his pain away, I wanted him to understand that to me he was perfect and so was our son. Wolf had been made of our love and our bodies.

"There is nothing for me to forgive, I love you and I love Wolf. But can you forgive me for leaving you? And for not telling you I was carrying your child?" I asked.

"As long as you promise never to leave me again," North whispered before he kissed me.

"Oh please," Birdy's voice interrupted. I looked up and saw him standing in front of us. "Give me my nephew," he told North, taking Wolf from his arms before turning and pacing his way around the fire making cooing noises.

I had never thought of Birdy as being a baby person, but seeing Wolf in his arms, I thought he would make an excellent father.

North wrapped his arms around me, pulled me onto his lap and kissed me with all the ferocity of a starving man. The heated buzzing sensation zapped through me in waves of pure light and pleasure.

"I love you," I whispered as we broke from the kiss and I looked into the firelight dancing in his dark brown eyes.

"I love you."

Wolf let out a tiny squawk from the other side of the fire.

"Give him here," I heard Beth say.

"But . . ." was the only reply from Birdy before I saw Beth giggling with Wolf on her shoulder. Birdy had no chance against Beth.

I smiled, then I felt Travis looking over at me. I saw him,

his russet-red hair aglow in the firelight. He looked sorrowful.

I slipped off North's lap and walked over to him. Travis's sorrowful eyes were full of unshed tears. I gently wrapped my arms around him, hugging him as he hugged me back. He rested his head on my shoulder and cried.

Sabastian undid his tie and slung it over the back of his office chair. All in all, tonight had been an interesting evening, and the prospect of becoming the new General of the Nation's Defence Network had him almost giddy with pride. He had thought his ideas for upgrading the computer systems and making compulsory service mandatory for all men had been sound, but he had never expected to be given the job.

Sabastian glanced at his tablet lying on the desk. Over the last few weeks, he had received one-hundred and forty-three photographs on his tablet from Agent Twain and the other MGD field agents that had been sent out to start the mandatary implants of females in the north, but none of the women had even looked similar to Harper. Certainly, none were as pretty or had those emerald-green eyes which haunted his dreams.

Sabastian sighed. He needed to find his dear wife before he took up his role as general in two weeks' time.

Sabastian looked at the latest lot of photographs with disgust. He had known Harper wouldn't be in the north, but he had been hoping that the agents searching might have found something that would give him a clue to where she might have gone.

He flicked through the images. "Small eyes, funny teeth, oh yuck," he mumbled, setting the tablet down on his desk before he got up to go have a shower.

He had only taken one step when his tablet pinged and an image of a blonde woman appeared.

"Now they weren't even trying," he mumbled to himself, picking up the tablet to look at the image.

The blonde was pretty with big breasts and a tiny waist, but she certainly wasn't his type, his type was Harper.

He was about to set the tablet back on his desk when he saw something hanging in the background. His heart almost did a backflip. He zoomed in on the white dress.

He knew that dress. It was the one Harper had worn at their last lunch together, back at her parent's house. He had seen her standing by the window in it, looking like an angel. He looked at the woman again. She was definitely not Harper, but she must have seen her.

Sabastian grabbed his phone, punching in Agent Twain's number.

"Are you still with the blonde?" he barked at Twain.

"Yeah, we were just packing up to leave."

"Where are you?" Sabastian barked as he headed out of his office.

"We're on a farm about fifty kilometres from the border."

"Send me the coordinates, and who else is there besides the girl?"

"Her husband and a farmhand," Twain said.

"Are either of the men in their twenties with either brown or blond hair?" Sabastian asked.

"The farmhand has blond hair but looks in his early thirties and the husband looks to be about fifty," Agent Twain told him.

Neither sounded like Bernard Crain or the Crain's farm boy, but still . . . that dress, it was etched into his brain. He had dreamed about her in that dress a hundred times, and he couldn't get it out of his mind.

"Hold them. I'll be there in a few hours," Sabastian ordered and disconnected.

He would go to the farm and make those people tell him

where she was.

"Kleve!" he shouted.

Kleve appeared in the kitchen door with a sandwich in one hand. "Sir?"

"We're going hunting up north, you have ten minutes to pack."

Kleve smiled. "I'm already packed."

North watched as Harper slipped silently from his lap before approaching the russet-haired Travis, wrapping her arms around him and hugging him. He hugged her back, resting his head on her shoulder.

Something burned inside North as he watched Harper hug the other man. It wasn't jealousy in the strictest sense—he knew by the way their bodies connected and by tiny Wolf laying in Beth's arms that Harper was completely and utterly his. What he felt was more envy toward Travis. Travis had seen Harper, spoken to her and been by her side when Wolf was born. He had spent the last six months by her side and watched their baby come into the world. That was what North envied. He envied him for being with Harper when he wasn't.

Travis suddenly pulled away from Harper, turned and walked away.

North half stood.

"Don't mind Travis, I think he fell in love with Crash the moment she broke his nose. But I did tell him from the start that her heart belonged somewhere else," Beth said, gently pushing North's shoulder down so he would sit before she handed Wolf over. "There are so few of her kind in the world. They might call your kind Unholy, her kind Angelic and the rest of us Normal, but in the end, we are all just humans."

North looked at Beth. "Angelic?"

"You know, the opposite to you." Beth shrugged. "I wasn't

surprised when Billy said you were an Unholy, but you must be an extremely strong one to capture her eye."

"I don't know what you're talking about," North told her in confusion.

Beth smiled. "I have an old geneticist's book that explains it. You and she are like positive and negative electron magnets, you attract each other, draw each other in, but unlike magnets, once you've bonded that connection can't be broken." Beth looked down at baby Wolf. "I'd say you two are definitely mated for life. No matter where you go in the world, you will be drawn to her as she is to you. To be honest, I was a little surprised you didn't come sooner or she didn't leave to find you, but I guess there was the baby to worry about."

"So, if you are saying I'm a mutant and you're a normal, then what's her genetic code?" North asked.

"It's perfect, without a single flaw. But despite what you have been told, you're not a mutant. You are an evolutionary step forward, brought on by the Pandemic virus. None of your genes have abnormalities. You have the exact same ones as me, but you have the bonus of having some extra ones too, which makes you stronger, faster and more attuned." Beth smiled.

North wasn't sure how to take that. He had always assumed his DNA was damaged, not that it just had extra on top of the normal. "So what about Harper's DNA?"

"By what I read, an Angelic is quicker at learning new skills, more adaptable, and has no genetic faults. They will never get sick and their DNA is stacked closer, unlocking extra abilities. The book said they can sense energy or feel it coming off other living creatures." Beth looked down at Wolf. "And their offspring will retain those traits."

North looked at Harper, who had her back to him and was now talking to Birdy on the opposite side of the bonfire.

Harper turned and smiled at him before continuing the conversation with Birdy.

"I bet she always knows when you're around or looking at her." Beth smiled.

"How do you know she's an Angelic and not just a Normal?" North asked, but somewhere in his head it felt like the pieces clicked together.

"I'm not a geneticist, but my grandfather was. He taught me many things about DNA sequencing, and he left me the book I was telling you about. He always said that the reason the first government after the Pandemic started hunting down the Unholys and gave them that name was because they were scared of them. They knew that if an Unholy and an Angelic had children, then the children would possess both sets of genes making, them almost the perfect human. They'd be faster, stronger, more adaptable, with the added ability to shapeshift and sense danger. And the government didn't want to compete with that."

North looked at Wolf lying in his arms. He thought his son was perfect, but he'd thought his genetics were flawed.

"So why are the Angelics rare?" North questioned.

"The simple answer is they always were," Beth said. "By what my grandfather told me, when the early geneticists discovered the Angelic DNA, they removed any they found from the general population so they could try to breed more. The problem was Angelics aren't like normal humans. It takes someone with their own exceptionally strong DNA to successfully breed with an Angelic, otherwise the Angelic's body rejects the fertilized egg, and then there are the chemicals that their bodies have to naturally produce. They must have overwhelmingly high levels of oxytocin, which is the chemical the body releases when humans are in love. The government tried for years to replicate the conditions for breeding more Angelics, but sadly many died in forced pregnancies or were poisoned by the heavy drugs the doctors used to stop the foetuses being rejected. Then when the program failed, many were executed to cover up what the government had done. Harper's Angelic DNA is likely a throwback, because I can tell her brother isn't one," Beth said.

Wolf wriggled in North's arms. "So would Harper have fallen in love with just any Unholy if I wasn't there?"

"Are you an imbecile? She has free will. She didn't fall in love with you because of your DNA, she fell in love with *you,* and that's what made the bond possible to produce Wolf. The strong genetic stuff is only for the breeding. The magnetic pull is something that only happens when there is attraction and love, otherwise it's just like any other person you meet.

"An Angelic can fall in love with anyone, just like you could have. The difference is that the genetics might not be strong enough to produce children, making her appear barren, but it wouldn't mean she wouldn't love him."

North looked down at Wolf. "So he is a miracle?"

"No, he is a product of love, which shows you that you two are meant for each other. Crash had to be deeply, madly in love with an exceptionally strong man to have had that gorgeous little bundle in your arms." Beth smiled. "And never doubt yourself, because Crash doesn't doubt you, and neither do I."

Sabastian surveyed the lake and the little house from his seat in the copter while Kleve circled the farm looking for a place to land in the early morning light. The house was situated well away from the road in a valley. He noted that although the house looked old, it appeared well maintained with a veranda on the rear overlooking the lake. A large four-bay shed sat at the front of the house, screening much of the front from the driveway.

It was remote, discreet and the perfect place for Harper to have hidden.

Sabastian had taken one of the quieter, faster copters with the extra seats in the back in case they found Harper hiding here. But even with the faster copter, it had taken just over four hours to fly from the Capital, and Sabastian was growing impatient as Kleve found a place to set down.

Sabastian was out of the copter and walking toward the house before Kleve had even set the skids firmly on the ground.

"Mr James, it's good to see you, sir," Agent Twain greeted, meeting him halfway across the lawn.

"Where are they?" Sabastian growled, ignoring the pleasantries.

"In the house."

"Names?" Sabastian asked, reaching the back steps.

"Mr and Mrs Duran, and the farmhand's name is Blane West. I checked with the MGD files. Mr and Mrs Duran were married about five years ago, and the farmhand has been here about two years," Agent Twain rattled off.

"Any sign of anyone else living here?"

"There are some men's clothes in two of the spare rooms, but Mr Duran said they were his old ones."

"What about women's clothes? Were there any in the spare rooms?" Sabastian asked, halting at the screen door.

"Nope, all the women's clothes were in the main bedroom either hanging up or packed away in boxes," Agent Twain said. "Oh, sorry, there was one dress hanging in one of the spare rooms where we found some of the men's clothes."

"I want to see that room," Sabastian ordered.

"Don't you want to talk to Mr Duran first?"

Sabastian just looked at the agent, wondering if they bred stupid into the MGD agents deliberately. Agent Twain lowered his head. Something in Sabastian's gaze must have made him reconsider questioning him, because Twain opened the door and led Sabastian down the hall, stopping in front of one of the open bedroom doors.

Sabastian surveyed the room. The white dress hung from a curtain rod.

He slowly walked over, admiring the lace and the way it curved in at the waist. It was Harper's dress. He remembered it so vividly on her. He ran his fingers over it for a moment before he leaned forward and sniffed it. The scent was faint, but it was definitely his wife's. He savoured her aroma for a few seconds before turning to the closet to look inside. Men's clothes hung neatly inside it, and a pair of size eleven men's work boots sat in the bottom.

Sabastian's mouth tightened. Why would Harper's dress be hanging in this bedroom which so obviously belonged to a man?

Someone had deliberately left the dress hanging in plain sight to admire it as he would. Sabastian hated the obvious reason. Harper had taken a lover. He ground his teeth. He wanted to know who the man was so he could slit his throat.

How dare someone else touch his property, his wife!

Sabastian yanked the dress down, gripping it tightly in his fist while he turned to Agent Twain.

"Where is Mr Duran?" Sabastian snarled.

"They're all in the kitchen," Twain said, motioning down the hallway.

Sabastian was going to enjoy this part. He even hoped they'd put up a fight. He wanted to make every last one of them suffer. How dare they let his wife have an affair under their roof?

An older man with salt and pepper hair and broad shoulders sat at the table next to a blonde woman with olive skin and an hourglass figure. He recognised the woman from the photo. Another younger man in his early thirties with a mass of curly blond hair and a round, almost pretty, face leaned against the counter with two MGD Agents standing guard.

"Mr and Mrs Duran, I presume," Sabastian said, putting on his amiable face while he set the dress on the table between them. "I'm terribly sorry for the intrusion, but the good agents are trying to find something that belongs to me, and I want it back."

Neither Mr or Mrs Duran spoke as they sat stiff-backed and stoic.

"Who does this garment belong to?" Sabastian asked, nodding at the dress.

"It's mine. I found a bag of clothes on the side of the road a while back. So I kept them," Mrs Duran said unapologetically, as if she was his equal.

He wanted to slap her for being so arrogant as to think herself anything other than her husband's property. Sabastian glanced over at the blond man's shoes. He guessed they were about a size nine before he deliberately lifted the tablecloth, taking in the older man's feet, which were also about a nine. The woman's feet were tiny. None of these three owned the size eleven work boots in the spare room. He dropped the tablecloth and leaned back in the chair as he thought about the other possibilities. Bernard Crain? Or the farm boy?

He thought back to when he'd seen the farm boy at the Crain property. He had been tall with broad shoulders, blond hair, and Harper had been looking at him.

"Do you even know who I am?" Sabastian asked casually, but no one spoke. "I am Harper's husband, and I know she was here, and now I need to know where she has gone."

"I'm sorry, but we don't know any Harper. My wife is the only woman who has set foot on this farm," Mr Duran said.

Sabastian glanced at the younger farmhand, then at Mr Duran.

Mr Duran looked like he had spent a lifetime in the sun,

but he had a feeling the younger man didn't do much outside work. His skin was tanned, but not the kind of tan he'd get if he spent hours fixing fences or chasing cows. No. His tan was an even bronze.

Sabastian stood and walked over to the knife block on the kitchen counter. "Tell me where she is," Sabastian said, pulling each knife out and testing their sharpness.

"I told you, we don't know any Harper," Mr Duran said.

Sabastian chose a knife and set it on the counter while he stole a glance at the younger man's hands. *No calluses. Interesting.*

The young man had either lied or was one of their lovers.

Sabastian looked the younger man over. Neat button-down blue shirt, clean well-fitting jeans and work boots that looked as if they hadn't touched dirt. He was betting the younger man was Mr Duran's lover. After all, he looked too pretty and effeminate to be the buxom blonde's.

"What's your name?" Sabastian asked. He already knew the answer, Agent Twain had told him.

"Blane West," the man said, sounding effeminate.

"And what do you do here, Blane West?" Sabastian questioned.

"I do whatever I'm told," Blane said, and Sabastian could tell he was trying to sound more masculine but failing miserably.

Blane was an idiot and likely knew the least out of all three of them.

Sabastian stepped around the blond man, went into the walk-in pantry and scanned the neatly arranged shelves. He took a large bottle of vinegar and a bag of salt out, sitting them on the counter next to the knife.

"Who was sleeping with my wife?" Sabastian asked, moving to the sink and opening the cupboard underneath.

"No one," Mr Duran said. "I told you, we don't know your wife."

"That is a pity," Sabastian said as he took out a bottle of bleach and set it beside the salt before casually closing the cabinet door.

"Mr Kleve," Sabastian called, knowing his right-hand man would likely be somewhere close by.

Kleve walked in, and all eyes seemed to be focused on the four-foot-tall man. Sabastian always enjoyed how people underestimated Mr Kleve due to his stature, but he was a ruthless, sadistic little bastard who knew how to get the job done.

Kleve looked at the assortment on the bench and smiled widely.

Chapter Twenty-one

I stared across at my beautiful family sleeping in bed beside me. Wolf was lying between North and me as the morning light filtered through the curtains.

If there was a heaven, this would be mine.

Wolf took a little shuddering breath. North's eyes snapped open as if jolted awake before he looked at Wolf, then at me.

"I half expected to be dreaming and when I opened my eyes you would both be gone," he whispered. He reached over Wolf and gently touched my face with his warm hand as if I might evaporate into thin air.

A light knock sounded on the door before the door opened and Billy looked in.

"Can I cuddle him?" he quietly asked.

I was about to tell him Wolf was sleeping when I looked down to see two beautiful dark eyes looking up at me.

"Sure, but he'll need a feed soon," I told Billy.

North scooped his son up and stood, then hesitantly placed him in Billy's arms.

North had barely let either of us out of his sight since he arrived two days ago, but at least he was starting to let me go to the bathroom without standing outside the door with Wolf to make sure I came out.

"When you get bigger, I'm going to show you how to shoot, and then we can hunt rabbits together," Billy told Wolf as he headed for the door.

"When you can shoot as well as his mother, you can teach him to shoot," Joe said as he passed by my open bedroom door.

"No one can shoot that good," Travis said as he followed Joe. "She is beyond amazing."

North glanced over at me, a smile touching the corners of his mouth while he waited for Billy to take Wolf out of the room, before closing the door and slipping back into bed beside me. He wrapped me in his warm arms as he pulled me against him.

"I can't wait to take you home and show Wolf off to Lloyd, Blane and Charli," North beamed.

I suddenly realised that I wanted to stay here. I wanted to raise our baby in this amazing community with other children. Beth and Joe would be supportive grandparents, and Billy and Travis would be wonderful uncles.

"I bet Lloyd and Blane will spoil him rotten. Lloyd told me once he almost turned straight because he desperately wanted a son. Guess I was the substitute one for a while," North said.

"What if we stay here instead?" I asked "Joe and Travis have been fixing up the old cabin next door. I could ask if we could have it."

North moved back a little so he could look at me. "Do you want to stay here?"

I didn't want to argue with him. I rolled away and sat up, slipping on the fluffy pink robe Beth had given me.

I moved to stand, but North grabbed my hand and tugged me back. "Talk to me Harper, I'm not a mind reader."

I turned to look at him as I bit my lip. "I want to stay. They have a school here, and kids for Wolf to play with, and we're safe."

Even as the word *safe* left my mouth I felt a terrible sense of foreboding wash over me, as if something dangerous was coming.

"If you want to stay, then I will stay," North told me. "I don't care where I am as long as I'm with you and Wolf."

I leaned over and kissed him. "I love you."

If it were up to me, I would stay locked away in my bedroom with North and Wolf forever, but Wolf was out in the kitchen with Billy and Beth, and I could hear both North's and my stomach growling for breakfast.

Everyone was in the kitchen, the coffee was brewing, pancakes were frying in the pan and in the middle of it was Wolf, quietly watching everything from Travis's arms while Birdy played with his tiny toes.

"My turn," Joe told Travis, taking Wolf from his son and he began cooing.

Birdy looked disappointed that it wasn't his turn to hold Wolf.

Beth chuckled while she flipped a pancake. "Nothing like a baby to make grown men gooey."

I smiled and went to work setting the table for breakfast.

This was the life I wanted.

Sabastian leaned against the kitchen counter in the old farmhouse. The blonde woman and the old man were handcuffed to the dining chairs at the table while the younger man had been given his own chair in the centre of the kitchen floor.

His face was bloody with dozens of neat shallow cuts and a few deeper ones. It wasn't enough to kill him, but the pain would have been excruciating.

"You're looking a bit messy there, Mr West," Kleve said, taking the lid off the vinegar bottle. "Let me help clean you up." He smiled, tipping it over the younger man's face.

The younger man cried out in agony, frantically shaking his head, trying to get away from the liquid.

Sabastian smiled. He thought Mr Kleve an artist with the neatness and symmetry of his handiwork on the younger man's face. Even if Blane West survived this torture, his pretty face would be scarred for life.

"Please stop it, we don't know anything." The blonde woman sobbed.

Sabastian turned his attention to the woman. "Oh, but I think you do, and I think you know who was screwing my wife." His voice came out a gravelly growl. They had been doing this for almost twenty hours, and no one had told him anything.

"Fuck you," the woman said defiantly.

Sabastian backhanded her, sending her and the chair toppling onto the kitchen floor before crouching over her.

"Tell me where Harper is and we will leave, you have my word," Sabastian said quietly.

He meant it, too. He didn't give a shit about these pathetic people or this dead-end hole of a farm, he just wanted Harper and he was prepared to keep torturing them one-by-one until he got his answers.

The woman shook with fear, but she didn't say a word.

Sabastian was impressed that a pansy man and a woman could endure the torture, but the one man he hadn't touched was the one he wanted to break. He knew that for some people, watching others suffer was more effective a torture than anything physical he could inflict, but he was starting to think the older, distinguished man wasn't the one he should be relying on for answers. He honestly didn't think a woman or a pansy man would be smart enough to be his fountain of information, but then again, he had underestimated Harper.

Sabastian stood and slowly walked over to the kitchen drawers, pulling out a meat tenderising mallet. Now which one would he use it on? The younger blond man seemed the obvious choice. He wasn't handcuffed, which would make it easier to tenderise one finger at a time.

Kleve seemed to read Sabastian's mind and grabbed the man's mop of blond hair, forcing him forward onto the ground. Blane landed on his hands and knees. Kleve quickly stepped onto his hand and pinned him. Blane yelped in pain, but Kleve only pressed down harder, a wicked smile playing on his lips.

"First I'm going to break every bone in your hands, then I'm going to slit your throat if someone in this god forsaken house doesn't tell me where my fucking wife is," Sabastian snarled, sounding demonic.

"Suck my dick," Blane jeered defiantly.

Kleve suddenly yanked his head back by his hair and brought his fist down punching him in his blood covered face.

Blane groaned pathetically, but still didn't say a word.

Sabastian crouched down in front of Blane, who was dripping blood, tears and drool onto the kitchen floor. "All you have to do to make this all go away is tell me where one little girl is and we will leave you all alone," he said, his voice softening.

Blane and the blonde woman sobbed openly while the older man slumped in his chair, like he'd been the one who had been punched. He was the man of the house. His role was the protector, but instead he was tied to a chair, powerless, having to watch his female and the farmhand being brutalised. This was what Sabastian had been waiting for, it wouldn't take much more to break the man.

"This little piggy went to market," Sabastian said, suddenly bring down the meat hammer, crushing Blane's little finger.

Blane screamed, trying to pull away, but Kleve had him pinned.

"This little piggy stayed home." Crack! Sabastian smashed Blane's ring finger.

The pain-filled scream didn't have a sound for a moment as the air caught in Blane's throat before erupting with choking tears.

"This little piggy had roast—"

"No!" Lloyd yelled, struggling to free himself. "She's in the mountains, two-or-three days south-west. I don't know the exact location," he blurted out as Blane looked over at him with sorrow in his eyes.

Sabastian saw it. The younger man would have taken ten beatings and would never have told them anything, but Mr Duran couldn't sit by and watch it any longer.

"Where?" Sabastian straightened while Agent Twain pulled a map out and laid it on the table.

Lloyd looked to Blane, then at the map, a look of resignation on his face as he nodded at an area of mountains. "She's there somewhere. I don't have the exact location. Please, let him go."

Sabastian was confident the older man was telling the truth. Harper had been seen on the road going in that direction, and it made sense she would hide somewhere remote. Perhaps he could use the Defence Network's satellite system and intelligence to locate her exact location.

Sabastian straightened his clothes. "Now that wasn't too hard was it?" he said mockingly. He picked the white dress up off the table before he walked toward the back door.

Kleve released the blond man's hair and removed his foot from his hand, then followed.

"What do we do with these three?" Agent Twain asked.

"I gave them my word that we would leave and they'd be free once they gave me the information I needed, so that's what we will do," Sabastian said, a grin twisting his lips. "But once they are outside, I want this place burnt to the ground."

He knew that they would lead him to her and all he would have to do was use the tracker in the unsuspecting blonde woman and he would have Harper.

North woke with a start as he looked across the empty expanse of bed beside him. Harper and Wolf were gone. He rolled out of bed and hit the ground running, bolting from the bedroom, down the hall to the kitchen, but it was empty and so were the living room and dining room.

Panic gripped his chest as he yanked open the front door and stopped.

Harper and Billy were sitting on the steps sipping coffee while Wolf lay on a rug between them, wriggling like a little worm.

"Morning." Harper smiled up at him.

North crossed the veranda without a sound and kissed her. He had to know she was real and not a dream. The electricity that sparked between them heated him to the core as she wrapped her arms around his neck. He broke from the kiss and looked at her, emotions overwhelming him.

"Wow, with you coming out here shirtless and kissing me like that, I might have to ask Billy to babysit for an hour," Harper told North.

He looked down at himself and realised he had run out of the room wearing only his sweatpants.

"Do you think I'll ever have a chest and stomach like North's?" Billy asked, unfazed by Harper and North's passionate kiss. "Or are you two like a superhero couple? North would be the Wolfman, and, Crash, you can be the girl that can shoot the dots off a ladybeetle's back at fifty metres."

Harper looked at North, then at Billy. "I don't think you need any more coffee."

North bent and kissed Wolf's head, then sniffed him, before he stood.

"Why do you always smell him?" Billy asked.

"So I can always remember his scent," North told him.

"Is that like a Wolfman thing?" Billy questioned, looking curious.

North shrugged. "I don't know, it's just what I do, but I don't know if it's an Unholy thing or a me thing."

Harper smiled at North and said to Billy, "I think it's cute, and he does it to me too."

"I'm going to go get dressed," North told them, a little embarrassed, but walked back inside with a smile.

Birdy was in the kitchen with Travis when North emerged from Harper's room in jeans and a plain grey shirt. He had only packed enough clothes for a few days, but they had already been in Haven for a week. He would have to do some washing soon, or his clothes might stand up and walk out in protest.

Travis looked over at North. "I heard you jump out of bed and thunder through the house this morning, I'm guessing Crash wasn't in bed when you woke up."

North felt silly, but he was so afraid of losing her, that even standing here while she sat outside felt like too much space was between them. He had to get a grip. He didn't want her to feel like he was smothering her.

"I used to wake up just to make sure she was still here," Travis said, pouring coffee into a mug and handing it to North. "So I understand, and she wasn't even my soulmate."

Birdy chuckled. "Even when we were kids, I used to do that. half the time I'd catch our mother and father on the landing outside her door with their ear pressed to it, listening to her breathe. There is something about Harper that makes people want to protect her, even though I'm positive she can do it herself and probably better than any of us."

"I know what you mean. t's like Harper is a fragile angel, but she's really tougher than she looks. I mean she sat there in labour as quiet as a mouse and only knocked on my door when it was pretty much time to push. Even then she only grunted and groaned until she called out your name, but that wasn't until Wolf was born," Travis said to North.

North had a feeling he knew the exact moment Wolf was born. He remembered the pains and the sound of his name being called out.

"Before I was a hundred percent sure Harper was pregnant, I had her doing the compulsory self-defence stuff and running the obstacle course. She picked it up quicker than anyone else I've ever seen. If she wasn't a girl, I'd say she was an elite soldier. And she did all that while pregnant and didn't miss a beat," Travis said.

North imagined his beautiful fine-boned Harper scaling walls and beating people up. It made him smile.

"It's like Harper is . . ." Travis started.

"Angelic," North finished.

Birdy and Travis both nodded.

Harper chose that moment to walk inside with Wolf, the bright morning light framing them both in the doorway and for a moment she seemed to glow.

North had to fight himself to stay planted where he was. He wanted to wrap his arms around her and kiss her. He always wanted to kiss and hold her.

Wolf made a happy, cooing noise as Harper brought him over to North.

"Would you mind taking him? I need to get dressed and brush my hair," Harper asked, slipping Wolf into his arms before kissing him quickly on the cheek and heading for the bedroom.

"If Crash was my girl, I'd want to have surgery to stitch us together so she couldn't leave my side ever," Billy said as he headed for the kitchen. With a cheeky grin, he called back over his shoulder. "Of course, Crash is too old for me, I like Jasmine."

"I thought you liked Felicity with the red hair?" Travis said, looking over at Billy.

"I do, but Jasmine with the glasses was wearing a pair of

jeans yesterday, and she has a real nice ass," Billy said with a wide smile.

"When you make up your mind, let me know," Travis said, rolling his eyes.

North jiggled Wolf and paced across the kitchen, resisting the temptation to pace too far or he might find himself down the hallway at her bedroom door.

"So, when are we heading back to the farm?" Birdy asked.

"Crash and Wolf can't go, they have to stay here," Billy interjected.

"Billy, that isn't up to us. If Crash wants to leave, she is free to," Travis said, sounding mournful.

Billy looked at Travis. "But Crash can't go. Who's going to teach me how to shoot? And what would you do if you couldn't see her every day? We all know you're in love with her even though she's insane about North."

Travis's cheeks turned pink.

North knew Travis was in love with Harper. Beth had said as much the first night he and Birdy had arrived, but he didn't hold it against him. Any man with half a brain would be in love with her. Harper was kind, smart and beautiful, but best of all she loved him.

"Have you talked about it? Does she want to leave?" Travis asked sheepishly.

"She wants to stay," North said as Wolf let out a long yawn.

"And you?" Travis asked.

"I'd live on the moon or at the bottom of the ocean if that's where Harper and Wolf were," North told him. "They are the centre of my universe and I don't care where I am as long as we're together."

"Well, the centre of your universe looks like he needs to be put down for a sleep," Billy said looking at Wolf.

"What about you Birdy, are you staying too?" Travis asked.

Birdy's cheeks blushed slightly. "I don't know. There's a woman back on the farm who I think I'm in love with, so I was going to head back in a few days."

North smiled at him. "Charli's a lucky girl."

"Well, North, if you're staying, I want to see what your skills are on the obstacle course and shooting range. I need to know if you're going to be useful in a fight or be a hindrance," Travis said, sounding almost professional.

Birdy let out a bark of laughter. "He is a one-man demolition crew."

CHAPTER TWENTY-TWO

Sabastian watched the old farmhouse burn from his seat in the copter circling above. Its three occupants stood huddled together on the lawn by the lake while the MGD agents drove away up the long driveway.

Sabastian had told the agents to leave the garage alone. He wanted them to have a vehicle so they could leave. So he could track them. It would take at least a few days for the trio to drive to the mountains that Mr Duran had pointed out on the map. It would give him enough time to get back to the Capital and start work on the new computer system that would give him access to every department and government file.

"Take us back to the Capital, Kleve, and I want you to monitor Mrs Duran's tracker. Tell me when they start moving," Sabastian said, resting his head back on the seat and closing his eyes. He brought the white dress to his face to sniff it.

He would have her soon, and she would be his. He would have his Harper, and then he would never let her out of his sight again.

The copter sped toward the Capital, the sound of the wind louder than the hum of the engine and blades. Sabastian loved his toy. It was stealthy compared to the old copters, but it could still use improvement. He would have to make some modifications when he was general and perhaps put in a remote guidance system. Sabastian was more than capable of flying a copter, he just preferred Kleve to do it. Kleve had been his most loyal employee, and Sabastian respected him. The fact that he was only four feet tall and people always seemed to underestimate his ruthlessness entertained Sabastian.

When they landed at Sabastian's sprawling mansion, he went straight to work on the new system. He had been considering the changes for months, and now that Praeses Irving Connelly had given him the highest-level clearance, he intended to use it. Once he finished the new system, he would have access to every secret document and intelligence report that the government had ever possessed.

A small icon blinked on his computer screen, a message from one of his own computer technicians at his main office. Sabastian tapped the icon, the screen flashed as it dialled into the technician's computer, and a man's face appeared. It was Harvey, who was one of the more proficient and discreet workers. They had spent time together in the army, and Sabastian had assigned him the task of monitoring General Lucas's audio transmissions from his GPS tracking unit, because he knew he could trust him.

"Good afternoon, sir," Harvey said as he tapped something on his computer.

"What do you have for me?" Sabastian asked.

"I don't want to bore you with the three-hour monolog the general had with one of his wives last night, but the overall gist is, he thinks you're getting too big for your britches and now you've done your job he wants to retire you," Harvey said flatly. "I can send you the audio, but I should warn you it's coma inducing."

"No, I've listened to his voice enough over the last six months, I can live without hearing it again," Sabastian said. "Where is he now?"

Harvey tapped something and an image appeared on Sabastian's screen. "It looks like he's driving somewhere."

Sabastian looked at the image and realised he was heading toward Praeses Connelly's mansion. Sabastian smiled.

"Thank you, Harvey, there will be a substantial bonus in your pay this week," Sabastian said and disconnected before grabbing his phone and tapping in the Praeses's number.

"Sabastian, what can I do for you?" Irving answered.

"I believe General Lucas is on his way to visit you to ask permission to assassinate me. I was hoping I might get in first and kill him en route."

Irving chuckled. "I was wondering why he sounded desperate to get an audience with me, now that I know he knows he's on his way out," Irving said. "Sure, you have my permission, but can you do it away from the house? I don't want the media swarming at the gates."

Sabastian tapped in General Lucas's code and pressed the skull and cross bones icon which was the kill button. The confirm box blinked up asking *yes* or *no*.

"Would eight kilometres be far enough away?" Sabastian asked, looking at the blinking dot on the screen.

"That would be fine."

Sabastian pressed the *Yes* and the heart rate monitor on General Lucas's GPS tracker sped up until it was almost a blur.

"I'm glad you called, I thought I might have to slit his throat if he insisted on talking too much," Irving said.

The red light which represented General Lucas on the screen suddenly veered left and jerked to a stop.

"I think he might have just had a car accident," Sabastian said calmly as the red light blinked two more times then faded out.

"Well, that is amusing. Is he dead?" Irving asked.

"Yes, sir." Sabastian smiled.

"Excellent, I will announce your appointment as the Head of Defence after the funeral, which will be next Tuesday," Irving said. "So that gives you six days before you're tied to the government."

Sabastian thanked Irving and disconnected.

Six days to find Harper—after that he'd be too busy to hunt her, and he didn't want to give anyone else that pleasure.

I watched while North vaulted effortlessly over the hurdles, shimmied up the rope wall and swung across the mud-filled puddle to land perfectly on his toes.

Beth had taken Wolf for the afternoon, leaving North and me to practice on the obstacle course and shooting range while Travis, Billy and Joe watched, timing and scrutinising every move we made.

Travis, Joe and Billy looked at the stopwatch with their mouths open.

"Your time beats the record by almost fifteen seconds," Travis said, looking shocked.

"I could probably do it quicker in half-form," North said casually as he came to stand next to me.

"Can you do it now?" Billy asked, excitement echoing in his voice.

Joe slapped Billy up the back of his head. "I explained this to you, the half-form is the fighting form and can only be maintained with high amounts of adrenaline in the system, which means he only shifts into that form when he needs to, not to show off on an obstacle course."

I looked at North. "Is that true?"

North shrugged. "I guess so. I can shift into animal anytime, but I have to feel like I'm losing control to shift into half-form."

"That's because animal is your other base form, whereas half-form is exactly that, half of both your base forms. Holding a form which wants to be either one or the other takes a lot more energy," Joe explained.

"Makes sense." North shrugged.

"Okay Crash, you're up next," Travis said.

I was a quick learner, but the way North had gone through the course with such proficiency made me reassess my approach. He was taller and quicker than I could ever be, but I had the advantage of being smaller and lighter, which meant there was less of me to have to throw around.

I moved to the start line.

"Don't worry if you're a little rusty, I had to stop your training when it became obvious you were pregnant," Travis said.

I had stopped doing the obstacle course when I was about four and a half months pregnant—had they all known for that long? I put it out of my mind. It didn't matter now.

"Okay, you ready? Go!" Travis yelled.

I sprinted, slid under the first bar then leapt up over the second before planting my hand on the third and vaulting over it. I sprang to my feet and grabbed the ladder which was suspended horizontally over a pit of mud. I had been grabbing each rung in the past, but after seeing North do it I snatched every second one, propelling myself forward before dropping down in a crouch on the other side to crawl through the concrete pipe. Next were the hurdles. I ran, planted both hands, pulled myself up onto the first round log before jumping atop the next, then the next. Every other time I had done this part, I had jumped over each one individually. When I reached the last one, I launched myself, gripping the rope on the climbing wall about halfway up before heaving myself over the top and grabbing the rope swing.

I landed as North had, on his toes.

Joe, Travis and Billy looked at me as if I were an alien.

"You did that only a second slower than North," Travis said, sounding shocked.

I had expected to do all right but doing it only a second slower than North thrilled me.

North smiled. "That's my girl, you'll beat me next time," he said and kissed me on top of the head. He was always so proud of me.

We moved to the shooting range next. Several people from the community had dragged down chairs and looked as though they were waiting to watch a show.

"It looks like we have spectators," Joe said. "Beth must have told them you were shooting today."

I looked to North, who was smiling at me. "So how's your aim?" I asked.

"Not as good as yours, but I can hold my own." North shrugged.

"Okay you both have fifteen bullets, try to get as close to the black dot in the centre as you can," Travis explained as I picked up the rifle and sighted the black inner dot.

I smiled as I heard the first *POP* of North's gun.

I aimed and hit the white paper that bordered the black dot, about a millimetre from the black on the left side, then did the same on the right side of the black dot. I continued around the edge of the dot, spacing the shots evenly, leaving only a millimetre gap from the black until I had spent fourteen rounds of my fifteen. I aimed the last dead centre, *POP.*

I looked over at North's target. The very centre of the black dot was riddled with a cluster of bullet holes.

North lowered his gun and looked over at me, then at my target and quirked an eyebrow.

"What? Travis said get close to the black dot." I smiled and North burst out laughing.

"Smart ass," Travis said, shaking his head while Billy went to retrieve the targets.

Not a single bullet hole on North's target was outside the black line, while on mine all but the last shot had been outside the line.

Travis examined both of the targets for a moment. "If you

two were in the army, I'm betting you'd be Black Ops or snipers," he said, shaking his head.

"Are we done?" I asked. "I need to go have a shower and find Beth."

"Sure. You two can go clean up. I think the rest of us need some target practice," Joe said dismissively, taking the rifles from us and handing them to Billy and Travis.

The small gathering of spectators clapped as North and I walked past them on our way back to the house.

It was the first time North and I had actually been alone in the house without someone being in the next room or in the kitchen.

I grabbed his hand and pulled him into the bathroom with me, before closing the door and beginning to strip.

I was a little concerned that my body wouldn't be as attractive to him as it was before I had Wolf, but North seemed to love it even more as he hurriedly stripped off his own clothes and stepped under the hot water with me.

North watched as Harper stripped off her dirty clothes and tossed them into the laundry basket before stepping into the shower.

Her perfect body had changed since having Wolf—she'd lost her lean, sharp edges, leaving her looking softer, fuller and more alluring. Her body had gone from mere perfection to goddess, and North was finding it hard to concentrate with all the blood in his body rushing south.

Harper looked back at him and smiled while he watched the water cascading down her sensual curves.

North knew he was done for as he hurriedly stripped off his clothes, almost falling over as his foot caught in his pants. He kicked them free and slid into the hot water with Harper, his hands slipping around her waist.

He had missed the feel of her naked skin against his and the electrifying buzz that they produced together.

She kissed his shoulder, then moved her mouth up his neck and along his jaw until Harper found his lips. Heat ignited in him and he pulled her closer.

Her hands tangled in his hair as their kiss became deeper, more sensuous.

He loved her with every fibre of his being, and she loved him.

North slid his hands down her back, cupping her ass and lifting her up. Harper wrapped her legs around him, pressing herself against him. The hot water ran over them, adding to the heat he felt building inside as he slid into her. Harper moaned with pleasure, biting his shoulder as she began to rock against him.

North couldn't hold back as he thrust into her, hot and deep, their bodies perfectly in tune as they built to a hard-smooth rhythm.

Her breaths quickened as she moaned with pleasure. North loved that sound, it made him wild.

The pleasure was becoming too much, then just as he thought he couldn't last another moment, she clenched around him, tipping her head back, her body pulsing around him as her breath caught in her throat. It was the most erotic thing he had ever seen. He thrust deep inside her, releasing in a rush of ecstasy and electricity.

She was his nirvana.

Satiated, they stood under the shower for a long time just holding each other, letting the water run over them. She didn't speak, but the way she smiled he knew she was as content as he was.

CHAPTER TWENTY-THREE

Sabastian watched the red dot blinking on the screen. It had stayed still for almost a whole day but had started moving south a few hours ago. If it turned south-west, he would have Harper in just a few days and be back in time for General Lucas's funeral and his appointment as Defence General.

He turned back to his work on his computer. He had already synchronised all the departments so he could look over their files, but they couldn't look at one another's. He felt like a voyeur peeping into the government's panty drawer, and he liked it.

He would have to go through the finances and personnel to determine what security upgrades each department needed, but it was clear that every single head had been squandering money. Some had been blatantly padding their own bank balances. He had figured, up until now, each department had been separated and only the heads of those departments had full access to the financial records, so they probably felt safe.

Sabastian smiled. He had no need to steal—he had plenty of money—but looking at the numbers on the screen he was sure he would be culling a few heads soon.

He pulled up the Head of Roads and Transport, Dennis Soterios. He remembered that Mr Soterios was a short, thick-set man with black hair and a chin that jutted out past his beak-like nose. Mr Soterios had been the greediest of all the department heads. By Sabastian's quick calculations, he had embezzled over two and a half million dollars in the past five years alone.

Next was his dear old friend Frederick Mills, who had given himself a new car and a holiday house on the coast.

He thought about it for a moment. He had no use for Dennis Soterios, but Frederick Mills was a handy man to have around, for now. Sabastian would most likely need the MGD agents to help secure his wife. He would have used the army, but he wasn't their general yet, and if there was an internal review of Frederick Mills, then he would likely have to deal with a new department head, who was as yet untested and likely not as easily manipulated, or worse, incorruptible.

Sabastian looked at the dot on the screen again. It flashed as it began travelling in a south-west direction. He smiled. His plan was coming together, and his wife would be home before the end of the week.

He picked up the phone and dialled Frederick.

"I have a strong lead on Harper. I need this to be discreet, but I want as many teams as you have available," Sabastian told him.

"I can give you three teams, four men per team, plus Agent Twain's team. That's sixteen men, any more than that and it won't be very discreet," Frederick offered.

Sabastian had been hoping for a less than helpful conversation so he could blackmail the man, but sixteen agents was a number he was comfortable with, plus him and Kleve.

"That would be fine, have them on standby in the north-west region. As soon as I have the exact location, I will call them in," Sabastian ordered.

"Yes, sir. And may I say it will be good to have you as general. I know the country will be in good hands," Frederick told him.

Sabastian smiled. His first brown-noser. He might keep Frederick around for a while after all, but perhaps pull in his budget.

I sat on the veranda, gently rocking Wolf in my arms while the late afternoon light leached from the sky, turning the world amethyst in its wake.

North had gone out hunting with Birdy and Billy, while Travis, Joe and Beth were at a community meeting leaving me alone with my precious baby.

All day I had felt a strange sense of impending dread looming over me, like something was coming, but I didn't know what.

Wolf stirred in my arms as I felt a gaze on me, and I looked up to see a giant black wolf standing on the tree line.

I smiled. "Did you catch anything?" I asked. Part of me knew I should have been scared, but I knew by his energy it was North in his animal form.

The wolf trotted up the path, and just as he reached the veranda step his body twisted, reshaped and North stood before me in all his naked glory.

"How did you know it was me?" North asked.

I laughed. "How wouldn't I? I can feel you. Can't you feel me?"

Birdy and Billy emerged from the trees behind him.

"Every heartbeat," North told me as Billy jogged up the path and handed him an armful of clothes.

"You should have seen him—he turned into this giant black wolf," Billy said excitedly.

North shrugged, pulling on his jeans. "He harassed me until I change shape."

"It was awesome." Billy smiled while Birdy dropped eight rabbits and a possum on the veranda. "If I could do that, I'd hunt down deer and bite their necks."

North rolled his eyes. "You'd do it once and realise it isn't easy when you have a mouth full of blood and fur and you wouldn't want a kick to the gut with one of those hooves. I'd rather use a gun to go hunting over running around the forest, any day. It's quicker and easier."

North tugged on his shirt, kissed my forehead and scooped Wolf out of my arms, doing that sniffing thing he did while he kissed his son's tiny nose.

Beth, Joe and Travis walked up the path.

Joe smiled at the mound of rabbits. "I'll have to send you three out more often," he said, picking the possum up to admire the neat head shot.

"It was North," Billy said. "He can shoot almost as good as Crash, and he moves so quietly, it's like he's a ghost."

"Is that so?" Travis said, looking like he had bitten into an apple and found only half a worm.

I'd have to talk to Travis. I knew how he felt about me, and having North staying in his own house must be rubbing him up the wrong way, especially with North staying in my room.

"We have some good news and some bad," Beth said. "First of all, Crash, you will have to move out with North and Wolf."

Shock slapped me. "What? Why?" I stammered, glancing at Joe and back to Beth. "Have I done something wrong?"

Beth and Joe both smiled.

"No," Beth told me, "You know that old cabin next door? The one Joe and Travis have been fixing up?"

I nodded.

"Well, Travis insisted they fix it up for when you had the baby, so you wouldn't be too far away from us."

I felt confused. "What?"

Joe laughed. "The cabin is yours."

I looked to Travis, but he was gazing at the ground as it registered. He had worked so hard on that cabin and had probably hoped we would live there together.

"Well?" Beth said.

"I . . ." Words failed me as I looked to North, who was positively beaming.

"I think she means *thank you*," North explained, leaning over and kissing the top of my head.

"I do. I'm just shocked," I said. "Thank you."

"Wow, you're going to be living right next door so I can come over and play with Wolf and go hunting with you." Billy beamed. "And Crash can come over and learn to cook, because she isn't a very good cook."

Birdy smiled. "Yeah, I've tasted my sister's cooking. Thank goodness North can cook, otherwise they'd starve."

Travis pushed past us and went inside.

I looked to Beth. "I think I have to go talk to him."

Beth nodded. "That's probably a good idea."

I left everyone on the veranda talking about the cabin and my lack of culinary skills and went inside.

Travis was in his bedroom sitting on the window seat, looking out into the falling darkness.

I tapped the door lightly. "Can I come in?" I asked softly.

He answered without looking at me. "Sure."

I stepped into his neat room and closed the door behind me. "I'm sorry Travis," I said as I joined him on the window seat.

"For what?" he asked.

"I know you worked hard on that cabin for me and Wolf," I said, unsure how to word it without sounding conceited or belittling.

"You don't have to apologise for that. I liked fixing it up for you, and now you're just going to be next door."

I reached out and gently touched his cheek. Travis closed his eyes for a moment, pushing his cheek against my hand.

"You're so wonderful and you're going to make some woman very happy one day," I told him.

Travis opened his eyes and looked straight at me. "It's just not going to be the woman I want, because her heart isn't free to love me."

"I'm sorry," I said again as I leaned over and kissed his other cheek.

Travis let out a weak smile. "I know that you love him, and I understand that you can't just turn that feeling off, otherwise I wouldn't still be in love with you. But if he so much as hurts one hair on yours or Wolf's head, I will kill him."

I took Travis's hand. "He isn't the one you should worry about, but thank you."

We sat in silence for a long time, his hand in mine as we both looked out at the darkness. Something felt like it was changing, but I wasn't sure what.

"What would you do if the Nation was different? If women were treated as equals?" Travis asked, still looking out the window.

"I'd probably live here," I said with a shrug. "And what would *you* do if the world was different?"

Travis shrugged. "I don't know. You were a prisoner out there, but now you're a prisoner here. We all are. We can't come and go as we please, because half of us aren't registered with the government and the rest are runaways or considered Insurgents."

"I'm not a prisoner here, and neither are you," I told him.

"Just because this place doesn't have bars doesn't mean we aren't trapped."

I knew what he meant, but this place gave me more freedom than any other place I had known, and I was happy if this was going to be my prison.

"At least the inmates in this prison look good in a dress." Travis smiled at me.

I laughed, "Yeah, I think you and Billy would look good in a dress, maybe some high-heels . . ."

Travis grabbed me and tickled me. I squealed and wriggled

while I laughed so hard, I almost wet myself.

Suddenly the bedroom door flung open and North looked in at us. "What the — ? I heard you scream."

Travis stopped tickling me. "She squealed, there's a difference." The tone in Travis's voice dripped with disdain.

"We were just mucking around," I told North.

North turned without a word and walked out.

"Guess you better go see what his problem is," Travis said.

I shot him a look and followed North.

Beth was in the kitchen with Wolf as I walked out, and she nodded at the door. "Out there," she told me, obviously knowing who I was looking for.

I stepped outside.

North was standing halfway down the path looking up at the stars.

"Do you want to tell me what that was about?" I asked.

North didn't look at me. "I used to watch the stars every night when I couldn't find you, worried that something bad had happened to you and then I found you here living in a house with people who think you're as wonderful as I think you are. They even fixed up a cabin right next door so you could be close to them." North turned to look at me as I stepped off the veranda. "I have nothing to give you. No money, no home, nothing."

"The only thing I will ever ask of you is that you love me. I don't need anything else," I told him.

"Harper, what about . . ."

"No," I said flatly. "No whats, ifs or buts. I love you, North, and that's that. I already made the biggest mistake of my life by leaving you once. You are not going anywhere, and neither am I. Everything else we can sort out when we need to."

North stared at me for a minute, "Geez you look sexy when you're being stubborn," he smiled and pulled me to him, kissing me with red-hot passion.

Sabastian watched the red light blink. Mrs Duran's GPS tracker had wound its way through the mountains, stopping on an unused old track. It had stayed still for a few hours but was now moving a lot slower. He guessed there must have been an obstruction on the road and they were now travelling on foot.

Sabastian brought up some old surveyors' reports on his screen. That area was known for avalanches, but of more interest there was an old holiday resort consisting of around fifty cabins and several halls, all powered by thermal springs. It was about forty kilometres from Mrs Duran's current location. At their current pace, he estimated that if that was their final destination, they'd be there by nightfall and he would be there by dawn.

He pulled up the topographical maps to look for landing sites. He would have to take in copters to have the best chance of surprise. He had enough copters in his company's fleet, but only two that were the newer, quieter models. He and Kleve could go in the quiet five-man copter with Agent Twain, which would have enough room for Harper. Two of the MGD Agents could use the two-man copter while the rest of the team waited for a signal to move in. They'd have one of the larger transport carriers, which could easily hold the remaining thirteen MGD Agents and his own pilots.

Sabastian wasn't sure what kind of resistance he would meet when they landed, but he was confident that he would find her and bring her back. There was no way he was leaving without her.

He sat back in his chair and considered what he would do with Harper once he got her back to his mansion. He could chain her, cuff her and beat her into submission, or he could simply use a shock collar on her. He had seen people use shock collars on dogs, and occasionally the government used them on convicts, although these days the government usually sentenced people to death for breaking the laws. It was cheaper and guaranteed no repeat offenders. It was also a great deterrent to anyone considering breaking the law.

Yes, a shock collar with electronic sensors around the perimeter of the house and a remote control, so if she stepped out of line, he would have control.

Sabastian rang Harvey.

"What can I do for you, sir?" Harvey bluntly asked.

"I want a lockable shock collar that can be synced with a wireless perimeter fence around my house and a remote," Sabastian said.

"How big is the dog?"

"About five foot seven inches."

"So human. Male or female?"

"Female. I will send you the stats," Sabastian said. "Can you have it all installed by lunchtime tomorrow?"

"Can't see why not," Harvey said, a smile in his voice.

Sabastian liked that the men who worked for him didn't ask questions. It showed their devotion to their jobs and made his life run smoothly.

"One more thing. I want you to increase security in and around my home, both the electronic monitoring and bodyguard detail. I am going to go and retrieve a very precious item which was stolen, and I am in no doubt that someone will want to steal it again," Sabastian explained.

"Not a problem. Do you need it tonight, or do you want it with the collar?"

"With the collar would be fine," Sabastian said and disconnected.

His next call was to Agent Twain to inform him of their precipitous departure and his plan to use his own copters to transport the MGD agents in and out of the mountains.

Sabastian pulled up the satellite images of the area. He was glad he had convinced General Lucas to direct a satellite toward the northern area before his untimely death. There was a cleared area in the centre of the old holiday resort that looked maintained, which indicated people were living there. It would be too blatant to land there, so the next alternative would be on the road which led along the side of the mountain. He would take a pilot and have him, Kleve and Agent Twain dropped on the road. The two agents in the other two-man copter could land and walk in with them. If all went well, they would grab Harper and have the pilot return to the road to retrieve them. If it didn't, his pilot could pick them up from the clearing in the centre of the old resort.

Sabastian glanced over at the dot blinking on the screen. It was still moving, but at a lot slower pace now.

If by some chance they weren't going to the old resort, but to some back woods hut, he would have to reassess his plans, but Sabastian was growing more and more confident he knew where they were heading, and when they got there, they would make a bee line for her.

CHAPTER TWENTY-FOUR

North sat quietly watching the road with Travis and Birdy. The alarm had sounded, letting them know that three people were approaching and were about five kilometres out.

"You did a good job fixing up the cabin for Harper and North," Birdy said, sitting between Travis and North.

Travis and North had barely spoken a word to each other, but Birdy could feel the tension growing.

"Yeah, well someone had to make sure Wolf and Crash had somewhere to call home," Travis said flatly.

"What's that meant to mean?" North growled.

"It means how the hell do I know she even wants you here? She ran away from you."

"You know nothing about Harper. She didn't even speak to you until we got here," North said, anger building.

"I know she is the most amazing, strong and beautiful woman I have ever known." Travis looked North over. "And she chose you, a fucking Unholy."

North suddenly realised everything Travis had said was said in jealousy. "Yeah, Harper chose me, and I feel blessed every day for it. And yeah, she is the strongest woman I've ever known, but Travis, if you ever chuck another jealous hissy fit or question any of Harper's choices, including me, I will cut off your balls and shove them up your ass You have no idea who she is or what she is truly capable of."

Travis looked sideways at him but didn't say a word.

North didn't completely understand Harper's Angelic DNA, but from what he had seen, she was like the perfect warrior, adaptable, fast and smart. And she was his soulmate.

He turned back to the road and smiled to himself. He had heard the term *soulmate* before and thought it was a word some bureaucrat had made up to sell the government's *Buy A Wife* scheme, but now he knew it went much deeper. It meant they were connected heart, body, and soul, forever.

North smelled the intruders before he saw them. Their scent was familiar, and for a moment he wondered if he'd imagined them, before he suddenly realised he could smell blood.

"Shit!" North barked, jumping from the hiding spot and sprinting down the road.

"What is it?" Birdy called after him.

"Blane, he's injured," North yelled over his shoulder as he rounded a corner, then another before seeing two figures walking.

Lloyd was carrying Blane on his back, while Charli plodded along beside him, their heads down.

North sprinted. "Lloyd!"

The big man looked up, relief plain on his face. "North, Blane's hurt," he called, staggering slightly as he tried to speed up.

Charli looked up, clearly unsure whether she should cry or laugh.

North slid to a stop in front of Lloyd. Blane's face was lying on the big man's shoulder. He looked like he had put his face through a glass window, except that the cuts were uniform and placed asymmetrically across his face.

"Who did this?" North asked as Birdy and Travis caught up.

Birdy wrapped his arms around Charli, and it was only then that North realised the entire left side of her face was swollen black and blue with tinges of purple.

"Sabastian James," Blane whispered. "He said he wanted

his wife back."

"Harper isn't his wife. We left the night before they were to marry. I made sure of that," Birdy protested, while North and Travis eased Blane from Lloyd's back.

"Well, he wants her," Charli said, looking as if she were so tired she could sleep for a month.

"He isn't having her," North snarled. He gently picked up Blane, making sure to hold him carefully without causing him more pain, then started back down the road.

"We'll take them straight to my house. Mum will know what to do," Travis said.

On this, at least, North and Travis could agree.

I sat at the dining table while Billy played on the floor with Wolf. Even though I now had my own little house and wanted to cook in my own kitchen, Beth had asked us over for dinner. I think it was more so she and Joe could snuggle Wolf in between stirring the rabbit casserole than for my company. I didn't mind—Wolf loved them and would coo and gurgle whenever they tickled his toes or blew raspberries on his little stomach.

"I was thinking of putting North on security and training with Travis," Joe said. "He has an in-built tactical ability that can't be learned."

"I think that's a good idea," Beth agreed. "I just hope they don't kill each other."

I smiled. "I'm sure they'd be fine. They will just have to learn to work together. Where will I be assigned?"

Joe shrugged. "I haven't figured that out yet. I thought you might go into the Insurgent Program, but I thought we'd wait until Wolf was a few months old before we decide."

"What's the Insurgent Program?" I asked.

"We aren't the only off-grid community in the Nation, and

there are many of our members out in the community. Our goal is to bring about change in the government, stop forced marriages and the dictatorship of the ruling parties," Beth explained. "The Insurgent Program focuses on how this may be attained."

"So, like a spy network?" I questioned.

"Kind of." Joe shrugged. "But like I said, we'll figure out how you can best be assigned when Wolf is older."

I had been hoping to be assigned wherever North was assigned, but I would go to wherever I was needed, although I had no idea what exactly a spy did.

I felt a tug. North was coming up the path, but he wasn't alone, and he was anxious.

"Billy, take Wolf into your room," I snapped as I jumped from my seat and rushed to the front door.

It was almost dark out, and I could see he was carrying someone. My first thought was Birdy or Travis, but they were behind him and so were two other people whose energies were familiar — Lloyd and Charli, which meant it was Blane in North's arms.

Beth and Joe followed me onto the veranda.

"What's going on? Who are these people?" Joe barked as North brought Blane up the front steps.

I took one look at his tortured face in the light and gasped. My hand shot up to cover my mouth. Birdy and Charli were next. Her face was battered and swollen.

"Harper." She sighed as she wrapped her arms around my neck. "I'm so glad North found you."

"Bring them inside," Beth ordered, and Birdy gently eased Charli into the house behind North.

Lloyd and Travis followed them in. Lloyd didn't look at me. He appeared uninjured physically, but I could see he was suffering inside.

North laid Blane in the lounge while Beth went to work

gathering medical supplies to begin cleaning his face.

"Help me in the kitchen," Travis said softly. "I don't think they've eaten in a few days."

We set to work making cups of tea and dishing out rabbit casserole, setting steaming bowls on the table. Charli wasn't shy as she sat down and began to eat ravenously, but Lloyd just stood guard over Beth while she worked on Blane's face.

"Sit," North told him sternly. "Beth knows what she is doing."

Blane smiled at his husband. "These are the good guys, we're safe here," he told Lloyd. "You can trust them."

Lloyd relented, sitting down at the table, but he still didn't eat, he just watched Beth as if she were a poisonous viper waiting to strike.

"What happened?" I asked, sliding a cup of tea in front of Lloyd.

"Your husband happened," he said angrily.

"What?"

"Your husband came to the farm with MGD Agents and tortured Blane to find out where you were," Lloyd said coldly.

I looked at North.

"Sabastian James," he said bitterly.

Shock washed over me. I hadn't thought about that man in months.

"Sabastian James? As in the next General of the Defence Network?" Joe asked.

"Wait, what?" I asked, confusion washing over me.

Travis set a cup of tea in my hands.

A million thoughts ran through my head, but I couldn't process any of them properly.

North looked to me. "Apparently I've been sleeping with a married woman," he told me flatly.

Birdy interrupted. "But that's why we left. It was so she

didn't have to marry him."

"If your father signed the paperwork, then she's married, and obviously Sabastian James intends on making her his wife," Travis snarled.

I saw Billy poke his head out of the doorway down the hall. I hurried to him to get Wolf. "It's all right, they're friends of ours," I said as he passed Wolf over and followed me back out.

Lloyd, Charli and Blane all looked at Wolf then me, then North.

"That must be North's baby," Blane said, half sitting up. "My goodness, he looks like his daddy."

"You had a baby," Charli said, forgetting her food as she rose and came over.

Lloyd just stared silently.

"What's his name?" Charli asked, extending her arms to hold him.

"Wolf," I told her as she cradled him.

"None of the cuts are deep enough to need stitches, but I'm afraid you are likely to have a lot of scarring, and two of your fingers are broken," Beth announced.

Blane nodded and managed to push himself up off the lounge chair and come over.

The pair gushed and cooed at Wolf, while he gurgled and cooed back.

Blane turned to North. "Is this why you were so desperate to find her?"

I blushed and lowered my head.

"Nope, I had no idea. I just knew I couldn't live without her. Wolf was a beautiful surprise," North smiled.

"Sit down, man," Beth ordered Blane. "You have a lifetime to fuss over Wolf."

Blane sat.

"There is something I should tell you all," Lloyd said,

staring into his cup. "I told Sabastian that Harper was here in the mountains."

Silence fell.

North looked like he was ready to tear the older man's head off. "You what?"

"Sabastian was torturing Blane," Lloyd said defensively while tears rolled down his cheeks. "He was going to kill him."

I stepped over to him as he lowered his head. "I would have done the same if it was North," I said quietly, gently stroking his hair.

After everyone had showered and eaten, North took me and Wolf back to our cabin.

Travis and Billy tried to be discreet about following us, but I felt them watching us, and North smelled them.

I couldn't see them, but I knew they were there. "If you two are going to pretend to be bodyguards, you might as well come in and make yourselves comfortable," I called into the darkness.

"How does she do that?" I heard Billy ask as he and Travis stepped out from the bushes.

"Damned if I know," Travis said quietly. "But I haven't once been able to sneak up on her, and trust me, I've tried."

North smiled while we all went inside.

CHAPTER TWENTY-FIVE

Sabastian smiled at the red dot that had stopped moving in the vicinity of the old holiday resort. He wished he had the hindsight to put a listening device into Mrs Duran's GPS tracker so he could hear any conversations, but by the look of the heartbeat monitor, she had been excited about something before her heartbeat slowed, so he assumed she was sleeping now.

He pulled up the blueprints of the resort, overlaying it with the satellite images he had accessed. By the looks of it, Mrs Duran was in one of the larger five-bedroom luxury cabins. It was the place Harper would most likely be.

Sabastian pulled on a pair of camouflage cargo pants and a khaki green shirt which stretched over his shoulders. They were clothes left over from his time in the army, where he had been a member of a small elite-squad. A few of the members had died on missions, a few more when they returned home and couldn't adjust, and now there were only himself and Harvey left.

Harvey had saved his army pay, and as soon as he left the army, he had bought a house and a plain looking wife, who was cheap but a good cook and an excellent housekeeper.

Sabastian had inherited some money when his father passed and he too had saved every penny he earnt in the army, but he wasn't going to throw it away on some boring wife and a cheap house. No. Sabastian built his empire by developing computer programs and gadgets which no government could resist. He knew that was where the money was, and the power.

Sabastian pulled on his boots, strapped his gun holster on and tidied his hair. He didn't want Harper to see him looking a mess, although he presumed she would look like a bush woman living in a squalid old mountain cabin. That didn't matter, though. He would have a personal stylist come in to tidy her up and make her presentable.

Kleve knocked on the door at precisely midnight. "Sir, the copters are waiting. We will pick up the MGD agents en route."

"Thank you, Kleve," Sabastian said. "Oh, and I took the liberty of securing tranquiliser guns for all the MGD agents as well as one each for us. I trust you wouldn't shoot Harper, but those idiot agents are another story."

"I'll make sure the tranquiliser guns are the only weapons the agents have," Kleve told him.

They loaded themselves into the five-man copter with their pilot already waiting. The smaller, quieter two-man copter and the larger cargo copter were already at the rendezvous point awaiting their arrival. The cargo copter sounded like a freight train in the sky and the pilot had been ordered to wait ten kilometres out from the resort with the bulk of the agents until instructed to move in. Sabastian, Kleve and Agent Twain would be dropped on the road by their pilot. He was to circle until he was told the pickup location, which would either be the road or the clearing in the centre of the resort, while the two agents in the smaller copter were to land on the road and walk in with Sabastian, Kleve and Agent Twain.

Sabastian hoped to be in and out with Harper without calling in the larger copter. But he had to locate her first without alerting whoever else lived in the resort.

The sun hadn't risen, but the sky was starting to lighten ever so slightly as the two quieter copters zigzagged through the mountains. The map of the terrain and their destination were projected onto the windscreen.

Sabastian checked Mrs Duran's GPS tracker again, but she hadn't moved.

"We will be setting down in two minutes," the pilot said as the copter swept along the side of the mountain.

Sabastian saw several vehicles parked on the road beside a large landslip and guessed that was the reason why Mrs Duran's pace had slowed. It was also a bonus for him, because if anyone tried to follow them or if Harper did try to escape, she would have a long way to run to get to the cars.

The pilot slowed, bringing the copter down on the road as the second copter landed beside them and cut its engine.

Sabastian, Kleve and Agent Twain stepped out, and their pilot took off immediately.

Kleve adjusted his rifle on his shoulder, and Sabastian noted it was almost as big as he was.

"We have a location for Mrs Duran, I am presuming Harper will be somewhere close by," Sabastian said, holding up an image of Harper for them all to see. "You have been given tranquiliser guns, so feel free to use them on anyone you see except Harper. I do not want her injured."

North woke with a start when the low sound of a copter vibrated through the air. If he were a normal person, he might not have heard it, but with his Unholy hearing, the sound was unmistakably clear in the still morning air.

"Harper." He shook her urgently.

Her eyes flew open. "He's here," she said, snatching up Wolf before jumping out of bed.

North was already at the bedroom door. "Travis," he barked, "we have incoming."

Travis and Billy sprang to their feet, rifles in hand.

Harper grabbed Billy's rifle, handing him Wolf instead.

"Get him out of here and don't come back until it is all clear," she ordered.

Billy stood frozen for a moment. "But . . ."

"Billy, I'm trusting you with the most precious thing in my life—take care of him for me. Please." Harper pleaded with her eyes as well as her words.

"Harper is a better shot than you. Your job is to keep Wolf safe," North ordered while Harper quickly kissed Wolf on top of his head.

Travis tossed Billy a bag with a bottle and some food. With a worried backward glance, Billy took off out the back door and disappeared into the woods.

North could see the anguish in Harper's eyes. "They'll be all right, he knows the woods."

Harper nodded.

Travis peeked out the window. "Harper, I want you in the tree line. I don't want them seeing you."

"But I'm your best marksman," she protested.

"Yes, but you are likely the target too," North reasoned. "Take out whoever you deem a threat, but only shoot to kill if necessary. I don't want you having nightmares again."

"Again?" Travis questioned.

North glanced at Travis. "You're with me. We need to sound whatever alarm system you have to evacuate this place."

Travis punched a number into his phone "Shit, there's no reception."

Harper opened the front door a crack, lifted her rifle, aimed at Beth and Joe's lodge and fired. The sound of breaking glass shattered the morning silence.

"I'm so telling them that was you and not me," Travis said with a smile.

North opened the back door and Harper slipped out. "Stay safe," he whispered, kissing her quickly before she slipped into the trees with Billy's rifle. She was wearing a pair of navy blue sweatpants, one of North's dark-grey shirts, which hung off her, and lavender coloured socks.

He had a sinking feeling that this would be the last time he saw her.

North smelled them long before he saw them, and one of them was definitely Sabastian James.

Four shadowy figures of armed men and what looked like a child all dressed in army fatigues slipped between the trees, making their way toward Beth and Joe's house. They must have thought Harper was there, but North knew Harper was about fifty metres away in the trees, halfway down the slope to the open field.

Joe suddenly burst out the front door, gun in hand with Lloyd and Beth behind him.

The five people stopped, and the lead man lifted his weapon. The *POP* of the gun bit the air and Joe staggered back.

North and Travis opened fire, taking out the two leading agents as Joe collapsed on the veranda.

A sharp tang bit North's nose — not blood. They were using tranquiliser guns.

The three men dove for cover, turning their guns toward Travis and North.

North heard a faint POP and knew Harper had fired, then a scream shattered the silence before a thunderous rumble began to quake the air, growing louder and louder until it sounded like a freight train hurtling toward them. A giant black copter appeared above the open field, spilling out over a dozen MGD agents in full fatigue.

North could hear the sound of people shouting and screaming as they ran from their houses in panic while the MGD agents picked them off, indiscriminately shooting women, men and children.

Rage erupted in North, his body twisting, reshaping into his massive half-form. He looked like a demon as he burst from the cabin and sprinted down the hill, tearing through any agent who came within reach.

Blood splattered while the sound of guns POPPED around him. He felt the sting of the darts, but they didn't slow him.

I watched as five men crept quietly up the path toward Beth and Joe's house. One of the men was short enough to be a child, but from where I lay amongst the bushes, I could tell he wasn't.

Another of the men turned, scanning his surroundings. His black hair was tidy, and he looked like he'd just stepped out of a photoshoot for *Army Monthly*, but I would have known his face anywhere—Sabastian.

I wanted to shoot him right there on the spot. I had his temple in my sight and my finger itched to pull the trigger.

The lodge door suddenly crashed open and Joe burst out onto the veranda with his rifle.

The leading man lifted his gun and shot. Joe staggered back, collapsing onto the veranda as two quick shots rang out and the two leading agents dropped to the ground, dead.

Sabastian dove behind a fallen tree, taking cover. He said something into a communications device while a red-haired agent lifted his gun to return fire. I took aim and shot him through the forearm. He screamed and dropped his gun.

The sound of rumbling thunder echoed off the mountains. A giant black copter came into view, disgorging uniformed men onto Haven's open field.

I heard North's roar as a giant half-human, half-wolf raced down the hill, swiping and tearing through four of the agents as he went.

I turned my gun, *POP, POP, POP,* and men fell as my bullets tore through three of the agents' brains, dropping them where they stood. But I couldn't stop all of them.

One, two, three, four bullets hit North.

I jumped to my feet, forgetting about Sabastian and the little man as I ran down the hill.

I shot another agent as Haven's people poured out of buildings. The remaining agents shot at the fleeing children as they tried to run away with their mothers and fathers.

I heard two POPs from the hill behind me and turned to see the little man who had been with Sabastian taking aim at North across the other side of the field. He fired and North stumbled, falling to the ground, his body shifting back into his human form.

"NO!" I screamed, turning my gun on the little man just as he swung his gun toward me. We fired at the same time.

I saw the bullet puncture the middle of his forehead, and his eyes went wide as I felt the sting of his bullet bite my chest. We both fell, my body limp, but the sounds around me became sharp. I tried to sit up. I couldn't move. My body felt limp as I lay motionless. I could see North lying across the other side of the field unmoving, his eyes closed, red stains covering his naked body.

He was dead. I was dead. My beautiful baby boy who I loved so much would be an orphan.

A large muscular arm came into view, sliding under my neck as darkness rushed in and swallowed me whole.

Sabastian saw Harper lying on the ground like a gift wrapped in hideous baggy clothes. He had given orders not to shoot her with the tranquilisers, so he wasn't happy, but at least he had her. He called in his copter and ordered the retreat of the remaining agents.

Once he was general, he would bomb this hell hole and flatten these mountains to rubble.

Sabastian looked around for Kleve, then spotted him lying lifeless on the ground halfway up the hill. Blood was trickling from a single bullet hole between his eyes.

Sabastian would have to find himself another right-hand man, which was a bloody nuisance. He'd had Kleve for years and he'd known his job.

A young russet-haired man sprinted across the field toward him.

A loud POP sounded next to Sabastian as Agent Twain fired, dropping the man instantly while the two copters landed. Sabastian noted that despite being shot in the forearm by a sniper who had been hiding in the bushes, Agent Twain was still an effective soldier.

Sabastian slid into the front seat with Harper on his lap while Twain climbed in the back, gripping his bloody arm as the remaining agents dragged their injured and dead comrades into the cargo copter.

Sabastian hated that the hillbillies got the jump on him. He had expected little resistance from a few people hiding out in the mountains, but instead he found an entire community, with the biggest, most ferocious Unholy he had ever seen.

He looked down at Harper lying limp in his arms. She had changed a little, her face looked slightly rounder, but his wife was still the most stunning woman he had ever seen and now she was all his.

"Drop Agent Twain off at the closest hospital. He's bleeding on the seat," Sabastian told the pilot.

Harper would be unconscious for at least six hours, which gave Sabastian plenty of time to get her back to his house in the Capital. *Their* house.

CHAPTER TWENTY-SIX

Sabastian stood waiting for the doctor to finish examining Harper. She had started waking up when they landed at the mansion, but his personal physician had sedated her so he could do a thorough examination without having to restrain her.

"I'm afraid to tell you Mr James, but your suspicions were correct, she isn't a virgin, in fact far from it," the doctor said. "Your wife has given birth, and quite recently."

"What?" Sabastian said feeling rage burning inside him. "My wife had a baby with another man?"

"It appears that way," the doctor said. "Would you like me to euthanize her for you?"

He had searched for months to find *his* wife and he wasn't giving her up now. He didn't care that she had another man's baby — she would never see it again, and she would give him beautiful, Angelic children.

Sabastian pulled his gun out without warning and shot the doctor between the eyes.

He hadn't particularly liked that doctor anyway. His hands always felt cold and clammy.

Sabastian took the modified electric shock collar Harvey had provided and fastened it around Harper's neck. It looked like a thick metal cuff. Then he took the syringe and injected a special GPS tracker he had made just for her into her upper left arm. The special tracker didn't just show location and heartbeat, but also estrogen levels so he would know the best time to make love to his wife. There was also a built-in tranquiliser and poison, giving him the option of killing her or merely detaining her, plus it had its own internal power source, so even if she died, he could locate her body.

Sabastian looked Harper over. She was the most beautiful woman he had ever seen, and she belonged to him. He smiled at that thought. No other man would ever touch her again. He would make sure of it.

Sabastian carefully lifted Harper's limp body and carried her into his bedroom, then laid her out on the bed before stepping back to look at his wife.

He wanted to strangle her and beat her until she surrendered herself to him, but watching her lying there so peacefully made him want to protect her, not hurt her. It was as if her very essence affected him, making him want to wrap her in bubble wrap and keep her safe. He would keep her close, and anything or anyone that tried to get near his wife, he would destroy.

North heard Joe calling his name, but he sounded so far away, and North felt so incredibly tired.

"I just need to sleep a little longer," North tried to say, but the words came out jumbled.

"He's coming around," Joe yelled, followed by the sound of feet rushing toward him.

A warm hand touched his wrist, and for a moment he thought it might be Harper, but there was no buzz or sense of connection.

A flash of memory came back — the MGD agents.

"Harper?" North groaned, forcing his eyes open.

He was lying on the grass. Around him lay chunks of red flesh and dead bodies.

"Take it easy," Joe said, the older man's face wavering into focus, his russet hair a mess.

North felt confused. He had seen Joe get shot on his veranda.

"Am I dead?" North mumbled, looking to Beth, who was wrapping a sheet over his naked body.

"No, not yet," Joe said, helping him to sit up.

North looked at the carnage around him. Dead bodies were scattered about, and among them, Travis sat with his head between his knees, a soft sob trembling in his throat.

Anxiety rushed over North as he looked around. There were people everywhere, but he couldn't see her.

"Where's Harper?" he asked, suddenly feeling wide awake.

Joe rested his hand on North's shoulder. "They took her."

The words took a moment to sink in. They didn't sound real.

"What do you mean, they took her?" North asked, pushing himself to his feet. His head still felt woozy and he staggered slightly, but he scanned the surroundings looking for Harper.

"I tried, I swear I tried," Travis said without looking up.

Beth stood next to Joe, her face mournful. "You'd better come and sit down. You were hit with eight tranquiliser bullets. Five is usually lethal to a normal human, lucky you aren't a Normal."

North didn't want to sit down, he wanted to find Harper.

Through the crowd of people, North saw Billy standing with Wolf, a lost expression on both the boys' faces. North ran to them, taking Wolf from him and pressing him against his chest.

"Thank you for keeping him safe." North choked out as tears welled in his eyes.

His baby was safe.

Beth, Travis and Joe walked over, and Billy flung himself into Beth's arms. She cuddled him against her. It was easy to forget how old Billy was, but in reality, he was only fifteen and still a child at heart.

"You did well," Beth told him softly. "Wolf is safe because of you."

As North held Wolf, he felt his heart shattering—he had only just found Harper, and now she was gone again.

"How the hell did they find us?" Travis asked.

North shook his head, unsure, only then remembering that Lloyd, Blane and Charli had arrived only last night. He swung around and grimly marched up the path to the lodge, baby Wolf in his arms. If one of them had led Sabastian here deliberately, he would rip their head off.

Birdy was sitting on the veranda step, a rifle resting between his knees with Charli beside him, while Blane and Lloyd rested in the seats.

"Which one of you led those bastards here?" North snarled as Travis and Joe caught him up with Beth and Billy only a few steps behind.

"What?" Lloyd questioned.

"You heard me. I want to know which one of you told them where the fuck this place was?" North said as Beth quickly slid Wolf from his father's arms and went inside.

Blane stood. "I have their torture etched into my face and two smashed fingers to prove I would never tell those assholes anything," he said, sounding offended, but North didn't care.

"What about you, Lloyd? Did you decide to save your own ass again?" Travis chimed in.

The distinguished man looked ready to kill something.

"Oh shit," Charli suddenly said, looking to Birdy, then North before pulling her shirt sleeve up to reveal a puncture mark on her upper arm. "I think it was me."

Everyone looked to her.

"What is that?" Joe asked.

Charli shook her blonde head. "I don't know, but it was the

MGD Agents who injected me with it."

North grabbed her arm, squeezing it in different directions.

"It's probably one of those GPS trackers the media has been going on about," Blane said, "I saw an article about them injecting all the soldiers and how they wanted to do the women next."

There was a group swearing session followed by North dragging Charli into the house, with Birdy objecting adamantly.

"Charli has a GPS tracker in her," North barked at Beth.

Beth didn't miss a beat as she handed Wolf to North and went to get her medical supplies.

"This might hurt a bit," Beth said.

"I don't care, just get that fucking thing out of me," Charli swore.

Beth pulled out a scalpel and pressed it skilfully into Charli's arm. Charli flinched, but didn't pull away, her face expressing the pain she was feeling. Blood trickled down her arm while Beth felt around with her fingers and finally a small cylindrical object slid out.

Joe swore.

"What is that?" Lloyd asked, as Beth deposited it on the table and they all leaned forward to take a closer look.

"It looks like a maggot," Billy announced.

Beth wiped the blood from Charli's arm and wrapped it with a gauze bandage.

"I need to contact the Insurgent group down south," Joe said, retrieving a small preserving jar to put the maggot-looking thing in.

"How do we find Harper?" North asked, as Wolf began to struggle in his arms.

Wolf barely ever cried. He was usually happy and content, but now he looked on the verge of tears. North cradled him against his chest and began to rock.

"Shh, it will be all right, we'll get her back," North promised.

Once Charli's arm was clean and bandaged, she finally broke down, crying, "I'm so sorry. I'm so, so sorry." She sobbed as Birdy put his arm around her and took her down the hall to his room.

"We are going to have to leave here," Beth said while Joe went to make a phone call. "We can't stay. The government knows where we are, and they will probably have the army here in a few hours. North, go over to your cabin and pack as many clothes and blankets as you can carry for you and Wolf. Billy, Travis, go into your rooms and do the same. Lloyd and Blane, since you both arrived light, I need you to pack as much food as you can manage."

"Beth," Joe interrupted. "We have a recovery team coming in for the object and they are sending in copters to evacuate."

"What if Harper comes back looking for us and we aren't here?" Billy asked.

Beth gave Billy a sympathetic look. "There are monitoring systems around the community and we can turn on the remote access CCTV."

North half-cleared his throat. He knew the chances of her returning on her own were slim to none. "Sabastian James won't just let her go. He has been hunting her for almost a year now, and he is obsessed with her."

"Like you," Travis said snidely.

"There's a difference," North snarled.

"All I see is similarities. She ran away from both of you, you both hunted her down and you're both obsessed with her."

"What the fuck do you know?" North snapped.

Joe stepped between them. "Both of you, knock it off," he said before turning to North. "You have a baby to worry about." Joe turned to his son. "And you should be coordinating the evacuation."

North and Travis stared at each other for a moment before they both turned their backs and stalked off.

North took Wolf to the cabin which Harper and he had lived in together for less than forty-eight hours. He laid Wolf on the bed, dropped to his knees, and began to cry. She was gone again, and he had Wolf to take care of, he couldn't just drop everything like before and go look for her.

A hand rested on his shoulder and he looked up to see Beth and Blane standing there.

"We understand, but your first priority is to get Wolf to safety," Beth said, going to the drawers to pull out nappies, clothes and blankets for Wolf while Blane offered North his good hand to help him up off the floor.

North looked at Wolf—he couldn't break down yet, his son needed him. "So where are we being evacuated to?" North asked while Beth handed him a large duffle bag.

"Home," Beth said, picking Wolf up and walking out.

Chapter Twenty-seven

My head throbbed. I didn't want to, but I carefully opened my eyes and looked around the dark, unfamiliar space. Slivers of daylight slipped through a gap in the curtains on the far side of the room and from around the edge of a closed door.

I slowly sat myself up, realising I was on a massive bed and there was something fitted snugly around my neck, almost choking me. I reached up and tried to pull it loose, but it was smooth and held fast.

"It is locked on you," a man's voice said from the darkness.

I jumped. I looked around, at last noticing a shadowy figure sitting in a chair in the corner. I hadn't felt him, but I instantly knew the voice—Sabastian.

Fear and anger rushed through me. Instinctively I scrambled backward up the bed, pushing myself against the massive, carved, wooden headboard, my head swimming and woozy.

A low laugh emanated from Sabastian as he stood, flicking on a light, illuminating his black hair and blue eyes. He seemed bigger than I remembered, with more muscle and a squarer jaw. If he wasn't a sadistic asshole, I would call him handsome.

I wanted to run, but my body was trembling, and my head wouldn't stop spinning.

"Are you going to kill me?" I asked my voice shaky.

Sabastian smiled. "Why would I kill my wife? I only just found you."

"I'm not your wife," I told him, my eyes darting around looking for a way out.

Sabastian held up a piece of paper. "This says you are. Your father signed it before his, um, untimely death."

Shock gripped me, holding me paralysed for a moment. "You killed my father?"

"Of course not. I believe he and your mother were killed in a house fire," Sabastian drawled stepping closer. "I'm not a monster."

I wanted to disagree, but I needed to figure out how to get out of here first, and making him angry would likely end in me finding out just how much of a monster he really was.

As if reading my thoughts, Sabastian lifted a small key-chain with a single key on it and what looked like a car's central locking device. "Your new necklace is actually an electric-shock collar. If you try to leave, it will send enough volts through you to knock you out. If I need to take you somewhere or if you misbehave, I can press this button and it will also zap you," he explained, holding up the remote mechanism for me to see. "And if by some miracle you manage to get past the wireless fence, keyed to your collar of course, which is set up around the perimeter of this house, then I have implanted a GPS tracker in you which can release a quick acting tranquiliser or a poison."

I sat horrified. If I tried to escape, he would electrocute me, knock me unconscious or kill me. I had to stay alive. I had to get back to Wolf and North.

Oh god! North.

My heart felt as if it had shattered into a million pieces. I had seen North fall. He was dead. That little man shot him.

I wanted to burst into tears, but I wouldn't let Sabastian see me cry. I would not show that asshole any weakness. Now I had to figure out a way to escape—I had to get back to Wolf, I couldn't leave him an orphan.

I had told Billy to hide in the woods until it was all clear, but goodness knew if anyone else survived the MGD Agents.

I thought about North for a moment, trying to concentrate on him. He didn't feel dead, but was that my intuition or my wishful thinking? I had seen him fall. I had seen him lying on the ground, unmoving, his half-form body shrinking back to human. And the bloody puncture wounds.

Sabastian was watching me with a small amused grin. He was letting me know he was the cat and I was the mouse.

I slowly rolled off the far side of the bed, making sure to keep the expanse of the bed between us when I realised I was wearing a hospital gown and not my own clothes.

A disturbing thought crossed my mind. "Did you . . ."

"No, I would prefer my wife be awake so you can enjoy it as much as I will," Sabastian interrupted, moving to a pile of clothes on a dressing table. "Please get dressed. You have a hair and makeup appointment before we attend General Lucas's funeral, after which you will accompany me to a media conference, where I will be appointed General in Charge of the Nation's Defence Network."

Was he serious? He'd just drugged me, kidnapped me and now wanted me to play his demure wife while we attended a funeral and media conference.

"Are you insane?" I asked him incredulously.

An electric buzz stung my throat, closing my airways as it choked me for a moment.

"No, my Angel, I am quite sane, but you do need to learn your place," Sabastian smiled.

"Fuck you," I snarled, and a stronger, more painful jolt zapped me, dropping me to my knees while I clawed at the collar, trying to breathe.

"That isn't very ladylike," he said, casually walking around the bed to lift me to my feet as my breath came back. "Now get dressed." His voice was calm, but his grip on my arm was tight.

I know I should have kicked him or punched him, but he was so much bigger than me, and he scared me.

You have to survive and escape for Wolf, I told myself. I would not leave my son alone in the world. I would find him and hug him and tell him how wonderful and brave and beautiful his Daddy was . . . is. I didn't know.

Sabastian let me go, motioning to the clothes. "If you would, Mrs James."

It took me a moment to realise he was talking to me. The thought of being Mrs James disgusted me, but I would play the game and bide my time until I figured out how I could escape. The GPS tracker he said he'd implanted with the tranquiliser and poison had me worried. I would have to find it in my body and cut it out, and I had to figure out how to get this horrible collar off.

I took a wide berth around Sabastian and walked over to the dressing table. Bra, panties, black stockings and a black dress, which reminded me of a white dress I used to have, even down to the lace detail. I looked at Sabastian.

"I liked your white dress so much that I had a black one made for you." Sabastian smiled. "I hope you like it."

He remembered my white dress? Well, that was weird. I didn't remember wearing it around him until a flashback came to me — I had worn it the day North and I had been in my parent's kitchen. North had been cooking because Sabastian was coming to lunch and my mother was going crazy.

I looked at the underwear in front of me, then at Sabastian. "Are you going to give me some privacy?" I asked.

"No," Sabastian said flatly. "You're my wife, I'm expected to know you intimately."

I fought the shudder. If he touched me, collar or not, I would claw his eyes out.

I turned away, slipping the black panties on under my

hospital gown. I couldn't figure out how to get the bra on under the gown, so I took a breath, straightened myself and with my back to him, I dropped the hospital gown before pulling on the bra and dress.

If he so much as took one single step toward me, I would wrap the pantyhose around his neck and strangle him.

Sabastian didn't move, but I felt him watching me with a smile on his face like a sick, voyeuristic pervert.

"Now the stockings," he said sounding like a cat purring.

I took them over to the corner seat where I first saw him and pulled them on. Sabastian smiled, then went to retrieve a pair of black high-heeled shoes from the closet.

I glanced at the closed bedroom door, wondering how far I would make it before he zapped me again. Maybe if I got far enough away, the shock collar wouldn't work. I needed to test it, then I would find the GPS tracker hidden in my body.

I jumped to my feet, sprinted across the room and wrenched open the door, I made it three steps out into the wide hallway before the electric shock buzzed through my neck, paralysing me, dropping me to my hands and knees.

I gasped for air.

I heard Sabastian laugh as his shiny black shoes came into view. "You are so full of spirit," he chuckled. "But I will break you," he said, gripping me under the arm and pulling me up to face him.

He was so tall and broad that I felt tiny as he loomed over me.

"Don't think for a moment I won't use the collar when we go out. And if I have to use it, I'll make sure you feel its full effects."

I knew it wasn't an empty threat. Sabastian James wouldn't bother with bluffing. He would zap me until my hair stood on end.

"Now behave," Sabastian said quietly, setting my shoes on

the floor in front of me.

Reluctantly I stepped into them.

He led me downstairs to where two men waited with an array of makeup and torturous hair devices.

"Oh my, what happened to your hair," one of the men asked as Sabastian took me over to a seat and sat me down.

"You have an hour," Sabastian told him, stepping back a metre and folding his thick muscular arms.

The two men went to work, one tugging at my hair while the other rubbed and patted makeup all over my face.

A year ago, I probably would have been vain enough to enjoy this and think it pampering. Now I just hated it.

"Close your eyes," the man with the makeup told me, setting to work on my eyelids while the man doing my hair poked me with hair pins.

Sabastian admired his wife sitting straight-backed while the men worked on her. He thought Harper needed little improvement, but they were going to be on television—every eye in the Nation would be on him while they scrutinised her, and he wanted every man to envy what he possessed.

The hairdresser sprayed Harper's brown hair, which he had artfully twisted into a French roll and accessorised with a silver and diamond encrusted leaf.

Harper coughed, choking on the thick hairspray in the air while the makeup artist finished applying mascara.

"I just have to do your lipstick, and we'll be all done," he said, pulling out a pale pink lipstick.

Sabastian thought his wife needed something more dramatic to make every man want her lips on theirs. "I want her to wear red lipstick." Sabastian smiled as Harper opened her eyes and looked at him.

The smoky grey eyeshadow and black eyeliner made her

emerald-green eyes look luminescent.

Harper stared at Sabastian for a moment before lowering her head to look at her lap.

Sabastian smiled. He could tell she was trying to form a plan in her head, but he expected that—in fact, he hoped she would try to run. He wanted her to know unreservedly that he was in control and the consequences would be painful if she disobeyed him.

"We are done," the makeup artist said, stepping back with the hairdresser to admire their work. "And might I say, Mr James, you have chosen a most exquisite wife. I'm sure you will be the envy of every man in the country after today's broadcast."

Sabastian smiled at the compliment, offering Harper his hand for her to stand. "I agree, she was a rare find," he said, noticing Harper's jaw clench as she hesitantly took his hand and stood.

Her skin felt warm and silky soft. His wife might not love him, yet, but she would give him beautiful babies, and he would have fun making them with her.

Sabastian walked her out to his waiting car, where four huge men with guns waited.

"This is your personal security detail," Sabastian said. "They have your GPS tracker programmed into their tablets and a remote control for the shock collar."

One of the men held up a small control-device, the same as the one Sabastian had shown her.

"If you try anything, these men have permission to use any force they deem necessary to contain you. If you act in an un-flattering way or disobey me while we are out, you will be rendered unconscious," Sabastian said, opening the passenger door for Harper while two of the guards headed for a black SUV in front of Sabastian's car and the other two went to a waiting SUV behind it.

"You know I don't like you and I will try to escape," Harper calmly commented.

Sabastian grinned viciously, gripping her arm tightly. "I look forward to it," he said, feeling his pants grow tighter. Her defiant nature turned him on.

Harper jerked her arm away and slid into the seat, staring straight ahead. Sabastian closed her door and slid into the driver's seat. After the funeral and his appointment as general, he would have his wife.

North cradled Wolf in his arms between Beth and Birdy while they huddled on the floor of the massive cargo copter. They were among the last of the evacuees to leave Haven.

The first of the Insurgent pilots to fly in had spotted a small two-man copter abandoned on the road. Joe and Lloyd were tasked with flying it out to Home, as they were the only people in the community who had taken part in aeronautical training.

North had no idea where they were heading, but if it were up to him, he would have stayed in Haven to wait for Harper. He sighed with resignation. He had Wolf to consider, and he knew Harper would never forgive him if anything ever happened to their son.

The copter flight took hours, and Wolf fidgeted and fussed in his arms. Wolf was usually a contented baby but was now unsettled without Harper, and whenever Beth or Travis tried to hold him, his bottom lip would quiver and he would start crying. The only person besides North who could settle him was Billy, and he'd fallen asleep, resting his head in Beth's lap.

North felt the cabin pressure change and knew they were descending. Then he caught the smell of the ocean. When the copter touched down, Wolf looked up at him, his eyes wide.

"It's all right," North told him. "You're safe, Daddy won't let anything happen to you."

Wolf let out a tiny coo, as if he understood North's words.

The back of the copter opened, and bright sunlight and hot air flooded in.

"Welcome to the south-east," Joe said, greeting them.

Beth hadn't said anything during the long ride, but it was obvious now that she had been worried about Joe. She let out a sigh of relief at the sight of him and Joe looked relieved to see her too.

North completely understood. He had almost exploded with relief when he'd found Harper. Now she was gone again, leaving him with the emptiness that he felt whenever they weren't together.

North unbuckled and stood with Wolf in readiness to follow Joe and the others out into the hot sun.

Wolf wrinkled his tiny nose. The smell of the ocean was strong here.

Yep, definitely a little Werewolf, North thought, although most Werewolves didn't develop their traits until puberty. North though, had developed them early. He'd been only five years old. North wondered if Wolf's traits came more from him, or more from Harper because she was an Angelic, or both. He considered it while he carried Wolf off the landing pad. He hadn't actually talked to Harper about being an Angelic, and he wasn't sure she even knew what she was. But Sabastian had access to the DNA facilities, so he was almost positive he would know.

A man in his sixties with white hair and wire-rimmed glasses approached. He looked like an utterly forgettable old man with a forgettable face and an average body.

"Everyone, listen up," Joe called out to the twenty or so who disembarked from the copter. "This is Captain Smith."

Even his name was forgettable, North thought of the man

who looked across the crowd, but in that moment, he saw something in the old man's eyes. He had just surveyed everyone and had probably formulated a defence strategy in the event of anyone turning on him. He had the eyes of a wolf, and North knew he hadn't missed a thing.

"Werewolf," North said aloud before he realised.

The older man smiled at him before turning back to the crowd. "Welcome to Home. In case any of you aren't familiar with us, we are the Insurgent stronghold in the south-east of the Nation," Captain Smith explained. "We have set up cabins as best we could at short notice, but I'm afraid you will all be sharing with eight to ten people per cabin. I want to apologise for the meagre accommodations, but until we can gather the materials to build more cabins, we will all be staying in close quarters."

Joe stepped forward with a list and began calling names, pointing people toward their allocated cabins until Beth, Travis, Billy, Lloyd, Blane, Charli, Birdy and North, who was still holding Wolf, stood alone with Joe and the captain.

"We're all bunking in together," Joe said, as he wrapped an arm around Beth and started walking toward the row of cabins.

"If you don't mind," Captain Smith interrupted as everyone turned to look at him. "I would like a few words with these men," he said, pointing to North and Travis.

"Can this wait? It's been a long day and my baby needs a change and a bottle," North said.

"I'll take him," Billy volunteered, knowing Wolf wouldn't fuss for him.

North rooted himself to the ground with his back straight. He didn't want to be separated from Wolf, especially here in this new place.

"He'll be fine. You're as bad as Crash when it comes to separation anxiety—anyone would think you were never going to see him again," Beth said, before a look on her face made her realise what she'd said. "Oh, I didn't mean . . ."

"It's fine. I'm getting her back," North said with conviction, sliding Wolf into Billy's arms.

"We're in cabin eleven at the far end, next to the trees," Joe said, as North watched them walk away for a moment before turning to the captain.

"Joe told me you two are quite the soldiers, and because of you two, there were no fatalities on our side," Smith said.

"They were using tranquiliser bullets," Travis said. "And we were using rifles, plus we had a seven-foot Werewolf going berserk."

North and Travis gave each other a sideways glance.

"Thanks for that, by the way," Travis said.

"It didn't save her," North said solemnly, sliding his gaze back to Smith.

Smith looked intently at them both. "Joe told me about the Harper girl. He said he was fairly certain she was the reason for the attack on Haven."

"Sabastian James is obsessed with her," North told him. "Evidently he'd been hunting her for months."

Captain Smith shifted, looking slightly uncomfortable. "We have something you need to see," he said, then turned crisply and strode toward a large concrete building which was painted in dappled greens, with plants and vines growing from the roof. Camouflage for the well-dressed Insurgent.

Captain Smith led them through to a control room where dozens of people sat at desks tapping on keyboards. The far wall housed a bank of televisions stretching along its entire length. Travis and North both stood for a moment with their mouths open. They had never seen anything like it before.

Smith tapped a woman on the shoulder. "Bring up the media footage from the funeral."

A screen in front of them flickered, and the scene of a

funeral appeared on the screen. The camera panned the crowd, showing men in expensive black suits and women in short black dresses, while a television presenter narrated the scene.

"As you can see by the turn-out, General Lucas was much admired as the leader of the Nation's Defence Network and we know that our new general"—the camera image changed to show Sabastian James—"will continue our great Nation's fine military traditions."

The camera panned out slightly showing a woman with a thick silver collar around her neck, wearing a simple black lace dress. Her head was down, and her brown hair was perfectly arranged into a neat twist. North felt his breath catch. It was Harper.

"As you can see, Mr James, soon to be General James, has brought his beautiful new wife. She looks exquisite in that simple gown and necklace."

Smith switched the television off and turned to North and Travis.

"What the fuck?!" Travis burst out, saying what North was thinking. "Harper was taken this morning and is standing there like nothing happened."

North thought she would have been clawing Sabastian's eyes out or at least trying to escape, but she was just standing there dressed up like a doll.

"Settle down," Smith said. "We had a couple of the tech guys look at the footage and examine the device you pulled out of the other woman. The necklace is a modified shock collar. They said it is likely capable of rendering her unconscious or even killing her, and the GPS device can be tracked almost anywhere in the Nation and has poison in it."

"She's the walking dead if she tries to run. Sabastian would kill her," North said, his heart sinking as the realisation set in.

"We have sent out a surveillance team, but James's house

near the Capital has cutting edge security, and the access codes are encrypted," Smith informed them. "I'm sorry, but we have no idea if or how we can get her out. Then we have the other issue. In about an hour, Sabastian James will become General James and will have the entire army at his beck and call."

North swore.

"We need to get her out of there," Travis ground out through gritted teeth.

"I'm sorry, but we can't just throw our people away just to save one woman," Smith apologised.

"Would you do it for an Angelic?" North asked, his jaw set.

Captain Smith snapped a sharp look at him. "How do you know about Angelics?" he asked.

"Because Harper Crain is an Angelic and the mother of my son," North told him.

Smith took a half a step back. "Are you sure?"

"Ask Beth, Joe's wife, she'll confirm it," North told him.

A stupefied look crossed Travis's face. Obviously, he had no idea.

Smith quirked a wry smile. "If this is true, you must be one hell of a Werewolf."

Chapter Twenty-eight

I stood stone still next to Sabastian with my head down, but it didn't stop people from staring at me. I could feel their glares boring into me, assessing me like a prize cow. It made me sick. These men couldn't give a crap about how a woman felt. Women were objects to possess and throw away when they were tired of them.

Sabastian stood straight-backed and tall beside me. The shock collar remote was discreetly tucked into his palm. I wouldn't give him an excuse to use it, not until I got the GPS tracker out.

I had felt a sharp pin prick of pain in my upper left arm earlier when he grabbed me, and when I looked, there was a small puncture mark. Now I just had to find a way to remove it and the collar.

"You look beautiful today. Lift your head so the crowd can see your face," Sabastian whispered.

I didn't move, although the urge to punch him in the throat was very tempting. No, I wouldn't show him anything I had learned in Haven, not unless I had to, and not with my body-guards and half the Nation watching.

When the funeral service ended, I was ushered to a podium between my hulking guards and Sabastian.

I chanced a furtive peek around and saw Praeses Connelly, the leader of the Nation, looking straight at me, a dirty smirk plain on his wrinkled, old face. I put my head back down. I was jostled into place next to a blonde woman behind Sabastian and Praeses Connelly. I had seen the woman before on television and I knew she was the Praeses's wife. I stole a glimpse at her. She looked tired and withdrawn, standing without emotion, looking at the ground a few metres in front of her. I did the same.

Was she what I would become if I didn't get away?

The crowd of spectators and media men hushed as Praeses Connelly approached the microphone.

"On this day of great sorrow for the loss of one of our Nation's most diligent members, General Lucas, we also celebrate the appointment of our new Head of the Defence Network, General Sabastian James," Praeses Connelly said as Sabastian stepped forward.

The men shook hands while cameras flashed and paparazzi shouted for them to look in their direction.

I closed my eyes and thought of North. He was gone, and I had to find my way back to Wolf.

Praeses Connelly stepped back to the microphone with Sabastian beside him. "We look forward to the future under the protection of our new general. Thank you, that is all."

The two men turned and walked back to where the blonde woman and I stood.

"I hope that wasn't too short, I hate doing speeches," Praeses Connelly said, stopping in front of me.

I could feel his glare boring into me as he reached over and gently ran a fingertip down my arm.

"She's pretty," Connelly said. "Perhaps I could borrow her."

I couldn't believe what I was hearing. I wasn't some poor *Bride of the state* prostitute, I was meant to be Sabastian's wife, although that thought disgusted me as well. My stomach churned with revulsion as the men continued their chat.

"I'm planning for her to bear my children as soon as possible," Sabastian said casually, as if I were a bitch he was breeding for pups.

"I don't blame you. She's got a pretty face, good bone structure and decent hips. I'm sure any daughters she produces will fetch a decent price, and any sons would make excellent soldiers," Connelly said.

The way they spoke so casually about breeding girls to sell while they sent boys off to be killed turned my stomach. None of us, not even their own children, were looked upon as human. We were mere commodities to be bought, swapped and sold.

I tuned out and my mind wandered to thoughts of Wolf and North.

It was strange, but I was sure I could feel North, although it was crazy to think such a thing after I had seen him die.

"So it's settled." Connelly's voice interrupted my thoughts. "You have a lot of work to do, and by the sounds of it you'd better get onto firebombing those mountains before the Insurgents scatter like vermin."

I looked up only to meet Sabastian's smile as he looked me over. I quickly lowered my head again.

"Thank you, my Praeses, I look forward to working with you," Sabastian said before leading me away, surrounded by guards.

"Take Harper back to my house and make sure she is secured," Sabastian ordered, loading me into a car with two of the guards. "I should be home by midnight."

North sat on the step of the little cabin looking up at the stars. It was too hot to sleep, and thoughts of Harper kept running through his head. She had looked so beautiful on the television, but the spark that made her so amazing had gone from her eyes.

What has Sabastian done to her?

The cabin door creaked open and Birdy slipped out. "It's nearly midnight," he said in hushed tones.

"I couldn't sleep," North admitted, feeling useless.

"You know she'll be all right," Birdy told him, leaning against the rail. "Harper is strong."

North dropped his head into his hands. "Sabastian is a sadistic egomaniac, if Harper doesn't do as he wants, he will hurt her."

"You will get her back. I know you will, you don't give up," Birdy said. "Just let me know when you need me."

The ocean wasn't far from the Insurgent camp. North and Birdy sat quietly, listening to the sound of waves breaking for a long time.

North was about to tell Birdy to go to bed when he caught the scent of Captain Smith coming toward them.

"Have you got news?" North asked.

Birdy looked at him in confusion before he suddenly saw the figure emerging from the darkness.

"You'll want to go grab Joe," Smith said solemnly.

Birdy hurried inside, quickly returning with Joe and Travis.

"What's going on?" Joe asked.

"We just got a report that Haven and everything in a twenty-kilometre radius has been firebombed by the army. General James wasted no time ordering the attack once he became Head of Defence," Smith explained. "There are still two surveillance cameras working on the outer perimeters, but by the look of it pretty much everything burned except for a few isolated cabins."

"That fucking bastard," Travis growled. "He isn't content with snatching Harper, he wants us all dead too."

"It's called strategy," North said. "If he takes us out, then there is no one to oppose the government or to fight for Harper."

"The boy has a point," Smith said. "If we didn't evac everyone out when we did, you'd all have been cremated."

North thought about that for a minute, "So Sabastian would now think we are all dead?"

"Most likely," Joe said.

North smiled.

"I'm guessing by that grin you want to use that," Smith said, folding his arms across his chest. "What did you have in mind?"

Sabastian leaned back in the large chair reading the report of the mountain community's firebombing. He'd ordered the air force to strike hard, obliterating the old mountain resort. He had set up copters with heat seeking weapons in a twenty-five-kilometre perimeter, to target any escapees who survived the firebombing and ordered them to stay in place for two hours, but no one had emerged from the forest.

He had annihilated the Insurgents' mountain base and killed them all, including Harper's lover and baby. Now even if she did escape, there would be nothing left for her.

Sabastian stood and stretched. He was going to go home and make love to his wife, or at least fuck her.

Sabastian's phone rang.

"Mr James, I mean General," Sabastian's Head of Security, Neil, stammered. "Mrs James tried to escape and rendered herself unconscious."

Sabastian smiled. "I take it the shock collar fence worked," he said happily.

"Yes, sir, however it might work too well," Neil agreed.

Sabastian felt his smile fade. "What do you mean? She's alive, isn't she?"

"Ahh, yes, sir. It's just when your wife fell unconscious, she was in the shock zone, and it kept shocking her until we pulled her back to the house. The doctor said another thirty seconds and she might have sustained a brain injury."

Sabastian wanted to hurl his phone at the wall and strangle someone. "I'm leaving now. I'll be there in half an hour," he managed to grind out. "And have someone come and fix that fence immediately and have whoever was meant to check it fired."

Sabastian disconnected and hurried home.

His first day as general and he had to rush home to his wife. He felt ridiculous, but the fact was he didn't care. Harper was his, he bought her, and he wanted her kept safe.

Sabastian pulled up in front of his home and rushed inside.

He found Neil, a tall muscular man with coffee brown skin and a buzz cut, standing outside the bathroom door.

"Where is my wife?" Sabastian demanded.

"In the shower," Neil answered, pointing his thumb at the closed door. "She's been in there about ten minutes."

Sabastian pushed past him and tried the handle, locked.

"Harper, open the door," Sabastian said, listening to the sound of the water running, but she didn't respond. "Harper, if you don't open this door, I'll kick it down!"

Still nothing.

Sabastian lifted his foot and with one kick the door flew open.

He saw Harper instantly wrap her arms around her naked body and drop to the shower floor, letting out a high pitch scream, her hair white with soapy bubbles.

"What are you doing?" Harper yelled. "Both of you get out!"

Sabastian suddenly realised Neil was standing behind him, looking at his naked wife in the shower.

"Out!" Sabastian ordered.

Neil quickly turned and left, but Sabastian stayed, closed the door and looked at his wife huddled on the tiled floor.

"Why didn't you answer me when I called out?" Sabastian said, stepping closer to the shower.

Her skin was smooth and wet, making him want to reach out and touch her.

"I was washing my hair. I didn't hear you," she said, sounding short with him.

Sabastian looked down at Harper huddled with her arms and knees tucked up tight, trying to cover herself.

"You tried to escape. I might have to punish you for that." He smiled.

"Kill me, if it makes you feel like a big man," Harper said defiantly.

Sabastian knelt down next to her, the knees of his pants resting on the wet floor while the huge shower head rained down on him and Harper. "Trust me, I have been tempted over the last year, but now I have you, I'm keeping you."

Harper flinched away as Sabastian ran his fingers over her smooth shoulder.

"Don't touch me," Harper snarled.

Sabastian laughed. "You're my wife, I'm expected to touch you," he said, then suddenly grabbed her soapy hair, pulled her to him and kissed her.

Harper struggled against him before biting down hard on his lip.

Sabastian let her go and without thinking, backhanded her across the face. Her head jerked to the side and she let out a small yelp.

He didn't feel bad about making his wife cry as he tasted his own blood and spat it onto the tiles, but if he bruised her face too badly, he wouldn't be able to take her out in public without calling in the makeup artist again.

"Don't ever do that again," he said calmly, watching the soapy bubbles running down the curves of her body for a moment.

He wanted Harper so badly. He could take her here in the shower.

A knock sounded at the door.

"Sir, Praeses Connelly is on the phone for you," Neil's voice called.

Sabastian thought about deferring the call, but it was his first night as general.

"I'll be right there," Sabastian called while he stood up, dripping wet in his expensive suit.

His pleasure with Harper would have to wait just a little longer.

Chapter Twenty-nine

My throat hurt as I stood looking at myself in the bath-room mirror, not recognising the makeup covered face looking back at me. I'd wanted to see if Sabastian was bluffing about the shock collar fence. I found the markers in the garden not far from the house, but when I tried to pass through them, the pain gripped me so suddenly and tightly that I couldn't move. My throat had contracted, choking me until I'd passed out. I had woken looking up at a dark-skinned guard and an ugly man in his forties or fifties with a nose that said he drank too much. He had told me he was a doctor, although the smile he gave when his stethoscope slid over my left breast to check my heartbeat made me think he was a pervert instead.

I needed to figure out a way to get out of here, to get away, to find Wolf and bury North.

Tears slid down my cheeks. My beautiful North. I had been so stupid, so selfish. If I hadn't run away, we could have had so much more time together. Instead he was dead, and our son was alone in the world.

I wrapped my arms around myself and sobbed quietly, even though something inside me said he wasn't dead, that he was alive. I would hold onto that. I needed to.

I stopped. My arms were still wrapped around myself as I felt something under my fingertip. I squeezed my left arm with my right hand, it had to be the tracker under my skin. I needed to get that thing out of me.

I dug through the drawers and found a shaver. I hurriedly pulled it apart and nicked my finger. Shit, if anyone saw blood, they'd tell Sabastian, and he'd have me examined. I wiped the drop of blood off the counter, hurriedly turned on the water in the shower and undressed

I stood for a few minutes trying to build up courage, the razor blade poised in my hand.

"Come on Harper," I told myself. "Cut it out before he decides to poison you."

I pressed the razor hard against my skin above the small hard lump, clenched my teeth and sliced a one centimetre slit into my arm. It stung, making me bite back a groan. Blood mixed with water, forming a rusty orange river down my arm as I squeezed. A tiny object slid from the hole and I caught it before it could wash away. I still needed Sabastian to think I had the tracker in me. If he knew I had cut it out, he would implant another one somewhere I couldn't reach.

A bang sounded on the door.

"Harper," Sabastian's voice called.

I dropped the razor on the floor putting my foot on it to cover it while I quickly tucked the tracker under the metal collar around my neck. I grabbed the shampoo and began desperately lathering my bloody arm and hair to cover up what I had been doing.

"Harper, if you don't open this door, I'll kick it down!" Sabastian yelled.

I lathered more soap onto my arm and into my hair.

The door suddenly crashed open, I grabbed my arm, covering the cut while Sabastian and one of the guards looked at me.

I dropped to the ground. "What are you doing? Both of you get out!" I yelled, trying to cover my body. I didn't have to fake embarrassment or outrage, at least.

Sabastian turned, looking at the guard as if he hadn't realised he was standing there. "Out!" he ordered.

The guard stepped back, and Sabastian closed the door,

leaving us alone in the bathroom. I don't know which would have been scarier — being naked and alone with Sabastian, or being in a room full of hungry lions.

"Why didn't you answer me when I called out?" Sabastian asked, moving toward me.

He frightened me. I wanted to curl into a ball and shrink to the size of an ant.

"I was washing my hair and didn't hear you," I lied.

Sabastian stopped so close that his black shoes were only centimetres away. I didn't look up, but I could feel him looking down at me.

"You tried to escape." I could hear the amusement in his voice, as he knelt down beside me in the running water, still wearing his suit. "I might have to punish you for that."

I didn't want to play his sick games. "Kill me, if it makes you feel like a big man."

"Trust me, I have been tempted over the last year," Sabastian said as if it were funny. "But I have you now, and I'm keeping you."

He reached over and touched my shoulder.

I jerked away. "Don't touch me."

Sabastian laughed. "You're my wife, I'm expected to touch you," he said. Then his face turned serious, he grabbed my hair, pulled me to him and kissed me. I struggled, trying to pull away, but he was stronger than me. I bit his bottom lip.

Sabastian released my hair and backhanded me across the face, sending me off balance as my foot slipped and I felt the razor dig into my heel.

A small cry of pain broke from my lips.

"Don't ever do that again," he told me calmly, spitting blood onto the tiles in front of me.

I was sure he was going to force himself on me right here in the shower. I thought about grabbing the razor blade to slit his throat.

A knock sounded at the door.

"Sir, Praeses Connelly is on the phone for you," I heard the guard call out as I glanced up into Sabastian's dark-blue eyes. There was some sort of calculation going on behind them, it had the hair on the back of my neck standing on end.

"I'll be right there," Sabastian said, looking me over as he stood in his soaking wet clothes, before he turned on his heel and left the bathroom, closing the door behind him.

I waited a moment before lifting my foot to see a cut, dripping blood. Shit. But at least the one on my arm wasn't running like a faucet anymore. I quickly washed my hair out and stepped from the shower, drying myself before sliding the razor blade under the bottom drawer in the cabinet to hide it. I might still need it again, and I certainly didn't want Sabastian or a guard to find it. I wrapped the towel around myself and found a plaster to put on my foot then cleaned up the drops of blood from the floor. I checked that the small tracker was still securely tucked between my shock collar and skin.

"Are you all right in there?" I heard the guard call through the door.

"Umm, I need clothes," I called back, realising I had none except the black dress I had worn to the funeral.

I heard the guard mumbling something which sounded derogatory toward women. A few minutes later there was a brief knock on the door before it opened a fraction and a set of pale mint green silk pyjamas slid onto the floor. I pulled on the pants and top and stepped out into the hallway, trying not to limp.

"Your husband wants you to be taken to his office. He is working," my guard announced, leading me down the hallway.

I hadn't actually spoken to the guard directly, but maybe if I befriended him, he might only shoot me in the leg if I tried to escape his custody and not the head.

"What's your name?" I asked.

The man glanced at me, looking unsure. "Neil."

"It is nice to meet you, Mr Neil. I'm sure you will do an excellent job watching over me," I smiled my most charming smile.

Neil didn't say anything, but I saw him stand just a little taller. I would have to work on him.

He stopped in front of a set of doors and motioned for me to go inside.

Sabastian was sitting at a large desk talking on the phone when I walked in. He waved his hand toward a lounge in the centre of the room, motioning me to sit, so I did. He typed something into his computer while I watched him bring up government files. I had seen computers before, but I had never used one. They were off limits to women.

Sabastian typed commands into the keyboard, and more things popped onto the screen, showing information about the Defence Network, while a map of the Nation sat in the corner with red dots blinking on it. I was sure the red dots were people who had the GPS trackers implanted. It suddenly made me very aware of the tiny lump pressed against my throat and the fact I could feel it with every heartbeat pulsing up my neck.

"Yes, of course, Irving," he said glancing over at me.

I dropped my gaze while he turned back and began typing again. It didn't look difficult to use, and I was sure I would be able to figure it out if I watched him for a while. Maybe I could use the map to find my way back to Haven, to North and Wolf.

Sabastian disconnected and punched something into the computer before pressing another button. The screen went blank while Sabastian stretched his arms.

"I think it is time for us to go to bed," he casually said, as I felt my eyes widen. He laughed. "Don't worry your beautiful head, you aren't going to bed with me tonight, you have your own room."

He moved to the door, motioning me to follow.

I wasn't sure if this was another one of his games, but if he tried anything, I would do my best to kill him.

I stood and followed him out into the hallway where Neil was waiting. They walked me down the hall, Sabastian beside me and Neil behind.

"My room is next to yours, and there will be a guard at your door," Sabastian informed me, leaving out *if you try to escape, you will either be rendered unconscious or killed.*

We stopped in front of a door as something sharp stabbed my neck. My legs instantly went to jelly. Sabastian caught me as I began to fall just as I registered Neil had a syringe in his hand.

The bastard had drugged me. I was really going to have to work on befriending him.

"Good night, my Angel," I heard Sabastian say while everything slipped into darkness.

North watched Wolf sucking on his bottle. Beth had offered to feed him, but North felt closest to Harper when he held their son. He was so scared he wouldn't find her in time or that Sabastian was doing horrible things to her.

Joe sat down next to him on the small lounge chair. The cabin was a tight fit with so many people having to share, but only Billy seemed to mind not having his own space.

"Captain Smith wants us over at the command centre this morning. He said he wants to talk to anyone who is willing to fight against the government," Joe said.

"Is he planning to attack them?" North asked.

"He wouldn't do it directly, that would be suicide," Travis interrupted.

"Do you know any of the targets?" North asked Joe.

"That's what Smith wants to talk about," Joe explained.

North looked at Wolf.

"Don't worry about him," Beth said, reading his thoughts. "Blane, Lloyd, Billy and I will be here to look after him."

"Where's Charli and Birdy?" North questioned, realising they were missing.

"They've already left for basic training early this morning," Beth said, gently freeing Wolf from his arms. "Now off you go. If we need you, I'll send Billy over to the command centre."

North had come to realise there was no point arguing with Beth. When she made up her mind it was set in iron and come hell or high water she wouldn't budge.

North kissed Wolf's head, whispered, "I love you" and followed Joe and Travis over to the large camouflaged building with the plants growing on the roof.

North smelled Captain Smith before he saw him. He was standing in front of a small crowd of men and women, some of whom he recognised, while others were strangers. But the thing that surprised him most was that he could smell three other Unholys in the room, one of which he recognised. He knew that scent.

"North," a tall broad blond man called with a smile. He pushed his way through the crowd toward North and caught him up in a fierce, joyous hug. "I heard a new Unholy flew in from Haven, but no one told me it was you."

"I guess you two know each other," Travis interrupted.

North broke from the hug. "Travis, Joe, this is Dace, my older brother."

Joe extended his hand. "Nice to meet you. If you're half the man your brother is, we'll get along just fine."

"So he grew out of his bratty stage," Dace joked.

"No, he's still an asshole," Travis shrugged. "But he's an

asshole I can call a friend."

North rolled his eyes with a smile. "Back at you."

"I'm glad to hear it." Dace grinned. "You always were the one I worried about, even though you have the strongest half-form I've ever seen. You just never seemed to want to connect with people."

The lights flickered on and off as Captain Smith moved to the front of the room. "Can I have everyone's attention?" Smith called and the room quieted. "Thank you for coming. As everyone must know by now, General James's first act as the new Head of Defence was to firebomb the Haven community last night, leaving a forty-kilometre-wide black-spot on the side of the mountain. We are grateful for the quick thinking of the community's leaders and to our pilots for getting everyone out safely. We had no loss of life."

Everyone clapped politely while North shifted uncomfortably. He was anxious to get back to Wolf, but he wanted to know if they had any more information on Harper.

"We have been sent intel that indicates that Praeses Connelly has already signed off on a list of changes to the Defence Network after James's new appointment, starting with mandatory military service for all men, the carrot being only men who have served get wives. All women and soldiers must have the GPS tracker imbedded," Smith said, holding up a glass cylinder with a tiny white tracker in it. "Our tech people found this GPS device has not only got a tracker in it, but a heart monitor and a lethal dose of poison that can be remotely activated."

"Shit, if someone hacks the system, thousands of people could just drop dead." Joe said

A hushed murmur went through the small crowd.

"That's part of what we're worried about. The other thing is, at this point we believe only a select few people have the access codes, and the poison is almost undetectable. We suspect General Lucas may have been killed in this way," Smith continued as an image of James injecting Lucas for a media event flashed on the big screen.

"So, Sabastian James or Praeses Connelly can potentially commit mass murder on a whim?" North asked.

"Essentially, yes," Smith said. "Our man on the inside has informed us that General James keeps a computer in his home that contains the access codes to the entire government network which he has been working on linking into one mainframe."

"That place is locked up tighter than the government's own headquarters. We'll never get in," a man in the front row commented.

Smith nodded solemnly. "Yes, but we already have someone on the inside — we just have to make contact."

North had a sinking feeling in his gut.

"The general's own wife is one of our own. If we can make contact with her, she might be able to access the files we need," Smith explained.

North fought not to explode with anger. Harper was already in danger, and now he wanted to risk her life for some files.

"How do you plan to get her and the information out?" Travis asked, his voice cold.

"We have been told there will be a dinner at the James's mansion to celebrate the new general's appointment. Praeses Connelly, as well as every department head, will be there," Smith explained. "We have several members who have already infiltrated the security, including some wait staff, but none have access to the general's private quarters. that's why we need to contact Harper James."

North wanted to rip the captain's head off for referring to Harper as Sabastian's wife. She'd never chosen him to be her husband. Sabastian had bought her, which in North's eyes made her his slave.

"We will need several teams for surveillance and recovery. Do we have any volunteers?" Smith asked.

North instantly raised his hand, followed by Travis and Joe.

"Good," Smith said before Dace and several more hands were raised. "Can those who have volunteered please remain behind? Everyone else can go back to work."

North stood stiff-backed while the crowd filed out of the room.

Dace leaned toward North. "I've seen pictures of Mrs James. She is smoking hot. I wouldn't mind rescuing her, if you know what I mean," Dace joked.

Travis chuckled. "She would tear you to pieces."

Dace raised an eyebrow.

"Harper is the mother of my son," North said flatly.

Dace stared at North for a moment. "Since when do you have a kid?"

"Since about a month ago," North told him.

"And you had it with James's wife?" Dace burst out laughing. "She must be hell in bed, if you were that stupid."

North felt his anger growing and he tried to keep it in check.

"Is the general's wife's bastard kid here?"

"Your nephew's name is Wolf, and yes, he's here," he growled through gritted teeth.

Dace laughed louder, "Wolf? Really? I thought you hated being an Unholy. Maybe you should have called him Doggy or Pooch."

North snapped, his right arm shifted into his half-form and his clawed hand whipped out, gripped his brother around the neck, and lifted him off the ground before he could react. "Don't you ever talk about my son or Harper like that again," North snarled, the sound of a savage wolf escaping him.

"Put him down," Captain Smith ordered calmly.

North hesitated for a moment, then finally lowered Dace to the ground and released him.

Dace rubbed his neck and smiled. "I told you he has the best half-form, but you just have to get him riled up first."

Smith smiled. "I'm sorry about that, North, but when your brother found out you were here in Home, he insisted you would be the best person for the upcoming mission. I just couldn't see it until he managed to piss you off. Guess it takes a family member to know how to do that properly." Smith paused, looking thoughtful. "I've never seen anyone turn just one part of themselves before. You must have amazing control over your transformation."

North looked daggers at Dace.

"I'm sorry about that, but you should have known I would never disrespect family, North, and I look forward to meeting my nephew," Dace apologised.

North knew Dace was right. Dace had always stuck up for him and his family when they were growing up, and he was the one who'd helped and supported him when he started to change at five years old.

"So assholism runs in the family," Travis said. "Good to know."

Joe smiled. "That's where you inherited it, along with your mother's sarcasm and quick wit."

Captain Smith clapped his hands together and rubbed them. "Okay, let's get started. North, Travis, do either of you know how to pilot a copter?"

CHAPTER THIRTY

Sabastian watched Harper's red light and heartbeat monitor on his screen. The heartbeat was regular, but not as defined as he would have liked. He assumed the GPS must have been out of alignment, although he could see she was still in her bed asleep. A good thing, really — he had an entire military force to overhaul, a presidential dinner to plan, and an Insurgent movement to crush.

He had thought about postponing the dinner, but it was tradition, and it gave him a reason to show Harper off. He'd already had Praeses Connelly and several other heads of departments ask for her time, but Sabastian wasn't going to share. He resented the fact that his wife had a baby with another man. He wouldn't risk that ever happening again.

Sabastian stood and began to pace across his office. He wanted to kill the sonofabitch that had dared to touch his wife, but he'd probably already done so in the firebombing, as well as killing the baby.

Perhaps he should have found the baby before he ordered the firebombing — after all, it would have had Harper's Angelic blood. *No.* She was his, and her only children would be his, because she belonged to him and only him.

Sabastian walked down the hall past Neil into Harper's room.

Harper lay on the bed in pale green silk pyjamas. Her brown hair looked a mess, and her face was squished against the pillow. Sabastian thought every woman should look her best at all times, but despite Harper's imperfections, he thought she looked absolutely stunning. The thought shocked him. He had thought Harper not just beautiful, but stunning. He had never used that word to describe anyone or anything in his life, but his wife truly was.

Sabastian closed the bedroom door and slipped off his shirt and shoes before sliding into the bed beside her. Harper moved slightly, snuggling against him, and he froze. She was still asleep, but the touch of her made him want to just hold her while he watched her sleep. He gently wrapped an arm around her as she wriggled closer, resting her head against his chest.

He had been intimate with women, many, many women, but not like this. This was different. Her skin smelled warm and fresh like her, and the very scent was comforting. Harper shifted slightly, her hair tickling Sabastian's chest, but he didn't want to move in case he woke her. He liked this. He liked his wife in his arms.

Sabastian closed his eyes, inhaling her scent as he held his wife against him.

I was so tired when I felt North slip into bed beside me. His usually warm body felt cool to the touch. I snuggled closer, trying to warm him with my own heat while he wrapped an arm around me, pulling me close. I rested my head on his bare chest and listened to his heartbeat.

Something about his touch and the sound of his heart was wrong. I didn't feel the usual electric buzz, and his heart didn't sound the same, but I was too tired to think clearly. North's breath slowed, and I could tell he was drifting off to sleep.

A memory suddenly flashed in my head and the sleep-filled haze evaporated. I wasn't with North. I was in Sabastian's house. I opened my eyes and looked down the length of the body my head was resting on — it wasn't North, it was Sabastian.

Sabastian was in bed with me, holding me. I wanted to scramble out of his arms and vomit, but I was too scared to move. If I did, he might know I was awake and expect other things, but if I stayed where I was, he might think I was accepting of him being in my bed. No, he would think me drugged out.

I lay perfectly still, listening to his breaths deepen while mine grew shallower. I thought being so evil, he would smell like fire and brimstone, but he smelled of sandalwood and sweet musk. I couldn't understand how a man as handsome and smart as Sabastian, who smelled so nice, could be so evil.

Most women would think him a perfect husband — if only they knew.

I started thinking about that. If I could just show the Nation how horrible and cruel he was, maybe the people would start really seeing him and not just what he wanted them to see. Maybe they'd look at the entire government and Praeses Connelly with different eyes. Perhaps I could find something on his computer or in his office that would show the world that our system of government was wrong. Oppressive. That selling women to the highest bidders and excluding the Unholy wasn't right.

I carefully and slowly slipped from Sabastian's arms, being careful not to wake him, thanking my lucky stars I was still fully dressed in the silk pyjamas.

I crept from the room to find Neil standing in the hallway.

"Good morning," I whispered, so as not to wake Sabastian as I pulled the door shut behind me, stopping just short of making it click.

"Where is Mr James?" Neil questioned, folding his huge muscular arms across his chest.

"Sleeping," I told him, inching the door open for him to see

Sabastian lying on the bed.

"You didn't kill him, did you?"

I innocently raised my eyebrows. "I'm a woman, and I don't think women possess the strength or skill it would take to kill a man, especially one of General James's calibre."

Neil looked me over, assessing me and shrugged. "Yeah, women haven't got the stomach to kill people. You're all too delicate."

Thank goodness for chauvinistic idiots. If I did manage to kill Sabastian, Neil would likely tell the authorities I was too delicate to commit such a crime.

I had killed the hideous skinny man at the farmhouse with a knife to the throat and shot several men in Haven, but they were all in the heat of the moment. I didn't think I would be able to kill even Sabastian in cold blood so easily.

"Would you be able to show me to the kitchen please?" I smiled.

Neil led the way, standing in the doorway while I poured two cups of coffee.

"How many sugars do you take?" I asked.

"I'm on duty," Neil told me flatly.

"And I am the lady of the house and I am offering you coffee, I think it only polite to take it, don't you?"

Neil shifted uncomfortably. "Two," he finally said, while I spooned in the sugar and stirred before adding the milk and handing it to him.

I leaned against the bench with my coffee. "Are you married, Mr Neil?"

"No, I am saving up to buy a wife. I already have a house and some money in the bank, but it isn't enough to buy a decent wife."

I smiled, even though the thought of selling women like slaves made me sick to the stomach. Worse, if the woman wasn't pretty enough, she was offered at a cheap price which many men considered *bargain basement* and wouldn't touch, leaving them to become Brides of the state.

"I'm sure you will find an excellent companion when the time is right."

Neil smiled and sipped his coffee.

I was about to start questioning him about security on the property when Sabastian strode into the kitchen. His hair was a little tousled, but it made him look less arrogant and more approachable. He was a handsome sonofabitch.

Neil put his cup down and stood straight.

I smiled politely. "Coffee?"

Sabastian surveyed me for a moment before glancing at Neil, who quickly retreated from the kitchen.

Sabastian looked back to me. "Is it poisoned?"

I smiled, poured him a cup and sipped it before handing it over to him. "No, but if you have any spare arsenic, I can put it in there for you."

"Harper," Sabastian growled.

"I learned my lesson," I interrupted. "I won't try to escape again," I told him, lowering my head in the submissive wife gesture. "I am your wife, and I belong to you."

Sabastian smiled at me, and I fought the urge to step back. "I'm glad you have accepted that. I'm sure you will find you'll be happy here."

I kept my head down. I would play his games if it meant I could have my freedom again.

Sabastian slowly sipped his coffee. I felt him watching me while I did the same.

"We will be hosting a dinner party in a few days with around a hundred and fifty guests," Sabastian said.

I momentarily forgot my act and looked up at him.

He smiled. "Don't worry, I'm not going to tell you to cook for them, but I need to go into work today, and I want you to meet with the florist, caterers and an entertainment director."

I bit my bottom lip. I'd wanted to have free run of the house so I could snoop, not to arrange dinner parties for assholes with too much power.

Sabastian frowned at me. "What is it?"

"I've never arranged anything like that before," I told him. "What if I do something wrong?"

He laughed and it sounded real. "You just have to meet them, point them in the direction of the hall and look pretty."

"You have a hall?"

Sabastian looked amused. "I have to go. Ask Neil if you have any questions." He sat his cup down, grabbed the front of my silk top, pulled me up against him, and kissed me.

I fought the urge to grab a kitchen knife and stab him, but instead I kissed him back, hating myself for it. I would have to brush my teeth and gargle acid to wash my mouth out later.

He pulled away and smiled down at me. "That's more like it," he said, tucking a loose strand of hair behind my ear before leaving me alone in the kitchen.

I will kill him one of these days, I promised myself. *But for now, I have to be smart.*

I knew he would be watching my GPS tracker, so I would play the good wife and bide my time, at least for a few days until I figured out the security stuff and worked out an escape plan.

CHAPTER THIRTY-ONE

North sat in the copter simulator, bringing it in to land for the thousandth time. It had been three days since the meeting, and he had only crashed the copter the first two times on landing. Since then it had been textbook landings all the way. He knew Harper was a fast study, but he was, too.

"Good job," the instructor said while North finished the shutdown procedure and unbuckled his belt.

North glanced over at Travis in the other simulator and could tell immediately he was coming in too fast. Travis had only landed the copter safely a dozen times and wasn't picking it up as quickly as North.

"Pull up," North said. "You're coming in too quick."

Travis twisted the throttle control inboard to drop the RPMs and worked the pedals furiously to adjust the pitch. The copter slowed before it hit the ground, a little too hard, but it didn't crash.

"This is fucking ridiculous," Travis complained, jerking off his harness without shutting the simulator down. "We've been at this for three days when we should be in the Capital finding a way to rescue Harper. I thought you would want to help her instead of playing on these fucking toys," Travis growled and made to storm off.

North grabbed Travis by the neck, slamming him into the wall. "Don't you dare. I am doing whatever I am told so I can get her back. If I have to become the best pilot, I will. If they tell me to jump out of a copter fourteen-thousand feet up, I will. If they tell me to swim a hundred kilometres in shark infested sewage, I'd do it twice," North snapped. "I will do anything I am told if it gives me even the remotest chance of getting her back. And what are you doing? You're fucking around. They won't put you on the mission if you won't even try to follow orders."

Dace walked into the room and leaned against the wall next to Travis. "Put him down, North."

North released Travis and stepped back.

Travis looked ready to kill somebody.

"Captain Smith wants to see you both," Dace said casually and walked out, North and Travis in tow.

When they walked in, Captain Smith looked up from where he sat at a large wooden desk, to peer at them from between stacks of paper and a computer. Dace took a position against the wall while Travis and North stood awkwardly in the centre of the room.

"When I was asked to help start a revolution, I didn't think there would be so much paperwork," Smith complained. "If I have to do one more inventory list or payroll schedule, I'm going to bump myself back down to a foot soldier and let someone else do all the bureaucratic bullshit."

Dace chuckled. "You love this shit. You just hate the computer."

"The darn thing keeps telling me there's an *error,* but not what the *error* is," Smith complained.

Dace pushed himself off the wall, walked around the desk, looked at the computer over Smith's shoulder then leaned over him and tapped a button. "You had the *caps lock* on."

Smith swore a few times and turned to Travis and North. "I hear you're both flying the simulator just fine, but only North's landing it."

Travis looked at him defiantly. "Well, if we need a pilot, use North."

"I wanted to have everyone going on this mission to be able

to fly if needed. If you run into trouble, the first one to the copter would be the pilot," Smith explained. "Just like the first one to run into trouble would be expected to take out the threat."

Travis dropped his gaze like a chastised kid.

"I know you are both capable soldiers, I've seen you in the training yard."

North and Travis had smashed each other across the training yard, barely holding back as they took their frustrations out on each other. They had spent every spare minute either in the flight simulator or the training yard, while Beth and Lloyd watched over Wolf with Blane and Billy. Billy was keen to join them, but Beth told him she needed his help, which was code for *I'm your mother and you're not fighting with the big boys.*

Smith looked to Dace. "We want to make sure we have people in place before James's dinner party, so Dace is taking a team to the Capital to meet up with the Insurgents there."

North held his breath.

"He wants you two on the team." Smith continued.

North could have hugged his brother, before he realised he was going to have to leave Wolf behind.

"When do we leave?" North asked.

"In a couple of hours," Dace said, his face solemn. "You might want to go hug my nephew."

North understood what he hadn't said — *You might want to go say goodbye, because you may not be coming back.*

North hurried back to the cabin with Travis, neither of them saying a word, but Travis made it through the door first and picked up Wolf. North realised Travis loved Wolf as much as he did, and he probably loved Harper that much as well. North was just the lucky man who captured her heart, and he knew it. Harper was smart, beautiful and had *something* that people were drawn to. North wasn't sure if it was to do with her Angelic DNA or because Harper was just Harper.

Travis kissed the top of Wolf's head and handed him to North. Wolf gurgled, cooed and smiled up at his dad.

"Daddy and Uncle Travis are going to go get your mummy back," North told him. "If all goes well, we'll be back by Sunday."

I pulled on a simple powder-blue dress and went downstairs to have my hair and makeup done. It was now almost a routine. Sabastian chose everything I was to wear and had John the hairstylist and Bert the makeup artist come in every morning before anyone could see me looking normal. Only Sabastian, Neil and a few of the house staff ever saw me without a full face of makeup and my hair done. It was like Sabastian wanted me to be a living doll that he could show off to the world. I didn't care. I was getting good at playing his game and avoiding him, but I had still been subjected to the evening tranquiliser and had found him in my bed three mornings in a row now. He hadn't tried to do anything other than sleep beside me, but it still creeped me out.

I'd sat watching Sabastian work at his computer for a few hours yesterday and was fairly confident if I had ten minutes alone with the device I could get into the entire network. He hadn't been careful when accessing his new security system or when he was working on the government files. He probably didn't think I could remember the codes or that I could even use a computer, which I couldn't, yet.

I sat down in the chair, allowing John and Bert to work on my hair and makeup.

"Did you hear about Praeses Connelly's wife? Kevin was doing her hair a few days ago, and she's going bald," John gossiped. "She had a big patch out of the back of her head, poor dear, and she hasn't even given the Praeses any children."

"I know, it's such a shame, I liked her," Bert said, as if she were already gone.

"I did, too. Her colouring and height suited the Praeses so nicely. He's going to find it hard to get another one that does that so well," John said, as if talking about a pair of pants or a suit.

Bert focused his attention on me, dabbing skin-coloured concealer around my eyes. "Oh dear, you look tired," he said, before turning to Neil. "Be a dear and go get Mrs James some coffee."

Neil looked at him, curling his lip into a sneer. "I'm a bodyguard, not a servant."

"Our great general will most likely be getting out of the shower about now, and Mrs James looks like she's had a bad night in hell. If I don't get her makeup on and make her look fresh and awake before he gets down here, then I'm blaming you," Bert scolded, reminding me of my mother's tone when I wouldn't do as I was told.

Neil made a disgusted face and marched into the kitchen.

Bert waited a minute before he spoke in a hushed voice. "We are from the Insurgents. People are coming to rescue you, just not yet. We need you to access James's home computer and upload everything on it to our home base computer."

I smiled at him. "This is a joke, right, did my husband put you up to this?" I half-laughed—if Sabastian thought he was going to trick me into revealing myself and my plans, he was wrong.

"We were told to tell you *the baby Wolf is safe and sound at Home.* I don't know what it means, but I was told you would," John whispered over my shoulder while he tugged at my hair.

Relief flooded through me—Wolf was alive and safe.

Sabastian didn't know about him, and if he did, he certainly wouldn't know his name.

"Was there a message with North in it?" I asked, anxious to know.

Both men looked confused and shook their heads. "There was nothing about a compass."

My heart sank a little. I had been so sure he was alive that I would have bet my life on it, but now it felt like I had been slugged with a sledgehammer. I wanted to cry.

"What do you need me to do?" I asked, but before they could answer, Neil returned with my coffee.

"You need to use extra conditioner," John said, as if answering a different question. "It will help with the tangles."

"Your coffee, Mrs James," Neil said, handing me the mug.

"Thank you, Mr Neil. You are so kind. You are going to make some lucky woman very happy," I said, laying it on thick.

Neil blushed a little while Bert and John worked on my hair and makeup.

"Mr Neil is saving for a wife," I told Bert as he brushed powder across my nose. "He already has a house."

"Oh, that's wonderful," Bert gushed. "Do you like the brunettes or blondes?"

Neil looked a little embarrassed. "Actually, I like strawberry blondes."

I looked at the big dark-skinned man and smiled. "I think a strawberry blonde would look good on your arm."

Neil grinned as he opened his mouth to say something, then Sabastian walked in. Neil shut his mouth, killing the conversation.

I took a sip of my coffee. "Good morning. I trust you slept well," I said, leaving out *you fucking weird, perverted sonofabitch, how dare you drug me and climb into my bed while I'm unconscious?*

"Yes, thank you," Sabastian answered without emotion

before turning to John and Bert. "I am taking my wife to lunch in the city today. Make sure she looks her best."

"General James." Bert smiled. "Your wife is already perfection—I'm not sure if I can improve on that."

Sabastian looked down at me, took my hand and kissed it. "I know," he said, then wandered into the kitchen.

He was taking me out of the house—maybe I could find a way to escape. If I got rid of the GPS tracking device, he wouldn't be able to track me.

I felt like I was in a no-win situation. If Sabastian caught me trying to run, he would zap me, and he'd never take me out of the house or trust me enough to leave me alone ever again. But if I didn't try to escape, when would I get another chance? I wasn't sure what I should do, but I had to have faith that the Insurgents had a plan that didn't end up with me dead and Wolf motherless.

"So, Mr Neil," I said to distract myself. "Have you started looking for a wife yet?"

"I have had a look on the DNA website, but I haven't seen any I'm keen on. If I could find one like you with strawberry blonde hair, I'd be a happy man."

"I don't think there is another one out there like my wife." Sabastian smiled while he leaned against the doorframe with a cup in his hand. "She is unique."

He looked casually handsome in his black dress-pants and cream-coloured long-sleeve shirt with the sleeves pushed up to his elbows. It showed off his broad shoulders that narrowed to his firm flat stomach. His dark hair was still wet from his shower and neatly combed while his dark-blue eyes assessed me

I lazily sipped my coffee, then looked over at Sabastian while John pinned my hair up.

"Do you have a lunch meeting?" I asked. "Should I change into something more formal?"

Sabastian looked at my plain dress. "No, you look perfect." He smiled, and for a moment his dark eyes softened, revealing the man beneath them and not the cruel monster I knew lurked within.

Bert brushed my eyelashes with mascara while John sprayed my hair with hairspray.

"You look gorgeous as always, Mrs James," Bert gushed, stepping back to hold up a mirror.

My makeup was done more subtly than the previous days and my hair was in a simple bun. Overall I didn't look showy or like a millionaire's wife, but more like me.

"General James, is this what you had in mind?" Bert asked.

Sabastian's lips curved. "Yes."

"Very good," Bert said, starting to pack up his makeup kit.

I had to figure out how I could get some alone time with Bert and John without Neil or Sabastian around.

"Sabastian," I said softly as he looked at me. "Could I please ask Mr Bert and Mr John to give me some lessons on how I can do my makeup and hair the way you like it?"

Sabastian shot a glance at John and Bert, then back at me. "When?"

"Perhaps they could start teaching me tomorrow morning when they come in," I suggested. "After a week or so of lessons, I may only need them to come in on special occasions."

"The dinner is the night after tomorrow," Sabastian said, offering me his hand to stand. "But I guess it wouldn't hurt for you to learn how to present yourself, and it will keep you occupied."

I smiled and took his hand. "Thank you."

Sabastian leaned in close to my ear and whispered. "You look beautiful, as always."

His warm breath rolled down my neck, sending goose bumps across my skin. It wasn't an entirely unpleasant sensation, just strange.

Sabastian could smell Harper's scent as he leaned into her and whispered in her ear. "You look beautiful, as always." And he meant it.

He had intended to sleep in his own bed, but found himself tossing and turning until he had slipped in beside Harper and she cuddled into his side. He had slept beside her every night and hadn't once tried to do any more than that, even though he desperately wanted to. He would have forced any other woman to make love to him by now, but not his wife — she was different.

Harper made him feel almost giddy whenever she looked at him and when she said his name in her soft voice, his knees felt weak.

Sabastian still wasn't an idiot. He didn't trust Harper not to run if he took her out in public. Today was a test. He would give her the opportunity, and if she did, he'd simply hunt her down. He had already checked the GPS tracker before he came downstairs, noting that the device wasn't working as well as he had planned. The hormone detector wasn't working at all, and though the heartbeat monitor was still active, it wasn't as strong as he'd hoped for. He wondered if perhaps he'd put too many complex functions into the tiny device and was glad he hadn't added the audio transmitter, or it mightn't have worked at all. He would deal with it after the dinner. until then he still had the GPS which functioned perfectly.

Harper's eyes went wide as Sabastian led her out to his waiting copter.

"Are we going in that?" she asked while he opened the door for her.

Sabastian smiled. "I hope you don't mind — it is easier than taking the car." He left out that it was also easier to track her from the air if she ran.

Harper slid onto the seat, and Sabastian reached across her to do up the seatbelt.

She smelled so good that he considered taking her back inside to do what he had been imagining from the first day he saw her in the elevator at the DNA sequencing facility. That was a year ago. He'd never been so patient with anyone before.

"Is it too tight?" Sabastian asked, tightening the straps. He was so close he could have kissed her.

Harper shook her head while Neil and a second guard climbed into the back seat

Sabastian forced himself to take a step back, closed the door and walked around the nose of the copter. He slid into his seat, started the engine and went through the pre-flight sequence ready for take-off. Harper watched him carefully as if in awe, and he felt his ego swell. She was watching him.

The copter shifted slightly as it lifted, and Harper gripped the seatbelt straps at her chest, eyes wide.

"There is nothing to worry about, I am an experienced pilot," Sabastian said, lifting the copter straight up until they were above the mansion and trees.

Harper glanced out the window for a moment, looking around before looking back to him for reassurance. Sabastian liked this. He liked her looking at him for comfort instead of with disdain.

"Are you all right?" Sabastian asked, moving the stick and the copter started forward.

"We are so high," Harper managed to mumble.

"Don't worry, we won't be up here for long. We should be in the Capital in about ten minutes," he told her while her gaze was fixed out over the hills at the concrete buildings, growing larger on the horizon.

Sabastian had thought Harper might have a *woman's moment* and burst into hysteria, but she looked awestruck instead. This made him admire her even more. He had seen grown men tremble like jelly at half this altitude, but the longer Harper was up in the air, the more relaxed she appeared.

"Do you want to go higher?" Sabastian asked, testing the waters.

Harper smiled at him. "Can we?"

Sabastian felt that tingle of giddiness at her smile as he pulled the stick, making them go higher while Harper watched him.

The city drew closer and Sabastian pointed to the top of one of the buildings with a large H on it. "That's where we are going."

Harper briefly studied the view of the roof tops, then looked back to Sabastian as he lowered the copter, lining up the skids with the H before he went through the routine to power down the copter and slide out to open Harper's door.

The two guards were already disembarking when he held out his hand for his wife.

"Did you enjoy that?" he asked.

"I felt like a bird," she said whimsically. "Will we be doing it again?"

Sabastian liked the *we* part of the question. "Of course," he said with a nod, leading her to an elevator, the guards keeping a respectful distance behind.

Sabastian looked over at Harper as he pressed the button and the elevator doors closed. She was standing in the corner of the elevator with her head down. The smile which had greeted him when he opened the copter door was gone.

"Neil, you can wait in the lobby. We won't be requiring either of you in the restaurant," Sabastian ordered as the elevator doors opened onto the extravagant restaurant floor of the high-rise building.

Sabastian held out his elbow, and Harper reluctantly took

it. He led her toward the restaurant, where a man in a black and white maître d' suit hurried forward to greet them.

"General James," he greeted Sabastian with a small bow of his head. "Please follow me."

He completely ignored Harper.

Even before he became General of Defence, Sabastian was used to being waited on, but he had never had a maître d' rush over to greet him. He liked it.

The room fell silent as he and Harper were ushered to a window seat overlooking the city. Low whispers started to circulate, most of which started off with, "is that General James?" before moving to, "that must be his wife, he chose well, she is gorgeous." The comments made Sabastian smile. He had deliberately wanted Harper to be plainly dressed to show off her natural and unique beauty. He also thought women should only dress up for special occasions and for their husband's pleasure in the privacy of their own homes.

Sabastian was feeling magnanimous, so he did the gentlemanly thing and held the chair for Harper to sit before taking the seat across from her.

A waiter hurried over to hand him a menu, but Sabastian had eaten here before. "That won't be necessary," Sabastian said holding up his hand in a stopping motion. "We will have the crusted oysters with charred fennel and prosciutto, the seasoned duck with parsnip puree, and a bottle of Krug champagne."

The waiter hurried away. Sabastian noted that the quiet chatter still circulated around the restaurant. He liked that the people thought him important and his wife beautiful, but that wasn't the reason he'd brought her here. He wanted to test her, to see her willingness to run. Part of him wanted Harper to run so he could chase her, while another part hoped she wouldn't and would stay with him of her own accord.

Sabastian waited for their server to return to pour the

champagne before he stood. "Would you please excuse me, my Angel, just for a few minutes? I forgot to talk to Neil about a matter of security," Sabastian said before he left her sitting at the table alone.

He walked over to where Neil and the other guard were standing and told them both to get into the elevator and ride up to the copter with him. He had explained the plan to Neil the previous night. Neil had brought his tablet so they could track her without her knowledge.

The elevator door opened and they stepped out onto the roof. Harper's GPS stayed where it was, unmoving for a few minutes before it suddenly moved across the screen, then stopped for a time in a room on the restaurant floor.

Sabastian wasn't sure what to make of it. He thought she would have been hurrying away as fast as possible without stopping. The little red light continued to blink, staying still.

Sabastian felt his pulse rise. He wanted her to know her place was with him, that she belonged to him. He wanted his wife to love him, because he suspected he loved her.

The red dot flashed, slowly moving back to their table by the window.

Sabastian handed the tablet back to Neil and stepped into the elevator, returning to the restaurant where Harper was sitting demurely looking out the window, a plate of oysters sitting on the table.

Sabastian smiled at his wife as she turned to him.

"I apologise for leaving you sitting here alone," Sabastian said as he took a seat.

Harper wrung the napkin in her lap. "I hope you don't mind, but I needed to use the bathroom."

So that's what she was doing. Sabastian smiled. "Of course not."

She was his.

CHAPTER THIRTY-TWO

The servers and waiters fell all over Sabastian while they ignored me — after all, I wasn't going to pay them. But too many eyes looked at me as though I was on the menu.

I hated being on display as Sabastian walked me through the crowded restaurant to a seat by the window. I was like the new neon sign that everyone wanted to catch a glimpse of.

I'd watched every move Sabastian made when he was flying the copter and would do the same on the return trip to the mansion. It didn't look hard to fly, but there was a sequence to follow, and I would have to memorise it fully if I wanted to use the copter as a means of escape. And it was a possibility.

I had felt the slight tingle of the shock collar fence when I had approached the copter, but it had stopped once we were five or six meters off the ground, which meant I could possibly get out of range of the shock collar fence and the remote as long as I was quick enough to avoid Sabastian.

Sabastian pulled out my chair, so I sat, feeling the stares of the entire room staring at me. I couldn't have felt more exposed if I were naked.

A waiter in a crisp white shirt and black pants hurried to our table with the menu, but before he had a chance to hand it over, Sabastian stopped him and began rattling off what he wanted. Oysters, duck and champagne.

I had never had oysters, and the duck dish sounded foreign, but I'd had champagne before and didn't like it. It was bubbly and tasted sour to me.

The waiter hurried away, returned with the champagne a

minute later, poured two glasses and set the bottle in a silver bucket full of ice by the table.

Sabastian stood. "Would you please excuse me, my Angel, just for a few minutes. I forgot to talk to Neil about a matter of security." Then he left me alone at the table to watch him cross the floor to talk to Neil and the other guard before they stepped into the elevator.

I was alone. If I just got up and walked out, I would be free. I could leave, and he wouldn't be able to track me if I left the GPS behind. I saw the sign for the bathroom—if I left it in there, he might not look for me right away, and I could get a head start.

I stood and crossed the room as twenty gazes followed me like hungry dogs watching a bone.

I locked myself in the bathroom as it dawned on me that this was probably some sort of test. Sabastian never left me alone. If he wasn't with me, then one of his goons was. He likely had people in the restaurant ready to pounce if I made one wrong move.

I stared at myself in the mirror. I could run, but then I wouldn't be able to help the Insurgents, and where would I go? I knew nothing about the Capital. But if I stayed, I might never get another opportunity like this.

I fought it out in my own head.

I had to stay. I had to get the information stored in Sabastian's computer, the Insurgents had to bring down the government, otherwise the cycle of cruelty and atrocities toward women and Unholys would never end.

I felt the GPS digging into my throat, a tiny pin prick under the shock collar. He was watching me right now. I needed him to trust me. I needed him to think I had accepted that I was his wife and was devoted to him. I had to go back to the table, but worst of all I knew I had to do what a man expected of his wife, I had to be intimate. The thought sent a cold shiver down my spine. I would have to let him touch me if I were to gain his complete trust. Yuck.

I closed my eyes for a long moment and just breathed, trying to settle my nerves, then I slowly straightened and left the bathroom.

Sabastian wasn't at the table when I sat down, but I could feel everyone's gaze still on me. I turned to the window trying not to cry at the thought of having Sabastian touch me.

I distracted myself by watching a large copter fly across the skyline.

For a moment I thought I felt North, but I knew it was just my guilt eating at me. I loved North so much, yet I wasn't sure if he was alive or dead, and there was nothing in the message John had given me to let me know either way.

An image of him lying lifelessly on the ground flashed into my head.

I had to find a way to get back to our son, to Wolf. He was all that mattered now.

I heard the murmurs and knew that Sabastian had entered the room. I gathered myself and turned to look at him.

"I apologise for leaving you sitting here alone," Sabastian said as he took his seat.

I felt nervous about my plan as I wrung the napkin on my lap. "I hope you don't mind, but I needed to use the bathroom."

Sabastian gave me a knowing smile, which confirmed he'd been watching the tracker. Fucking bastard, it *was* a test, but at least I passed.

We ate with minimal conversation. I slowly sipped on my glass of champagne, despite the fact I wanted to drink the entire bottle to numb myself for what I was going to have to do later.

"Have you had enough to eat?" Sabastian asked while I glanced down at my plate. I had barely touched any of the duck in front of me.

"I'm sorry, I don't think I'm very hungry for duck," I said. "I've never had it before."

Sabastian shrugged. "Would you like to return to the house?"

No. But I didn't like sitting in the restaurant being a conversation piece for the spectators, either, and it would offer me another opportunity to see how he operated the copter.

I smiled. "In the copter?" I asked, trying to sound hopeful.

"Of course," he said as he rose and offered me his hand.

I took it without hesitation and stood like a good obedient wife. The spectators fell silent.

Sabastian leaned over to my ear. "Hold your head up when we walk through, my dear. I want every man to desire you and every woman to want to be you."

The thought churned my stomach, but I did as I was told, holding my posture perfectly like I had been trained by my mother.

North saw the Capital from the front seat of the copter Dace was piloting. It was huge, with concrete skyscrapers and straight black roads crisscrossing it in a grid pattern that stretched off into the distance.

He had no idea where Sabastian James's house was, only that it was just outside the city. Most of the wealthiest people lived outside the city in the surrounding countryside.

"We will be landing in a few minutes," Dace said through the head set.

The copter was a cargo mover and didn't have any stealth ability, unlike the small two-seater craft Sabastian had left behind at Haven. No, this copter sounded like ten freight trains in a thunderstorm.

North gazed out across the rooftops of the buildings,

noticing a copter sitting on one. Someone had actually landed on the roof of one of the high-rises. But something about it made him think of Harper, like that copter was somehow connected to her.

Dace brought the copter down in the centre of a ring of tall buildings, landing on a wide metal platform in the middle of a fenced enclosure while people rushed from a nearby warehouse with a small truck-looking thing and chains, working quickly to hook up the platform to the truck.

"What are they doing?" North asked.

"Getting the copter into the warehouse," Dace said, as though it were obvious.

The truck started pulling and the copter shook a little as it was dragged inside, stopping between two more copters.

"Why?" North asked.

Dace looked over at him, eyebrows furrowed. "This entire suburb is owned by a few of the Insurgents' wealthier sympathisers, and this is our official landing area inside the Capital, but we aren't about to advertise it, and we certainly don't want a defence copter flying over and asking questions. So we have ground crew to move the copters under cover. Then they can do the maintenance and the refuelling away from unfriendly eyes."

The ground crew manoeuvred the copter into position before Dace and North slid from the cockpit, opening the back doors so the rest of the team could get out.

North was impressed by the size of the warehouse—from the outside it looked big, but inside it was enormous. It must have stretched out under the surrounding buildings. It was brimming with people, who were all busy working.

"Dace, Joe," a short, thin man said, approaching the group. "Good to see you both again."

North thought the man looked vaguely familiar, but he couldn't quite place him.

"Tom," Joe said, stepping forward to shake the man's hand. "It's been a while."

"Only about twenty years," the man said with a smile. "How's Elizabeth?"

"She's good. She's back at Home with our youngest boy and grandson," Joe said, sounding proud and a hand onto Travis's shoulder. "This is our oldest boy, Travis."

North knew that Beth and Joe loved Wolf, but he found it surprising that he had called Wolf his grandson.

Some pleasantries passed between Joe, Tom and Travis before Tom looked to the rest of them. They had brought North, Dace, Travis, Birdy, Charli and Joe, as well as three other men, Carter, Austin and Kaden.

Kaden was also a Werewolf, and Dace had told North that Kaden was also a security expert.

"I understand you are the team assigned to the James job. I don't mean to be disrespectful, but a couple of you aren't completely human, are you?" Tom said with a smile.

North saw him wink at Dace.

"You got the briefing then," Dace said.

"Of course, I got the briefing, Dace. I just thought I'd stir the proverbial shit," Tom said while he looked at North. "I'm guessing that one is your brother—you two have a similar build and colouring. Now let me, see who's the third one," Tom paused, looking everyone over before stopping at Charli.

Charli had her blonde hair tied up into a bun and was wearing a black stretchy top and a pair of army-green cargo pants. The outfit showed off her generous breasts and her tiny waist.

"Well, I know you aren't the third Unholy, but I'm betting the guy over there with the black hair is," Tom said, gesturing his hand at Kaden without looking. "Hi, my name's Tom. I would love to give you a personal tour of the facility, and maybe later I could show you my quarters."

Charli smiled nicely, stepped forward, then in a fluid, practiced move gripped Tom's arm, twisted it and threw him on the hard concrete ground. "I'm not here to be hit on by an old pervert," she said flatly.

"I see you still haven't learned the art of subtlety," Joe said, looking down at Tom lying on the ground.

North and Birdy chuckled softly. They knew Charli might look soft and pretty, but she had run a farm and had hauled bales of hay heavier than Tom.

Tom pushed himself off the floor and smiled. "Got to love a girl with spunk."

"I wouldn't love her too close," North said, "I don't know what city women are like, but Charli's a farm girl and she can hog-tie you and castrate you in under a minute."

Tom's hands went to his groin. "Okay then, how about everyone follows me to the briefing room," he said, stepping back when Charli and Birdy passed.

"Actually," Charli said, giving North a wink as she passed Tom. "I can do it in under thirty seconds."

North saw Tom's face turn a shade paler.

North thought about telling Tom that he'd never once seen Charli hog-tie a cow. They had a cattle crush if they needed to hold the beasts still, and they used a special device that put rubber bands around the young bull calf's testicles, so they would go numb and eventually drop off without hurting the animal. But if he told Tom that, he might try to hit on Charli again, and North was scared Charli might actually castrate him.

The team was taken through to a conference room where a woman with salt and pepper hair was waiting.

"Lady Anastasia, may I present the team from Home?" Tom said greeting the woman as she looked them over.

North sniffed the air. The woman standing in front of them had a faint scent of gunpowder and something else, something similar to Harper.

"An Angelic," North said without thinking.

The woman smiled at him. "One sixteenth," she told him. "You must be Mrs James's Unholy lover."

North resisted growling at her. "Her name is Harper," he said, while everyone took a seat at the large table.

The woman nodded. "We have made contact with Mrs Ja — Harper, but our men were unable to give any instructions to her. However, Harper was resourceful and has set up a meeting with our men in the morning."

"Why couldn't they do a snatch and grab when they saw her?" Travis asked.

Anastasia shifted uncomfortably. "General James has her implanted with a GPS tracker which also contains the poison we are worried about and . . ." her voice trailed slightly as her glance flicked to North. "He also has an electric shock collar on her."

North swore. "We suspected that fucking asshole had a dog collar on her and was shocking her."

Anastasia nodded. "We have been informed that there is both an invisible fence around the house and a remote control that activates the device. Mrs James, I mean Harper, has attempted to escape several times. One time she came close to dying after she passed out in range of the fence and the collar made her throat close over so she couldn't breathe."

North stood and began to pace.

"We are hoping that with the security being stretched for General James's dinner party in two nights' time, we may have an opportunity to smuggle her out, but with the shock collar and GPS in place, we are unsure how far we will get," Anastasia said. "It could be a suicide mission."

"Why is this woman so important?" Kaden asked.

"General James has access to every department of the government. We need that access to bring down the government from the inside and show the average person what the government is doing, but we need Harper as a spokeswoman. The Nation now knows who she is. Women are dressing like her and men are drooling over every photo they see of her," Anastasia continued. "We know today General James took Harper to lunch at an exclusive restaurant, and before they had even been served the champagne, there were more photos of her uploaded than of the Praeses."

A screen ignited on the wall showing a picture of Harper sitting alone at a table, looking out the window. North stopped pacing and looked at the image of her wearing a simple pale-blue dress with her hair twisted into a bun.

North studied his goddess, backlit by the sky and city.

"Wow. I can see why men are obsessed with her, she's completely fuckable," Tom said. "Do you think she would fancy an older guy?"

"Good luck with that," Travis said. "The Unholy there is her man." Travis pointed his thumb at North. "And she only has eyes for him, even had a baby with him."

Anastasia smiled. "I saw Harper's DNA file. She is a pure Angelic, a throwback. It is almost unheard of, and beyond rare after the government slaughtered most of us during their experiments," she told him. "Is the child healthy?"

"Yes," North said evenly. He wasn't going to talk about his son with complete strangers. He still wasn't absolutely sure they were the good guys and weren't just trying to use Harper for their own gain. He knew Harper hated being the centre of attention, and their plan to make her a spokeswoman would likely not sit well with her, but he still needed to get her out of Sabastian's clutches, so he would go along with their plans for the time being.

"Good," Anastasia said, "Now let us get down to business . . ."

I had watched Sabastian carefully in the copter, memorising the buttons and the way he moved the stick in his hands when he wanted to move it up and down, the way his feet moved the pedals to control the yaw by altering the pitch on the tail rotor.

Instead of taking me straight home, Sabastian had done a lap around the city, pointing out landmarks and the government buildings like a tour guide.

"So where do you work?" I asked, faking interest. I didn't actually care, I just wanted to watch how he manoeuvred the copter.

Sabastian smiled, his ego swelling as he flew over a large grey stone building that looked more like an armoured tank than an office building. It had guns and cannons on the roof, thick bars on the windows, and was surrounded by armed military personnel.

The sun had set by the time Sabastian landed back at the mansion, and I felt the familiar tingle of the fence against my throat, which was close to the copter's landing pad.

Neil and the other guard slid out while Sabastian opened my door and helped me down.

We had only taken a step inside when one of the servants brought Sabastian a phone. "Praeses Connelly for you, sir."

Sabastian took it. "Irving," Sabastian greeted, before listening to the man on the other end for a moment. He looked down at me and smiled. "Yes, I'm just going to turn the television on," he said into the phone as he ushered me into one of the downstairs sitting rooms and flicked on the large screen mounted to the wall.

A picture of me sitting in the restaurant looking out the window filled the screen while a man's voice filled the quiet room. "Our new general certainly knows how to pick a wife.

We know that fashionable men will all be dressing their wives in her chic *dressed down* look. This attire is set to become the new trend for the season, but we doubt many women will make *simple* look quite as spectacular as Mrs James."

I couldn't believe it—they were talking about me.

Sabastian's voice interrupted my thoughts. "Yes, I was sure the media network would love her, her face is perfect for television."

The image on the screen changed to one of Sabastian and me walking out of the restaurant. My head was up, and Sabastian was smiling.

"They make such a handsome couple," the TV host said. "And make sure you tune in this time tomorrow, when our cameras will be there to capture every moment as our new general and his beautiful wife host a dinner for the elite of our Capital, our heads of government and Praeses Connelly himself."

"I have already organised increased security for the dinner, and armed soldiers are to be stationed along the road for twenty kilometres out, in case the Insurgents try to attack any guests," Sabastian said into the phone. "I have also arranged for both a dummy convoy and an armoured car convoy for you and your wife."

Sabastian looked over at me and grinned.

I dropped my head, looking at a spot on the carpet.

"I'll see you tomorrow," he said and disconnected.

I felt awkward and uncomfortable. Well, at least more than usual.

Sabastian's black shiny shoes came into view as he stood just in front of me. "Is there a problem?"

I shook my head.

"Harper," Sabastian said, his voice laced with almost caring tones. "What is it?"

I shook slightly, scared I was going to make him angry.

"You are General of Defence and I'm just your wife, but" —I hesitated—"I don't understand, why is anyone interested in me?"

Sabastian laughed. It was unexpected. I had been expecting an outburst of rage or even a backhand, but he laughed.

I stood silent, unsure what to do.

Sabastian placed a finger under my chin, lifting my face to meet his. "You have no idea how rare or beautiful you are, do you?"

I wanted to pull away. His touch made me uneasy, but I had to gain his trust so I could recover my freedom. We stood staring into each other's eyes for a moment. Sabastian moved closer, and I was sure he was going to kiss me—a prospect I wasn't looking forward to.

A knock sounded at the door. Sabastian stopped, his gaze still locked on me.

"What is it?" he called without moving.

"Mr Harvey is on the phone, something about a security breach in the GPS manufacturing plant," Neil said.

I bit my bottom lip, and his glance caught on my mouth as he let out an inaudible sigh before answering the phone.

"What kind of security breach?" Sabastian said, walking away.

I walked to the sitting room door and watched him climb the stairs to his office while Neil stood guard over me.

"I'm getting a hot chocolate. Do you want one?" I asked Neil as I turned for the kitchen.

Neil followed me. "If it's all right, I might have a coffee. I'm doing a double shift again tonight."

I made coffee and hot chocolate, then we both sat down at the table.

"If you drug me every night so I sleep through until morning, why do you have to stand guard as well?" I asked.

"Mr James doesn't want anything to happen to you."

I didn't hear Sebastian, but I could feel him looking at me — he must have finished his call and come back downstairs.

"I'm in a heavily guarded house and my husband has been sleeping in my bed beside me. I would think I'd be safe without you watching me every minute of the day and night. I'm sure my husband is more than capable of keeping me safe," I said, playing to Sebastian's oversized ego.

"That isn't my call to make, Mrs James," he said, taking another sip of his coffee.

I saw the moment Neil's eyes widened before he quickly stood up, and I knew Sebastian must have made his presence known.

I turned and looked at him. "Would you like a hot chocolate?"

"No, thank you," Sebastian said, before looking to Neil. "I have to go out for a few hours, so when my wife has finished her drink would you escort her up to her room and go through the usual routine with her?"

"Of course, sir." Neil nodded.

"And once she is in bed asleep, would you please go down to the guard house and double check the security protocols?"

"Yes, sir," Neil said, looking slightly confused.

"You're going out?" I asked as I stood and faced him.

"I'll be back before you wake up," he said with a small smile. "Just some work I have to take care of."

I had a feeling the security stuff at the GPS factory had something to do with the Insurgents. I didn't know what I could do to help, but then again I did, and I hated what I was going to do next. I stepped a little closer pressing my breasts against his chest.

Sebastian stiffened slightly under my touch, his eyes widening.

"Thank you for today, I had a wonderful time," I told him with a smile before pushing myself up on to my tiptoes to kiss his cheek.

I wanted to scrub my lips with bleach.

I stepped back while Sabastian stood frozen for a moment, obviously shocked I'd actually kissed him.

"I'll see you in the morning." I smiled, picking up my cup of hot chocolate.

"Yes, of course," Sabastian said dazedly.

I was going to hell, and I wasn't even dead yet.

CHAPTER THIRTY-THREE

Sabastian disconnected from his call with Harvey. A small group of men had broken into his GPS manufacturing plant and damaged several of the machines. It was fixable, but having the General of Defence's own factory being damaged would be embarrassing if word got out. It was the timing that he thought most amusing — they had struck just one night before the dinner was scheduled.

Sabastian went downstairs, following the voices to the kitchen. He stopped when he saw Neil and Harper sitting at the table together sipping coffee. Harper had her back to him.

"If you drug me every night so I sleep through until morning, why do you have to stand guard as well?" Harper asked.

Neil made a small shrugging motion. "Mr James doesn't want anything to happen to you."

Sabastian had been waiting almost a year to possess Harper, and there was no way he was letting something happen to her now. They hadn't even made love yet.

"I'm in a heavily guarded house and my husband has been sleeping in my bed beside me — I would think I'd be safe without you watching me every minute of the day and night. I'm sure my husband is more than capable of keeping me safe."

Neil looked a little uncomfortable discussing such things and so he should. He was getting paid to protect and serve, not sit at Sabastian's kitchen table drinking coffee with Harper. But Harper did have a point — he was sleeping next to her, and with his training, he was more than capable of protecting her.

"That isn't my call to make, Mrs James," Neil said, taking another sip on his coffee.

That at least was true. It wasn't Neil's place to give the orders, just to follow them.

Sabastian made his presence known to Neil. Neil's eyes went wide as he scrambled to his feet, looking shame faced.

Harper turned to look at him with a smile. "Would you like a hot chocolate?"

"No, thank you," he told her, before turning to Neil. "I have to go out for a few hours so when my wife has finished her drink, you will escort her up to her room and go through the usual routine with her."

Sabastian didn't like having to drug her, but he wasn't having her sneak downstairs in the middle of the night and grab a knife to slit his throat.

"Of course, sir." Neil nodded.

Sabastian thought about what Harper said. "And once she is in bed asleep, you will go down to the guard house and double check the security protocols for tomorrow."

"Yes, sir." Neil nodded.

Harper looked mournfully at Sabastian. "You're going out?"

"I'll be back before you wake up," he told her, wishing he could stay. "Just some work I have to take care of."

Harper moved in close to him. The smell of her skin was mesmerising as her perfect breasts pressed against his chest. Sabastian hadn't expected her soft touch, which sent a rush through him.

"Thank you for today, I had a wonderful time." Harper smiled before she suddenly kissed his cheek.

Sabastian stood watching her for a moment. The sensation of her warm lips against his cheek lingered there long after she had moved away.

"I'll see you in the morning." Harper smiled as she picked

up her cup of hot chocolate.

The sooner Sabastian left, the sooner he would be back again. "Yes, of course." He smiled, planning to be in her bed beside her in a few hours.

Sabastian hurried out to his car, then had a sudden thought—if the Insurgents knew that Harper would be alone then this was likely a set up so they could snatch her tonight.

Sabastian pulled his phone out, tapping in Neil's number.

"Stay with Harper in the house, I'll send someone up to keep you company," Sabastian told him before disconnecting.

Next, he called the guard house. "I have to go out, but I want you to send two men up to the house to guard my wife with Neil and commence the security protocol for maximum threat. Expect the situation to stay that way for at least a few days. If you want extra men, call it in to the Defence Office and tell them it is for me," he ordered.

If the Insurgents wanted him to leave the house, he would stay.

Sabastian slid from the car and dialled Harvey, giving him instructions to email all the video surveillance to him.

He didn't physically have to be there to look at the footage, which meant he could keep a close eye on Harper. He knew he might be overreacting to some hooligans, but he didn't care. He had Harper, and he was keeping her.

Sabastian went upstairs and found Neil standing in his usual position outside Harper's bedroom door.

"Has she been sedated yet?" Sabastian asked.

"No, sir. She wanted to have a shower and put on her pyjamas first," Neil told him.

Sabastian nodded and went in. He could hear the water running in the bathroom as he walked over and pushed the bathroom door open.

Harper was standing with her naked back to him in the steamy glass-framed shower, washing the soap from her hair.

She stopped and glanced over her shoulder at him. "Are you just going to stand there and stare at me?"

"I was thinking about it," Sabastian told her, admiring the curves of her body as the water made her bronze skin glisten.

Harper smiled. "You could join me."

Sabastian felt like a kid let into the candy shop. "Are you sure you want me to?"

"No," Harper answered honestly. "But you are my husband, and I need to be a good wife, don't I?"

Sabastian hesitated for a moment. He wanted Harper so desperately, but not if she was only doing it out of wifely obligation. He stood watching her for a little longer while she bent over to rub soap down her legs.

Just because I get in the shower with her doesn't mean we have to have sex, Sabastian reasoned with himself while he stripped off his clothes, releasing his rock-hard erection which led the way as he stepped into the shower.

North crouched by the chain link fence that circled the GPS factory with Travis, Kaden and Birdy. They had just completed their assignment, which was to go in and cause some minor damage while they planted a remote-activated detonation device on a key piece of manufacturing equipment. They would need it the next day as a diversion to get Harper out. They also needed to time how long it would take security forces to get there and to see if James would respond to the break-in in person. If he came running, that would be perfect. If not, they'd work with it.

North's ears pricked at the sound of sirens. "Let's go," he ordered, leading the group down an alleyway.

North wanted to stay just in case Sabastian James was arrogant enough to bring Harper, but he knew he wouldn't. Sabastian would have her under lock and key, surrounded by guards.

The four men jogged down the alleyway to where Joe and Dace were waiting in a van. The sirens were getting louder as North pulled the door closed and Joe casually drove away.

"Glad to see you are all present," Dace commented, looking over his shoulder from the front seat. "Any problems?"

North shook his head, "No. Once Kaden shut down the electronic door locks, we went straight in, and I planted the device on the gas line as instructed."

If it were up to North, they would have attacked the James's mansion directly, but once he saw the layout of the building and the security surrounding it, he thought he would have better luck snatching the Praeses himself than getting to Harper.

Dace took a call. "So he hasn't left the mansion." He paused, listening for a moment. "Yeah, we'll head there now."

North didn't like the sound of that.

"James never left the property, and he's increased security around Harper."

North cursed. They'd been hoping to draw security away from the mansion, but Sabastian was too clever for that.

"So where are we going?" Joe questioned.

"The James's mansion. We need to do a recon to find out exactly how much more security has been added," Dace informed them.

They had studied the layout of both the grounds and the mansion. North had it all memorised.

They took a road that ran parallel to the James's estate, parking about two kilometres from the western boundary.

"I want to make this clear," Dace said as they stepped out into the darkness. "This is a purely recon mission. If you see Harper, smell her or hear her, you are not to engage. Her safety must not be compromised."

"North, Travis, he's talking mainly to you two," Joe interceded. "Harper is a smart girl, and from what we have been told, she is trying her best to gain James's trust."

North tightened his fists. He'd heard the speculation about Sabastian sleeping in Harper's bed and hoped it wasn't true, but if it was, he understood why. Harper would do anything to get back to Wolf.

They spread out in teams of two, Joe and Dace, Birdy and Kaden and Travis and North.

Joe figured if each team had a Werewolf on it, they would have half a chance of scenting an approaching guard before they saw them, and if all else failed, the wolves could transform and tear them apart.

North and Travis moved quickly and silently through the forest that surrounded the estate, stopping at the edge of the lawns that surrounded the massive mansion.

North felt his skin tingle and realised they must have been close to the electric-collar fence. He hated Sabastian even more.

They skirted the invisible boundary, heading for the eastern corner. They had Intel that Harper's room was next to Sabastian's on the second storey, so they went looking for the windows of the main upstairs bedrooms. They'd been told to stay away, but neither North nor Travis were inclined to do that.

North was distracted, focussed on trying to catch just a glimpse of Harper through the windows when he suddenly smelled something. Two guards.

"Drop," he hissed, grabbing Travis and pulling him down. Both men hit the ground hard and pressed themselves flat.

If North had been paying attention, he would have caught their scent earlier and found a better place to hide—as it was, they were semi visible. The guards would only have to flick a torch in their direction, and they'd be seen.

"If you ask me, I think the general is a little obsessed with his wife. Yeah, she's beautiful and all, but to be worried that people are going to sneak in and snatch her, I don't think so." one of the guards said.

"Don't complain, it's an easy job, all we have to do is walk the boundary every two hours then go back to the guard house, drink coffee and play cards," the second guard said. "I feel more for Neil. That poor bastard is pretty much glued to the wife's ass. Wherever she goes, he has to go. I don't think he's slept in days."

The two guards didn't even look sideways as they continued around the house.

"So much for the security team," Travis whispered, while they got to their feet and continued around the house.

North saw a light in one of the large upstairs windows and felt sure it was either Harper's room or Sabastian's.

They stood in the shadows looking up as someone moved in front of the window. Sabastian. He was bare chested and looked as though he'd just stepped out of the shower.

North felt his blood boiling. He wanted to rip the man's head off.

He was about to move to the next window to try and find Harper when he saw her. His breath caught in his throat as she stepped in front of the window wearing nothing but a towel.

She was smiling at Sabastian.

She wouldn't.

Sabastian pulled her close, lifted her chin and kissed her passionately.

North started to move, but Travis grabbed his arm, stopping him.

"No," Travis whispered. "You'll blow our cover."

North growled, "I'm going to kill him."

CHAPTER THIRTY-FOUR

My back pressed against the cold tiles while Sabastian ran his hands down my naked body, his hard length pressing against my stomach while he kissed his way down my neck.

Even under the hot water, Sabastian's hard muscular body felt cool against mine.

I ran my fingers through his hair, caressing it as his lips brushed my bare nipples and I fought the urge to ram his head into the tiled wall.

"You are so beautiful. I want to make love to you right here," Sabastian whispered raggedly as I pulled his hair, dragging him back up to my lips.

I smiled and kissed him while his hands moved down over my stomach, moving lower.

"In the bed," I told him, nipping his bottom lip.

I needed him to trust me, to think I would be his good little wife. I needed to get back to Haven and find Wolf. I would do whatever I had to do to see my baby boy again.

I swallowed back the nausea. I was going to prostitute myself to a man I couldn't stand.

Sabastian smiled and turned off the shower before stepping out. I followed, wrapping a towel around myself.

Sabastian walked over to the large window. I spotted the tranquiliser syringe, which was meant for me, sitting on a tray on the dressing table. I quietly picked it up and hid it behind my back.

"Kiss me," I purred, allowing him to pull me against him

for a kiss, his tongue licking mine. If he wasn't such a sonofa-bitch, I would have enjoyed him kissing me—he was good at it.

Sabastian's lips traced a line down my neck while I wrapped my arms around him, digging my nails into his back.

Sabastian moaned. "Do it harder," he whispered, his hot breath against my neck before he sank lower, kissing my shoulder.

I dug my nails in until I thought I would draw blood, covering the moment I slid the syringe in and injected the tranquiliser.

Sabastian instantly went limp against me, falling to the floor at my feet. I put my head back and laughed. I really hated that arrogant sonofabitch.

I was reeling with relief, trying to think of what to do next, when I felt *him*.

I turned to the window. He was out there. I ran over and looked down. It was too dark to see him, but still I just knew he was there, I could feel him. He was alive and so close.

Tears spilled down my face while I pushed my palms against the glass trying to reach out to him, the forgotten syringe still in my hand.

I wanted to smash the window and jump out so I could look for him, but I knew I had to stay a little longer, and now that I knew he was alive I would find the strength to do it.

A shadow moved, and suddenly I couldn't feel him anymore. He was gone, but at least I knew he was alive and that was all that mattered.

I turned back to Sabastian lying naked on the floor. In hindsight I probably should have gotten him on the bed before I tranquilised him.

I took his arms and started to drag him across the floor, grunting and groaning as I went, but somehow, I managed to keep my towel on. When I finally managed to get him over to the bed, I propped him up while I caught my breath. I was about to try to lift him, when my elbow hit the side table knocking a small lamp off which crashed to the ground.

A knock sounded as the door opened. I dropped to my knees, straddling Sabastian and he let out a groan under my weight.

I looked over and saw Neil looking in at me on top of Sabastian's naked body.

His dark cheeks blushed red, before he quickly withdrew, closing the door behind him.

Note to self – There is nothing like catching the boss in a compromising position to make a grown guard run for the hills.

I stood and struggled, heaving Sabastian up onto the bed, dragging him up so his head lay on the pillow, and covered him with the blanket. Hopefully when he woke up, he wouldn't remember any of tonight.

I slipped on my panties and pulled on pyjamas before heading for the door.

Neil and two other guards were standing in the hall when I stepped out.

Neil looked embarrassed.

"You will apologise to my husband in the morning," I ordered.

Neil nodded vigorously.

Sabastian would wake up in my bed naked, receive an apology from Neil about walking in on us, and he'd have no memory of any of it. It made me want to burst out laughing.

I wished my guards a *goodnight* and went back to my bedroom. Sleeping next to a naked Sabastian would be uncomfortable, but if he woke up and I was on the sofa, it would be hard to explain.

I inspected the empty syringe. The remnant of the liquid was clear like water, so I took it into the bathroom and filled it from the tap before placing it back on the tray where I'd found it.

I crossed the room thinking of Wolf and North. I had felt North, he was alive, our baby was all right, and now I needed to help the Insurgents access the government mainframe — then maybe women and Unholys might be seen as equals.

I stopped pacing and looked at Sabastian. I hated him, but I still needed him.

I lay down on the bed beside Sabastian and looked at him. He was handsome, smart and vicious. I had a sense he was actually developing genuine feelings for me, but his cruelty, be it innate or learned, made him undesirable.

I reached over and switched off the light. I would find a way to access Sabastian's computer as soon as I could, and then I would escape.

Sabastian woke in a haze with Harper's arm draped across his bare chest. He was naked, but she was wearing silk pyjamas. He couldn't remember much after stepping out of the shower with Harper, but he was sure he hadn't gone to bed.

Harper stirred beside him. Her eyes fluttered open. "Morning, my husband," she said softly before giving his bare chest a quick kiss.

Sabastian didn't remember a thing, but the way she smiled at him made him think something had happened.

Harper rolled out of bed and trotted to the bathroom.

"Watch yourself when you get out of bed, that lamp you broke is still on the floor," Harper called out before shutting the door.

Sabastian looked over the edge of the bed at a broken lamp lying on the ground. He couldn't remember breaking it — had he been angry?

Sabastian slid out of the bed and stood naked, looking around the room in confusion. He wasn't accustomed to being uncertain—everything he did, he did with methodical planning, except for last night. He had seen Harper in the shower and had to have her.

Sabastian looked at the tray that was still sitting on the dresser with the syringe on it. Harper had slept next to him willingly without being drugged and hadn't slit his throat.

The bathroom door opened, and Harper stepped out in plain grey pants and a white top. His wife looked him up and down as she walked over, then ran a finger down his bare chest. "As tempting as you're making it, I have a makeup lesson soon. But maybe you could do that thing you did last night to me again, later—but this time you might not want to be so rough. I only have one lamp left."

Sabastian was confused. "What thing?"

Harper giggled. "I'm not saying it, that wouldn't be lady-like, but I liked it." She blushed, standing up on her tiptoes to kiss his jaw before she walked over to the bedroom door and opened it, sticking her head out.

Sabastian felt himself swell with her touch, but for the life of him he couldn't remember anything. He had been in the shower with her before they stepped out to move to the bed. The last thing he could remember was Harper's nails on his back while he kissed her neck, then nothing.

"Mr Neil, would you please ask one of the servants to fetch my husband a change of clothes?" Harper ordered, sounding like the lady of the house before she closed the door and turned to Sabastian. She bit her bottom lip as her gaze settled on his erect length.

"What exactly happened last night?" Sabastian asked.

Harper's blush deepened. "If you're upset about me not sleeping naked, I couldn't. I didn't feel comfortable after Mr Neil walked in and saw us doing that *thing*," Harper said, dropping her gaze to the floor.

"What *thing* are you talking about?" Sabastian asked.

Harper just looked at the ground. "Do I have to say it?"

"Yes."

Harper shifted uncomfortably. "The thing when I . . ." Her voice wavered.

"When you what?" Sabastian asked, his voice short.

Harper shifted again. "When I sat on your . . . you know," she said, her cheeks flaring bright red with embarrassment.

"You sat on my penis?" Sabastian asked.

"You don't have to be so vulgar. And besides, it was your idea, and you said you liked it."

Sabastian didn't remember any of it, not a single moment. How had he forgotten being inside Harper? "What else did we do?"

Harper crossed her arms. "If you're going to make me verbalise what we do every time we are intimate, then you can forget me ever doing it again."

A knock sounded at the door and Harper opened it, took the clothes from the servant, and dropped them on the bed, looking annoyed.

"I know I'm your wife, but I'm not talking about this anymore. It's crude to talk about intimacies," she told him impatiently. "I will be downstairs in the kitchen when your mind leaves the gutter."

Sabastian watched her leave. How had he had sex with Harper without remembering any of it? How was that even possible? He thought her the most beautiful woman in the universe.

Sabastian pulled on his clothes and went downstairs to the kitchen, where Harper and Neil were sitting at the table with their coffees while two other guards stood by the door.

Neil instantly stood as always when Sabastian entered.

"I need a few minutes alone with my wife," Sabastian ordered.

The two new guards left instantly, but Neil seemed to

linger.

"Mr James, sir," Neil said sheepishly.

Sabastian looked at him. "What?"

Neil shifted uncomfortably, "I just wanted to apologise for walking in on you and your wife last night. It was just that when I heard something break and you groaning, I thought something was wrong. I mean, I didn't expect to see Mrs James on top of you like that, in fact I didn't know you could have a woman sit on your . . ."

"Mr Neil," Harper said, stopping him. "We get it. You are sorry you walked in and saw me and Mr James being intimate. I don't think it needs to be discussed further."

"Yes, Mrs James," Neil said and left the kitchen in a hurry.

Sabastian wondered if perhaps something in Harper's Angelic blood had given him amnesia, or maybe he had a mini stroke.

"Sabastian," Harper said. "Please don't be angry with Mr Neil. After all, he was just doing his job, and you did station three guards outside the door to keep us safe."

Sabastian wished he could remember what they had done last night. He took Harper's hand, kissing her palm. "As you wish, my Angel." He turned and left the kitchen, still confused. He would have to find out more about the Angelics and their special abilities, he thought, heading up to his office.

Sabastian tapped in his code, bringing his computer to life. The email icon blinked with a message from Harvey, and he remembered the break-in at the factory.

Sabastian opened the file marked *CCTV footage*.

Four men in masks could be seen in the grainy footage, doing damage to several of the machines. The message attached from Harvey told him that what the intruders had done was minimal and easily fixed, but it didn't make Sabastian feel any better. He was the Head of Defence, and four men had slipped into his factory to damage his equipment.

Sabastian watched the footage again as a sense of familiarity came over him. He felt like he knew at least two of the men. It was in the way they moved, but he couldn't think from where.

He ran his hands through his hair. First Harper, and now the CCTV footage—he felt like he was losing his mind.

CHAPTER THIRTY-FIVE

North watched the mansion from a distance until almost dawn, memorising the layout of the gardens and the guards' routines from a safe distance. He knew that as soon as Harper had uploaded the information the Insurgents needed, he would get the go-ahead from Anastasia to go get her.

"We have to go," Travis whispered, pointing at the fading night sky.

North knew the others would already be back at the van, but he didn't want to leave Harper in there with that monster, even though he knew she could defend herself well enough.

He smiled when he remembered seeing the syringe in her hand. Harper was beautiful, smart and occasionally a little scary.

North pushed up from their hiding spot amongst the shrubs and followed Travis back through the woods to the van, where the others were waiting.

Dace climbed into the driver's seat with Joe beside him, but no one said a word for a long time as they headed back toward the city. The long night stretched into morning, making the fatigue feel heavier with the rising sun.

"We saw her," Travis finally announced, breaking the silence.

Joe turned back in his seat. "Did she see you?"

Travis shook his head. "No, I don't think so, but it was like she knew we were there somehow."

Dace let out a bark of laughter. "She's an Angelic, she can

feel an ant crawl across the ground a kilometre away if she is tuned into it. And she is definitely tuned-in to you, North. For goodness sake, she had your kid."

"It probably wasn't a good idea to bring you, North. We don't want her to deviate from the plans the Insurgents are setting up," Joe said.

"If anyone tries to stop me from rescuing her, they'll find out what a half-form can really do," North said coldly.

He didn't care about the Insurgents or the mission, he only cared about Harper, and if anyone put her life at risk, he wouldn't hesitate to kill them.

"We know she means a lot to you, and no one is going to hold you back when it is time to go in and get her," Joe told North. "I just meant I'd forgotten how strong your bond is and how Angelics can feel people, especially their soul-mates."

Dace drove the van through the city to the Insurgents' garage. "I think we all need some rest. If all goes well, tomorrow is going to be a big day."

North wasn't sure he could wait twenty-four hours to see her again, but he would try.

I smeared the skin-coloured cream over my face, making sure to get it into my hair line and blending it down my neck, while Neil and the two other guards Sabastian had so thoughtfully assigned watched on.

"I can't do this with everyone watching me," I complained. "Can't you all stand outside the door?"

Neil shook his head. "Sorry, Mrs James, General James said we had to have eyes on you at all times."

I put the creamy sponge down and stood, looking to John and Bert. "Would you please excuse me for a few moments? I need to have a word with my husband." I then walked upstairs to find Sabastian.

I tapped on the office door and let myself in as Sabastian looked up from his computer, a puzzled look on his face before I remembered I had only the foundation on, making my face look featureless.

"I've been trying to learn how to do my makeup," I said by way of explanation. "But I have Mr Neil and those other guards watching every move I make, and it is very distracting."

"That's their job," Sabastian said flatly, leaning back in his chair.

"I know, but can't they wait out in the hallway, so I can concentrate? I don't want to look terrible for you."

The corners of Sabastian's lips curled up. I had stroked his ego, and he liked it.

"Fine, they can wait in the hallway." He relented as I walked over to the door, motioning Neil in with my finger.

Neil looked annoyed as he stepped into the doorway.

"My wife requires some privacy while doing her lady stuff, please make sure to wait in the hallway." Sabastian sighed, as if this level of management was beneath him.

I walked over and kissed his forehead with a smile. "Thank you," I told him, stealing a glance at the computer screen where a blueprint of some kind of aircraft was displayed, before I left.

Neil and my other babysitters followed me back downstairs, stopping outside the door as I closed it behind me and smiled at John and Bert.

"You should show me how to apply the contouring powder now," I said, a little too loud so Neil could hear me while I sat down in the chair.

I had learned how to do makeup from the age of eight in preparation for becoming a wife. It was almost a mandatory lesson for young women in the Nation.

I started powdering my face, blending the darker and lighter tones quickly and methodically while Bert watched on in astonishment.

"So, tell me what I have to do," I whispered, moving onto the smoky-eyeshadow pallet.

"You need to find a way to access the mainframe on James's computer, then upload the files to the Insurgents," John explained quietly.

"Can't I just give you the access codes?" I questioned while I brushed the eyeshadow on.

"Do you have them?" Bert asked, sounding shocked.

"Yes."

"It won't work," John told me. "The government computer network is a closed network, so we need you to send the files through one of the connected computers so we can open it."

I stopped working on my eyeshadow and looked at him. "Did you notice the armed guards following me around? I had to pretty much act like a spoilt brat just to get them to stand outside the door while you're here."

"You're doing well, now try the eyeliner," Bert said loudly and for a moment I was confused until I realised he was saying it for Neil and the others.

"You'll have to figure it out," John whispered. "Once you open the network, send the files to the Rebellium website."

I had never used a computer, and now I had to figure out how to send stuff and go to websites. I was certain this entire thing was doomed and Sabastian would kill me.

I picked up the eyeliner with a shaky hand. "I don't know if I can do this," I told them. "I'm worried I'm going to mess it up."

The door suddenly opened, and Sabastian walked in.

"Of course, you can do it. You just have to go slow," Bert said encouragingly, clearly aware that I hadn't been talking about the stupid eyeliner. Sabastian stood in front of me to see what I was doing.

"You look much better now," he said with a smile. "But do something with your hair."

I nodded at him. "Do you prefer it up or down?" I asked, giving him a half-smile while inside I shook like a leaf, hoping he hadn't heard any of the earlier conversation.

John took hold of my hair and held it up, then let it back down to demonstrate how it would look.

Sabastian thought about it for a few moments. "Up," he said, "I have to go into one of my factories today."

"Will I be accompanying you?" I asked while I applied the eyeliner, then reached for the mascara.

Sabastian looked as if he hadn't considered taking me but was thinking about it now. "I'm afraid today you have a full schedule — you have your makeup and hair lessons this morning, a dress fitting for tonight's dinner, as well as the extra staff and caterers who will be coming in to setup."

I lowered my head and stuck out my bottom lip. "So I won't see you all day," I asked, putting on my best sulky voice.

Sabastian looked at John and Bert. "I need a moment with my wife."

The two men nodded and left the room.

I lowered my head further, looking into my lap. "I'm sorry," I apologised. "I am being selfish and ungrateful. I know your work is important, I will just miss you when you aren't here."

I caught a glimpse of Sabastian smiling out of the corner of my eye as he reached over and stroked my hair lightly.

"Was there anything else?" Sabastian asked.

I thought about how I could get rid of the guards. "May I make a request that the guards stay downstairs when you're not here? I don't think it is right to have men standing outside my bedroom door when my husband isn't home and I'm naked in the shower or having a nap."

Sabastian's fingers tightened in my hair, pulling my head up to face him. "You have guards for a reason, Harper."

"Yes, I'm sorry I questioned you," I apologised, wanting to rip his throat out as he eased his grip on my hair. "I just thought if I'm the only person allowed upstairs, then they could stand at the bottom of the steps so no one can come up to my room, and I wouldn't feel so vulnerable."

"Vulnerable?" Sabastian questioned.

I nodded. "They're big men and they scare me when you're not here to protect me," I told Sabastian, doing my innocent voice.

Sabastian released my hair, but his face was unreadable.

I was going for the best actress award, and his face was indecipherable.

"I apologise and I won't speak of it again. I know a wife shouldn't trouble her husband with such trivial things," I said, ducking my head low again, unsure if I had crossed the line of his ego and started down the path to his cruelty.

Sabastian slipped his hand under my chin and lifted my head until his dark-blue eyes met mine.

"You are too valuable to leave completely unguarded," Sabastian told me. "I will concede to one guard staying with you while you are upstairs, but while you are anywhere else in the house or garden, you will have all three with you. Is that understood?"

"Yes, Sabastian. Thank you, Sabastian," I said meekly. It wasn't exactly what I wanted, but it was better than having all three of the guards with me.

Sabastian glanced at his expensive gold watch. "I have to go," he said, leaning forward and kissing me.

I kissed him back, wrapping my hands around his neck, hoping he would think it real, but it made me want to vomit.

"Have a good day." I smiled, pulling away, wishing very

much that I had superpowers that involved making his head implode.

Sabastian smiled, looking satisfied with himself, and left.

John and Bert came back in and looked at me almost crossly.

"What was that?" Bert whispered.

"Strategy," I told him. "I got myself down to one guard while I'm upstairs, and I know Neil has had about ten minutes sleep in the last three days."

"So what are you going to do?" Bert asked.

"I already gave him decaf coffee this morning and I plan on offering him a comfortable chair while I file my fingernails or read or do something mundane."

Both men smiled.

North stood looking at himself in the changing room mirror. He was wearing a full camo-green army uniform which the Insurgents had supplied.

"I feel like a gimp," Dace growled as he came up beside North dressed in an identical uniform.

Travis, Joe, Birdy and Kaden had the same uniforms as well. Charli was upstairs, but they could hear her through their earpieces, snarling like a pissed off cat because she couldn't go. Instead, she would be staying at the base, monitoring the computers and feeding them Intel.

Joe strode over, holding himself erect. He looked like a career soldier, while Birdy looked like the newest recruit as he fidgeted with his gun holster.

"I feel like an idiot," Birdy announced.

"That's because you are an idiot," North told him with a smile.

"Ha, ha, very funny." Birdy rolled his eyes.

Travis and Kaden were the last to emerge in the army

uniforms.

Kaden shrugged his broad shoulders while he looked to Dace and North. "I really hope we don't have to change into half-form in these outfits — they don't have much give."

"Hopefully, Harper gets it done and we can get her out tonight without a fight," Joe said, but he looked sceptical.

No one was expecting this mission to be easy.

North had heard Joe talking to Travis earlier. He had asked his son to stay behind in case there was fighting. North thought he'd probably have had the same conversation with Wolf if he were in Joe's position. Travis of course had said *No* and that he was going to get Harper home to Wolf no matter what. Joe accepted his son's response, although he looked worried, something North could relate to as a father.

"I've been told we have transport waiting to take us out," Joe announced, heading for the door.

North took one last look at himself in the mirror before following Joe down the hall to the huge warehouse. Tom was there with a group of men, dressed in the same uniforms as themselves, waiting by a massive tank-like truck. The thing had thick metal mesh over the doors and enough weaponry to start a war and probably finish it as well.

"Gentlemen, meet Betty." Tom smiled, patting the side of the truck affectionately with his palm. "Isn't she gorgeous?"

"You seriously need to get a woman." Dace grinned.

Tom folded his arms. "There are plenty of women who don't mind my company."

"Yeah, but do any of them actually exist, or are they all make believe?" Birdy asked with a straight face.

"Fuck you. I'm a good-looking man."

"You're a sleazy gnome." Charli's voice crackled in everyone's ears. "And Birdy, if you so much as get a scratch on you, I will kill you because you, promised you would do that thing I like."

"What thing?" Tom asked eagerly, with a smile.

"Charli, we can all hear you," North told her with amusement. "And besides Tom, none of us wants to hear about your and Birdy's private life."

Travis and Kaden let out a choking laugh, while Tom's cheeks blushed bright red.

"Okay, listen up," Tom said, regaining his composure. "Tonight's dinner is our best chance at snatching the girl."

North folded his arms across his broad chest. "And how do you propose we do that? Sabastian will have eyes on Harper the entire time."

Tom smiled wickedly. "Don't you worry about that — I will be providing the distractions."

North looked to Travis and Joe, but neither of them gave anything away.

"Okay, here is the plan." Tom grinned. "We will be going in in two teams. The Haven group will be team one and the Capital group will be team two. Team one's assignment will be to get in as close as possible to the mansion. If you can infiltrate the grounds, that would be even better, while team two will be stationed along the boundary for backup."

"Lucky that us dogs don't mind a bit of fresh meat on the barbeque," Kaden said, grinning at North and Dace.

"I prefer my meat well done with a side of dead general," North said coldly.

"This isn't an assassination mission," Tom told North flatly.

North shrugged. "You mean it isn't meant to be."

"North," Dace growled. "We get in, grab your girl and get out. If everything goes to plan, we won't have to bring him down, the people of the Nation will, along with the rest of the government."

"Shall I continue?" Tom asked without waiting for a response. "I'm going to wait for the go-ahead before I set off the distractions. They'll be about two kilometres east of the mansion, they'll be the signal for you to go in, snatch the Angelic, and rendezvous back at the drop sight to the west. If all goes to plan, we'll be broadcasting the entire retrieval live to the Nation and be back in time for dessert. If it doesn't go to plan, then the simple rule is to shut your mouth if you're caught and wait for help to arrive."

"You sure do know how to make a guy feel confident," Travis said, slouching against the truck.

Tom sniggered while he retrieved a tray with fifteen small button-like objects on it, "These are cameras, and the footage will be sent straight to the control room. Everything you see and hear, the control room sees and hears, so I want you all to run a clean and professional mission."

CHAPTER THIRTY-SIX

Sabastian sat at his wide oak desk on the top floor of the defence building in the centre of the Capital, watching the monitor with the little red dot blinking on it. Harper was in her bedroom next to the window. She was probably watching the servants bring in the tables and chairs for tonight's dinner in the hall.

Sabastian desperately wanted to remember what he and Harper had done last night, but all he could do was draw a blank. She was too beautiful to forget making love to. Could there be something in her DNA that caused his memory loss? After all, Neil had said he walked in on them in the midst of intimacy.

Sabastian tapped in the code for the DNA sequencing database looking for any information he could find on Angelics. Most of the information had been destroyed after the Angelic breeding program had failed and they tried to wipe all knowledge of their existence from the history books, but there were still some remnants left. Sabastian read through page after page of obscure manuscripts, picking up small snippets here and there.

They are smart . . . Have a high level of adaptability . . . Are easily trained . . . Hard to breed due to physical characteristics including the need for increased naturally released chemicals in the blood stream which can't be manufactured, but must occur naturally, AKA they must be in love with their mating partner to obtain viable offspring. Sabastian read on. Most of this he knew. He was training Harper to be the ideal wife and she was adapting well, but breeding seemed to be a problem.

Sabastian tapped his fingers on the table. He needed Harper to be in love with him so she could bear his children.

He was under no illusion that she loved him, not yet anyway, although he was certain he was in love with her. She had been in his thoughts ever since the first time he had seen her, and he doubted that he would have passed her up, even if she weren't an Angelic, although that was the icing on his Harper cake.

Sabastian glanced at the red dot blinking on his tablet screen and smiled. She was his property, and tonight the entire Nation would be watching the media broadcast of the general's dinner and would admire his gorgeous wife.

"Working hard I see," Praeses Connelly said.

Sabastian looked up to see the older man standing in his office doorway.

Sabastian tapped the screen, reducing Harper's GPS tracker feed. "Irving, it's good to see you," he said, moving to greet the Praeses.

"Cut the bullshit. Neither of us likes pleasantries," Irving said. "How are the arrangements going for tonight's dinner?"

Sabastian rolled his eyes. "As well as can be expected, considering I have a house full of incompetent moronic servants, the overworked Head of Security, and a hundred and fifty assholes arriving at my house for dinner with a camera crew."

Irving laughed and slapped Sabastian on the shoulder. "Welcome to politics. Wait until they all start sucking up your ass, you'll need a colonoscopy and colonic irrigation to get the bastards out."

"Am I allowed to shoot them?" Sabastian asked, only half-joking.

"Well, you are Head of Defence, so technically yes, but even you had better have a darn good reason for it," Irving said with a smile. "Speaking of which, I have a list for disposal

I want you to take care of. General Lucas usually outsourced the jobs, but I have a feeling you may like to get your hands dirty."

Sabastian smiled. "I have a feeling you wouldn't mind if you could as well."

Both men laughed.

Sabastian didn't mind the older man. He thought himself a lot like him, and perhaps after a few years of running the Defence Network the old man might have an unfortunate accident, and he would have to step up into the Praeses position, but he was getting ahead of himself. First, Sabastian just wanted to get through this nightmare of the dinner party, then he wanted to make love to his wife, and after that he would consider his future career advancements.

Irving glanced at his watch. "You should be finishing off your work for the day and heading home. The media crew will be arriving in a few hours to do an interview with you and your wife before the dinner."

Sabastian sighed. He had seen the schedule for his afternoon and evening, and he hated it.

"Don't worry, once this dinner is over you only have to do media releases when they are necessary," Irving informed him. "And even then, you can often get an underling to do it."

Sabastian would have to find himself an efficient underling whose career advancements were little to none.

Irving left, and Sabastian returned to his desk, bringing up Harper's GPS tracker. She was now downstairs in the front sitting room, no doubt with either her hair and makeup men or the fashion designer.

Sabastian tapped in Harvey's phone number.

"Sir," he answered.

"How is the army personnel deployment going?" Sabastian asked.

"We have army personnel stationed around the house as

requested, and every hundred meters down the roads leading in for ten kilometres."

"I said twenty kilometres," Sabastian growled.

Harvey sighed. "I'll see what I can do."

I leaned my back against the windowsill, watching the men carrying tables and chairs across the lawn to the hall at the rear of the mansion. When the guests arrived, they would have to walk through the ornate manicured gardens to the hall.

I glanced over at Neil dozing on the large soft sofa in the centre of the room. In another five minutes he would be sound asleep.

I turned my back to Neil and discreetly dug the tiny GPS monitor out from under the shock collar. It was only the size of a large piece of cooked rice, but that tiny thing had the potential to wipe out every woman and soldier in the Nation. Even so, the scariest thing about it was that Sabastian James had the codes to do it.

A faint snore echoed through my quiet bedroom. I smiled, gently sat the GPS tracker on the windowsill, and slipped off my shoes before tiptoeing over to the door.

My heart pounded in my chest, beating so hard I was sure people on the next continent could hear it as I slowly turned the handle and inched the door open to peek out. The hall was empty. I slid out. I was so nervous that every footstep seemed as loud as an elephant walking across bubble wrap.

Come on Harper, if you can do an obstacle course in record time, you can tiptoe down a hallway. I reached the office door, turned the knob and let myself in, then closed the door behind me.

I had given myself ten minutes and had already used up two tiptoeing down the hallway.

I turned the computer on as I had seen Sabastian do and tapped in the passcode when prompted. The screen flashed blue, then filled with small icons. I stared at them, unsure which one I should press. One of the icons was titled *WOMEN*, so I clicked on it. The screen filled with pictures of women. They all had brown hair similar to mine and were naked. Scrolling down I stopped on one of the images. It was a young woman with her legs splayed apart, fully exposed, but her eyes looked strange, then I noticed the bruising around her neck. She was dead.

I felt my gut heave.

Had Sabastian killed her? I scrolled through more pictures and found several more women who had the bruises on their necks and the same lifeless expression in their eyes.

I covered my mouth to prevent a scream of horror escaping. He had killed them and taken photographs of their dead, naked bodies as if they were trophies to be admired. He was truly a monster.

My entire body shook with fear and disgust.

I had to gather myself. I closed the file and looked at the other icons. I had four minutes left, and I wasn't sure what I was meant to do as I opened another folder that read INVEN-TORY. The folder held files which were individually named with every head of a government department, topped off with Praeses Irving Connelly.

I pressed on the Praeses's file. An image of the white-haired older man popped up in the top left corner with a lot of writing down the right side of the page—his name, date of birth, place of birth, parents, military service, all of his wives' names, etcetera. I scrolled down further, looking at his finances, followed by his real estate dealings and so on. I had little interest in any of it, but I had no idea what any of it even meant except for the fact that all six of his previous wives had died before their fortieth birthdays from accidents at home.

I closed the file, took out a storage stick thing I had seen Sabastian use to transfer files, and downloaded the entire contents of the folder onto it before stuffing it up under my breast to hide it.

I still had no idea how to transfer the files to the Insurgents. It had looked so easy when Sabastian was doing it, but I had no idea what I was doing.

I looked at the time. I was already running over my self-imposed ten-minute time limit — any longer, and I ran the risk of being caught. I had to get out of there.

I quickly shut down the computer and hurried back to my room before I would be missed. Neil was still asleep on the sofa as I inched in and made my way back to the windowsill, stuffing the hideous little GPS tracker back under my collar before adjusting the computer stick, which was digging into my breast.

A knock suddenly sounded at the door, making me jump.

Neil immediately opened his eyes and looked at me as if checking I was still there.

I smiled at him. "Would you like me to get that?" I asked, moving to the door, but Neil beat me to it.

One of the big dopey-looking guards who was meant to be waiting downstairs was standing in the hallway. I was lucky he hadn't seen me sneaking around.

"The man with your dress is here," he said, sounding as dopey as he looked.

"Thank you." I smiled. "It's so good of you to come and tell me, I really appreciate it." I was laying on the gratitude so thick you could have used it on toast. I figured the guards might be less inclined to shoot me if I was nice to them before I tried to escape.

The dopey guard looked as if he blushed at receiving a nice comment. He must not have received many in his life, which made me feel bad for him. I followed him down to the sitting room, which looked out over the rose garden as Neil, half-asleep, plodded behind me.

A man in his forties with a balding head and thick eyebrows stood in the centre of the room assessing me, while a younger man with mousy blond hair stood by three full racks of dresses in different colours and styles.

"I want to see her in the red dress with the opal trim, the black dress with the crystal sequins and the cobalt blue dress with the gold brocade," the older man said, while the younger man pulled dresses from the racks.

I looked to Neil and my other guards. "Would you please wait outside?" I asked.

Neil shifted, looking uncomfortable.

"I am about to strip down to my underwear so I can try on dresses," I said plainly before leaning into whisper. "Besides, you look like you could use a cup of coffee."

Neil scrutinised the two men before looking back to me. "Call if you need us," he said before all three of my guards stepped out, closing the door behind them.

"Take off your clothes," the older man told me.

I glanced around the room. There was no privacy screen or bathroom to go into. "You want me to get undressed here, in front of you?"

"I have dressed thousands of women, and you all have bodies and breasts, so unless you have a penis hiding under those pants, then I have seen it all before." The older man sighed. "Actually, I even saw the penis on one rich man's wife. I guess money can buy anything."

I wasn't sure how to react to that last comment as I sheepishly stripped down to my bra and panties while both men watched.

The older man tilted his head to the side. "I changed my mind. I want the plain black dress with the slit."

The younger man hurriedly returned the dresses to the racks and pulled out a plain floor length black dress with a flowing skirt which became fitted at the hips, with a scooping neckline, elbow length sleeves and a slit up the right side that stopped just short of breakfast time.

"You will need to remove your bra and panties," the older man ordered.

I raised an eyebrow. I had the stick thing stuck down my bra and besides that, the balding man gave me the creeps.

"I don't think so," I told him flatly. "If you want to see me naked, you'd best talk to my husband, General James."

The older man looked at me with disgust. "I am a professional designer, I have dressed thousands of women and . . ."

"And you enjoy perving on them," I finished for him.

"You cannot speak to me that way. I am a man, which makes me superior to you," the older man snarled.

I snatched the dress from the younger man as I looked at the older man with disdain. "You are a dirty old pervert who gets his kicks from telling women to strip for him."

The older man's eyes bulged with anger. "How dare you," he snarled, raising his hand to slap me as the door suddenly opened and the six-foot, dark-skinned Neil stepped into the room, looking angry.

"Mrs James, I heard a commotion in here, is everything all right?" Neil said, without taking his glare off the older man, who I was fairly certain had wet his pants. I probably would have too, if I was on the receiving end of Neil's anger.

"The bald man wanted to see me naked, I told him he was a pervert, so he was going to slap me," I told him, giving the older man a smile. "Did I forget anything?"

The man didn't say a word.

I turned to the younger man, who was looking at Neil like a deer in the headlights. "Mr Neil will be staying in here with us. Now will you please help me get into this dress?" I asked.

It took a moment for the younger man to respond before he cautiously helped me into the dress and zipped it up, then produced a full-length mirror from behind the racks of dresses.

The dress fitted me perfectly, giving me curves and cleavage. The slit was higher than I would have liked, although if I needed to kick someone in the head it would accommodate it.

I turned to Neil. "What do you think?"

"Mrs James, I don't get paid to make fashion choices," Neil said, not looking at me.

I smiled. "Are there shoes to go with this?"

The balding man stood to the side sulking while the younger man ran around finding the perfect shoes to go with the outfit, as well as a gorgeous aquamarine and gold filigree necklace with a matching bracelet and earrings.

A knock sounded at the door before one of my other guards stuck his head in. "Your makeup and hair men are here."

"What do you think?" I asked, doing a little wiggle dance.

He smiled. "I think I'd get fired if I said what I thought," he told me with a blush, before withdrawing.

I turned to the younger man. "What is your name?"

He looked at me with a puzzled expression. "Why?"

"Because when people ask who dressed me, I can tell them your name."

"He didn't dress you, I dressed you," the older man suddenly protested.

"No. You acted like a sleazy old man who wanted to catch an eyeful, then when you were called out you wanted to slap me, until my wonderful guard Mr Neil came in, and since then you've been standing there sulking while your assistant and soon-to-be partner helped me," I said in my sweetest voice, before turning back to the younger man. "Your name, please?"

The younger man gave the older man a sideways glance. "Mervin."

"Thank you, Mervin. I appreciate you taking the time to

help me dress and for making me feel comfortable." I smiled before I went to meet with my hair and makeup artists.

Neil was hesitant to leave me with Bert and John after the incident with the bald man, but I reassured him I was safe and I knew he would be just outside the door.

I watched him leave, worried he would return shortly and I wouldn't have a chance to give them the stick thing with the files on it, so I stuck my hand down my top and started fishing around.

Bert and John both stared at me with wide eyes before I managed to pull it out and slapped it in John's hand.

"I didn't know how to do the upload thing, so I just stuck some stuff I found onto that thing," I said. "I haven't given up trying, I just haven't figured it out yet"

Both men looked at the device in John's hand, then at me.

"I thought you said you knew the codes," Bert said quietly.

"I do, but I don't know which thing I have to push to get into the network and upload," I told them. "Until today, I had never used a computer."

John looked confused. "Let me get this straight, you've never used a computer before, but you managed to copy files onto a stick. How?"

"I saw Sabastian do it the other day." I shrugged.

Both men looked like they were going to pull their hair out.

Bert started wiping off the day's makeup and applying fresh concealer. "We have word that a team will be extracting you tonight, but only if the computer access is opened."

I raised my eyebrow. "Well unless you can show me how, I'll have to wait"

I wanted to get out of here more than anything, but I had no idea how to do what they wanted me to do.

John pulled his tablet out of his bag and began showing me how to access the network he was connected to.

"Why can't we use your tablet to do it?" I asked.

"Different networks. The one James is on has a secured line, which means we can't access it from a different computer or tablet, and then there are the passcodes," John explained while he tapped a few buttons and the screen filled with pictures of hairstyles.

It would figure a hairdresser would have hairstyles on his tablet.

John went through the process of uploading files from his tablet to the hairdresser site twice, explaining that there might be slight differences in the process on different computers, but it shouldn't be too difficult to figure out.

A cold sensation crawled down my spine, and I knew Sabastian was here.

I pointed carelessly at the screen. "Can you do something like that with my hair, but maybe a little fancier?" I asked just as the door opened and Sabastian strolled in with a smile.

I suddenly realised the picture I had pointed to was of a woman with half her hair shaved off on one side.

John quickly tapped the screen and an image of a woman with her hair elaborately braided and twisted appeared. "I was thinking maybe something like this," he said, without missing a beat.

I looked to Sabastian and smiled. "What do you think?" I asked, taking the tablet and turning it so he could see.

Sabastian looked at the image, then at the black dress I was wearing. "I think your hair is too short for that style," he said, with something unreadable in his tone. "And besides, I want your hair down tonight."

The images of the dead, naked women flashed into my head—they had all had their hair down. I did my best to smile at Sabastian while I fought not to scream or cry or show any genuine emotion.

"Did you have a good day, my husband?" I asked sweetly.

"Yes, thank you," Sabastian said, looking down at the slit

in the dress which stopped just short of exposing my panties.

I wanted to cover myself, but I just smiled instead. Now that I knew how to upload the files, it was only a matter of time until I could bring Sabastian's cruel world crashing down around him.

Sabastian leaned in close. "I like the dress," he said, breathing against my neck while his hand slid up my thigh.

His touch made my skin crawl.

"We have an audience," I whispered back.

Sabastian sighed. "If we didn't have a television crew arriving in twenty minutes I would . . ."

It didn't take a genius to know what he was thinking. I took his hand. "Later."

Later I would be dead or gone. Either way, he would never touch me again.

Chapter Thirty-seven

Sabastian wanted to make love to his wife right there in the front sitting room, but she had said, "Later," and he would hold her to that. He kissed Harper, holding back the desire to tear her clothes off, and went upstairs to dress in his tailored black dinner suit. It was cut perfectly to show off his muscular body and broad shoulders. He and Harper would look like the perfect couple tonight.

His phone rang, displaying Harvey's number.

"What is it?" Sabastian answered while he admired himself in the mirror.

"I just thought I would inform you that the troops are in position along the road and around the house," Harvey told him.

"How long until the media crew arrive?" Sabastian asked, turning to catch a glimpse of his broad muscular back in the mirror.

He was wearing a white shirt, but he thought a black one was more his style. It would match Harper's dress better and make him look more severe, a perfect image of power.

"They are about twenty minutes out from the house," Harvey said. "I will be there in around forty minutes to go over the security system one last time. The guests should start arriving in an hour and twenty minutes."

"I need you to check my wife's GPS tracker and shock collar when you get here."

"Not a problem."

"Please be discreet about the GPS, Harper doesn't know

where it is in her body."

"Discretion is my middle name," Harvey joked.

"I'll see you when you get here," Sabastian said, disconnecting before he changed his white shirt for a black one, adding a deep-blue tie which matched his eyes. Sabastian smiled to himself. He was about to host the grand event of the year with his gorgeous wife, and it would be telecast across the Nation, making him the envy of every man.

Sabastian straightened his dark hair in the mirror before going to his office, stopping when he reached his desk. The top drawer was slightly ajar. Sabastian looked across his desk, nothing else seemed out of place, but he knew someone had been in his office. He would never leave the drawer open. He was too precise to do that.

Sabastian quickly opened his computer, noting an image of one of the girls he had strangled hadn't been closed properly. Sabastian smiled to himself. Could it have been Harper on his computer? Anyone else would have made sure to close the file completely instead of just minimizing it. She must have taken a flash drive and downloaded the image. But how would she know how?

Sabastian thought about it for a moment. She had sat with him while he worked—she must have watched how he'd done it, but what would his wife gain from downloading a picture of a dead girl? If she tried to show anyone, he could easily refute it and say it wasn't his, or maybe she was going to try to blackmail him with it.

Sabastian sat back, curling his fingers together.

He found the thought amusing, but either way, he would have to keep a close eye on his wife.

He didn't want to kill Harper. She was too valuable an asset, but he couldn't keep her under lock and key. He would have to fix her GPS tracker, perhaps even modify it with an alarm system, so if she went somewhere in the house she shouldn't, he would be notified. In the meantime, he would keep his office door locked and have her room searched for the flash drive.

A knock sounded on his office door, and Neil poked his head in. "The media people are downstairs. Mrs James directed them to set up in the pergola by the rose garden."

Sabastian examined Neil for a moment as a thought came to him. Neil should have been watching Harper, but where was he when the computer had been accessed? Had he done it? But he had been a loyal servant for a long time. Sabastian hoped for Neil's sake that he wasn't reporting to someone like the Praeses.

Sabastian sighed. He had employed Neil a long time and he didn't want to have to replace him now that Kleve was dead. It was so hard to find good loyal killers. For now, Sabastian would keep an eye on Neil.

"Did you leave my wife alone with the reporter?" Sabastian questioned

"No, sir, I have two guards with her," Neil answered.

Sabastian nodded, shutting down his computer before following Neil down to the rose garden.

He heard an unfamiliar man's voice ask, "So Mrs James, what do you think of General James's appointment to Head of Defence?"

Sabastian sped up, unsure of what Harper would say in response.

"Well Mr Ryker, to be honest I rather wish he didn't get the job," Harper answered, as Sabastian rounded the corner and saw her sitting on a bench opposite a thick-set older man, "Not because my husband isn't the best man to lead our Nation's defences, because I know he is, but because as a wife, I now have to share him with the rest of the country, and I don't like to share." Harper smiled.

The man laughed a little. "Well, we couldn't expect a

lovestruck wife to want to share her husband," the man said as Harper turned to Sabastian with a smile.

Harper rose from her seat, looking like the Angelic creature she was, and stepped over to Sabastian, giving him a quick kiss before turning back to Mr Ryker.

"May I introduce my husband, General Sabastian James," Harper said as Sabastian noted the sound of pride in her voice.

The television host rose and shook Sabastian's hand. "A pleasure to meet you, General. I hope you don't mind that we started the interview without you."

Sabastian wrapped his arm around his wife and smiled politely. "Of course not."

Harper led him over to the bench seat before sitting down and crossing her long lean legs, allowing the split to fall open. Sabastian sat beside her while she took his hand and rested it in her lap against her bare thigh.

Mr Ryker's eyes almost bulged out of his head.

"Are you all right, Mr Ryker?" Harper asked with concern.

Sabastian thought it amusing. If Mr Ryker, the television host, was almost having an embolism at seeing her thigh, then the rest of the Nation's men would likely do the same.

"Yes of course, Mrs James," Ryker stammered and cleared his throat, taking his seat across from them.

Sabastian had a fair idea that the host would have a clear view up Harper's dress, so he adjusted his and Harper's hands to discreetly cover her. That was his and only his area to admire.

"Just a moment, I just need to pull up the preapproved questions I was sent for the interview," Ryker said, fiddling with his tablet for a moment.

Sabastian leaned over to Harper's ear. "I know you were on my computer," he murmured. She suddenly stiffened. "Did you enjoy looking at the naked women?"

My heart stopped in my chest as I stiffened.

"Did you enjoy looking at the naked women?" Sabastian had whispered and my brain executed a full stop.

I could deny it, but he probably had proof it was me. *No. Go on the attack.*

"Did you fuck them because they looked like me?" I questioned softly, feeling sick to the gut but trying to sound confident.

"None of them looked like you. You are far more beautiful than any of them," he whispered.

"So I don't need to be jealous than?" I asked, nipping his ear seductively.

Sabastian closed his eyes for a moment as I felt a shudder run through him.

"I don't like to share, Sabastian and I won't share you with any other woman," I whispered, trying to sound possessive before he suddenly turned and kissed me.

The kiss was hot and seductive. Sabastian might have been an evil sonofabitch, but he knew how to kiss.

"Umm, we are live from General James's Mansion on the outskirts of the Capital. And here with us is General James and his wife," Ryker interrupted as we separated.

"Sorry, but as you said earlier, my wife is a little lovestruck with me." Sabastian smiled. "She can hardly keep her hands off me."

I blushed, looking at the ground demurely.

"Well, you certainly do make a handsome couple. I think every man, woman and child in our nation would agree. And personally, if my wife kissed me like that, I'd never leave the house."

For fuck's sake, I thought, I had just wanted him to get off the subject of me snooping in his computer, not have the entire nation watching us kiss. Oh hell, what if North saw it?

He'd hate me.

I tuned out while Sabastian talked about the house, the guest list, some of the new security protocols he was going to implement in the coming months, before I suddenly heard my name being mentioned.

"Harper James, what is it like being married to the Head of Defence?" Ryker asked as I glanced up at him, then looked to Sabastian sitting beside me.

I wanted to tell him it was like living in a nightmare, that I couldn't escape, but instead I had to play the doting wife, at least for now.

I smiled up at Sabastian. "Well, I have to admit it has been different to my previous life."

Ryker laughed, and Sabastian squeezed my hand tightly, warning me.

"You see, I grew up on a modest farm," I continued, but Sabastian's grip didn't ease. "So marrying Sabastian, I mean General James, was a big change for me."

It felt like every bone in my hand was about to be ground to dust. It hurt as I battled to keep a straight face.

"And how is that?" Ryker asked.

I thought about it for a moment, trying to find words that wouldn't result in my hand being crushed. "Well, I thought we had a nice house on my family's farm, but after coming here" — I moved my free hand, indicating the house and gardens — "well, I'm sure you can see what I mean."

"Yes, most definitely," Ryker said as the cameraman moved the camera to capture the house and garden. "I'm sure many of the young women out there are envious of your new position and your powerful husband."

"I'm sure they are. I am living the fantasy all women have before they marry. I have a wonderful home, my own personal hair and makeup men, and amazing clothes, but it is my husband that has truly changed my life to what it is now."

"And what about you, General James, what has been the biggest adjustment you have had to make being married to this gorgeous wife of yours?" Ryker asked, turning to Sabastian as he eased his grip on my hand slightly.

Sabastian looked over at me. "Sleeping on the right side of the bed for starters," he said jokingly before his face turned more serious. "Going to sleep next to Harper still feels surreal, then there are the small things," he said, still looking at me. "Like watching her make my coffee in the morning, or the way she looks when she is absently gazing out at the garden."

I could tell by the way his eyes softened that he meant it. Sabastian James was in love with me. I had hated him so much that I wanted to destroy him, and he loved me. Sabastian must have been so screwed up as a kid, he thought this possessive, dominating thing he did was what you had to do to love someone. I felt a little bad that the person to love him was never going to be me.

I gently reached over and touched his cheek, smiling at him. He took my hand, kissing my palm.

"There you have it, ladies and gentlemen, General James and his lovely wife really are the perfect couple," Ryker announced to the camera. "Now let's head back to the studio to have a look at the guest list for tonight's dinner, with the first guests starting to arrive in around half an hour, so stay tuned."

"Are we done for now?" I asked Ryker.

"Yes, but I would like to do a short interview with just your husband before we move to the dining room to set up," Ryker told me.

I turned to Sabastian. "Would you like me to stay? Or should I go and check on the preparations?"

"Actually, I have an old friend arriving any moment, by the name of Harvey. I would like you to go greet him and offer him a cup of coffee," Sabastian told me, then gave my forehead a quick kiss. "I'll be in as soon as we are finished here, my Angel."

I gave him a smile, leaving him and Ryker to do their interview.

I was halfway to the house before I saw Neil and my two other guards lurking behind the trees, trying to be discreet.

"Coffee?" I called out.

Neil nodded, following me into the house with the two other men in tow.

I had just finished pouring four cups of coffee and handing them out when I caught a glimpse of a shiny gold car pulling up in front of the house. Neil looked over at me, placing his cup on the table.

"I believe it will be Mr Harvey, a long-time friend of Sabastian's. He told me I was to make Mr Harvey a coffee and keep him company while he was doing the interview," I explained with a sigh.

Neil raised an eyebrow. "Keep him company?"

And I was instantly aware what Neil was asking. "Eew! No. I have only ever made love to one man in my entire life, and I plan to keep it that way."

Neil looked almost thankful at the correction. "Mr James is a lucky man."

I didn't bother to correct Neil's assumption that it wasn't Sabastian, but North that I was talking about while we walked to the front door.

A man with thinning sandy blond hair, a fit but soft body. and a nose which looked like it was shaped like a Z walked up the front path. He looked me over with a slight grin.

"So, you must be Harper, the troublemaker," he said with a smile. "I'm Harvey."

"A pleasure to meet you Mr Harvey," I said politely, unsure what he meant by the *troublemaker* comment.

"It's just Harvey," he corrected.

I gave him a half-smile. "Would you care for a cup of coffee?" I asked, leading the way back to the kitchen. "My gentlemen overseers and I were just having one while we wait for my husband to finish his interview with Mr Ryker."

"Actually, Mrs James, I want a few minutes alone with you," Harvey said, looking at my guards.

"I'm afraid we have orders to keep an eye on Mrs James at all times," Neil told him, crossing his arms over his broad chest.

Harvey gave the big man a look that made Neil uncross his arms. "You know who I am, don't you, Neil? And I also have my orders."

Neil and the other men hurried out of the room. Whatever they must have seen in Harvey's face had made them nearly wet their pants.

I tried to look uninterested, but the truth was if the big guys who protected me were scared of this unassuming looking man, maybe I should be too.

Harvey sat his bag on the table and pulled out several gadgets while I sat down across from him with my coffee.

"My husband told me you are old friends," I said conversationally.

"We served in the army together," Harvey said, without looking up. "And he gave me a job when we got out."

I didn't know much about Sabastian's younger life. To be honest, I didn't care to ask.

Harvey picked up a device and tapped a code into a keypad.

The shock collar tingled around my neck, tightening slightly. I gasped, grabbing at it.

"It's working," he said flatly, tapping another button, and the sensation of being choked vanished.

"I could have told you that," I told him. "Anytime I walk too close to the fence, I can feel it."

"Is it as strong now as the first time you tried to escape?"

I had no idea. When I'd tried to escape, I ran straight out the front door and thought I could make it through it, but was choked unconscious. I wasn't paying attention to how strong it was.

"I don't know, I learnt my lesson and I won't be trying it again," I said simply. "My place is here with my husband."

Harvey looked almost amused as he pulled out another gadget and began running it over me, before stopping at my neck where the collar was.

"Did he inject it in your neck?" Harvey questioned, looking a little confused.

The tracker! Oh no—he must have been looking for the tracker.

Harvey tapped something on the device and smiled. He looked up from the small screen. "You cut it out and have it stuffed under that collar, don't you?"

"I'm sorry, Mr Harvey, but I don't know what you are talking about," I said, trying to sound convincing.

"Your heart rate is increasing and you're starting to sweat," he told me. "You are a clever girl, aren't you? You cut the GPS tracker out of your own arm but kept it on you so Sabastian wouldn't know."

Harvey put the device down, leaned toward me, reached out and ran his finger across the skin at the top of my shock collar. "You know, I don't have to tell Sabastian about this, but it will cost you."

He had me, and he knew it.

"And what cost will that be, Mr Harvey?"

"Well, I've been looking at pictures of your pretty face for a year now, and I wouldn't mind seeing what's under that skirt."

I wanted to kill him. "Can I think about it?" I questioned, standing and walking over to the coffee maker to pour myself another coffee.

He followed.

"No, I doubt my dear old friend would let us be alone again for a while," Harvey said as I felt one meaty hand slip around my waist while the other moved up over my breast.

I spun around and kneed him between the legs. He bent, grabbing himself, so I kicked him in the face.

Harvey staggered back. "You fucking bitch," he roared, lunging forward and grabbing my hair, jerking my head down. I grabbed for the coffee jug. His fist closed ready to punch me. I swung, smashing the jug into the side of his face, glass and scalding coffee sprayed everywhere. Then suddenly Sabastian was there, pulling Harvey away from me before slamming his head into the kitchen counter again and again.

Harvey fell limply to the ground at Sabastian's feet.

Sabastian stepped over him. "Are you all right?" he asked, genuine concern in his voice.

I looked down at myself. I was shaking, and I still had the handle of the broken coffee jug in my hand, but I was otherwise uninjured.

"I—I—I think so," I stammered as Sabastian took the handle from me, sitting it on the counter.

"What happened?" Neil asked, looking down at Harvey lying bleeding, burnt and unconscious on the ground.

"He came up behind me when I was getting coffee and grabbed my breast," I told Sabastian. "He said he had been looking at pictures of me and wanted to see what was under my skirt."

"That sonofabitch. He never could keep his hands to himself," Sabastian growled

I buried my head in his chest. I didn't have to fake being scared or the shaking that the adrenaline had caused.

"Clean this mess up, discreetly. We have people arriving in less than fifteen minutes and a media crew walking around the grounds," Sabastian told Neil as he led me out of the kitchen and half-carried me upstairs to clean up.

A small sob escaped me as I looked in the bedroom mirror. I had glass and coffee all over me, and there was blood splattered on my face.

Sabastian hugged me to him. "It's all right, Harper, no one will ever hurt you again."

I pulled myself together. "I'm all right," I told him, pushing myself away to retrieve a tissue to dab my eyes. "We have guests arriving in ten minutes and I need to change and fix my hair and makeup. We don't want people thinking our general married a mess," I half-joked, sniffling.

"There are some formal dresses in my closet for you," Sabastian said, kissing my forehead before leading me into his room.

He pulled out a soft-pink dress and laid it on the bed before stepping around me to unzip me.

As Sabastian undid my dress, his hands carefully ran down my spine, sending shivers through me before he leaned in to kiss my shoulder.

"We have guests arriving any minute," I told him with a giggle.

"Let them entertain themselves," he whispered, tugging my dress down to reveal my bra.

I had to stop this.

"We have the rest of our lives," I told him as he ran a hand down over my bare stomach.

I grabbed his hand, stopping him from going any further south.

"Later," I told him as I gave him a quick kiss.

Sabastian sighed. "Later."

I sure as hell hoped I would be rescued before *later* came.

Sabastian turned to the door. "I'll go meet our guests. Come down when you're ready," he told me, giving me a once over with his eyes.

I almost did a happy dance when he closed the door and I saw his tablet still sitting on the dresser.

I could hardly believe my luck.

I walked over and turned it on. The screen lit up, and I entered the code I knew. I scrolled through it and realised it was connected to the home computer and the Defence Network. I just prayed I remembered everything John had shown me.

CHAPTER THIRTY-EIGHT

North sat with his back against the wall of the truck. In a few hours, if all went to plan, Harper would be on her way to Home with him. North held onto that thought.

"Check out what that guy is wearing," Dace laughed. He and Kaden sat opposite North with a small tablet watching the media broadcast of the James's dinner.

They had been laughing for the last fifteen minutes over the ridiculous outfits the guests were wearing, occasionally flashing the tablet around for everyone to see. Some of the outfits looked ludicrous, but North didn't care. He was focused on getting Harper out and home to their son.

"We are now going to cross over to Ryker, who is live at the James estate with General James himself," a man's voice announced as both Dace's and Kaden's eyes suddenly widened and their mouths dropped open.

"Umm, we are live from General James's mansion on the outskirts of the Capital. And here with us is General James and his wife," a man's deep voice said, as Dace glanced up at North.

"Sorry, but as you said earlier, my wife is a little lovestruck with me, she can hardly keep her hands off me," North heard Sabastian say.

North looked at his brother. "Is Harper on there?"

"I don't think you want to see this," Dace said, almost apologetically.

"Well, you certainly do make a handsome couple. I think every man, woman and child in our nation would agree. And personally, if my wife kissed me like that, I'd never leave the house."

North snatched the tablet so fast even Dace and Kaden had to blink.

Harper was dressed in a black dress with a slit so high only the fact that Sabastian was holding Harper's hand in her lap stopped everyone from being able to see her panties, but at least she looked all right.

Sabastian and the host talked *shit* while Dace, Travis, Kaden and Birdy gathered around North to watch the media coverage.

"Are you sure that's your girl?" Dace asked. "Because I'm certain you're batting way above your average with her."

North didn't reply, but he knew he was the luckiest son-ofabitch in the world to have Harper love him.

"Harper James, what is it like being married to the Head of Defence?" the host asked as Harper looked to Sabastian.

Harper smiled. "Well, I have to admit it has been different to my previous life."

North didn't doubt that comment for a moment—she had been ripped away from her son so she could be a rich man's trophy.

Harper's face tensed slightly, and North noticed her fingers turning white in Sabastian's hand.

"That sonofabitch," North growled, tapping the screen. "He's fucking hurting her right there on national television."

Seeing her fingers, Birdy and Travis also swore.

"You see, I grew up on a modest farm, so marrying Sabastian, I mean General James, was a big change for me."

"And how is that?" the host asked.

Harper paused for a moment as if considering the question. "Well, I thought we had a nice house on my family's farm, but after coming here"—she waved her free hand around, the strained smile evident on her face—"well, I'm sure you can see what I mean."

"Yes, most definitely," the host said as the camera panned around the house and gardens. "I'm sure many of the young women out there are envious of your new position and your powerful husband."

"I'm sure they are," Harper said, sounding bitter while plastering a smile on her face. "I am living the fantasy all women have before they marry. I have a wonderful home, my own personal hair and makeup men, and amazing clothes, but it is my husband that has truly changed my life to what it is now."

North wanted to reach through the screen and rip Sabastian's head off.

"And what about you, General James, what has been the biggest adjustment you have had to make being married to this gorgeous wife of yours?" the host asked.

A slight bit of colour began returning to Harper's fingers — Sabastian must have approved of her answer enough to discontinue torturing her.

"She is a tough woman," Dace said, as the host turned to James. "I thought he was going to break her hand if she didn't answer the questions correctly and smile."

"He would have," Birdy said, with bitter conviction.

"Sleeping on the right side of the bed for starters," James smiled.

"That fucking asshole," North snarled

"Going to sleep next to Harper still feels surreal, then there are the small things," James continued. "Like watching her make my coffee in the morning, or the way she looks when she is absently gazing out at the garden."

North suddenly realised Sabastian really was in love with Harper — he just had a seriously sick way of showing it.

Harper suddenly reached over, cupped James's cheek and kissed him softly.

Dace grabbed the tablet out of North's hand.

"Wow, I know that touch," Travis interrupted as all gazes turned to him. "That's the *I'm sorry, but I'm in love with North* touch. She did it to me, too, before you even came back on the scene."

Dace snorted. "Holy shit on a stick, that hottie is in love with my brother, and I'm the good-looking one in the family," he joked.

"You only *think* you're the good-looking one," North replied with half a smile as the truck jerked to a stop.

"Okay boys, time to roll," Tom called out. "Just remember you're meant to be soldiers, not bickering housewives."

Joe opened the back door and teams one and two jumped out.

"Team two, take up position along the high ground," Tom ordered. "Team one, move in, get in as close as possible, identify your target and wait for the distraction before you grab her."

"Yes, sir." Joe nodded.

"Once the distraction is set off, you'll have thirty minutes to grab her and get back here. Any longer and we risk being caught," Tom added.

North nodded and headed into the woods toward the mansion, with the rest of his team following. North could feel his skin prickling with readiness to transform at a moment's notice. He was on the edge of losing control. He usually hated the sensation, but when it came to Harper, he would tear anyone apart that stood in his way, and he didn't care if he was in wolf or human form when he did it.

North could smell the soldiers hiding in the woods close to the mansion, so moved his team away from them, stopping on the edge of the large gardens which surrounded the house.

Everyone went to ground, hiding amongst the undergrowth to wait for the signal.

From North's position, he had a clear view of both the driveway and the walk up to the hall, but not the hall itself. He would have to move in closer if he was going to get sight of Harper.

A big man with chocolate-brown skin walked out of the side doors of the house, moving toward the trees close to where they were hiding, before stopping and looking around.

North was sure they couldn't be seen, but his stomach clenched anyway.

"I need two soldiers," the man announced, still scanning the woods above their heads.

North knew they were the only ones in this sector, and the man in front of him smelled of coffee, blood and Harper.

"Come on, I know you're there," the man said impatiently.

North tugged on Dace's sleeve before he stood up silently to reveal himself.

The chocolate-skinned man looked at him almost shocked. "Anyone with you, soldier?"

Dace stood up beside North.

"Ahh, good, I have a job of utmost discretion for you both," the man said, turning and walking back toward the house.

North looked to Dace, who shrugged and mouthed *I don't know* as they both followed the man.

"I'm sorry to pull you both off your assignment, but we had an incident, and we need it cleaned up," the man told them, leading them inside the house and down a hall to a large state-of-the-art kitchen, where a man was lying on the floor with pieces of broken glass, coffee, and blood covering his mangled face.

Two more big beefy men in guard uniforms laid plastic on the floor beside the man before rolling him onto it and wrapping him.

The chocolate skinned man looked at North and Dace. "This man attacked Mrs James earlier. She was lucky enough to break the hot coffee jug in his face before she was saved by Mr James," the man explained.

"That sonofabitch, is she all right?" North asked, before remembering he was meant to be a soldier and not ask questions or have an opinion.

One of the other guards nodded. "Yeah, just shaken up. But we're all a bit surprised she managed to fight off a Special Ops guy with barely a scratch."

North wasn't surprised. He knew Harper was good at anything she tried — except cooking. She was terrible at that.

The chocolate-skinned man glanced at his two men, then at North and Dace. "I need you to clean this up. The guests will start to arrive in five minutes." He glanced at his watch. "You and you," he said, pointing at North and the chatty guard. "Take the body down to the cellar and lock it in the cold room, we'll dispose of it later." He turned to Dace and the second guard. "You two clean up this mess. I don't want anyone wandering in here and seeing this."

North glanced at Dace, then to the plastic wrapped body. He picked up one end while the chatty guard got a hold of the other. North could have easily carried the body by himself, but he was meant to be a human soldier, and he wouldn't give his Unholy status away to the house guards.

They shuffled across a short hallway into a small service elevator, where they unceremoniously dropped the body on the floor.

North was sure the man was still alive. He could hear a faint heartbeat, but after what he'd done to Harper, he wouldn't tell anyone. The man could rot in hell, for all he cared.

The elevator doors closed, and the chatty guard propped himself against the back wall. "So, you been in the army long?"

"No, I'm pretty fresh at this stuff," North said in all

honesty.

"Yeah, thought so. So why did you join up?"

"I just want to serve long enough to save for a girl." North shrugged.

The guard smiled as the elevator doors opened into a cellar lined with wine bottles. "Yeah, us average guys got to work our butts off to get an average wife, while rich guys get the cream of the crop, like Mrs James."

North gave a small smile. "Is she pretty?"

"She's beautiful. She makes my day just by walking down the hall, and she's real nice to us guards. She even makes us coffee and asks us to sit with her when we're on duty."

North smiled. "Sounds like you've got yourself a good position here," he said, lifting his end of the plastic roll so they could drag it over to the large cool room.

The guard's phone rang, and he dropped the bag to answer it. He nodded at North to stay, walking away to talk.

North heard a muffled voice from inside the plastic and pulled it back to see the man's face, his eyes open but groggy.

"Tell Sabastian I'm sorry I tried to have her, but she cut the tracker out of her own arm," he said in a gasping wheeze.

North smiled at the thought of Harper cutting out the tracker. She was smart, and he loved that about her.

"Please tell him I'm sorry, I won't do it again," the man begged.

Charli's voice crackled in his ear. He'd almost forgotten she was there listening. "You have orders to eliminate him."

North didn't hesitate to form one razor sharp clawed finger and puncture the man's carotid artery in his neck before quickly pulling the plastic back over the man so the blood wouldn't spray him.

North turned, leaving the cool room and closing the door behind him. He knew the man in the plastic would already have passed out from blood loss, and in another minute his heart wouldn't have anything left to pump.

The chatty guard had his back to North and didn't seem to notice him standing there as he contemplated slitting the guard's throat as well.

"Not yet, North," Charli's voice said in his ear.

The guard disconnected as North re-formed his hand back to normal.

"Come on, we're needed upstairs." The guard sighed. "General James is worried someone might try to steal his wife."

CHAPTER THIRTY-NINE

Sabastian stood by the door of the huge hall admiring the white marble floors, ornate crystal chandeliers, the elegantly set tables dressed with royal blue satin tablecloths, and the black glass vases holding huge sprays of silvery white roses and ivy which cascaded down onto the table top.

It looked perfect.

Sabastian wished Harper would hurry up. He had a sinking feeling in his gut that something was going to happen tonight, and he wanted to make sure she was secure.

He pulled out his phone, dialling Neil.

"Sir," Neil answered crisply.

"Have you taken care of that mess?" he asked, looking down the long garden path at the first of the cars to pull to a stop.

"We're just finishing up," Neil answered.

"Good," Sabastian said distractedly. He watched a leggy blonde woman in a tight red dress slip from the passenger seat of the sports car. "I have a feeling that something is going to happen tonight, so I want you to commandeer a few soldiers and add them to Harper's detail. I want her safe and secure."

"Yes, sir," Neil answered. "I already have two helping with the clean-up."

"Fine, use them. Oh, and hurry her up, she was getting cleaned up in my room, and we have guests arriving," Sabastian ordered, disconnecting.

The leggy blonde woman and Frederick Mills, Head of the

MGD, posed for the waiting media cameras while the valet drove the car away. Another car pulled up and another pretty blonde slid out in a skin-tight red dress. She looked like a clone of Frederick's wife.

These men are so predictable. A smile crossed Sabastian's lips. They all drove fancy shiny sports cars in bronze, gold or silver, and the majority had pretty blonde, big breasted wives who were completely forgettable.

Sabastian wasn't a clone of the Capital. He had a sports car, but he flew copters, and his wife wasn't a carbon cut-out of every other man's wife in a position of power. No, Harper was a beautiful brunette with a presence that enchanted people at first glance.

More cars began to queue, disgorging the powerful men and their glamorous wives, all jostling for their moment in front of the camera with Ryker. The scene reminded Sabastian of a feeding frenzy, and he smiled to himself. If he and Harper were to attend one of these functions, he wouldn't crowd around like these morons. He'd just walk on through, leaving the media wanting more, making them chase him.

Frederick and his wife started up the extravagant garden path toward the hall, leaving the jostling mess before several more couples began to follow.

Harper walked through the door looking slightly flushed. Her hair was down, and she was wearing a long dusty-pink dress which was cinched under her breasts, leaving its diaphanous fabric to float to the floor around her. It wasn't as sexy or revealing as the black dress with the long slit, but it did make her look softer and more feminine than every other woman here. It wasn't the dress he had chosen, but this one was more elegant and sophisticated, which made him smile.

Harper came to stand next to him, her head dipped toward the ground. "I'm sorry I took so long, and I hope you don't mind that I chose a different dress to wear from your wardrobe. This one just looked so pretty," she apologised. "I hope it meets your approval."

Sabastian slipped his finger under her chin, lifting her face to meet his. She had taken off the smoky dark-grey and black eyeshadow, replacing it with a shimmering silver-white, which made her emerald-green eyes sparkle.

"You look perfect," he whispered, leaning down and kissing her soft pink lips.

Harper gave him a coy smile. "As do you, my husband," she returned, running her fingers down his suit front as if wiping away an invisible wrinkle.

Sabastian smiled. Harper really was perfect, and she belonged to him.

I hurriedly tapped on the tablet while I tried to pull on the dress that Sabastian had chosen for me.

I wasn't sure how long I would have before Sabastian sent Neil to come and get me.

The tablet made a faint ping as it started to upload the files to the Rebellium network. I continued to tug when I suddenly heard the fabric of the dress tear. I looked down—I'd put a rip in the fabric under the armpit.

"Shit," I growled, dropping the tablet on the bed and running to the wardrobe. I snatched the first dress I saw and pulled it over my head, careful not to tear this one.

It was long, pink, and reminded me of Cinderella. I surveyed myself in the mirror and realised my makeup was too heavy for such a delicate dress. I sprinted back to the bed to check the progress of the bar on the tablet screen, which read only two percent uploaded and was crawling along like an old snail with a wheelie walker. *Shit.*

I ran to the bathroom, soaked a wad of toilet paper and began wiping the makeup off before grabbing the first eyeshadow I saw. It was a shimmery white, I smeared it on, redid my eyeliner, and brushed on a thick layer of mascara before quickly running my fingers through my hair to flatten it. I was passable, but not photo perfect. I didn't care, and if anyone asked, I'd tell them my stylist wasn't around to help. Everyone in the Capital seemed to have a stylist and didn't sneeze unless it was choreographed.

I ran back to the tablet and looked down—three percent uploaded.

This was going to take too long.

A knock sounded at the door.

I snatched up the tablet, half-burying the thing in the layers of material behind my back as the door opened and Neil stepped in with a blond man dressed in army fatigues on his heels.

He looked so similar to North at first glance that I had to look twice, but it wasn't him.

I missed North and Wolf so much that my chest hurt just thinking about them. I would do anything to see them, to hold them.

"The general asked me to hurry you along, your guests have started arriving," Neil told me while I looked down at my bare feet.

I needed more time to upload this darn stuff off the tablet, but by the way it was going it was going to be a month before it was done.

I felt a sudden electric tingle rush through me. My heart faltered in my chest while my breath caught in my throat.

He was here.

I glanced over Neil's shoulder past the blond and my two other normal guards to see him standing at the back of the group with his head down as if trying to hide from me.

He could never hide from me—I could feel him.

He was wearing a military uniform and looked the part of

a soldier, but it was him.

North looked up at me, his beautiful brown eyes locking with mine for an instant, and it felt like I was home.

I had no idea what he was doing here or how he'd managed to get himself assigned to my personal security team, and I didn't care. He was here, and it took all my willpower not to dive into his arms.

I needed to get rid of the other guards.

I couldn't help but smile as I looked to Neil. "I need you to go downstairs and get me a few headache pills, please."

Neil looked wary, "I don't think . . ."

I leaned in close, interrupting him. "The earlier events have given me a terrible headache, and I only trust you to get me the pills so I'm not poisoned."

Neil nodded. "Of course," he said solemnly before hurrying off.

I turned to my other two guards when Neil was out of sight. "Go to my room, I need my silver shoes, the bottle of perfume from the dresser and my hairbrush," I told them.

The two men shook their heads.

I needed them gone so I could speak to North. I needed to touch him to know he was real and not a figment of my imagination.

"You will go and get me what I need, General James is waiting for me," I demanded sharply. "And I'm not sending the army boys to do it — they've never been in my room, and I don't want them to be. They can watch me while you both go." I put on my best *do as I say* voice, but neither of them moved. I lowered my voice. "Go now and get my things," I growled with authority.

"But . . ." one started.

"Now!" I barked and both men turned and hurried down the hall past North and disappeared.

I looked at the blond man, unsure how to get rid of him,

but before I could think of something to say North rushed into the room, wrapping his arms around me, pulling me to him and kissing me. A million volts of electricity seemed to explode between us. I kissed him back, wrapping my free arm around his neck.

It was him. He was here.

I pulled back, grabbing his face in my hands. "I love you," I stammered, as I heard the door click and looked to see the blond man leaning against it.

I stumbled back, but North caught me.

"It's all right," North said. "This is my brother, Dace—he's here to help."

Dace gave me a smile and a finger wave.

"Harper, really it's all right," North reassured me.

I pulled the tablet out from behind my back and looked down at the screen. Five percent uploaded.

"I'm uploading the files now, but it's taking forever," I said, holding the screen up for North to see.

Dace stepped over and took the tablet from me, tapping something on the screen before frowning. "Shit, we can't just take it and run, it has to be connected to the house network to upload the files," he said with disgust. "It's going to take another hour at least."

North and Dace simultaneously touched their fingers to their ears.

"Yeah, I'll let her know," North said, looking to me.

I looked at him, unsure who or what he was talking about.

"Charli is back in the command centre. She said you are going to have to stay here until it is completed, or they might not get all the files," North told me while Dace unbuttoned his shirt and tucked the tablet inside.

I shook my head at North. "I'm not staying here any longer. Sabastian expects me to sleep with him tonight, and I won't do it. I don't care how important these files are, I'm not a Bride of the state, and if he touches me, I will try to kill him."

North's jaw tightened. "If he lays a hand on you, it will be the last thing he does before he dies."

"Don't worry, we'll have you out before dinner is over. We just need enough time to get this uploaded," Dace interrupted.

I tapped the shock collar tightly fastened around my neck. "I can't just walk out of here. This thing will choke me as soon as I get close to the fence line, and Sabastian has a remote control."

North swore and pulled me close, hugging me to him. "I'm going to kill that sonofabitch."

"Not if I do it first," I told him. "Where's our son?"

"Safe. He is with Beth," North told me.

If Wolf was with Beth, he was in good hands. She would likely love and spoil him beyond belief. No one would hurt him as long as she drew breath.

Footsteps sounded in the hall outside the door and I quickly leaned forward, kissing North again.

"I love you," he whispered, stepping back just as the door opened.

"So, you must see some interesting places being in the army," I said as Neil stepped into the room.

He scrutinized us all for a moment, then crossed the room and handed me a glass of water and two small white pills.

"Thank you, Mr Neil, I don't know what I would do without you." I smiled as my two other guards returned with my shoes, hairbrush, and perfume.

I quickly slipped on the shoes, ran the brush through my hair, and sprayed the perfume Sabastian liked me to wear.

"How do I look?" I asked, without looking at North.

"Very nice, Mrs James. Now if you would please hurry downstairs, your husband is waiting for you," Neil said, ushering me out the door with my guard detail, including North and Dace at the rear.

Sabastian was standing in the extravagant doorway watching the couples making their way up the ornate garden path, past the perfectly trimmed hedges and flower-filled gardens.

I felt nervous and flushed as I approached. I had taken too long. I wasn't wearing the dress he had chosen for me, and I could feel North watching me from a distance.

I didn't know if Sabastian would recognise North if he saw him. He'd only ever seen him once or twice at my family's farm, but Sabastian seemed to have a mind like a steel trap — once information went in, it didn't escape. I knew North would be smart enough to stay out of sight just in case he was recognised, but it didn't make me feel any less uneasy.

I ducked my head, not wanting Sabastian to see my flushed face while I apologised for wearing a different dress to the one he had chosen.

"You look perfect," he whispered as he leaned in and kissed me.

I wanted to rip his heart out, and I was sure it was taking every ounce of North's self-control not to do it. The thought made me smile slightly.

"As do you," I told him, running my fingers over his chest, wishing I had a knife to plunge into his heart.

The first couple reached us. Sabastian instantly went into host mode, greeting the older man with a friendly handshake while the blonde wife looked me over with a disgusted smirk. She obviously thought herself better than me in her red dress, but I didn't care. North was here, he loved me, and that to me was all that mattered. The blonde, who looked like every other woman walking down the path, could strip naked and do a dance, and I knew North would still be looking at me.

The first couple left us to go find their table before Sabastian and I turned back to the path. There was a line of couples heading toward us, with most of the women being platinum blonde or a variation of it. Most were also wearing either red or black dresses which were so tight I could see every curve of their bodies. My dress looked like a tent in comparison.

I leaned into Sabastian. "Am I wearing the wrong outfit?" I asked, not that I really cared, but I was wondering if he did.

Sabastian smiled at me. "No. You look perfect," he told me, wrapping an arm around my waist as we greeted the next couple, then the next and the next.

Every woman seemed to give me an assessing look, like they were appalled at my attire, while every man looked as if he wanted to lift my skirt to see what was underneath.

Sabastian leaned in close, his hot breath rolling down my neck, "You look beautiful," he whispered, kissing my neck just below my ear.

"You will make me blush, Sabastian," I said, giving him a coy smile.

I could feel North watching us, and I was sure if Sabastian didn't get away from me soon, North would break his neck in front of everyone.

I was grateful when the next couple approached and Sabastian had to put space between us.

An hour later, we were still standing in the doorway watching the last of the guests, Praeses Connelly and his blonde wife, who was surprisingly wearing a pale-blue gown with a fitted top and a diaphanous skirt similar to mine, came walking up the path.

I stole a glance, looking for North. I couldn't see him, but I could feel him still watching me from the wings, so next I looked over at Dace, hoping it was time to leave, but he shook his head ever so slightly.

"Irving, it is good to see you," Sabastian greeted as the old man reached us.

Most of the women had looked at me with irritable disdain,

but the Praeses's blonde gave me a quick up and down glance, then smiled before returning her gaze to the ground. I looked down too as the cameras and Ryker moved in to film the two men shaking hands and smiling.

"First Lady, Mrs James, please raise your heads for the camera — the people at home would want to see our Nation's two most powerful couples," Ryker instructed as Sabastian turned me to face the camera.

The Praeses's wife looked as uncomfortable as I did. She had the air of a battered woman who had resigned herself to living a life of misery. It made my blood boil with anger.

"Look up, Harper," Sabastian whispered in my ear, his hot breath rolling across my cheek.

I looked up, straight into the camera. I hated this. I hated being on show, and I hated the fact that average people had no idea what was really going on or how cruel and depraved the people in power really were.

Suddenly without warning, I caught sight of Dace covering both ears.

BOOM!

A huge fireball erupted behind the house, billowing up into the sky like a giant fire-filled mushroom.

The Praeses's wife screamed as people began yelling and running.

I saw Dace hit the ground, bracing for another explosion. I grabbed the Praeses's wife, throwing us both into a garden bed as a second fireball erupted.

Sabastian grabbed me, hauling me to my feet as Neil rushed in.

"Get her out of here," Sabastian yelled.

"Get the First Lady," I yelled at Sabastian.

"Sir, the GPS factory has been destroyed," Neil yelled, snatching my arm.

Sabastian growled, hauling the Praeses's wife to her feet. "Take them both," he ordered before running toward the fireball.

Men in military uniforms rushed from the surrounding tree line, while Ryker and his crew continued to film the chaos.

"This way," Neil yelled, pushing us toward the door of the house.

I wasn't going back in there.

"I'm sorry," I said apologetically before I swung my elbow up, smashing Neil in the face. Something crunched. He buckled forward, then I grabbed the back of his hair and drove his head into the door frame.

The First Lady stopped, her eyes wide with shock as my other guards ran at me. I ducked as the first one reached to grab me before striking out, kicking his knee out. He fell to the ground, screaming in pain as I stood and spun, punching the second guard in the face. He staggered back, and I kicked him between the legs. He instantly dropped to his knees, grabbing himself, and I kneed him in the face, laying him out cold.

"That's my girl," North smiled, grabbing my hand.

"The First Lady?"

"Dace has her," North told me as I saw the camera man. He had been filming the entire thing for the Nation to see live.

North tried to pull me toward the woods, but I wrenched my arm free. I wanted the Nation to know what I really thought of Sabastian, the Praeses, and the way they treated both women and the Unholy.

I marched back to the cameraman and Ryker.

Ryker looked petrified.

"Are we live to the Nation?" I asked, wiping my bloody fist down my pale pink dress.

CHAPTER FORTY

Sabastian sprinted through the gardens toward the fire with a team of soldiers on his heels. The Insurgents weren't going to get Harper. He could see the flames through the trees while thick black smoke billowed up into the sky.

Sabastian stopped at the edge of a large charred-black clearing. There was no one there.

He swore.

"General, what is it?" one of the soldiers asked.

"It's a decoy," Sabastian snarled. "Get back to the house and find my wife!"

Sabastian ran back through the woods. He would kill anyone who tried to take Harper from him. She belonged to him. She was his.

The sound of gunfire and screaming women echoed through the woods as Sabastian burst into the gardens and sprinted around the house.

Neil had better have secured Harper or I'll snap his neck. Sabastian rounded the corner and found people running in every direction. He noted some of the pathetic heads of departments cowering under tables while their wives ran around in circles like headless chickens.

"Sabastian," Praeses Connelly called, striding through the mayhem, his nose and head bloody. "When you catch that traitorous wife of yours, you are to execute her on sight!"

Sabastian wasn't sure what had happened.

"Where is she?" he asked, glancing around.

A gust of wind suddenly buffeted him, and he looked up

to see his stealth copter rising above the house.

"Kill that fucking bitch and anyone who's with her!" Irving screamed, his face mottled with rage.

Sabastian grabbed the first soldier he saw. "Get me a copter here now," he ordered before running upstairs to his office so he could track her GPS.

Neil staggered into the office after him, his face bloody and swollen.

"Where is she?" Sabastian yelled.

"I don't know, I got knocked out," Neil answered.

Sabastian tapped in his passcode, bringing up Harper's GPS. The red dot blinked on the screen showing Harper was in the house. He zoomed in and realised it indicated she was in the office and should have been right there in front of him.

"Where is she?" Sabastian asked, looking around the room before he suddenly noticed the small rice-sized object sitting on the desk in front of him.

Something clicked in Sabastian's head as he realised why her tracker hadn't been working properly — she must have cut it out of her arm.

Harper's two other guards limped in, looking like they had been hit by a train.

"Who did that to you?" Sabastian asked coldly, suspecting he knew the answer.

All three men looked sheepish.

"Mrs James," Neil answered slowly.

Sabastian leaned back and laughed. He loved the fact his wife had beaten up Harvey, probably when he discovered the GPS wasn't where it was meant to be, as well as three trained guards.

Harper was magnificent.

Sabastian couldn't track her by the GPS, but he could track his copter.

He smiled, tapping in the code as his screen switched to a

map of the Nation, before zooming in on the Capital and the surrounding region. A red light steadily blinked as the copter flew in a north-easterly direction.

Suddenly it dawned on Sabastian. They were heading toward the mountain resort he had ordered to be firebombed.

Sabastian's phone rang.

"Sir, your copter is here," a man said.

"I'll be right there." Sabastian grinned, looking at the red dot.

They had a half hour head start on him, but there would be no safe hiding spot in the mountains.

"Neil, get us food for two days and meet me at the copter," Sabastian ordered, heading for his room to find his tablet.

He searched the dresser and the bedside table. Harper must have taken it, or perhaps one of the Insurgents had.

"Sabastian," Irving's voice barked from the door. "They took my wife."

Sabastian didn't give a shit about the First Lady — he needed to find Harper. He was mildly surprised when he looked up to see Irving's bruised and battered face but didn't care enough to find out why. "My copter is here, I'm going after them now."

"I mean it, Sabastian, if you find that wife of yours, you kill her, or I'll have you both executed on site," Irving growled, turning to leave.

Sabastian felt rage bubbling up inside. He would never hurt Harper. He pulled a short-bladed knife from his sock drawer and buried it into the side of Irving's throat.

"No one will ever touch my wife," Sabastian snarled.

The Praeses's eyes widened as he turned to Sabastian, gripping his neck as blood burbled from his mouth.

Sabastian stepped back, not wanting to get blood on his good suit and calmly watched Irving crumple to the floor, coughing and choking on his own blood.

"Damn, now they will be even further ahead," Sabastian groused, heading for the door without looking back.

Thirty minutes earlier

North watched Harper speaking into the camera. She was the voice of the Insurgents, and she chose what to say on her own terms.

"Most of you know me as Harper James, wife of General Sabastian James, Head of the Defence Network, but to me I am just another victim of our society. A society which justifies selling its own people into slavery. We persecute and reject anyone who isn't considered perfect after their DNA test and any man without a fat bank balance.

"We live in a society that forces parents to sell their children and watch them be turned into a Bride of the state or even be killed, because we as a nation have been fed the lies that females are inferior and Unholy are lesser beings. Well, I'm here to tell you neither is true.

"An Unholy has exactly the same DNA as every other human plus more. They are the advanced versions of the rest of us, not our inferiors. They are fighters, protectors and lovers, not monsters like the government has been telling us." Harper looked at North. "I know this because before I was forced into being Sabastian's wife. I lived in a peaceful settlement where women and men chose each other, and I chose my Unholy lover. He is a man of honour and devotion, and he didn't purchase me like a loaf of bread. Instead, we chose each other, and he gave me a son born of love, not obligation. Then my life, my soulmate and my child were torn away from me and I was forced to come here to live as a rich man's trophy. No person should watch their son die or should have to sell their daughters into misery."

A tear ran down Harper's cheek as North took her hand,

giving it a light squeeze.

"Stop selling your children to the highest bidders, stop hurting people because they are different to you, and stop listening to the bullshit the government tells you. Those men in power only care about keeping the power, not helping the people of this Nation. We need to rebuild our Nation, and to do that we need to clean up the government from the ground all the way up to the Praeses, before he kills another one of his young wives." Harper took a deep breath. "I have been hunted, tortured and terrorised — this collar I'm wearing isn't a fashion statement, it is a shock collar so I can't run away, but I will never give up fighting. My children will not grow up in a world where their dad will sell them or people shun them because they are different, or where the men in the seats of power have no respect for the average person.

"Women, find your voice, and men, find your balls and change this atrocity that our country has become!" Harper moved to leave, then turned back to Ryker. "By the way, Mr Ryker, you may want to warn your viewers that the GPS tracking units that the government implanted into every female and soldier in our Nation all have a remotely activated, fast acting poison in them. I recommend that everyone who has one cut it out immediately, before someone pushes the release button and kills the Nation."

Ryker's mouth dropped open as he felt his arm. He likely had been implanted.

"So much for our government taking care of us," Harper spat out, looking directly into the lens of the camera.

The sound of gunfire broke from the woods as Travis, Birdy, Kaden and Joe burst from the trees, running toward them.

"We have to get out of here," Joe yelled.

North grabbed Harper's hand, pulling her toward the woods, while Dace scooped up the Praeses's wife and sprinted after them.

Harper suddenly jolted to a stop, gripping her throat. "I can't," she gasped, stepping back, "The fence."

North suddenly realised the collar was choking her.

"How do we get you out of here?" North asked, feeling almost panicked. He had to get Harper as far from here as he could.

"The copter," she rasped.

North turned to the rest of the team. "Get back to the rendezvous point, I'll fly Harper out."

"I'm coming," Travis said, as Birdy gave Harper a quick hug.

"Don't get yourself killed," Joe told Travis before he, Birdy and Dace sprinted for the woods with the blonde woman.

"Kaden?" North questioned, looking at the dark-haired man.

"I live for this shit, and besides, I want thirty seconds with James's home computer."

Harper laughed at Kaden. "Werewolves."

Kaden looked at her, shocked, wondering how she knew he wasn't human. "How did you . . ."

"It's a gift." North smiled.

"The office is upstairs," Harper said, pulling off her shoes. She hiked up her dress and sprinted into the house with North never more than a few steps behind her.

He wasn't going to let her out of his sight until he knew she was safe, and probably not even then.

Harper grabbed the door handle and turned, but it was locked so she stepped back, lifted her foot and kicked, sending the door flying open.

"That's my girl." North beamed, glancing over at Kaden, who still had a shocked look on his face.

"You don't want to see what she can do with a gun," Travis said, pushing Kaden through the door and over to the desk.

North stood by the door watching the stairs. He would protect Harper with his life if need be.

Kaden sat in front of the computer, turned it on and swore. "Shit. I need the passcode to get in."

Harper started rattling off letters and numbers as if it were nothing, while she fiddled with the thick silver collar around her neck.

North hated looking at that collar. He hated that Sabastian James had put it on her like she was a disobedient dog.

"I'm in." Kaden grinned, tapping frantically on the keyboard.

Harper pulled out a tiny white object from under the collar and placed it on the desk in front of Kaden.

North walked over to look at it. He knew it was the tracker—he'd seen the one they'd dug out of Charli back in Haven, and the man he'd dumped in the freezer had said she had cut it out of herself, but still.

North kissed Harper's temple. "Have I told you lately you are amazing?"

"No." Harper smiled and kissed him. "But I think I might have forgotten to tell you that as well."

Travis blew air out through his nose. "Are we done?"

Kaden tapped a few more buttons and stood. "Yes." He smiled. "I just uploaded a virus into the government network. It will destroy every record . . ."

A loud shot rang out as North tackled Harper to the ground.

I hit the ground hard, with North landing on top of me. Kaden's blank eyes stared at me from under the desk, a single red hole puncturing the left side of his forehead as a trickle of crimson oozed out, running down into his dark hair.

The weight of North's body suddenly disappeared. I

looked up to see a giant black half-human, half-wolf disappearing through the open door. The sound of gunshots boomed as Travis crawled over, covering me with his body like a shield.

Vicious snarls and screams filled the air then suddenly, silence. It was so abrupt it was deafening.

"North," I yelled, pushing Travis off me as I sprang to my feet and ran into the hallway.

North stood in half-form, blood dripping from his claws and maw, as chunks of red flesh lay sprawled in the hall around him.

"Are you all right?" I asked.

North nodded.

"We have to get out of here," Travis said, glancing back into the office. "Kaden's dead."

I ran past North, snatching up a blood-soaked gun from the floor. Travis and North followed. We sprinted down the stairs and out the back door.

Women were still screaming. The sound of gunfire erupted in the woods around us. I just hoped they weren't firing at Birdy and the others.

North suddenly stumbled, grabbing his stomach. His body shrank back down to his human form and Travis caught him.

He had been shot.

I hadn't seen it with all the fur and blood in the hall.

"Get him to the copter," I yelled, just as two soldiers rounded the corner.

I lifted the gun, pulled the trigger, but nothing happened. *Shit*. I sprinted across the stone path toward them, they lifted their weapons, but they weren't aiming at me. They didn't think I was the threat, but they would kill North or Travis if I didn't stop them.

As if in a slow-motion dream, my body took over. I stepped sideways and jumped. Bouncing off the wall, I came down on the first soldier's head with my elbow before dropping to the ground, sweeping my leg out and dropping the second man. He landed on his back and instantly I was on top of him, pinning him as I punched him as hard as I could, over and over again in the face. He fell limp under me, so now both men lay unconscious on the ground.

I stood looking at the copter where Travis was loading North into the back seat.

A gun shot rang out so close I flinched, covering my ears for a moment as I saw Travis slump against the copter gripping his arm.

I turned to see Praeses Connelly pointing a gun at me.

"I thought we eradicated your kind," he said, looking amused. "No wonder Sabastian has been so obsessed with you. You are the diamond in a bucket of shit."

I chanced a glance back at Travis. The wound didn't look fatal, but his face had turned ashen from shock and adrenaline.

"If I'd have known what you were, I would have ordered your execution a year ago," Connelly said. "Your kind and those Unholy are mutant vermin."

"You and your government are the vermin," I snarled at him while I slowly stepped to the side, moving him away from North and Travis. "You have lied to the people, forcibly enslaved the women of this Nation, and killed anyone who dares to call you a dictator. This country deserves better than you."

Connelly laughed. "You're a naive child if you think that any of this will change the country. Men control this Nation."

"Is the government so scared of females having freedom that you think it justified to forcibly enslave us?"

"Women are weak," he snapped.

I lunged forward, knocking the gun from his hand.

Connelly grabbed my hair and spun me around into the

hard stone wall, his forearm pressed against the back of my neck, pinning me there.

"Sabastian is a fool to think he could have controlled an Angelic," Connelly crowed in my ear. "If I were him, I would have strapped you to a bed, fucked you and killed you, then fucked you again."

His hot breath ran down my face, bitter and putrid.

For an old man, Connelly was surprisingly strong and quick.

"You say the nicest things, Praeses Connelly," I said sweetly, before suddenly pushing off the wall with all my strength, catching him off-guard.

He stumbled back.

I spun, connecting the back of my elbow with his cheek. Then his head snapped to the side as I moved to his back, kicking him forward, his face smashing into the stone wall where he crumbled to his knees.

I wanted to kill him.

I took a step forward, ready to snap his neck.

"Harper!" Travis yelled.

I turned to see him leaning against the door of the copter. I had to get them out of here.

"Get in," I yelled, running back to the copter.

"I can't fly it, my arm's useless, and North's out cold," he said.

I ran around to the pilot's seat and began pressing buttons in the order I'd remembered seeing Sabastian do it.

Travis climbed into the front passenger-seat, watching me as the blades began to hum above us.

"I didn't know you could fly," Travis exclaimed as we lifted off.

It felt weird, but it was easier than I thought. "This is my first time."

"Oh fuck," Travis said, hurriedly strapping his seatbelt on.

The buzz of the shock collar fence tingled against my throat. I gritted my teeth.

I heard Praeses Connelly roar with anger. I sincerely wished I'd killed him as we lifted above the house. I glanced down, seeing the people scurrying around like ants and a huge fire burning in the woods, the thick smoke funnelling up into the sky. I moved higher then forward, away from the mansion.

"Where are we going?" I asked when we were clear of the house and smoke.

Travis didn't answer, so I glanced over. His eyes were shut and his face was pale, but I could see his chest rising and falling in long even breaths. I glanced back at North lying naked on the back seat. The wound in his stomach had already began to knit itself back together, thanks to his Unholy DNA, which gave his body accelerated healing. He would likely be up and around in a few hours, but in the meantime, I had a problem. I had no idea where I was meant to be going. With both Travis and North out cold and the Nation's army likely after us, I didn't want to set down on the ground. The dying light of the evening felt heavy. The lights of the distant Capital dotted the horizon ahead.

I didn't want to go to the Capital. I wanted to go home to Wolf. I wanted to hold my baby and kiss his soft little nose.

I looked at the control panel in front of me, remembering that Sabastian had tapped in the GPS coordinates for the restaurant he had taken me to and the return trip had automatically come up when he was taking me home.

I tapped a screen and a map appeared with a list of commands down the right side.

Home. New destination. Previous destinations.

I pressed *Previous destinations.* A list of names with phone numbers popped onto the screen like a phone book. I looked down the list, stopping at one which simply read Harper. I pressed on my name, and the screen switched to a map of the entire country with a red line heading up to the north-east. To an area which looked mountainous.

"Haven," I whispered to myself.

I turned the copter to meet the coordinates on the screen as we skirted the edge of the Capital. I was going home to see my baby, to see Wolf.

It had been almost three and a half hours since I had left the Capital lights behind, following the red line. Neither North nor Travis had stirred, but at least they were still breathing.

I would have felt better if I could see, but at night with only dots of light below and stars above, I felt blind, and it frightened me. I could be heading straight for a mountain and I wouldn't know.

Lightning suddenly flashed off in the distance, outlining distant mountains. At least there wasn't one right in front of us, but by the look of it, we were flying right into a storm.

The map on the control panel said it was only another thirty minutes to our destination. I crossed my fingers and toes that we'd make it to Haven before the storm hit.

More lightning flashed as we drew closer to the mountains.

Without warning, a flash of lightning burst across the sky, illuminating a huge granite cliff only fifty meters to our left before a sudden gust of wind buffeted the copter, shaking it violently. I fought with the stick and pedals to keep from blowing into the rocky mountain side.

The image on the screen blinked, showing me the copter's position between the mountains. More wind buffeted us, and lightning flashed again.

I followed the screen, zigzagging through the mountains, glancing up from the screen with each bright flash to make sure I wasn't too close to the steep mountain sides which seemed to loom over us.

Fear gripped me. I wasn't scared for my own life, but for North and Travis. If I crashed the copter, they'd die.

"Destination, two kilometres ahead. Please follow landing coordinates," a woman's voice suddenly said from the screen, making me jump. It had been the first thing outside the hum of the blades I had heard in hours.

The copter jerked with another gust of wind.

North let out a faint moan from the back seat.

I glanced back. "North?" I questioned, hoping he was awake, but he didn't answer.

"Destination reached," the woman's voice said.

I looked out the window, looking for house lights or a fire or anything, but all I could see was darkness.

A flash of lightning burst above us, the thunder so loud it shook the copter, but it was what I saw in that millisecond of light that frightened me.

It was gone—only charred black sticks of trees and crumbling black buildings littered the hillside.

My breath caught in my chest.

How could it all be gone, and where was my baby? I was told he was safe, but this looked far from safe.

Panic rushed through me.

Rain started to beat against the copter as the violent bursts of lightening came perilously close. I had to land this thing, at least until the storm passed.

I needed to get on the ground. I needed to find my baby, my Wolf.

I flicked on the searchlight, spotting the flat field area everyone used as the community meeting place.

I began descending as the wind and rain picked up, vicious downdrafts skewing us sideways while I fought to hold the copter from hitting the blackened trees around the field. The skids bumped on the ground, once, twice and we were down.

I quickly went through the shutdown procedure I'd

remembered Sabastian doing before leaning over to check on Travis. The bleeding had stopped, but he needed medical help. Next, I climbed over the seats to North. He was still out of it and naked, but he had colour in his cheeks and the wound looked well on its way to healed.

I looked around the copter for a blanket or a first aid kit and found a gym bag under the front seat with a pair of Sabastian's sweatpants and a shirt in it.

He was so arrogant he must have flown himself to the gym to work out.

I took the clothes out and laid them over North—they weren't exactly a blanket, but hopefully he wouldn't freeze to death.

Another bright flash burst across the sky. I caught sight of the remains of Joe and Beth's house up on the hill. I had to know if my son was in there and if he had been killed.

I kissed North's forehead. "I love you," I whispered, pushed open the door and stepped out into the icy rain.

CHAPTER FORTY-ONE

Sabastian's grim face was lit by the LEDs on the dash of his stealth army copter as he flew over the dark countryside. He glanced down at the monitor which showed exactly where his stolen copter and stolen wife were located. He'd been closing the gap and was now only twenty minutes behind them, but they were slowing, negotiating their way through the mountains.

A flash of lightning lit up the sky as his passenger, Neil, gripped his seatbelt tightly. For a big, muscular, scary-looking man, he sure was scared of a little lightning. The other two guards in the back seat looked unfazed by the weather. Obviously, they had spent more time in the air.

Sabastian tapped a button on the console bringing up the weather radar. A heavy storm was coming in from the north, but by the looks of it, that should clear by morning. Once they landed, they wouldn't be able to take off again until the wind and rain eased. It also meant whoever had taken Harper couldn't take off either, giving him a chance to kill his wife's kidnappers.

Sabastian just hoped the pilot was competent—if they crashed and killed his Harper, he would be absolutely furious.

Another flash of lightning erupted across the sky as the wind picked up, buffeting the copter in the narrow gorges. Sabastian had flown in worse conditions when in the army and the loud cracks of thunder and lightning would help conceal his approach, not that the stealth copters made much noise.

The red dot stopped moving on the screen as heavy rain began beating against the windows. The stolen copter had slowed coming through the mountains and it was now only ten minutes ahead.

Sabastian felt in his pocket for the shock collar remote, which she would still be wearing. There was no way for her to take it off without him.

He thought about the GPS tracker Harper had removed herself and the way she had accessed his computer. she was smarter than he had given her credit for. Or had someone helped her? He glanced at Neil and wondered about him again. No. He was a muscle-bound moron.

It had to be Harper. She was smart and cunning, a predator wrapped in fine silk.

Sabastian thought her intelligence a good thing. Their children wouldn't be morons, at least. He had seen the offspring of intelligent men who had married pretty but stupid wives, resulting in pretty but stupid children. He wouldn't have that problem. His children would be both beautiful and intelligent. It was a good thing, too, or he would be forced to discard them out of principle. A man in his position couldn't afford to have half-witted offspring.

Another flash of lightning illuminated the mountains as a loud boom of thunder crackled through the air.

"Target two kilometres ahead," the audio voice announced as Sabastian flew in low, just above the trees, and turned on the infra-red scanners.

Sabastian didn't want to use his landing lights. It was bad enough they were already on the ground giving them the tactical advantage, but he had the infra-red which gave them nowhere to hide.

Neil reached between his legs, pulling out four sets of infra-red night vision goggles and four guns, dispensing them in readiness for landing.

The heat signature of the stolen copter sitting on the ground glowed red as Sabastian hovered two hundred metres away. He tapped the screen again, looking for somewhere to land. The field where his stolen copter sat was the only flat spot around. He would have to land there. He changed the screen back to the infra-red and noticed someone exiting the copter. The figure was smaller than most men and looked to be holding up the hem of a long dress while running across the field and up the hill toward a half-ruined cabin.

Sabastian was sure it was Harper. He smiled — no one else left the copter, even though he could make out two more heat signatures inside the copter, but neither was moving.

Harper must have incapacitated them when they landed.

Sabastian slowly came in to land on the edge of the field behind his stolen copter, while Neil watched the monitor for any movement. The copter the army had hurriedly supplied wasn't equipped with external weaponry, so until they were on the ground, they would be sitting ducks.

Still, no one moved as they touched down.

Neil and the other guards immediately slid from the copter with their goggles on and guns drawn in a defensive move, while Sabastian shut down the engine.

Lightning flashed violently overhead, illuminating both the copters.

Sabastian slipped on his goggles and stepped out into the heavy rain as more lightning exploded across the sky, followed by a deafening crack of thunder.

"Stay here," Sabastian ordered. "I'm going after my wife. Give me ten minutes to locate her, then shoot the people in the copter. If anyone stirs before then, you know what to do."

Neil and the other guards nodded. "Yes, sir."

Sabastian jogged across the field and up the hill toward the large half-destroyed cabin.

Another flash of lightning lit the sky. The bright flashes

played havoc with the goggles, their automatic adjustment setting changing to flickering black for a moment or flashing blinding white with every lightning bolt. Sabastian would have taken them off, but he needed them to make sure no one except Harper was here.

He caught movement from a small almost untouched building to the left. He turned and saw Harper stepping inside.

Sabastian jogged over to the shack before lightly tiptoeing up the steps. The sound of the rain on the tin roof was almost deafening as he stepped onto the small veranda, holding the remote in one hand and his gun in the other.

He slowly stepped through the open door, glancing around the small cabin, noting that it was smaller than his bathroom.

Had this been where she was hiding? The thought shook him — she was an Angelic, not a scullery maid. She deserved the best of everything.

A faint glow came from one of the rooms as Sabastian lifted his goggles and stepped cautiously toward the door to peer inside.

Harper was sitting on the edge of a bed with her back to him, her hair and dress dripping water as she stared into an empty baby's cot.

"Did you do this?" Harper asked, without turning.

Sabastian froze, unsure if she was talking to herself or him.

"Did you destroy Haven, Sabastian?" she asked, answering his question.

He wasn't sure how she'd known he was there. Sabastian tucked the gun down the back of his pants as he moved around the bed to where he could see her face. Rain and tears dampened her cheeks, smearing her makeup.

Harper looked up at him, pain filling her emerald eyes. "I just want my son, Sabastian — please tell me where he is." Her voice trembled as more tears flooded down her cheeks.

Harper looked so sorrowful, and he was the one who had done that to her. He shook his head. "I don't know."

Two loud bangs rang out, one after the other and even over the thunder and rain Sabastian could tell they were gunshots.

Harper quickly stood, turning to the door.

"It's time to come home, Harper," Sabastian told her.

Harper turned her glare on him, a look of pure hatred in them. "I am home," she said, losing all pretence of sweetness.

Her sorrow had turned to rage.

My hair dripped onto my lap as I sat staring at Wolf's empty cot. A layer of cold, black soot had coated everything. I had been so sure Wolf would be here. North had told me he was safe with Beth, but this place, my home, looked as if it had been destroyed weeks ago.

Had North lied to save me the heartbreak, or didn't he know?

I felt a familiar cold sensation creep up my spine and knew Sabastian was here. I knew he would be. He would hunt me to the ends of the earth, and for some reason the universe had seen fit to make us connected. I could feel him now as clearly as I had always felt North, even though all I wanted was to be free of him.

I felt Sabastian coming up the stairs and into my small cabin.

I knew I should run and hide, but I just felt hollow.

Sabastian moved into the doorway behind me. I didn't bother moving, I just stared at Wolf's empty bed, sorrow filling me.

"Did you do this?" I asked Sabastian.

He didn't say a word.

"Did you destroy Haven, Sabastian?"

He moved closer. I lifted my head to look at him, tears rolling down my face, but I wanted to look him in the eyes.

"I just want my son, Sabastian. Please tell me where he is." My voice quivered.

For the first time since I first saw Sabastian, he genuinely looked remorseful as he shook his head. "I don't know."

My heart sank.

Two loud gunshots rang out from the field where I had left Travis and North in the copter. A rush of panic erupted in me as I stood, turning toward the door.

"It's time to come home, Harper," Sabastian told me casually.

I looked to him, feeling pure hatred. "I am home." My voice came out angry and savage.

Sabastian held up the shock collar remote, sending a small buzz through my neck, making my jaw clench.

"We can do this the easy way or the hard way, but either way you are coming home with me," Sabastian said.

"Let's do it the hard way," I told him coldly before I spun, kicking the remote from his hand and sending it bouncing under the bed.

I lunged forward, aiming to punch him in the side of his face, but Sabastian blocked me, grabbing my arms as he pulled me up against his rock-hard chest.

Sabastian smiled. "There is my defiant wife," he said, before suddenly kissing me.

I bit his lip, tasting his blood in my mouth before he released me, pushing me back on the bed. I rolled off the other side, putting the mattress between us.

Sabastian grinned, wiping the blood from his mouth with the back of his hand.

I sprinted toward the door, but Sabastian got there first, blocking me. I lashed out, punching him as hard as I could in the side of the face, snapping his head sideways.

He turned to me, still smiling. "I love it when you play rough," he said, before backhanding me.

I stumbled back, gripping my cheek which felt as if fire had exploded under my cheek bone.

The only other way out of the room was through the window on the other side of the bed, but it was closed and locked. He would grab me before I could unlock it and jump out.

I had to get past him, out the door and run.

I lunged forward, grabbing his hair and wrenching his head down, then kneed him in the gut.

Sabastian grunted, grabbed my thighs and lifted me up, my hand still tangled in his hair before he threw me onto the bed. I pulled him down with me. His big body landed on top of me, winding me.

I released his hair as I tried to punch and scratch him, but he grabbed my arms, pinning me to the bed. I bucked under him, trying to get him off me, but he was too heavy.

Sabastian's face was close to mine as he smiled down at me. "God, I love you Harper."

I suddenly realised how much he meant it as he looked down at me.

For a moment I was shocked. I wanted to kill him, and he was telling me he loved me.

I head-butted him in the nose, blood sprayed my face as he toppled off me grabbing his face, swearing.

I jumped to my feet to run, but Sabastian grabbed my arm, spinning me into the wooden wall. Pain erupted in my head and I dropped to the ground while the world shifted sideways.

I tried to stand as I pushed myself up the wall, but everything seemed off balance and I collapsed back down.

Sabastian squatted down in front of me, wiping his bloody nose on his sleeve.

"You are mine, Harper," he told me calmly, grabbing me

under the arms and lifting me. "You are the only woman I have ever loved, and you will always be mine."

My head swam, spinning at a million miles an hour. "Fuck you," I managed, although it came out slurred.

Footsteps sounded on the wooden floor outside the bedroom door.

Sabastian turned, half-shielding me before I saw the gun tucked down the back of his pants.

Neil appeared in the doorway, holding his gun at Sabastian and me.

"You can lower your gun, I have her," Sabastian said, holding me tight against him.

"I'm sorry, sir, but I have orders from the Praeses himself to eliminate Mrs James on sight," Neil told him.

I hadn't suspected Neil of being loyal to Praeses Connelly, but from Sabastian's body language he had.

"Neil," Sabastian barked. "I order you as Head of Defence to lower your weapon!"

Neil shook his head. "I'm sorry, sir, but I can't do that."

Sabastian shifted his grip on me as he pushed me back against the wall, putting himself between me and Neil.

I wrapped my fingers around the gun at Sabastian's back.

"Please step aside, sir, I have orders to shoot anyone who gets in the way of my mission, including you," Neil announced.

"No," Sabastian said firmly. "You will have to kill me to get to her."

Neil lifted his gun, aiming for Sabastian's head as I pulled the gun from his back.

Suddenly a huge beast appeared behind Neil. Massive claws wrapped around his throat, shredding it in one swift swipe, sending blood spraying into the room.

There was a thunderous boom from Neil's gun as his lifeless body slumped to the ground.

Sabastian staggered, slumping forward onto the ground in front of me.

I looked up at North in half-form, then back to Sabastian on the ground.

"Harper," Sabastian rasped, blood trickling from his lips, his eyes full of pleading.

I dropped to my knees, rolling Sabastian's head onto my lap as I saw the tattered fabric and the dark stain spreading across his stomach.

He had put himself between me and Neil, he had saved me. Hot tears blurred my vision.

Sabastian smiled up at me as he shakily raised his hand to my cheek. "I love you, my wife," he said, before moving his hand to the back of my neck. "Release."

The collar clicked, loosening around my throat.

He had freed me.

"We would have made beautiful babies," he said.

I leaned forward and kissed his forehead. "The most beautiful, my husband," I whispered.

Sabastian smiled faintly, his eyes closing and his breath stilling.

I felt North rest a clawed hand on my shoulder. "As twisted as that sonofabitch was, he genuinely did love you, didn't he?"

I gently rested Sabastian's head on the ground, brushing his dark hair from his face before wiping the tears from my cheeks and pulling off the collar.

North offered me his hand, lifting me up as he shifted back into his human form. His arms wrapped around me, holding me against his warm body, his gentle hand cradling my throbbing head against his chest as that electric buzz tingled between us.

"Seriously?" I heard Travis say as we both turned our gazes to him leaning in the doorway dripping wet and clutching his shoulder. "You are standing in a blood-soaked bedroom with two dead guys, hugging."

I glanced down at Sabastian, then to the cot. "Where is our son?"

"At Home with Beth," North told me.

I raised an eyebrow. "We are at home?"

North smiled. "No, we're in Haven, Home is in the south-east."

I stepped around the blood to a set of drawers and pulled out clothes for North. "Well, I guess you'd better fly this time," I told him, tossing him the clothes.

We took what we wanted from the cabin and loaded it into the copters while Travis went through the remains of his home. He found a few undamaged books, pots and other random stuff in Billy's room, which seemed to be mostly untouched by the firebombing but was still its usual teenage mess.

At dawn, North took some of the reserve fuel from the copter's tank, using it to set fire to our cabin with the bodies of Sabastian, Neil and the other two guards inside.

I wasn't in love with Sabastian. He had tortured, enslaved and hunted me, but watching the cabin burn in the early morning light made me realise that I didn't hate him either. He had loved me the only way he knew how. It just wasn't the way someone should love, and no matter what, North would always own my heart.

"Guess it's time to go," Travis said, looking up at the burning cabin as North jogged back down the hill. "I'll see you both at Home." He grinned, walking over to the army copter.

"Maybe you want Harper to fly that—she can land it, at least," North said as he reached us.

Travis flicked him the bird over his shoulder and kept walking.

I hugged North tightly. "Let's go see our son."

EPILOGUE

After the initial breakdown of the chain of command, there was rioting in the streets, first over the GPS trackers, then over the mass corruption in the government, before the Insurgents stepped in and took control. They quickly brought about order under Lady Anastasia's command and promised to deliver a free government, voted in by every man and woman of the Nation.

There was a lot of opposition to women and Unholys being able to vote at first, but it was short-lived.

Harper and North were asked to help build the new government, but they both graciously declined, opting for the simpler life with their son.

On the day of the first free election, Harper and North strolled hand in hand along the beach near their house in Home, watching their five-year-old Wolf jumping and running along the sand. His little body shifted fluidly between human and wolf as he darted in and out of the water.

North smiled proudly at his son.

"I think Wolf needs a play mate," Harper said, watching Wolf.

"Dace and Emily said to bring Wolf around to play with Noah anytime," North said.

Dace and Praeses Connelly's wife, Emily, had fallen in love almost instantly, with Noah being born eleven months after the infamous dinner party. They lived in a house just down the road.

It was wonderful having family close. In fact, Birdy and

Charli lived in the small house beside Harper and North and were expecting their second daughter any day now, while Joe and Beth lived opposite them and were happy just to sit on their front porch watching all their adopted grand babies playing in the front yard.

Harper knew Beth and Joe missed Travis and Billy. Travis was now the new Head of National Security, and Billy was training to be a sniper in the new army — they both came home regularly, but it wasn't the same as having them living there.

Harper stopped walking, placing North's hand on her stomach. "I think Wolf will enjoy having a new playmate." Harper smiled, biting her bottom lip as she waited for North to catch on.

It took North a moment before his eyes widened. He looked down at Harper's stomach, then back at her face. "You're . . ."

"I am." Harper smiled, leaned forward and kissed him.

North let out a loud *Whoop*, picked Harper up and spun her around with excitement before setting her back on the ground.

"What's going on?" Wolf asked, running up to them with a smile.

"You're going to be a big brother. Mummy's having a baby," North said excitedly.

"I know. She smells like Aunt Charli," Wolf said with a shrug before dashing off again.

Harper laughed. "Werewolves."

North shook his head, wondering how he had missed the change in Harper's scent, but he didn't really care. He was going to have another baby with the woman he loved.

Harper cupped North's face, kissing him softly. "I love you."

North smiled. "And I love you."

YOU MAY ALSO ENJOY THE FOLLOWING FROM EXTASY BOOKS INC:

Frost and Fyr
Viola Grace

Excerpt

Fehniel drummed her fingers on her desk and scowled at the man across from her. "I understand that the seer shot her mouth off, but I don't see why Lord Thosnas would make the assumption that it was us."

The frost giant sat back in his chair and gave her a smirking grin. "You have to admit that the coincidences are a little thick on the ground."

She tented her fingers in front of her. "Tynir, is it?"

"Yes."

"Are you insane, is that it?" She cocked her head and blinked.

He snorted. "Hardly. Thosnas had a seer on hand and all of his grandchildren were allowed to visit. When I went, Morgarn and Ragnar were waiting. She told us that our women would travel in a set of three as well, would be found in the sky and each would be an elemental born of a new world."

Fen scowled. "Unfortunately, that does sound like us. Why did Thosnas try to buy our bar?"

"It was a move to flush the other giants into threatening you. Once you were on the alert, you would be more receptive to having bodyguards and once close to you, it would be easy to see if the attraction was mutual."

"Which it was in the first case and probably is in the second." She went back to drumming her fingers on the table.

"What about the third?" He leaned back to display his bluish grey skin and dark hair. His white-blue eyes had an everpresent amusement that shook her grim, logical outlook the moment that she saw him. His physique certainly was more than acceptable, his chest wide, belly flat and thighs impressively muscled. The only thing that kept her libido under control was the waves of cold coming from him.

"You are impressive, but I have a little problem with the cold you radiate."

"I am a frost giant. It's what I do."

"I am a fire elemental. You don't see me scorching folks as I pass." Fen held still and sent a short, sharp stab of inquiry to his mind. She was deflected, but not before she caught a glimpse of his internal heat.

"Did you just send a mind probe?"

She cocked her head and glared at him. "I don't know, did you feel one?"

"I did."

"Then perhaps I did." Her mother hadn't raised a liar, but her father taught her diplomacy at all times. She always wanted Aleyn and Baileez to be proud of her and she wasn't sure that this man was the right fit for her.

"You have mental talents?"

"Of a sort. Nothing like my elder siblings. I am the runt of the litter." She chuckled at the turn of phrase. She was physically the smallest of her brothers and sisters, the royal family of Hickom.

"I see. Would you consider coming to my home and assessing it for suitability?" He was very forthright.

"You are being direct. Where is the attempt to weasel me

to the surface under false pretences?" She felt her lips twitch in amusement.

"Time is of the essence. You don't want to leave your business unattended while it is in operation, so this week off is the only time available."

"Morgarn told you."

"Of course. He is my cousin, after all."

"Squealer."

He chuckled. "You are very controlled for someone whose base is fire."

She laughed. "In my family, you didn't get too far if you didn't have self-control. Being able to keep my emotions in check enabled me to reach adulthood."

"So, will you come to the surface with me?"

She ignored his raised eyebrow and thought about it. Her mind ran through all permutations and combinations, analyzing all possibilities of going down to Jotunheim with this giant that she had just met. Sex, she had no objection to, it was the living among giants that gave her pause.

The Hickom had their own seer and it had told her that she would find a man to cool her fire. It had been very vague, but a frost giant did fit the bill.

She would have to contact her parents and let them know where she was going, alert the management that the bar would be closed until further notice and pack a bag.

"I will go but only to check out the accommodations." Yeah, right.

"As you will, lady."

"I have a few things to take care of before we leave, so if you will meet me in my quarters in a few hours, we can leave then."

"I will escort you there and wait for you. The hired thugs are still on the station. Thosnas has not been able to recall them all yet."

She twisted her lips into a smile. "Just trying to make sure I don't bolt, aren't you?"

"Perhaps. Shall we begin our journey with a few steps?"

She stood and shook her head. "I am a little perturbed by your lack of romantic instinct. I always wanted to be swept off my feet."

"Romance will follow, Fehniel. First, I need to get you in my clutches."

She chuckled and came around the desk, he stood and Fen took his arm. "I will have to settle for you being in my clutches for now."

He raised his eyebrow again, but led the way out of Elymyntyl and into the halls of Raven's Rest space station. Fen kept her lips pressed tightly together to hide her smile. A simple look from her companion sent the fire giants scurrying for cover.

"My quarters are—"

"On the eleventh level."

He wasn't guessing, making her narrow her eyes at him. "Have you been spying on me?"

"Studying a likely candidate. I am sure you would have done the same." Tynir checked the lift and when he was sure they would be the only occupants, he escorted her in.

She fought the urge to whistle while they waited for her floor to be announced. It was a sign of nerves and she acknowledged it. Her parents always stressed self-awareness and to be standing next to a man who bore all the hallmarks of her promised mate definitely struck a number of chords inside her, not all unpleasant ones either.

Her rooms were the same sparsely decorated ones that she had left that morning. "Please, be seated. I have to tell my parents where I am going."

He looked around her common area and took a seat on the couch. "I will be waiting."

About the Author

Rowena lives on a small property on the Mid North Coast of New South wales with her husband, children and copious amounts of chocolate.

Rowena has always loved the written word, but she had been reluctant to put her work out there due to her dyslexia, however after her multiple cancer surgeries she decided life was too short for what ifs.

www.ingramcontent.com/pod-product-compliance
Lightning Source LLC
Chambersburg PA
CBHW060143260626
47160CB00001B/99